Also by D. M. Pirrone

No Less in Blood

Shall We Not Revenge

D. M. Pirrone

WITHDRAWN

ALLIUM PRESS OF CHICAGO

Allium Press of Chicago
Forest Park, IL
www.alliumpress.com

Book/cover design and maps by E. C. Victorson

Front cover images:
"Chicago in ruins after the Fire of 1871" [State and Madison Streets] *New York Times;*
detail from "boats sepia" by Amir Bajrich/Shutterstock;
"antique blood stained paper" by Ryan DeBerardinis/Shutterstock

Title page image:
Chicago Fire refugees living in a building foundation
Harper's Weekly, November 4, 1871
Illustration by Theodore R. Davis

ISBN: 978-0-9890535-3-2

Library of Congress Cataloging-in-Publication Data

Pirrone, D. M.
Shall we not revenge / D.M. Pirrone.
pages cm
Summary: "Shortly after the Great Chicago Fire of 1871, Irish detective Frank Hanley is assigned the case of a murdered rabbi. He is aided in his investigation by the rabbi's daughter, Rivka. They uncover political corruption involving Irish gangsters and a prominent relief organization"-- Provided by publisher.
ISBN 978-0-9890535-3-2 (pbk.)
1. Murder--Investigation--Fiction. 2. Political corruption--Chicago--Fiction. 3. Jews--Chicago--Fiction. 4. Irish Americans--Chicago--Fiction. 5. Chicago (Ill.)--Fiction. I. Title.
PS3616.I76S43 2014
813'.6--dc23

2014011252

To Steve, for all the many reasons why

If you wrong us,
shall we not revenge?

William Shakespeare, *The Merchant of Venice*

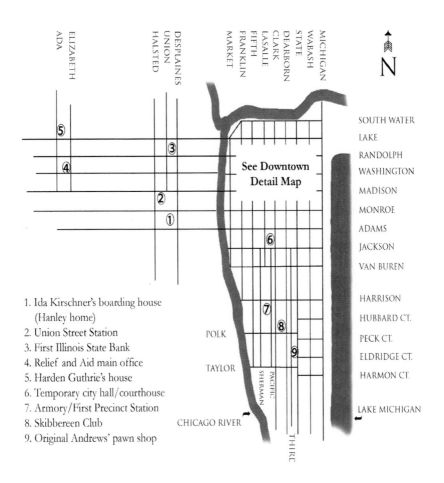

N

SOUTH WATER
LAKE
RANDOLPH
WASHINGTON
MADISON
MONROE
ADAMS
JACKSON
VAN BUREN

HARRISON
HUBBARD CT.
PECK CT.
ELDRIDGE CT.
HARMON CT.

LAKE MICHIGAN

ADA
ELIZABETH
HALSTED
UNION
DESPLAINES
MARKET
FRANKLIN
FIFTH
LASALLE
CLARK
DEARBORN
STATE
WABASH
MICHIGAN

See Downtown
Detail Map

POLK
TAYLOR
SHERMAN
PACIFIC
THIRD
CHICAGO RIVER

1. Ida Kirschner's boarding house
   (Hanley home)
2. Union Street Station
3. First Illinois State Bank
4. Relief and Aid main office
5. Harden Guthrie's house
6. Temporary city hall/courthouse
7. Armory/First Precinct Station
8. Skibbereen Club
9. Original Andrews' pawn shop

Downtown Detail Map on Following Page

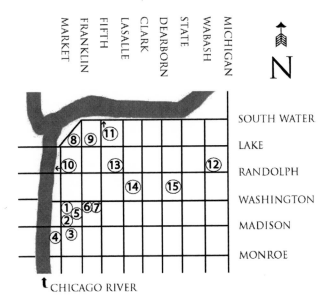

1. Synagogue and Kelmansky home
2. Nathan home
3. Klein's butcher shop
4. Nathan & Zalman tailor shop
5. Pavlics' bakery
6. Jamie Murphy's house
7. Callaghan's grocery/saloon
8. Lake Street Station
9. Lily Stemple's
10. Lind Block
11. Relief supply warehouse
12. Harden Guthrie's office
13. Randolph Street barracks
14. Court house ruins
15. Muskie's Chop House

Downtown Detail Map

Shall We Not Revenge

PROLOGUE

July 14, 1861

Once, Frank Hanley had thought the worst that could happen to him was jail. Now he knew different. He struggled in the grip of the bully boys that held him, ignoring the burn in his shoulders from his arms twisted behind his back and the throbbing pain in his ribcage where they'd worked him over. From the upstairs room at Sean Doyle's lakeside saloon, where customers sometimes paid to take women, Pegeen's screams lanced through the night air. Each one cut Hanley like a knife, straight through to the bone.

"Calm yourself, boyo." Sean Doyle, the sharp lines of his foxlike face visible in the glow from a kerosene lamp, raised a glass toward Hanley. "You'll get her back when Billy's done with her. Well shut of any notions she's too high-and-mighty to whore for me when I tell her to."

"Damn you to hell!" The words came out in a low growl as Hanley bucked and twisted against his captors. Both were new to Doyle's employ, and he couldn't put names to their faces. Half drunk as he was on the whiskey Doyle had fed him, he couldn't budge them. One fellow—Hanley's own height but a good thirty pounds heavier—yanked his arm so hard, it felt like his shoulder might pop from its socket. The pain made him gasp and he sagged in the thugs' hold.

"I'm sorry about this, Frank. I really am." Doyle didn't sound it. He tilted his head back and sipped, the lamplight gleaming off his red hair. "But you've got to learn, the pair of you. When I say something's to be,

1

you *don't say no.*" He dragged out the last three words, making each one ring like a hammer blow.

A thud followed by a slap came from upstairs. Then Charming Billy Shaughnessy's rough voice. "You don't shut up, I'll do it for you." Pegeen's sobbing was muffled abruptly, as if Billy had clamped a hand over her mouth.

Terror and rage gave Hanley new strength. He lurched forward, throwing one bully boy off balance, and stomped on the man's foot. The thug yelped and loosened his grip. An elbow to the ribs broke his hold. Hanley heard a chair scrape across the floor and fought harder against the remaining thug, Pegeen's cries spurring him on. Then her voice choked off. The creak of bedsprings, hard and fast, filtered through the ceiling along with Billy's grunts. Panic shot through Hanley. *Got to win this now, before—*

A stunning blow caught him across the chops. He staggered, tasting blood. The thug he'd injured grabbed his free arm again and twisted it near to breaking. He clenched his jaw against a cry of pain and glared at Doyle, who stood in front of him.

"God, but you try my patience," Doyle said, wiping blood from one knuckle where Hanley's teeth had cut into it. "All I've done for you the past five years, and it's down to this."

Hanley spat blood at him. A wet, red gobbet landed on Doyle's white shirt.

"Ah, Frank." Doyle sounded regretful, though Hanley knew better now than to believe it. "You shouldn't have done that." Without warning, his fist slammed into Hanley's stomach. The bully boys' grip kept Hanley from doubling over and he fought not to heave up his guts. An uppercut to his jaw made his head ring. Dizzied, he would have fallen, if not for the thugs holding him up.

A shout from Billy, hard and triumphant. The rhythmic creaking ceased. Hanley choked down bile, tasted stale whiskey at the back of his throat. *Pegeen. God.* He could hear Billy getting off the bed, then his steps crossing the floor. The thud of his feet, as he descended the rickety stairs by the serving counter, struck Hanley's ear like a death knell.

Billy sauntered into view, one hand buttoning his fly. In the lamplight,

Hanley made out scratches on his smirking face. One red line snaked from beneath an eye past his flattened lump of a nose. Through the horror inside him, Hanley felt a flicker of pride in his girl. Pegeen had damaged the son of a bitch, at least. Which was more than he'd done. A wave of shame washed over him, dizzying in its impact.

"Sweet piece you had there, Frank," Billy said. "You could've made plenty off her, you'd seen sense. Guess you're not so smart as our Sean always says you are, eh?"

Dazed and sickened as Hanley was, it took a moment for Billy's meaning to sink in. "You…God, you…"

"Ah Christ, Billy." Doyle threw him a disgusted look, grabbed his whiskey off the table, and threw it back in a gulp. "I'd wanted you to go that far, I'd have said."

Billy shrugged. "Had to shut her up. Don't know my own strength sometimes. Sorry, Sean."

Hanley lunged toward them both, heedless of the bully boys who still held him fast. Stabbing pain shot through his arms and chest. "Fucking bastards, I'll kill you, I'll kill you with my bare hands—"

Billy snickered. He rolled his broad shoulders and shifted into a fighter's stance with negligent ease. "Go ahead and try. You're beaten and you know it."

"Take off, Billy," Doyle said. "You and me, we'll settle up later."

For a moment, Billy's bravado deserted him. "Sure. Sure, Sean. Sorry again." He gave Hanley a final sneer, then walked out of the saloon into what was left of the night.

The fight went out of Hanley and he sagged in the bully boys' grasp. He had no strength left, no will to fight or curse or do anything except hang there as silence crawled by, his mind hurling itself against a blank wall of denial. Pegeen couldn't be dead. Thick-as-a-post Charming Billy, so stupid it was a wonder he knew day from night, he didn't know anything, not *any goddamned thing…*

Doyle nodded to his thugs. "Leave go of him. We're done."

The moment their grip slackened, Hanley tore away from them and raced for the stairs.

⋈

The room was near pitch-dark, scant moonlight seeping in around the makeshift curtain over the window. Hanley stumbled over a warped floorboard on his headlong rush toward the bed. Pegeen lay there, a huddled shape barely visible. She felt warm under his hands when he reached her. Relief shot through him as he pulled her up into his arms. "Pegeen? Sweetheart? I'm here, I won't let them hurt you anymore..."

She was limp in his hold. Not a movement, not a sound. Not a breath.

He said her name again, shifted one hand to cradle her face. Her slack mouth felt swollen beneath his fingers. Heart pounding, he eased her back down on the mattress, then strode to the window. Heedless of the pain spiking through his ribs, he tore the curtain aside.

Moonlight flooded the room. Its pale gleam caught Pegeen's eyes, open and staring upward. Unblinking.

Hanley staggered back to the bed and sank down on its edge. Pegeen's lips were puffy and bruised, her slender throat stippled with the marks of Billy's hands. He pulled her upright again, cradled her lifeless body in his arms. *No. No. No.*

As if from a vast distance, the sounds of Doyle's departure drifted up from below. The closing of the saloon door drew all Hanley's grief and rage into a white-hot pinpoint.

Damn you to hell, Sean Doyle. God help me, I'll send you there.

ONE

January 26, 1872

The darkness was nearly total, pierced only by the ever-burning pinprick of gold above the Ark. The stench of human waste and the rancid sweetness of blood blotted out the safe, familiar scents of the synagogue—new-cut pine, old beeswax, the faint smoky smell of the lamp oil. Rivka's stomach heaved, but there was nothing left in it to bring up.

She pressed the crumpled prayer shawl to her nose and breathed deep. Her father's scent, a blend of cherry tobacco and sun-dried grass, clung to the cloth. The blood smell also remained. She tasted it, thick and bitter, at the back of her throat.

For a time, she knew only the hoarse catch of her breathing and the rocking of her body. Cold crept through her bones from the hard floor where she sat. The clouds passed and moonlight returned. Thin, cold, as insubstantial as a wandering soul. She saw the pale blue of her nightdress, a narrow stripe of the wood beneath, the edge of the sticky dark pool under her father's head. His face, looking up at her. Broken. Empty.

One hand crept out from the stained prayer shawl and closed his still-whole eye. The other eye was gone, socket and surrounding skull shattered by the force of the killing blow.

She tucked her hand back inside the wadded cloth and bound the clean portion around her fingers as she swallowed the burning in her throat. She began to recite the Mourner's Kaddish, each syllable of the Hebrew falling from her mouth on a cloud of cold white air.

❧

"Tell me how you found him," Frank Hanley said gently.

"It was very late." The girl—Rivka—hadn't moved from her spot on the floor, next to the obscene halo around the corpse's battered head. The sheet someone had laid over the body didn't completely cover the darkened blood. Rivka's face was turned away from it. Hanley watched her toying with a corner of the wadded white cloth she held.

"Rivkaleh, you should not be talking to him." The interruption came from Jacob Nathan, who'd brought Hanley here from the Lake Street police substation. He strode over and squatted by the girl, his heavy gray coat brushing the floor. "Go with Hannah now," he said, patting her cheek and then gesturing toward the door. A middle-aged woman in black stood there, concern written on her patient face. "See, she has been waiting for you."

"No." Rivka drew away from Nathan with a headshake. A hank of black hair slid out from under the kerchief she wore and brushed across the navy wool blanket someone had draped over her shoulders.

"Rivka—"

Hanley spoke up. "I need to hear what she has to say, Mr. Nathan."

Nathan shot him a disapproving look. "I can tell you—"

"You told me she found him. I need to hear it from her."

Nathan gave a sharp sigh and stood. He hovered near them in front of an empty bench. Similar benches of polished wood surrounded three sides of a low platform. A lectern stood near the front of it. Other details registered as Hanley glanced around the little temple—the body by the platform, a small table some distance away from it draped in a white runner cloth, a long white curtain near the back of the room that gleamed in the sunlight from the plain glass windows. In front of the curtain sat three silent men in heavy coats and skullcaps. Nathan had said they were here to tend to the dead, once Hanley was finished.

He returned his attention to Rivka's face. Strong jaw, sharp cheekbones. Gray eyes shadowed by pain, with circles beneath them that shone like bruises. Their color emphasized her pallor. Hanley felt a flash of sympathy. She'd been here for hours, according to Nathan. All night, or a good part of it, alone with her father's dead body. He'd known soldiers during the War for the Union who faced a similar ordeal with less courage than this slip of a girl.

"Papa left before supper," she said. "He told me he might be gone some time and I shouldn't wait up. I went to bed a bit after nine. I woke much later. It was very cold and I got another blanket. I went to Papa's room to see if he wanted one, too. He was not there.

"The kitchen clock struck, two times. I put on my boots and shawl and came over to the *shul*—the synagogue. I saw no light, but sometimes my father prays in the dark when he's troubled. He says the moon gives enough light to see, and what better candle to use than the Holy One's own?"

Her voice trembled on the last words and she huddled deeper into the blanket. "I came into the shul." Her grip tightened around the cloth bundle against her chest. "I should have brought a lantern, but kerosene is so dear...The moon shone through the clouds. I saw the curtains of the Ark, the shape of the *bimah*. The blood. And Papa. There." She jerked her head toward the low platform. "Thrown down by the bimah, like a sack of washing."

She closed her eyes. Anguish drew her upper body inward, curling around the bundle as if shielding it from some terrible threat. Hanley moved instinctively to steady her, then crushed the impulse. He had no business offering comfort here—to a strange young woman, a murder witness. She might be involved, for all he knew. He needed to listen and observe, without emotion clouding his judgment.

"I went to him," she said. "I saw—" A quick nod of her head toward the corpse. "The blood was on the *tallis*. On one edge. I wanted to save it. Keep it clean. So I lifted him and took it."

Her fingers worked against the crumpled white cloth. Silk? Hanley's mother would know at a glance. *Tal-eess.* Hebrew, he guessed. "What is that? What's it for?"

She didn't answer. Maybe she couldn't. "A prayer shawl," Nathan said. "He must have been praying when—" He broke off, as if speaking the rest of his thought might choke him.

A queasy pang made Hanley swallow hard. He'd seen his share of death, as a soldier and in the past six years patrolling Chicago's streets, but the idea of murdering a man at prayer shocked him. It seemed an especially brutal crime, one that shouldn't happen to a harmless old rabbi.

"The clouds came then," Rivka said. "The dark. And after them, Jacob." Her dulled gaze flicked to Nathan. "By then it was morning. Jacob and the *minyan* came and saw."

"Minion?"

"A gathering for prayer," Nathan said. "Ten men, sometimes more. We come early every morning, to pray with our rabbi, Rav Kelmansky…" He trailed off, eyes fixed on Rivka, burly arms wrapped around his chest, as if even his wool coat couldn't keep out the chill. He avoided looking at the dead man.

Hanley addressed his next question to Rivka. "Did you see anyone or hear anything before you came here last night?"

"No."

He waited, but she said nothing more. He thanked her gently, then straightened up and shook the kinks out of his long legs. "You had your prayer gathering—your minyan—yesterday morning, Mr. Nathan?"

"Yes."

"Did you see your rabbi afterward that day?"

Nathan took a moment to answer. "I saw him in the afternoon. We study together."

"Was that the last time you saw him alive?"

"Yes." The word came out shakily, as if it took all Nathan had to say it.

"When was that? Early afternoon or later?"

Nathan closed his eyes and pressed his fingers to them. "Mid-afternoon. I'm sorry, I cannot be more precise. To speak of my Rav—" He broke off and turned away.

"I know this is painful," Hanley said. "But the more you can tell me, the better chance I have of finding the murderer."

Nathan's nod was barely noticeable. He'd likely be more helpful once the worst shock was past. A look at the body was Hanley's next step, but he didn't wish to add to these people's distress any more than he had to. It could cause problems later, when he'd need their trust. He moved to catch Nathan's eye and gestured toward the sheet. "May I…?"

"This is necessary?"

"Yes."

Nathan gestured to one of the men by the door, a lanky youth with eyeglasses and a scraggly beard. Together, they pulled the sheet back. The younger man returned to his seat.

Hanley thanked them and fished a small sketchbook and pencil from a pocket of his overcoat. His first clear look at the corpse made him suppress a shudder. It reminded him of bodies he'd seen on the battlefields—soldiers in blue and gray sprawled in the dirt, their heads half blown off by rifle balls.

He took a slow breath and began to draw the body. He heard Nathan walking toward the door, then voices. Nathan, the woman he'd called Hannah—his wife, Hanley guessed—and the others, talking quietly in a half-familiar tongue. Nathan sounded calmer now. Before long, the creak of the door told him someone had left. He glanced up and saw Nathan standing alone, watching him.

He returned to his work. The body had fallen just in front of the platform. What had the girl called it? Bimah. A powerful blow had crushed the upper left side of the dead man's skull. He knelt for a closer view of the wound, detailing the shape and angle of the staved-in bone. Seeing it as lines and shadows helped the horror of it recede a little. The undamaged right eye was closed. The left hand bore a gold wedding ring, and the dead man's clothing appeared undisturbed. Closer inspection of the hands showed no defensive wounds. Hanley finished the last few lines, put his sketching materials away and began searching the dead man's pockets.

"Detective!" Nathan snapped. "Stop!"

Annoyed, Hanley took a moment to master himself and then looked over at Nathan. The man's distress, written on his weathered face, made him soften his tone. "I need to know if a thief might have gone through your rabbi's pockets already."

Features pinched with distaste, Nathan slowly nodded.

Hanley resumed his search. He found only a crumpled cotton handkerchief. The victim's trousers, coat and vest were fine wool, more expensive than Hanley's own garments and little worn. Carefully, Hanley slid one arm beneath the dead man's shoulders and turned the body sideways. The stiff, cold flesh shifted in a single motion from armpit to toes. No bending at the waist, nor the immense dead weight of a snoring drunkard. Rigor mortis, friend of corpse retrievers.

Behind him, Rivka made a small, pained sound. Hanley paused, then went on with his examination. He pulled the coat lapel out far enough to read the tailor's mark inside—*Nathan and Zalman.* Then he lowered the corpse and unbuttoned the vest for a look at the shirt beneath. Plain cotton, it bore marks of darning and the collar had been turned at least once.

"You made this suit?" Hanley asked Nathan.

"I made all his suits. Good wool. My best work. What more should our rabbi...and my friend...deserve?"

"Worth something, then." Especially in this harsh winter, with so many people desperate for a little warmth.

"I charge a fair price." Nathan looked even more perturbed. He scratched under his flowing beard. "I would not cheat anyone—Rav Kelmansky least of all."

"I didn't suggest it." Hanley kept his tone mild with an effort. He put his next question to Rivka, who was watching him now instead of the floor. "Did your father carry money, or a pocket watch?"

"A few coins. He sold his watch for food after the Fire."

"Someone robbed him?" Nathan said. His eyes flicked to the dead man. "That could be. These are dangerous days." He shifted his weight, as if restless.

Something was definitely bothering him. The mere fact of violent death, or more? Some knowledge of it, maybe. Or maybe he was simply afraid. Martial law had ended scarcely three months before and tensions still ran high among the desperate, burned-out thousands who called Chicago home. This small Jewish neighborhood appeared to be surviving all right, from what Hanley had seen on his way here. These days, that could make them a target.

He looked around, seeking hints that anything valuable might have been taken. It struck him for the first time how different this little pine-board temple was from his parish church, Saint Pat's. The room was a simple square, its unadorned walls the straw-yellow of new lumber. Where the altar should have been sat a tall cabinet with curtains instead of doors. The little table he'd seen earlier was empty of whatever might have stood on it. The only valuable thing he could see was a silver candelabra, lying some distance from the corpse.

Nearer by, a trail of thin, dark smudges led from the blood pool around the dead man's head toward the door, with what looked like a detour toward the table. "Was anything missing when you arrived this morning?" Hanley asked. "Any valuables or relics?"

Nathan shrugged. "A spice box, silver, about so big…" He held out one broad hand that measured a short distance between thumb and fingers. "And one menorah. Like that." He nodded toward the fallen candelabra. "There should be two of them. We have little worth stealing. Our Torah survived the Fire, thanks be to the Holy One."

"How much are they worth, would you guess?" The fallen candelabra looked sizable. If the stolen one was just like it, that much silver should fetch a decent sum. Enough to spend a few evenings gambling it away… or to house a family for a few weeks at least, someplace that didn't smell of old smoke, unwashed bodies, and yesterday's cabbage.

"In money?" Nathan spoke the word with contempt. "I don't know. What is your hand worth? Or your eyes? How should we put a price on things that are priceless?"

"If someone came to rob us, they've done it." The taut anger in Rivka's voice startled Hanley. "Only at no profit to themselves." She began to shake. It took him a moment to realize she was laughing, a bitter sound with no mirth. "No profit. Only a life, only my father…" Her laughter turned to sobbing—a harsh, tearing sound, like the cry of a crow.

Hearing it made his throat hurt. He turned away, toward the bloody smudges. As he moved, he saw Nathan go to Rivka, lift her from the floor with one brawny arm and maneuver her toward the nearest bench, as easily as if she were a little child.

Hanley sketched the marks, then knelt and traced one. Thinner than his pinky finger, each mark had a curve at either end. Blood on the side of a shoe or boot-sole. He placed his own booted foot against one of the marks, lining up with where the toe should be. The heel curve reached to just behind his arch. Not too tall, whoever had walked out of here with a dead man's blood on his shoe.

He glanced at Nathan, who sat with Rivka—gone quiet now—huddled against his shoulder. The man likely wasn't more than five-foot-six. His boot soles were impossible to see. Hanley hadn't noticed blood anywhere on the uppers during their walk here from Lake Street—but he hadn't been looking then.

"You found something?" Nathan said.

"May I see your boots, please?"

"What for?"

"I need to see them."

"Why—"

"Onkl Jacob." Rivka's roughened voice stopped Nathan in mid-word. "*Ikh bet dikh.*"

Nathan looked at her, face drawn, then edged away and pulled off his boots. He held them out toward Hanley and dropped them. They hit the floor with a thunk. "Here. For whatever you expect them to tell you."

"Thank you." A close examination showed no blood. Only a little mud, dried clumps caught in front of the heel. Exactly what he'd expect if Nathan had been walking around any number of places yesterday afternoon, during the warm spell. *Warm* being a relative term in a Chicago winter.

He handed the boots back, then debated with himself over whether or not to demand Rivka's. The tracks led out the synagogue door, and she'd said she hadn't left the place since finding her father's body in the wee dark hours. It felt indecent to ask if he could check her boots for blood.

But he didn't have the luxury of sensitivity. Especially on his first solo homicide case. If he botched it the commanding officer of the West Division would savage him—and promptly replace him with the commander's own protégé at Lake Street Station. Hanley's promotion had been touch and go as it was. Considering his background, it was a miracle he'd gotten the job.

He had to do everything right. Better than right, just to show the people who expected him to fail. "Miss Kelmansky? I'd like to see your boots as well, please."

"She has nothing to do with this." Nathan stood up, one boot still in hand. "Isn't it enough that you make her tell you the horror she found here? That she stayed all night with, so her father's soul would not go back to the Holy One alone? Leave her. She has suffered enough."

Rivka touched his arm. "*Onkl.*"

The word—*uncle?* That was what it had sounded like—brought Nathan up short. He sat heavily on the bench, his back to her. She worked one-handed at her boots, all the while keeping her grip on the tallis.

Finally she rose and padded forward, boots held out toward Hanley. The motion dislodged the blanket, revealing a heavy shawl of chocolate-brown wool over a blue flannel nightdress. The fabric was worn enough to hint at the shape beneath, with just enough curves to spark Hanley's interest. He felt heat rise in his face and coughed to hide his embarrassment.

He took the boots, careful to avoid brushing her fingers, and examined them. No blood. No mud, either. He handed the boots back. She put them on, still one-handed, more hair falling around her face as she bent over. Her awkward movements displayed a ragged dignity that made him want to apologize. She looked exhausted. She must have managed to stand though sheer force of will.

He glanced around the room again, offering her what privacy he could. More blood spatters caught his eye, this time near a front corner of the platform, arcing away from the body in shrinking dots. A larger dark splotch and a smear pointed in the opposite direction, toward the menorah. It lay some distance from the body, as if it had rolled or been thrown.

He picked it up. The frigid air had chilled the metal. Six arms curved outward, three on each side, from a central column. The column base was streaked with blood and matted hair. The menorah felt heavier than the truncheon he'd once carried on his hip. To hold it comfortably required two hands.

"Is that how they—" Nathan broke off, staring at the menorah.

"'They'? You have some idea who—"

"No." Nathan rubbed his arms as if for warmth. "I am...this is... upsetting. I spoke without thought. Forgive me."

The words to form a sensible question wouldn't come. *Later*, Hanley thought. Jacob Nathan wasn't going anywhere.

He went to the corpse and held the menorah base next to the shattered portion of skull. A good fit, it looked like. Will Rushton, the police surgeon at the city morgue, could tell him for sure. He set the menorah down. When he sent more men to retrieve the corpse, he'd tell them to take this, too. Rushton and the coroner would want a look at it.

He knelt by the first blood droplet and fished out his pencil and some string. He set one end of the string at the edge of the droplet, stretched it across and then held the string down at the other edge while he marked the spot where they met. He did the same with the rest of the droplets and the larger blood splotch. The droplets were getting smaller the farther they'd landed from the corpse. Spatter from the killing blow, he guessed. Rushton could confirm that, too.

The sound of the door made him look up. The young man with the eyeglasses came in and went over to Nathan, who had gone back to Rivka and was standing with a hand on her shoulder. She leaned against him. The two men spoke briefly, then the younger one resumed his seat on the bench.

"You are finished with us now?" Nathan asked.

"Almost. Who's that you were talking to, and what about?"

"Moishe Zalman. My assistant. We were discussing arrangements for our dead."

Hanley thanked him and let them go. Nathan and Rivka left the synagogue together, but Zalman stayed behind. Maybe something to do with tending to the body, Hanley thought, though it seemed odd that he just sat there.

On his way outside, Hanley spoke to the patrolman waiting by the door. Square-built and sandy-haired, Rolf Schmidt was a competent officer, despite being only two years on the force. This Market Street neighborhood was part of his beat. "I'll send more patrolmen to help with the body," Hanley told him. "Tell these people they can have it back after the coroner's finished."

Schmidt nodded. Hanley strode into the thin sunlight and took a deep breath. The cold, fresh air banished the smells of death. A taste of smoke lingered, a reminder of the October fire. Almost four months after the Great Conflagration, as the newspapers called it, its traces still stained every breeze in Chicago's burned-out district. At least it wasn't ash any longer. Most of that had long since been washed to earth by rain and snow, turning the ever-present mud beneath the streets and sidewalks into a gritty mess that stuck to everything it touched.

He gazed across the muddy yard between the synagogue and the scattering of frame buildings opposite. Like the temple, their clapboards looked barely weathered. Through gaps where houses and shops had once stood, he could see passing traffic—horsecars, peddlers' wagons, carts and drays of every size. The empty lots, their blackened earth dotted with dirty snow crust, drew the eye like missing fingers. Before October eighth, they'd been greengrocers, dry-goods stores, saloons, homes. Parts of a city that had lived and breathed. Now they were gone. Some might never be rebuilt. Either way, Chicago would never be the same.

He blew on his fingers to warm them, then glanced down at the churned-up mud by the boardwalk that spanned the yard. A patch of tiny ridges caught his attention. He knelt for a closer look. Frozen by the overnight temperature drop, the stiffened muck formed a footprint, large and deep, with a thick heel and a wide, flat sole. Grains of snow furred the tops of each ridge. The print's position suggested a missed step off the boardwalk, heading away from the synagogue.

Carefully, Hanley brushed the snow away. Beneath it, he saw a swirl of tiny lines too small to make out. He sketched the footprint as best he could with stiffening fingers. The print took shape, dark pencil lines forming a pattern. A boot sole, a man's from the size. Jacob Nathan had muddy boots, he recalled, and apparently no chance to clean them yet. Hanley, like most people, cleaned his boots every night.

He closed the sketchbook, taking care not to smudge the drawing. Then he turned up his coat collar and set off toward the station. Sergeant Moore would want his report.

TWO

Pellets of snow stung Hanley's face as he neared Lake Street Station, a skipping-stone's throw from the curving bank between the South and East branches of the Chicago River. Jagged chunks of dirty ice bobbed on the gray water, which was churned up by the wind. Beyond it, the Chicago and Alton railroad tracks hugged the western shore. This portion of the line had escaped the Fire, which had jumped the river near Monroe Street and blazed its way east until it reached Lake Michigan. Memories swept over Hanley—standing chest-deep in lake water with his arms tight around his mother and sister, shivering like a fever victim from the bone-aching cold, while the roaring fire scorched his back and burning cinders fell in his hair. Crowds all around them doing the same thing—some weeping, some praying, others deathly silent. Until finally, mercifully, rain began to fall.

He hunched deeper inside his coat. The damned thing still didn't sit right on his broad shoulders, but he felt grateful for it nonetheless. Like everyone else lined up outside the Second District relief depot during that first awful week in October, breathing ash and trying not to look at the charred ruins around them, he'd been glad to take anything he could get.

Beneath his feet, the rough planks of the sidewalk felt spongy. The dull thud of his boot heels mingled with the clopping of hooves and the rattle of wagon wheels. Down Lake Street to the east, above the few scattered pedestrians who'd braved the morning's chill, he spotted three workmen high in the air, clinging to a half-finished office block. Fascinated and unnerved, he stopped to watch. The workmen stood tight-roped on thin boards, hoisting a load of bricks by pulley. The unwieldy stack, likely salvaged from the rubble after the Fire, nearly covered a square of dusty planking. The contractor must be in a hurry, to have men laying brick in weather too cold for the mortar to set right. Come spring these walls would collapse and God help anyone unlucky enough to be inside or walking by.

The heavy load swung as it rose in the frigid air. The plank tilted abruptly, brick scraping against wood. Hanley caught his breath as one man's foot slipped. The workman grabbed the pulley rope and his mates hauled him back upright.

Hanley began to breathe again. A pair of workers caught the edge of the load and unhooked it. None of the men wore anything heavier than a shirt. Likely several, layered to keep warmth in their bodies. An old trick for workingmen too poorly paid to afford decent clothes. Hanley had used it himself, during the war and before.

Some distance behind him, a muffled boom announced a crew blasting away a mountain of melted iron that had once been the bones of a building. Another hazardous job, but with no lack of takers in this hard winter, when a day's wage meant at least one night's food and shelter. Nowhere near enough, but better than nothing. Just. Anger rose in Hanley, blunted by familiarity. This was the way things were, had always been. The Fire hadn't changed that.

He walked on toward the station. Against the gray sky, its red brick façade gave off a warm glow. It and a few other buildings in the burned district—including the water-pumping station, in a prime example of the Almighty's misplaced humor—had miraculously survived the disaster. Hanley strode through the front doors, spoke to the desk sergeant about retrieving the murdered rabbi's body, and headed up the central staircase to Sergeant Moore's office.

He found the chief of detectives looking out the window at the eastward view down Lake Street. Hanley followed suit as he moved toward the fire in the office grate. His attention was caught by the line of half-finished stone and brick buildings that receded into the distance, sharing the streetscape with the burnt shells of their predecessors. Amazing to think that most of them had started going up between late

October and November, with the embers from the Fire barely cooled. Come spring, workmen would be swarming once more on the scaffolding and walls. For now, only the desperate and driven still toiled there.

Moore spoke without turning around. "It's freezing cold and the wind could blow a man into the river, but they never stop working."

"Three of them *were* blown into the river. Last Friday. Drowned." Hanley watched the distant moving specks. He imagined the chill of fingers too frozen to grip the scaffolding, the weight of bodies held in space by no more than a hank of rope. "But they need to eat. So do their children."

"I see promotion hasn't smoothed you out." The sergeant turned to face Hanley. His neat mustache twitched above a wry smile. Behind it, Hanley read regret for the lost lives his remark had conjured up. Moore had never been a laborer's son, but he gave a damn anyway. Not for the first time, Hanley blessed the luck that had brought this man to him as friend and mentor a decade ago, and had now won him a place serving under Moore on Chicago's twelve-man detective force. This case was his chance to justify Moore's faith in him.

He matched his sergeant's light tone. "My mother says that, too."

Moore ambled to his desk and leaned against it. His dark brown hair looked as if a mouse had nested in it. "What can you tell me so far?"

"The dead man is Asher Kelmansky. A rabbi—that's what they call their priests." The warmth from the fire made his chilled legs prickle. "Sixty-odd years old, a little less than my height—five foot ten or eleven, maybe—and not much bulk." He steeled himself for what he must say next. "He was praying when he was killed."

A mix of revulsion and sadness flitted across the sergeant's narrow face. "Go on."

"I thought at first it was a robbery gone wrong. It still could be. Jacob Nathan—the man who came here to report it—said they didn't have much worth stealing, but he did describe a little silver box and candelabra. Menorah, he called it. Mate to the one the rabbi was killed with. If anyone tries to fence them, they should turn up in the next few days. No lock on the door. Anyone could've wandered in. The daughter said Kelmansky carried no cash, but she might not've known whether he had any last night."

He thought of Rivka as he rubbed feeling back into his stiff fingers. He'd felt her emotions from the moment he walked into the synagogue— pain, shock, and exhaustion so deep it had tired him just to look at her. She'd seemed fragile, bent under the weight of her grief. Yet she'd stayed there the entire time. That took strength and grit. More than he'd have expected in a girl who looked no older than his younger sister. A smile crossed his face as he wondered what Kate would make of her. Then he sobered. *He* still wasn't sure what to make of her.

Moore leaned forward. "Something else?"

Hanley shoved his warmed hands into his coat pockets and paced away from the fire. "The victim's daughter. Rivka Kelmansky. She was there when Nathan and I showed up. She discovered the body late last night."

"You think she's involved?"

No came straight to mind, but he made himself think it through before answering. "I don't know," he said instead. He paced in the opposite direction. "I don't think she killed him. His skull was crushed with the menorah's base—about as big around as my arm. There'd have been a lot of blood from a blow like that and there wasn't a speck on her. But I saw some things that didn't add up."

"Such as?"

"Marks on the floor, for one." He showed Moore his sketch of them. "Whoever made these likely stole the clean menorah and the little box, then got out of there. Yet the thief who throws away the murder weapon keeps enough of a cool head to scoop up a little plunder on his way out? Why not take both menorahs? He already had the one in his hand.

"Then there's what *wasn't* stolen, but should have been. Along with the murder weapon there was the wedding ring the dead man wore. And his clothes. They were good quality. Why batter a man's head in and then balk at dealing with the mess if it means a better take?"

"Maybe he heard the daughter coming."

Hanley nodded. "Her or someone else passing by. Some drunk

headed home from Callaghan's saloon, maybe—that's the nearest one I know of, and it was well past midnight from what she said." He thought of Nathan's odd reactions at the synagogue. "Or the rabbi might've been killed by someone he knew. I found a boot print in the mud outside, looked like it could be around the same size as Jacob Nathan's feet and deep enough for what I'd guess he weighs. His boots had dried mud on them. And he looks strong enough to have hefted that menorah."

"Of course, given the cowpaths all over the city, who's to say where any muck on your man's boots came from? And the print may not be the killer's."

"Timing's right, though. It was frozen in the mud. Remember how cold it got after the rain last night? The downpour would've wiped out everything from earlier in the day. By sunrise this morning, the ground would've been frozen too hard to take prints. So, whoever stepped there must have done it sometime yesterday evening, between the end of the rain and the cold snap."

"Time of death should help you there."

Hanley nodded. "Some of his people may know something about it…if this wasn't a robbery. Or they might have seen or heard something in either case."

Moore gave Hanley a sober look. "If one of their own did it, you'll have a hell of a time getting anyone to say a word. I have friends among the German Jews and, from what some of them tell me, these new arrivals from Eastern Europe are a remarkably clannish lot. Most of them don't have much truck with outsiders, not even their fellow Jews."

"Some ways, we'd be lucky if one of his own killed him," Hanley said slowly. "That's a mixed neighborhood around Market and Franklin. Bohemians, Irish, a handful of Germans and the Jews, all in the same few blocks. And not getting along so well lately, with work short and relief shorter." He moved closer to the window. "Just last week, a drunk Bohemian in Callaghan's thumped the daylights out of some poor German boy over a card game. Schmidt told me it damned near turned into a riot. If some German or Bohemian or Irishman killed this rabbi…or even comes under suspicion for it…" He trailed off, not wanting to put the worst into words. As if saying it might make it happen.

"I don't envy you this case, Frank."

"I'll get the job done. You backed me for it and I'm damned if I'll prove Captain Hickey right." Hanley grinned. "And then there's the worst thing. How in the name of Mary and Jesus would I face my mam if I let you down?"

ဆ

The wind had picked up and it hit Hanley's face like a bowl of ice water. The short walk back to the synagogue suddenly seemed like miles.

He sighed and trudged down the sidewalk. The cold kept the planks from sinking into the frozen mud beneath and dampened the pervasive odors of moist lumber and rotting vegetables. The light was thin and gray, like the remnants of snow on the ground, and flurries swirled in the air. Not enough to cover the dirty snow-crust and muck, unfortunately. Hanley picked up his pace. He loathed winter, the harshness and ugliness of it. Especially now, with the city's scorched bones still bared to the sky and the taste of smoke in the air.

As he headed south, clopping hooves and creaking wheels blended with the ring of hammers and workingmen's shouts. The riverfront was busier here, where burned-over lots were still being cleared of rubble and new buildings were going up. He passed Z. M. Hall's Wholesale Grocers, its painted sign standing out against the pale stone of the five-story Lind Block. The massive building had survived the Fire, thanks to the strip of bare land around it that the flames hadn't jumped. Beyond it were a new dry-goods store, a locksmith's, a wheelwright's. No gambling houses that he knew of yet. Most of those had moved south since the Fire, though a few lay further east in what had been Gambler's Row on Clark Street. Hanley's old stomping grounds. In spite of himself, he felt the pull of habit. *A stiff drink, a good hand of cards, a pile of coins on the table…* He gritted his teeth and forced his mind back to his surroundings.

They'd nearly finished the giant warehouse on one corner of Randolph Street. He watched a group of laborers tacking down its tin-strip roof. Beyond the warehouse rose several barracks, hastily put up by the city to house the legions of newly homeless—a thicket of drafty, badly built pine-board structures fiercely protested by the Union-Fireproof Party during last November's election. Mayor Medill would surely order them torn down before long, in accordance with his favored ban on wooden buildings within city limits. Above the barracks to the south, the charred brick walls of the gasworks loomed. The blackened stone above the bright new wood gave Hanley a hollow feeling in his stomach. He walked faster, anxious to reach his destination and have something else to think about.

He arrived at the synagogue and found pandemonium. Four patrolmen stood near the front steps of the sanctuary, holding a sheet-covered stretcher that bore the corpse. Several men wearing skullcaps, along with a few women, had nearly surrounded them and Schmidt, gesturing and shouting in what Hanley guessed was their native tongue. Among them, Hanley recognized Hannah Nathan and the three men he'd seen earlier that morning. Jacob Nathan stood between the angry people and the policemen, trying to make himself heard.

Hannah's voice rose above the rest. "He is our rabbi! He stays with us!"

"No." Rolf Schmidt's bass rumble reminded Hanley of a bull steer. "We take him to the morgue. Or you go to jail."

A louder shout erupted from the crowd. The word *jail*, or at least Schmidt's tone, had gotten through the language barrier. The depth of the patrolman's anger surprised Hanley. Schmidt was normally rock-steady under pressure, a trait that served him well on the job and out with other coppers at local beer gardens. Hanley had lost more than one drinking game to him. Not that he minded, much. Schmidt was one of the few beat cops who'd seemed to trust him wholeheartedly from the start. For that, Hanley was glad to buy him a few rounds of beer.

He pitched his voice above the din as he strode into the muddy yard. "All right! Everybody calm down!"

Angry, frightened faces turned to look at him. He spread his hands in a peacemaking gesture. "Whatever the problem is, I'm sure we can settle it." Then he beckoned Schmidt aside. "What's the trouble?"

"We came for the body. They said no. Tried to stop us doing our job. We supposed to let them?"

Hanley clapped him on the shoulder. "I'll see what I can do." He stepped away from Schmidt. "Mr. Nathan? Can you explain what's going on?"

"You must understand. Our law—" Nathan broke off. One hand went to his forehead, as if easing a headache. He glanced down at the snow-dotted dirt, then back at Hanley. "You are Christian. You could not know. Our ways are not yours. We treat our dead with reverence. There are things we must do—"

"And there are things *we* must do." Hanley heard the sharpness in his voice and reined in his temper. As the man had said, there were things he didn't know—including whether or not Nathan had meant to imply that the police lacked respect for the dead. "We don't intend any offense to you," he continued, choosing his words with care. "But we need to examine the body to help us find the killer. Your people would want that, surely."

"Of course." Nathan's weary reply robbed Hanley of his anger. "I tried to tell them it is permitted to wait when it cannot be helped, but…" He looked at Hanley, his eyes moist. "We loved our rabbi. They are grieving."

"Then tell us what you need."

Nathan eyed the sky. "Shabbos—our Sabbath—begins this evening. Can you bring our rabbi back to us before then? With enough time to bury him before sundown?"

Hanley shook his head. A mutter arose, but subsided when Nathan raised a cautioning hand. "There'll have to be a coroner's inquest," Hanley said. "We'll need to keep him at least a day."

"Then we can wait until after Shabbos. One day, sundown to sundown. But no longer. It is not permitted to leave him unburied once Shabbos ends." He locked eyes with Hanley. "You understand this? Our law demands that he rest by then, in the earth from which he came."

Motion caught Hanley's eye as someone moved into his line of sight. Rivka Kelmansky had reached the gathering. Her face looked haggard, framed by her dark kerchief and coat. Nathan looked startled at her presence.

Hanley was thinking of her as he replied. "Send someone to City Hospital. That's where inquests are held. I'll be there. I can see to things."

Some of the tension went out of Nathan, as if he were setting down a burden. Then he spoke to the gathered people. As he finished, the men and women shuffled away from the stretcher-bearers. Hanley noticed some of them glancing at Rivka and whispering together. As if she'd done wrong by being here, though he couldn't think how. He found himself wanting to defend her, an absurd notion. He didn't know these people or their ways. Jacob Nathan had made that clear enough.

As the patrolmen moved off with their load, Hanley did some quick thinking. If the fracas in the synagogue yard were any indication of local English skills, he'd need someone to translate for him on his first canvass. Asking Nathan to do it was a risk—if the man knew anything about Rabbi Kelmansky's death, he might well try to conceal it—but watching his responses now might show where to dig for more information later. He could always come back and talk to people again, once he found someone else to help him.

"I need to know if anyone saw anything last night," he said. "Can you come along and interpret for me?"

The stretcher-bearers were continuing their slow walk toward Market Street. Nathan threw them a panicked look. "I can't. I must stay with the Rav, to watch—"

"I can," Rivka said.

Hanley stared. "You?" Beyond him, he saw Nathan standing still in apparent shock. All murmuring from the others in the yard had ceased.

The corner of her mouth rose, though the brief lightness didn't reach her eyes. "I speak English and Yiddish well. That is what you need, yes?"

"Rivka—" Nathan said.

"Please, Onkl Jacob. Let me do this for my father."

"No, Rivka. You are *onen*. In mourning. It is not your place."

"Then whose?" Defiant, she turned to Hanley. "I will help you. However I can."

Nathan let out a harsh breath. "Then on your head be it." He turned and hurried away after the departing stretcher.

Briefly, Rivka's gaze followed him. Then she adjusted her kerchief and turned back toward Hanley. In her eyes he read lingering regret, likely for Nathan's sharp words. Also a hint of nervousness, coupled with fierce determination. "Well then, Officer Hanley."

"Detective," he corrected. And then felt foolish. What did it matter what she called him, as long as she helped him out?

"Detective. Where shall we begin?"

THREE

till nothing, Rivka thought as she and Detective Hanley left the Kleins' butcher shop. *I should have known.* Discouragement settled on her like a weight. They'd been at this all afternoon and had nothing to show for it.

She'd had some hopes of the Kleins, which made it all the worse. Lazar Klein served as cantor at the shul, leading the people in chants and prayers. That, along with his easy manner toward his customers, made him unlikely to feel cowed at the prospect of talking to a policeman. Lazar's wife, Sisel, was a friend and would gladly aid them if she could. But Rivka's own presence, which she'd hoped would help, had proved a hindrance instead.

"I have customers," Klein said when he came to the shop door. He eyed Hanley briefly and managed to look past, rather than at, Rivka, even though she stood next to Hanley on the threshold. "I cannot talk now." The bemused look on his face made Rivka wonder if he found it as strange as she did, to see a grown man bareheaded and clean-shaven like a boy too young for *bar mitzvah*. Not that she would dare ask him. He was clearly shocked to see her with a strange man when she ought to be home tending to her mourning duties.

The chill wind ruffled Hanley's dark brown hair, giving it a wild look at odds with his sober expression. "Mr. Klein, the sooner I speak to everyone, the more likely someone will remember something. Too much time passes, people forget."

Klein looked regretful, but shook his head. "I don't know anything that could help you. I'm sorry." He stepped back and started to close the door.

Rivka spoke up, keeping her gaze modestly lowered. "May we speak with Fray Klein, then? Only for a moment."

He pursed his lips, then stepped aside. "Sisel is in the kitchen. She may speak if she will." He gave Hanley a sharp look. "Mind you don't distress her. This has all been bad enough for a woman in her condition."

Rivka thanked him and led the way through the shop to the rooms at the back where the family lived. "Sisel Klein is with child," she murmured to Hanley as they went. Speaking of such a private thing to a man, let alone a near-stranger, made warmth rise in her cheeks, but he had to know. Not just for Sisel's sake, but for their inquiry as well. If Detective Hanley caused offense because Rivka failed to safeguard him from it, no one would tell him anything, even if they knew it to tell.

They found Sisel peeling potatoes, her eight-year-old daughter Chava scrubbing more and adding to the small pile on the kitchen table. Surprise crossed Sisel's face at the sight of them and she edged forward in her chair. "Rivka! I'm so sorry…it's terrible, so terrible what happened." She struggled to rise, barely able to manage the weight of the baby. She must be near her time, Rivka thought.

"Please, don't get up," she said, as she crossed the room and bent to receive Sisel's one-armed embrace. Her eyes stung and she blinked back the threatened tears. Her friend was upset enough on her account already. She pulled back enough to see Sisel's face. "You've been well? The baby, too?"

Sisel's hand drifted to her swollen belly. "As far as I can tell. He moves a lot. Much more than the last one." A shadow darkened her eyes and Rivka squeezed her hand. After a moment, Sisel managed a smile. "Who have you brought here?" she murmured. "Lazar said there was a policeman at the shul."

"Yes." Rivka glanced over her shoulder at Hanley, who waited near the doorway, his eyes missing nothing as he looked around the room. He caught her gaze and she beckoned him over. "This is Detective Hanley. He wants to ask you a few questions. Is that all right?"

Sisel looked nervous. "I can't talk to a *goy*. I don't understand them well enough."

"I do." Rivka's gaze shifted to Chava, who was watching everything with wide eyes. "Chava can help too. She's a good student in my English class."

Delight at her teacher's praise flashed across the girl's face. She set down a potato and drew herself up as straight as she could. After a moment's hesitation, Sisel nodded.

Hanley moved forward. Just a few steps, as if aware that coming too close would make Sisel more uneasy than she already was. Patiently, like a doctor in a sickroom, he asked the same questions he'd asked everyone else. Hopeful at first, as she let Chava translate, stepping in only when the child faltered, Rivka's heart sank as Sisel gave the same answers. No, she hadn't seen or heard anything unusual last night. She had slept well, waking only once to use the chamber pot. She blushed as she said that, but Rivka read truth in her face and voice. No, she knew of no one who would harm the rabbi or even contemplate such a thing. "We all loved him," she said, with a mournful glance at Rivka. "No one would say a harsh word about him, let alone..." She trailed off with a shudder. Tamping down her own grief, Rivka laid a consoling arm around her shoulders.

Later, as they walked east down Madison Street, Rivka stole a glance at Hanley. It must be getting to him, too, this endless round of talking without success. Then again, maybe he was learning plenty. Who knew what was useful to a policeman investigating a murder? She shied away from that thought and focused again on Hanley's face. All bones and angles, but somehow handsome anyway. Because of the eyes, she thought. Wide and deep-set, they were slate blue, like storm clouds. Eyes that saw things other people missed. Was that what had made so many people reluctant to talk—a sense that Hanley could see through them, figure out things about them that they didn't want known? Or was it only that he was an outsider and police?

In his place, she would have given up long ago. Part of her wanted to now, but she had promised Hanley help, and help he would get. She pulled her coat tighter at the neck and kept pace with him, determined more than ever to do her part.

Useless, Hanley thought bitterly as they neared Franklin Street, passing yet more pine-board frame houses and storefronts with painted signs amid scattered empty lots. All put up in defiance of the new fire codes that took no notice of what city residents could afford to build with. *An absolutely useless waste of time.* He'd hoped Rivka's presence might make her neighbors more willing to talk. Instead, they'd gotten muttered apologies followed by closed doors, or tearful praise for Rabbi Kelmansky with not a scrap of useful information attached.

Despite their fruitless efforts, Rivka's determination hadn't wavered. The devotion of a daughter to her murdered father? Or did she want to keep an eye on him? He'd caught her sneaking looks at him. Maybe she didn't trust him to do a good job. *Or she has other reasons for wanting to know who tells me what.*

He walked faster, as if physical activity could banish such thoughts. He didn't like to think of Rivka being involved in her father's death, even though cold cop logic told him not to make assumptions this early on. He'd even begun to hope he'd found an ally, at least with the language barrier. But Moore had been right, and Hanley realized he faced a bigger challenge than the usual immigrant clannishness. He felt frustrated and ignorant and suspicious of everything, even more than a good cop should.

I just want to find the truth, he felt like shouting into the freezing air. *I'm not an enemy. I'm here to do a job.* Even as he thought it, he realized how futile it sounded. Jacob Nathan's words floated into his head—*You are Christian. You could not know.* As if that alone placed him so far from these people that no tie could exist between him and them.

"Have you eaten yet today?" Rivka asked as they reached Madison and Franklin.

"What?" The unexpected question halted Hanley in his tracks.

"Have you eaten yet today? Or am I speaking Yiddish and don't know it?"

"Tea for breakfast. With milk." He gave her a quick, wry grin. "It's not supposed to show."

She nodded toward the west side of Franklin. "Pavlic's Bakery is over there. They're Bohemian. Ever since the Fire, we've sometimes bought from them, even though they don't follow *kashruth*—Jewish dietary laws. They need the money as much as we do." Sadness and pride washed over her face. "After the Fire, once we had rebuilt a little, my father told us to buy what we could from here. Anything except bread for Shabbos." She took a breath, then let it out. "Mira Pavlic makes good onion rolls. As good as our own baker does. I've been buying them since November."

The small, dim shop brimmed with the scent of yeast. A board had been nailed over a brick-sized hole in one corner of the front window. Rivka glanced at it and frowned, but said nothing. Children's squabbling echoed from a back room. The bakery's only visible tenant stood bent over in front of a brick oven, wisps of blonde hair straggling over her thin neck and brushing the shoulders of her cotton dress. She turned at the sound of their entry, gripping a long-handled breadboard. Then she saw Rivka and some of the tension left her face. Hanley wondered who she'd been expecting. Friends of the brick-thrower, maybe.

She slid a browned loaf onto a cooling rack, propped the board against the side of the counter and came forward. "You are buying today?" she asked in a thick Bohemian accent.

"An onion roll, please, Mira." Rivka managed a small but genuine smile. "How are the children?"

Mrs. Pavlic shrugged. "Little Anton is over his chest cold. Thank God no doctor." She plucked a large, shiny roll from a nearly bare tray and dropped it into a brown paper bag. Hanley, stepping closer to hand over a penny, noticed careful patching around the shoulder seams of her dress. A fading bruise marked her cheek and the weariness in her face spoke of more than long hours slaving over dough. *That could explain the breadboard*, he thought with a jolt of sympathy. Nothing to do with brick-tossing hooligans, just a husband too quick with his fists.

He fished up another penny. "Two rolls, please, ma'am." He glanced at Rivka. "I'm not the only one who hasn't eaten enough today."

"I can't—" she began, but broke off as the woman dropped another

31

roll into the bag. Rivka's expression changed to guarded respect and Hanley felt a small, warm glow. At least he'd accomplished one thing today.

The sharp, fresh taste of the warm onion roll made him think of spring. He ate it in four bites. Mrs. Pavlic had turned her back to them again. He heard the soft *whuff* of punched dough, a familiar sound from childhood Saturdays. Somewhere in the back, a door closed with a *chunk*.

He looked around the bakery, noting details by long habit as he dusted crumbs off his hands. From years ago as a bunco-steerer to his days walking a beat, he'd long since learned it paid to be aware of his surroundings. The shelves by the oven held a tin of baking powder, a box of salt, and a few spice jars. Beneath them stood two tall canisters, likely for flour and sugar. A small wooden ice-box shared the long back counter with three mixing spoons stuck in a washed-out tea tin, a dough-rolling board, and a rolling pin. In a corner he spied a sugar barrel and a twenty-pound burlap sack of flour. From the sack's forlorn sag, he guessed it was almost empty.

He looked up to see Mrs. Pavlic watching him. He nodded toward the flour bag. "Must go through a lot of that in a week."

She scooped her dough out of its bowl and laid it on the back counter, then draped a white towel over it. "We manage."

The display trays said otherwise. Besides the one from which his roll had come, Hanley could see another one half full, plus one more that held four loaves of plain brown bread. The loaf just out of the oven made five and the dough she'd just finished might make another three. He could see nothing else for sale.

"The Aid help much? My mother's still waiting for a sewing machine."

"The Aid!" Mrs. Pavlic yanked open a drawer beneath the back counter. It gave with a screech. Out came another bowl and a pair of scoops. She picked up the larger scoop, along with one of the canisters, and approached the flour sack. The canister thunked on the floor as she set it down. "The Aid does not help. No one helps. Only the rabbi—" She glanced at Rivka. "I am so sorry for you. Sorry for us, too." She knelt and began scooping flour from the bag into the canister with sharp, jerky motions.

Did she think Kelmansky's people would stop buying from her with him gone? She must have other customers. But maybe not enough to get by. Hanley watched her digging in the flour sack. A twenty-pound bag and not from the Aid. From where, then? "Relief and Aid's given you nothing?"

"Nothing. Why do you ask this?" Before he could answer, her guarded expression gave way to cautious hope. "You are a reporter, maybe? You are writing a story? You can say how it really is. Make them do more. Better. Give us food, give us work so men don't fight and throw stones through windows."

"Tell me," Hanley said. He saw Rivka's sharp look in his direction, but ignored it.

Mrs. Pavlic rested her arms across her upraised knee. The scoop dangled from her fingers. "Big Anton…he is a good man when there is work. Not bad, you understand? Only worried, because there is no work. I told the reporter who came last week to talk to Anton about the saloon fight. That German boy started it anyway, cheating and lying." Contempt came over her face. "But those rich ladies, they see the bottle. They hear the baby cry for hunger. They think we are bad and they say no food. No clothes. No help. We have no one else to help. Even our church, it has nothing. Too many people, not enough to give. Only the rabbi could help us."

"How did the rabbi help you?"

She nodded toward the flour bag. "He gave us that. Flour, salt, food for the children, for the bakery. Clothes for Anton once. New shoes for Lilia—red shoes, no buttons gone. He helped everyone, everyone." She closed the canister and stood, her eyes on Rivka. "Your father was a blessed man. We are Christian, but he gave to us. I pray God will be good to his soul."

Hanley glanced at Rivka. She looked confused, even disturbed. A strange reaction to hearing her father praised, especially in light of her earlier pride in his request to buy at this store.

He turned back to Mrs. Pavlic. "Did the rabbi give you things often?"

"Three times since Advent. Others, too. I saw him go to their houses."

She returned to the back counter, where she set down the canister and began measuring flour into the clean bowl. "He brought baskets, food sometimes, clothes. A winter coat for Mr. Murphy across the street. I saw it on Saturday when Murphy came for bread. Before that...Nathan the tailor...he came to us with the rabbi and brought the flour. For Christmas baking. That big bag full, on his shoulders like a sheep."

"And he last brought you provisions...?"

"A week ago, Friday. Salt, cornmeal, a shirt for Little Anton." She shook her head. "How can someone kill such a man?"

He thought of the stolen silver, but said nothing. The saloon fight she'd mentioned must be the one at Callaghan's, which was Schmidt's case. He would ask Schmidt about Anton Pavlic. "You live in back of the shop?"

She nodded.

"Does your house overlook the synagogue? The Jewish church," he elaborated at her blank look. "You might have seen something, if—"

"We saw nothing." She flushed and reached for the baking powder. "We ate supper, we went to bed, we slept."

"Ma'am, if you'd just let me have a look over the yard. It may be important."

"Please, Mira," Rivka said.

After a moment, Mrs. Pavlic put down the baking-powder tin and beckoned. "Come."

FOUR

They followed her into a small room divided by half-drawn curtains. The scent of new pine boards mingled with stale coffee, bread, and unwashed linen. From somewhere past the curtains came a baby's thin wail.

The familiar sound chilled Hanley. Hungry babies cried like that. Babies weakened and miserable from the dull ache of a never-full stomach. Conley's Patch, the rough Irish neighborhood where he'd grown up, had been full of them.

Mrs. Pavlic strode to the bed just visible through the curtain gap and bent to pick up her child. Its wails subsided to whimpering as she cuddled it against her shoulder. She rattled off a question in Bohemian as she marched the baby around the alcove. The answering voice belonged to a small girl. An impulse came over Hanley to charge through the curtain, snatch up the woman and her children, and spirit them away somewhere full of comforts. Ridiculous. He couldn't even offer the five-cent piece in his trouser pocket without shaming her.

He choked down familiar anger at the injustice of it and looked around the larger part of the room. A dingy iron stove stood near a provision cupboard, a rough-built board table, and four chairs. A lumpy straw pallet on the floor—covered in a mouse-nest of sheets, blankets, a boy-sized nightshirt, and a trailing white sock—told him where the older children slept. A wooden washtub with brass handles sat upended in one corner by the back door.

Mrs. Pavlic and her infant appeared at the curtain gap. "You can see from here," she said.

The alcove held even less than the outer area—only the bed and a dark wood dresser that clearly came from better times. The window in the back wall gave a clear view of the muddy yard. The synagogue stood in the distance partway across it. Much closer to them a young boy, fair hair blowing in the stiff wind, knelt and hacked at the snow-flecked earth with a wooden spoon. His wrists stuck out from the sleeves of his homespun jacket. Several yards beyond him and a bit to the south, Hanley saw the curve of a pump handle marking what must be the neighborhood well. Through gaps where no one had yet rebuilt he could make out the line of the boardwalk and passing traffic along Market Street, about a hundred yards away.

He turned back toward Mrs. Pavlic. A few feet behind her, Rivka and the little girl huddled in a corner talking softly, their heads bent together. To his surprise, Rivka handed over the paper bag with the remaining onion roll. With a wide-eyed glance toward her mother, the child tucked the bag away in a skirt pocket.

Hanley brought his attention back to the matter at hand. "You're sure you didn't see or hear anything last night? Didn't wake up for a drink of water, look out the window without paying much attention?"

"We all slept." She offered the baby a finger to gum. "Even Laszlo."

"What about after supper? Anything then?"

She shook her head, all her attention on the baby.

"What about your husband? Was he home?"

She bit her lip, then nodded. Clearly, she didn't want to talk about him. Out of shame for what Hanley and Rivka had seen or guessed about how the Pavlics lived? Or had Anton been out?

He would check the saloons and talk to Schmidt. In the meantime, there was nothing more to be learned here. He thanked Mrs. Pavlic for allowing him into her home and returned with Rivka to the shop. It appalled him that the Relief and Aid had come here and refused this family help, refused them even enough flour to bake the bread that earned their keep. He had to do something about that. A word in some do-gooder's ear, testimony to the character of the hardworking mother, something.

He could do one small thing now. As they reached the street door, he palmed his five-cent piece. Rivka preceded him outside, which made it easier. He glanced over his shoulder to make sure Mrs. Pavlic was out of sight and dropped the nickel as he stepped over the threshold. By the time she found it, likely when she swept up for the evening, she wouldn't know whose it was. Found money, enough to buy a little milk for the children. For one night. Even swill milk, tainted with brewery slops fed to a distillery's bony-ribbed cow, would be better than nothing.

He saw Rivka frowning as he reached her. For a moment he wondered if she'd seen his subterfuge and disapproved. *Not likely*, he thought, *considering she gave her onion roll away*. He was curious about that. "You never ate your roll," he said. "Not hungry?"

She shook her head. "I am in mourning. A mourner does not eat for a day after—" She broke off, blinking hard as if to keep tears back.

"Oh." He gave her a moment to collect herself, then started down the street. "Your father seems to have been a generous man."

"He could not have done what she said." Rivka fell into step beside him, pushing stray hair back under her kerchief. "Our people lost nearly everything in the Fire. What aid we get goes to them...and it is not enough. A few things he might have given...a little of what we ourselves had. But not so much."

"Could all your people together have...?" He trailed off at her vigorous headshake.

"Who could spare twenty pounds of flour? One or two meals to share, buying onion rolls and plain bread, that is how we helped. I don't understand this."

"Who might?"

She took some time to answer. "Jacob Nathan," she said finally. "He and my father were friends, from back in Wroclaw before I was born. They were all young together—Onkl Jacob, Tanta Hannah, and my parents. I grew up calling the Nathans my uncle and aunt."

And Nathan was still with the rabbi's body. Or maybe not. They'd have reached the morgue long since. Nathan was likely making funeral arrangements by now. "Would Mr. Nathan be home yet?"

Rivka looked startled. "He is with my father. He will stay with him until Papa is buried." She paused, her expression troubled. "You do not watch over your dead? You leave them alone?"

"Not exactly. We have—" He broke off, unable to imagine describing an Irish wake in a way that wouldn't distress her further. The gulf between them suddenly seemed huge. "We have our own ways. They're just different."

They rounded the corner onto Washington, heading back west toward Market Street. Hanley hunched inside his coat against a fresh blast of wind. Rivka flinched from it, for the first time appearing to fully feel the cold. The sunlight had nearly gone, the sun itself a shrouded patch of red-gold behind a thin cloud bank.

"I must go home for Shabbos." Rivka sounded as chilled as Hanley felt.

"We're about done anyway. Thank you for your help." He wished he dared offer her his overcoat. A gentleman would give it away without a second thought. Of course, a gentleman wouldn't be spending the next several days tramping the streets, hunting down leads. Like finding out who'd left the bloody boot marks behind in the synagogue and where the stolen silver was. He should find out more about the rabbi's charity visits as well. It seemed unlikely they'd led to murder, but Rivka was clearly uneasy about them—and Hanley couldn't afford to ignore anything that stood out.

He wanted a talk with Jacob Nathan, who wouldn't be at his home or business until sometime Sunday at the earliest, after the inquest and the burial. Unless Hanley spoke with him at the morgue—which was where he'd be, staying with the body until it went in the ground. Hanley shook his head at the strangeness of it. He knew Will Rushton would at least set Nathan up with a cot and some blankets.

They walked on toward Market Street. A train whistle shrilled from the tracks on the riverbank. More lumber for the yards, or donated food and clothes for the poor and hungry. A woman passed them, bareheaded, only a shawl over her patched dress to keep out the cold. Her face was drawn with fatigue and she avoided meeting their eyes. Hanley heard objects bumping together in the basket she carried. A few potatoes, maybe, or carrots. Not many, from the sound. As Hanley watched her go by, he saw Rivka watching too. The sight of the woman seemed to deepen her distress. Hanley reached out to her on instinct, then let his hand fall. What was there to say?

Market and Lake lay to the north. He should head that way if he meant to check for messages at Lake Street Station. Instead, he turned south at the intersection and kept walking beside Rivka. She seemed scarcely aware of him. "What did your father tell you yesterday? Before he went out?"

"That he was going to see a friend. And not to wait up."

They walked on in silence. They had reached the houses nearest the synagogue when Rivka stopped. "I want to know what happened. I do not want to sit at home and wait, and have someone else decide what I may know when the truth is finally found. I want to help. Will you let me?"

Startled, it took him a moment to retrieve his wits and answer. "You're not a policeman."

"That is not what I asked."

He should say no. He should tell her to go inside and eat and sleep, and forget any other thought.

"Help how?" he heard himself asking, as though his mouth had gotten ahead of his brain. He wanted to call the words back, but it was too late. A murder victim's daughter, helping to solve the crime? Preposterous. And he knew so little about her. He couldn't even rule her out as a suspect—though he stood by what he'd told Moore earlier, that he doubted she'd done the killing. The cold-blooded nerve needed to have cleaned herself up, changed clothes, and then masqueraded through the morning's scene in the synagogue didn't fit with the shock and anguish he'd seen on her face. Or with the woman he'd been observing all afternoon.

"I have been some help today, yes?" Her attempt at a smile slipped away as she continued. "You do not know my people, Detective Hanley. I do. They will tell me things they would not dare say to you."

"No one said much today."

"Because..." She looked away, toward the dying sunset.

"Because I'm a copper."

"And a Christian."

Silence stretched between them. To his surprise, Hanley found himself thinking over her proposal. He would need help, at least with the language. And, right now, he wasn't sure where to get it. His landlady, Ida Kirschner, might speak Yiddish. But she hailed from a small town near Munich. The rabbi's people were from elsewhere. They might not accept her any more than they had him, even if she *did* agree to translate for him.

"If you knew what they had seen, you would not blame them," Rivka said.

"I don't. As you say, I don't know them."

"They loved my father. They will talk to me."

"With or without my being there?"

"Does it matter?"

He brought up the last objection he could think of. "How will you reach me? I can't exactly drop by your house."

"The police station is not far from here. A good walk on a clear day."

Neither of them brought up the scant likelihood of clear days in a Chicago winter. Hanley shoved his hands deeper into his pockets. The whole notion was crazy. Captain Hickey would have his head if he ever found out about it. But Hickey wasn't standing in front of him, waiting for an answer that might break him if it was no.

To hell with Captain Hickey. His case, his decision. "All right," he said, and her face brightened. "Day after tomorrow, then. Can you come by in the morning? I can be there by half past ten or so." He'd have to rush from Sunday Mass, but it would be worth it if she learned something that could give him a real place to start. And he found he liked the thought of seeing her again.

She hesitated. "Afternoon would be easier."

"One o'clock, then. Will that do?"

Her tentative smile almost reached her eyes. "I will be there."

SHALL WE NOT REVENGE

℗

"You should have been here." Tanta Hannah sat in the parlor in Rivka's house, her needlework across her lap. Rivka wondered how long she'd been waiting and braced herself for a scolding, which wasn't long in coming. "The girls and I took care of things. Again. You cannot be so heedless all your life, Rivka. You have obligations. One day you will have to see to them yourself."

Stung, Rivka replied with unintended sharpness. "Is it not an obligation to find out who killed Papa?"

"Such things should be left to the men." Hannah put her embroidery aside and picked up her coat. "Come along. My girls have Shabbos dinner waiting."

The mention of food made Rivka's empty stomach grumble. There could be no mourning on Shabbos, so she would be allowed to break her mourner's fast. She grabbed the back of the sofa to steady herself. Tanta Hannah's arms, warm and strong, slid around her. "It's all right. You're home now. I shouldn't have snapped at you. Poor *maideleh*. Such a terrible day."

Rivka held tight, her face pressed against Hannah's shoulder. The older woman's quiet weeping, the smooth silk of her best dress over her sturdy body, the tang of polish from the afternoon's cleaning, all threatened to overwhelm her. She should have helped to prepare her home for *shiva* instead of going off with Detective Hanley.

The thought of Hanley brought confusion. She couldn't make sense of what she'd learned in his company. She pulled away from Tanta Hannah. "Is there anything left to do here?"

"Only the candle," Hannah said.

The small silver holder stood on the dining room table, the shiva candle next to it. Rivka picked the candle up. It would be her task to light it when they returned home after burying Papa. *More than a day from now.*

Clumsily, she set the candle in its holder. It toppled out and rolled off the table. She clenched her hands and pressed them to her forehead.

After a moment that felt like an hour, she retrieved the candle and turned it in her fingers. Papa had gone to see someone yesterday and never come home. Who?

Onkl Jacob knew. He must. She wedged the candle into its holder and hurried back to where Hannah was waiting.

FIVE

Hanley overslept the next morning. No time for a decent breakfast, just a thick slice of soda bread handed to him by his mother as he dashed out of Ida Kirschner's boardinghouse on West Monroe at five to eight. He wolfed the bread as he strode down the sidewalk, eying the neighborhood as he went. Two- and three-story frame buildings as far as he could see. The Fire had barely touched the West Division. There were no burned lots raked clean of rubble, no piles of scorched bricks and blackened stone. No hint of smoke in the cold, crisp air. And there were trees, whose bare branches would put out new leaves come spring. Not like Conley's Patch where the blaze started. Hanley's old home, and everything around it, had burned to the ground.

Ida's three-floor house looked much like its neighbors, with weathered clapboards, fading paint, and a weed-sprinkled patch of winter-brown grass. Here and there as he walked, Hanley saw small kitchen gardens, identifiable by the frozen remains of cabbages and wilted onion stalks. Henhouses and pig sheds took up space in several yards. The wind carried the smell of them everywhere, but Hanley had learned to ignore it. A few homes, their occupants blessed with somewhat higher wages, sported leafless rose bushes near their front stoops.

A lumber cart rattled past, heading east toward the yards by the bank of the Chicago River. Closer by, the patter of tiny hooves and a woman's startled shriek split the morning air. "Daisy! Bad girl! Hiram, get your pants on! She's loose again!" Three houses ahead, a large black-and-white pig shot through a gate and dashed in Hanley's direction. He flattened himself against a nearby board fence as the pig ran past, followed by a plump woman in a brown work dress. Her dark hair, hastily pinned, was falling down. She shouted the pig's name again, along with dire threats in language no lady ought to use. Hanley bit his lip to keep back the laughter until she'd gone well past him.

The luckless Hiram came out next, a spare fellow still struggling to fasten one suspender as he ran. "That way," Hanley said, with a nod up the street, where pig and woman had gone. Hiram gasped a thank-you and gave up on the suspender in favor of greater speed. Still chuckling, Hanley went on his way.

The four-story tenement at the corner of Monroe and Jefferson was a bordello, but as no children were employed there and it had never been a site of violence, Hanley followed the custom of the police department and left it alone. With so many work-seeking newcomers offering fresh victims for footpads, confidence tricksters, and bunco men, Chicago's finest had more serious affairs to deal with than a relatively quiet whorehouse. As he neared its bright red front door, a late-departing customer came staggering out. A farm boy by the look of him, with straw-thatch hair and a freckled face. He gave Hanley a sheepish grin as he tucked in the tail of his homespun shirt and then headed west up the street.

Hanley watched him go. The memory of a face rose in his mind—delicate as a cat's, with a cloud of dark hair and deep blue eyes. Pegeen. Another face came then, bony and cold-eyed with a wolf's smile. *Sean Doyle.*

He clenched his hands into fists. Bad enough that he still dreamed of Pegeen whenever he'd had an especially grueling day. Worse that Sean Doyle was still alive and free, ruining lives in his brothels and gambling hells. *Should've done for him when I had the chance.*

Down that road lay ruin. He knew it. He walked faster, concentrating hard on the sound of his footsteps until he turned onto Jefferson Street, leaving the whorehouse and the memories behind. The rhythm of his own motion soothed away the roiling anger that thoughts of Pegeen and Doyle had raised. With his mind back under control, he felt able to finish the long, cold journey to the county morgue.

SHALL WE NOT REVENGE

ᘓ

Rivka lay in bed and stared out the window at the early morning sky. A sunny day, clear and cold. A Shabbos day, a day for joy even in the midst of grief.

The day Papa's body would come home.

Her throat felt tight and her eyes burned. She had hardly slept, save for a light doze every couple of hours. Even being in her own bedroom, where she'd insisted on returning after last night's meal at the Nathans' next door, had brought no solace. At the moment, she didn't even have the energy to cry. Just as well it was Shabbos, she thought dully. No work could be done, no food prepared or cooked. All that had been seen to yesterday. Hannah had set carrots and honey to simmer all night, and stew with barley and beans. Rivka need do nothing, though she could leave the house with Tanta Hannah to attend the day's services if she chose. She could listen from behind the women's curtain, tucked away where no sight of her could distract the men from prayer. She hated it. It made her feel far away from Hashem's sight, too. A son would be expected to pray in the open. Why not a daughter?

She rolled over, restless. A small lump beneath her pillow pressed against her cheek. She reached under, pulled out Papa's second-best tobacco pouch, and pressed it to her nose. It smelled of leather and cherries and smoke. She had snuck into his room last night and taken it from the pocket of his old, worn suit. A childish thing to do, but it gave her a little comfort. The scent took her back to a long-ago afternoon, herself eleven years old and finished with morning lessons and chores, sitting in Papa's study while he taught her to play chess, the aromatic smoke from his pipe wrapping around them like a blanket. It had become their tradition. Every Friday before sundown, a game, a talk, his pipe, and a pot of tea. For that hour, no one could interrupt them—not her mother or brother, not any of their neighbors, not even Onkl Jacob.

She sat up, bracing herself against the sudden chill, and slid the pouch back under the pillow. There was one thing she could do today—talk to Onkl Jacob. Alone, without the Nathan daughters there to change the subject. They had been painfully obvious about it during Shabbos dinner at the Nathans' home the night before, the girls following their mother's lead and Tanta Hannah looking more disapproving with every attempt Rivka made to ask where Papa had gone late on Thursday afternoon. According to Tanta Hannah, she had no business raising such questions or even thinking about who might have killed Papa. She should mourn him like a dutiful daughter and leave the thinking—and doing—to others.

She threw back the blankets, swung her legs out of bed, and pushed her feet into her knitted slippers. She couldn't leave it to others. Tanta Hannah knew her well enough to know that by now.

Fatigue made her stumble as she went to the washbasin. She broke the thin ice on the water in the pitcher, then poured some into the bowl and splashed her face. The icy water cooled her burning cheeks and sharpened her resolve against the familiar guilt of her failure to be a properly docile Jewish girl. Onkl Jacob would come home with Papa's body after sundown. She might have a chance at him then. Or after the burial on Sunday morning, while people gathered for the meal of condolence. Somehow she would help Detective Hanley find out who killed her father, no matter what anyone thought. Deep within and barely acknowledged, she felt a spark at the thought of seeing Hanley again.

♋

The warmth of the City Hospital, where the morgue was housed, came as a relief when Hanley finally arrived. His ears and fingers burned as the chill left them, but he welcomed the feeling. A patch of frostbite that had nearly cost him his little finger during the war had taught him to be grateful for the pain that proved flesh was still alive. He lingered in the hospital lobby until his hands and ears no longer stung and his feet had regained feeling, then headed down a back hallway.

The morgue itself felt almost as cold as the outside, except for the absence of wind. The sharp sterile smells of carbolic and formaldehyde failed to mask the stink of dead flesh. Hanley forced himself not to gag.

He wasn't looking forward to the autopsy. Maybe he'd get lucky and the coroner would have decided to skip it.

He found Will Rushton in the examining room, bent over one of three long tables, working on a body. Not the rabbi's. Even from the doorway, Hanley could tell it was too large. The rabbi's corpse must still be in the adjoining deadhouse. He coughed at the stench as he stepped into the room. The sound made Rushton look up. He nodded in greeting, then returned to his work. Stains Hanley didn't care to identify dotted his canvas apron. His hands were rock-steady as he pushed aside a long flap of skin and muscle he'd cut from the dead man's chest. Underneath, Hanley saw the white curve of ribs.

"Drowning victim," Rushton said as he peered beneath the exposed ribcage. "Damned fool must've walked out on the lake ice until he hit water and went under. Drunk as an alderman at election time, I'll wager."

Hanley moved closer, morbidly drawn to the body in spite of himself. He watched as Rushton sliced neatly through the thin tissue between two ribs, then lifted the sliced bit out and poked gently with his scalpel at the grayish mass underneath. He set the scalpel down, picked up a nearby record-book and wrote something in it. "You're here about the fellow in the deadhouse? Schmidt said yesterday he's your case."

Hanley nodded. "I thought you'd be done with him by now."

"You *hoped*." Rushton grinned, green eyes bright in his olive-hued face. His looks favored his Spanish mother, he'd once claimed with a laugh, but Hanley sometimes wondered if he had Indian blood somewhere. "I know you. You'd just as soon miss the whole thing."

"True enough." Hanley grinned back. "And now I've no excuse not to watch."

"My notes from the external exam are in the inquest room. You can get them while I finish up."

Hanley made his temporary escape and found the book of notes at one end of the long table where the coroner usually presided. The table, the witness chair, a few scattered seats, and two narrow wooden benches in the rear, where spectators sat, nearly filled the small chamber. Hanley lingered there, reading about Rabbi Kelmansky, happy to breathe air that smelled of nothing worse than dust and mice. As he read, he thought of Kelmansky alive, going around Market and Franklin streets handing out flour and clothing and coal. He'd found two more families, during a brief visit to the neighborhood he'd made earlier, who'd confirmed receiving donations from the rabbi. Too many and too often for Kelmansky or his people to spare. Then again, maybe the rabbi knew better-off people who regularly gave to the poor. Chicago had some wealthy and prominent Jews. Maybe they were the source of Kelmansky's gifts.

Too soon, he finished reading and headed back to the examining room. Rushton had spread a sheet over the drowning victim and pushed the table to one side. He leaned against a second table, his eyes on the deadhouse doorway. A murmur reached Hanley from the other room—someone reciting in a throaty, unfamiliar language. He listened and placed the voice as Nathan's. The strange words sounded like some kind of prayer.

He walked over to stand beside Rushton. Written notes were all well and good, but he got more detail when the police surgeon talked it out. Might as well do that while Nathan got on with praying. "So what can you tell me about the rabbi, Will?"

"Nasty wound. Drove bone splinters from the skull into his brain. He was likely knocked unconscious from the moment the blow connected."

"Only one blow?"

Rushton nodded. "Your killer didn't need more. Not with that big candelabra Officer Schmidt brought in."

Hanley nodded. "Menorah they call it. I found it in the sanctuary where he was killed."

Rushton raised his eyebrows, but a sudden silence from the deadhouse forestalled whatever he'd meant to say. "Help me move him out here," he said instead.

Kelmansky's body, still draped in its sheet, lay on a shelf against the morgue's far wall. The air was cold enough for Hanley to see his breath. Nathan stood facing the dead man. He wore a prayer shawl and small leather boxes strapped around his head and one hand. A short distance away was a cot with blankets on it, pulled straight and neatly turned down.

He must have heard them enter, but made no sign of it until he'd taken off the boxes and tucked his prayer shawl back beneath his gray wool vest. When he finally looked at them, Hanley saw his eyes were red-rimmed. "It is time?" he asked.

Rushton nodded. "The coroner will be here soon. We need to take your rabbi to the examining room."

Nathan looked puzzled and drew breath as if to speak, then seemed to think better of it. He moved to stand by the dead man's head and, together with Rushton, slid his arms underneath the shoulders. Hanley noticed the care he took to cradle the rabbi's head against his own body.

The three of them carefully carried the corpse out and laid it on the empty examining table. Rushton checked his pocket watch. "Gone half past nine. The jury should be here soon."

"Asbury didn't want to be here?" Hanley asked.

Rushton laughed as he took the small leather case that held his autopsy kit from where it lay next to the drowning victim. "He had plans last night. Involving old friends in town and several bottles of well set-up port, he said. Viewing an autopsy is the last way he'd want to spend this morning. He'd have made the inquest later if he could, but we got two more accidental deaths yesterday afternoon." Rushton looked grim as he opened the case. "One fell off a scaffold and snapped his neck. Other fellow blew his hand off blasting iron. Bled out before anyone there could think how to stop it."

"Excuse me!" Nathan spoke sharply. He was staring at the scalpels inside the open case. "What are those for? What are you going to do?"

"Perform the autopsy," Rushton said. His voice gentle, he added, "It's all right if you'd rather not watch. Most folks don't. The inquest room's that way. You can wait in there and we'll let you know when things are over."

"You are going to cut him open." Nathan's face had gone bloodless. He moved around the examining table until he stood between Rushton and the body. "You cannot do this. It is desecration."

"I wouldn't call it that." Rushton kept his tone mild. "We do this for every unnatural death, unless the coroner says otherwise. There's no desecration intended—"

"You cannot do this!" Nathan shot a look at Hanley. "Tell him he cannot do this. Cut up a human being like an animal at slaughter. It is against God!"

Rushton and Hanley exchanged glances. Rushton's expression said clearly, *Do you know what he's on about?*

Hanley turned to Nathan. "Autopsies are against your law?"

"Against any—" Nathan gripped the table's edge, visibly struggling to control himself. "Yes. To...to damage the body that once contained a human soul is an offense against the Creator who made them both. It dishonors my rabbi to treat his body this way. Like an object. He is not an object. He is a man. Not even death can rob him of that!"

Nathan seemed close to tears. Hanley felt sorry for him, but doubted there was anything he could do. The coroner ran the morgue as he saw fit and autopsies were part of the routine. One man's anguish couldn't be allowed to derail the usual procedure without a damned good reason.

Hanley shifted his weight. Maybe there *was* a good reason. An autopsy wasn't likely to tell him anything he didn't already know from Rushton's notes and his own observations. Moore would accept his word for that and he felt confident of his own judgment. He glanced at Nathan, who was still staring at him in mute appeal. If he could persuade the coroner to forego the procedure, Nathan—and all the rest of Kelmansky's people—would be in his debt. A debt he could call in later if he needed to.

"Ah, good. All ready to start." The new voice, deep and hearty, belonged to Asbury himself. Hanley glanced up as the coroner walked in. Portly and balding, he looked surprisingly alert. A mild pallor was the only sign of the festive evening Rushton had described. "Mr. Rushton," Asbury said, nodding in the surgeon's direction. Next, he looked at Hanley. "And you'd be?"

"Detective Frank Hanley. This is my case."

"You're here to testify, then, as well as observe? Excellent." He caught sight of Nathan. "And you, sir? Witness? Family member?"

"Jacob Nathan." Nathan could barely get the words out. "May I ask who you are?"

Asbury looked astonished. "The coroner, of course. Are you quite all right, Mr. Nathan? Detective, could you be so kind as to take this man to the inquest room—and get him a glass of something. He looks like he needs it."

Nathan spoke a fraction of a second before Hanley could. "You decide what is done here?"

"Yes." Asbury gave him a questioning look.

"Then I ask you not to shame my rabbi." He took a deep breath. "We cannot permit an…autopsy…of Rav Kelmansky. His body must not be mutilated. I—"

"Mutilated?" Asbury sounded offended. "I hardly think, sir, that you're qualified to say such a thing about a routine procedure in a criminal case—"

"Please!" Nathan's voice shook. "You cannot…it…" He backed up against the examining table and spread his arms wide, as if to block any move toward Kelmansky's body.

Hanley stepped forward. "Mr. Rushton kindly lent me his case notes on this body and they support what I saw at the death scene." He gestured toward the corpse, with its gaping head wound. "The manner of death is clear and I found the weapon used. Mightn't that be enough for a jury to establish whether or not a crime was committed? More than that isn't needed, as I understand it."

Asbury frowned. "Procedures must be followed, Detective. I'm sure you're aware of that."

"Yes, sir." Hanley moved closer to him. "But you might consider making an exception here, as the law allows." He lowered his voice. "Frankly, sir, I need all the help I can get with this case. This man was a priest to his people and they're wary of police to begin with. I have to talk to them in order to solve the killing, but I won't be able to if we harm their rabbi's body. They'll shut me out. These are the people who're most likely to have seen or heard something that'll point to the killer. I can't afford to lose that information."

Asbury's frown turned thoughtful. "And you're satisfied the external exam tells you everything you need to know about the manner of death?"

"In this case, yes." Hanley glanced toward Nathan, who was watching him with a mix of fear and hope. "Skipping the autopsy will make my job a lot easier. The police department'll appreciate that. Unsolved cases don't look good."

"An excellent point." Asbury rocked his oversized frame on the balls of his feet. "It'd make the inquest go quicker, too. Some of the jurors might appreciate that." He thought a moment more. "You're sure the Department will be satisfied with what you have?"

"Yes, sir." Moore would be, at least. Hanley knew his boss trusted him and for now that was all he needed.

"All right, then. Mr. Nathan, I'm going to grant your request. On the word of this officer here." He pulled out his pocket watch and glanced at it. "The jury should be here by half past ten. Anyone care for a quick walk to get a coffee?"

SIX

With Asbury gone on his brief errand, Hanley tried to persuade Nathan to sit awhile in the inquest room. Shaken as he was, however, Nathan refused to budge. Hanley finally brought him a chair and a glass of water. Then he went over to Rushton. He kept Nathan within his line of sight. Nathan's insistence on remaining for what was likely to be a painful experience—even without the autopsy— might be an act of courage on behalf of his dead friend, or he might have a personal interest in learning more about that death. Either way, Hanley wanted to watch his reactions.

"So tell me more about what you found," he said.

Rushton folded the sheet back. Underneath it, Kelmansky's naked flesh looked pale and shriveled, like a mackerel fillet left too long in the icebox. Force of will kept Hanley from flinching. The head wound had been bad enough in the sanctuary. It was worse seeing the victim here, stripped and laid out on the examining table, identity and dignity gone along with his clothes. Nathan seemed to be having similar thoughts. The lines of grief in his face deepened.

Rushton lifted one of the corpse's hands and showed it to Hanley. "Not a mark on either hand, no bruising or swelling like you'd expect if there'd been a struggle. Though there is this." His fingers brushed the edges of a shadowed patch on the back of the dead man's wrist. "A matched set, one on each arm. Not rope marks or anyone grabbing him here. Wrong shape, and those would go all the way around in any case. He didn't fight off his attacker, exactly, but something happened. I'm just not sure what."

He set the hand back down and gestured toward Kelmansky's

shoulder and hip. Two irregular dark patches stood out against the white skin, above the purpled areas where blood had pooled after death. "There's bruising here and here, but only where he fell." He put the sheet back and touched the edge of a purplish blotch the size of a half-dollar on Kelmansky's right temple. "A bruise here too, most likely from the fall as well."

Hanley frowned. The wrist marks were a puzzle, though he agreed with Rushton that without other bruising, they didn't point to a fight. "Could he have been struck from behind, while turning?"

"You mean was he hit before he saw his attacker?" Rushton shook his head. "He was struck from the front and slightly to the left." One slim finger traced the edges of the shattered eye socket and skull bone. "See here, how the wound is deepest near the front? That's where the greatest force was. Whoever hit him, the man saw it coming."

Hanley saw Nathan frown and his hand tighten on the water glass.

So the rabbi either knew his killer or the assault happened so fast that he hadn't had time to put up his hands. Unless...

"Those wrist marks," Hanley said. "Could he have tried to block a blow?"

"Not from that murder weapon. Wrong size and shape." Rushton frowned as he raised the dead man's wrists, one after the other. "And most people ward off blows with their palms out. These look more like someone had hold of him and he broke their grip. Only why no worse of a scuffle or fistfight, in that case..."

"Anything under his fingernails?" Chicago's morgue had a microscope and he knew Rushton routinely took fingernail scrapings and looked at them. Most of the time they were just dirt or bloody bits of skin, but sometimes they found things that pointed toward a likely assailant—cloth threads, or hair of distinctive quality and color, or substances like grease or coal dust from an attacker's dirty hands.

Rushton shook his head. "Nothing. Which is what I'd expect with no real fight involved."

Hanley eyed the bruise on the temple. It looked like the mark a cosh would leave behind. Anton Pavlic, Schmidt had told him, didn't own one. Pavlic was a drunk with a temper, not a professional criminal. He couldn't have killed Kelmansky during a botched robbery anyway. According to Schmidt, Pavlic had been in lockup at the Armory jail from four o'clock Thursday afternoon until late Friday morning. "Any chance he got hit twice?"

"It's possible." Rushton sounded doubtful. "Though I can't imagine why. That blow from the candelabra base was more than enough to kill him. And it did."

Rushton was probably right. "Find any tears in the clothes? I didn't."

"Me either." Rushton moved to stand by the head wound. "Here's another thing. Your killer was taller than the victim by four inches or so. See how that edge goes almost straight across?" He pointed to the rim of cracked bone where the eye had been. "That means the blow was nearly straight across, too. The killer struck from shoulder height."

Nathan stood up. Still clutching the water glass, he turned his back to them and took a few steps toward the deadhouse door. As if suddenly aware of where he was heading, he stopped. His shoulders worked as if he were breathing hard.

What was that about? Hanley watched him a moment, then turned his attention back to the body. "You'd be wrong about the height, Will. Didn't Schmidt tell you? He was killed while praying."

Rushton's look of shock gave way to concentration. "So...shoulder height and nearly straight across...victim's five-ten, take away the shinbone..." He took a folding ruler out of his apron pocket and measured the corpse's leg from knee to toe. "Sixteen inches. That'd make your killer five-feet-four, give or take. Say anywhere from five-two to five-five. You're looking for a short man. Or a woman, if she was strong."

The morning's soda bread suddenly felt heavy in Hanley's gut. Rivka Kelmansky stood about five feet four. The same height as Kate. *But there was no blood on her clothes. And there'd have been plenty from a blow like that...*

Nathan's slow footsteps and the creak of the chair as he sat back down recaptured Hanley's attention. Nathan wasn't much taller than Rivka. Five-foot-six? He'd behaved oddly yesterday, too. He still was. As if he knew something and it scared him.

Hanley let out a breath. He looked at Nathan, who set the water glass down and rested his head in his hands. Sympathy for him warred with Hanley's cop instincts. What did Nathan know and when would be the best time to tackle him about it?

Not here and now, he decided. Not without a clearer idea of what to ask. After what Mira Pavlic and her neighbors had said, he wondered if one thing Nathan didn't want to talk about was relief supplies. The larger question was whether that had anything to do with Rabbi Kelmansky's death—or whether Nathan just thought it did.

Hanley had one more question for Rushton. "When did he die?"

"A while before you saw him. With that temperature drop late last night, the body'd have lost heat faster than normal. I'd say sometime between three in the afternoon and nine at night...most likely toward the later time."

That was like Rushton—to be cautious—but Hanley knew his speculations were worth more than a lot of people's certainties. The time frame fit with Rivka's story that her father went out in the late afternoon and hadn't come back before she went to bed. Had anyone else seen the rabbi leave? Or seen Rivka—or Nathan—anyplace that meant they couldn't have killed him?

He needed to narrow the time down. Find out who might have seen Kelmansky around in the late afternoon or evening, or gone to the synagogue and found no dead body there yet. He looked at Nathan, who hadn't moved. No time to ask him anything now. The sounds of footsteps and voices told him Asbury and the jury were approaching.

The inquest went as he'd expected. The jurors accepted his testimony and Rushton's without question. Nathan testified as well, when offered the chance, his statements brief and stark.

He left Nathan and Rushton to work out arrangements for returning the rabbi's corpse back to Market Street while he thought over his own next move. Finding someone who'd seen Kelmansky alive between three and nine made the most sense. Six hours was a long time to account for.

Back to Market Street, then. With a detour home to see if Ida Kirschner could help him out.

SEVEN

Mam had made potato pancakes for lunch. The aroma of them surrounded Hanley as he stepped into the dim front hall of the boardinghouse. Feminine voices and the clink of china led him toward the kitchen. As he passed the half-open doorway to the dining room, a glint of silver caught his eye. Ida's Shabbos candlesticks and spice box were in the center of the table.

He walked into the room and picked the box up. A tiny silver model of the Holy City of Jerusalem, it barely filled his palm. He wondered if the missing box from the synagogue looked anything like it. A distinctive thing like that would be hard to fence. He'd meant to ask Jacob Nathan, but got sidetracked.

He set the box down and continued toward the kitchen, where he found Ida and his mother halfway through a platter of potato pancakes, apple butter, and strong tea. He thought of Mira Pavlic, the struggling baker on Franklin Street, and his own good fortune briefly shamed him. He, Mam, and Kate earned enough between them to buy their own food, rather than look to the Relief and Aid, and he could sit here and stuff himself because of it.

He shook off the feeling. Depriving himself wouldn't do Mrs. Pavlic or anyone else any good. "Any of those left for a hardworking man?"

"What brings you home in the middle of the day, Frankie? Not enough breakfast?" Mam's teasing grin and bright eyes softened the sharp lines of her face. The childhood nickname made him wince, but there was no point in objecting. Mary Rose Hanley let habits go hard, a legacy of the stubbornness he was often proud to think he'd inherited. He smiled his thanks at her as she poured him tea, her work-roughened hands graceful with Ida's delicate china cups. Were it not for that stubbornness, he wouldn't be here to fortify himself with a hot meal, warmth, and company, before once again tackling the job ahead of him.

Ida, softly rounded where Mam was all angles, gestured with her fork toward the cloth-covered platter in the middle of the table. "Bring a plate. There's plenty."

"Kate working today?" He fetched himself a dish, fork, and knife. Steam curled off the pancakes as he slid three of them onto his plate.

"At the Kings'." Mam scowled. "Terrible people. Not worth the extra dollar and a half a week."

"You say that every day she goes there." Hanley bit into a pancake, savoring the crisp potato and browned onions.

"And I'm right!" Mam snagged a pancake and slathered it with apple butter. "Her very first day, that Mrs. King told her specially that they always kept their spirits locked up and only Hodge the butler had a key."

"Kate laughed about it. And we need the money."

"Don't I know it. Would the Aid only send that sewing machine. End of October I sent in the paper for it, and here it is nearly February with no machine and no one from the Aid Society in sight. How in the name of Heaven do they get anything done?"

She'd been going on about the sewing machine since mid-November. Hanley exchanged an amused glance with Ida. Their landlady picked up a plate of sugar-dusted cookies. "Have a brandy snap," she said. "It'll settle the indigestion you're going to get if you don't stop about the Aid. They'll come when they come."

"Which will be when I'm eighty and dead."

"Mary Rose." Ida gave her The Look. Hanley had seen her give it to piano students who hadn't practiced and to tenants she liked who'd been careless once too often about their dirty dishes. It combined affection and flat refusal to put up with nonsense, and was one of the few things that could squelch Mam once she got going.

After a moment, Mam grinned and slid a cookie from the plate. Ida held the plate toward Hanley, who shook his head. He ate three more pancakes, relaxing in the simple comfort of a warm kitchen, good food, and two gently gossiping women. Hard to believe they'd only met Ida at the start of November, when Kate's small maid's salary added to Hanley's had made them too rich for their allotted few square feet at the squalid barracks on Randolph Street. Others worse off needed the space, meager though it was. Exorbitant rents for even the worst of the slum buildings spared by the Fire had made winter on Chicago's streets a frightening possibility, until the chilly evening when he'd come home from work to find Mam and Kate packing up their few salvaged belongings.

"We've a place in the West Division," Mam told him, brimming over with excitement. "Two rooms plus use of the kitchen. The landlady's an angel, a positive angel. Reasonable rent, too. It's a bit far from your station, but otherwise it couldn't be better."

The Kirschner house, and Ida herself, had surpassed his mother's rosy portrait. It surprised him how much his tiny room felt like home. He wanted their own roof and kitchen and a bit of garden as much as Mam and Kate did, but he knew he'd be sorry to leave when the time came.

"Penny," Ida said as she pushed the brandy snaps toward him.

"I was just thinking how much I'll miss this place when we finally have enough for our own house again." He took a cookie as he thought about what to say next. "There's a case I've just started. Got a problem I thought you might help me with."

He described the situation with the rabbi's people between bites of cookie. "There's so much I don't know and I'm not sure how to find out. Most folks in this city I can talk to, even if I don't know their language that well. We work it out. But these people..." He struggled to put his impressions into words. "It's not just that a lot of them don't speak English. There's an ocean between us I don't know how to cross. There's no ground where we can risk trusting each other. And if they don't trust me, at least a little, they won't talk. If they won't talk, I might as well hand in my badge for all the good I'll do solving this case."

"That Captain Hickey." The look on Mam's face as she named the West Division's commanding officer would have curdled swill milk.

"There's that, too. He'd love to see me fail. He's been waiting for it ever since I served under him. Plus, it'd be a big black mark against Sergeant Moore."

Mam's anxious glance acknowledged what they rarely spoke of—that Hanley had become a cop only after Moore vouched for him. He owed his job as much to Moore's reputation as to the shortage of men after the war. And there were plenty on the force who still saw him as a gambler and a thief. He couldn't tell them why he'd given up that life. Couldn't speak of Sean Doyle, who taught him to prosper in it before betraying his trust, without blind rage overtaking him. And he knew what could happen if he gave way to that.

Ida toyed with a brandy snap. "Are they city people? From back in Europe, I mean?"

Hanley brought his mind back to the current conversation. "Rivka... Miss Kelmansky told me her father and Jacob Nathan used to study back in Wroclaw. That's a big city, isn't it? I don't know about the rest of them."

"My second husband grew up near Wroclaw. He sold cloth to *yeshiva* students there before he came to America."

"So you could translate for me? They'd accept you?"

She shook her head. "I don't know. I wasn't raised there. My parents left the Russian Empire when I was small. We resettled in Munich, away from the pogroms. So I'm not sure how much use I can be. Especially if your rabbi's people come from the *shtetl*, as my parents did. Little villages tucked away from the rest of the world. Full of chickens and children and people who've learned not to trust anyone they don't know. My mother told us stories sometimes..." She curled her hands around her cup, as if for warmth. "Dov—my husband—came from a shtetl. He was one of ten survivors. Nine years old. He hid in a potato bin. Those who came to kill Jews didn't want to dig through the potatoes. Too much work for their fun, and there were so many other Jews to hunt down. They would do that—police, soldiers—ride into the shtetl and kill anything that moved."

She fell silent briefly. "I didn't live through that," she said. "Dov told it to me and, even so, I can't think of it without hurting. My parents never spoke of the pogrom that sent us to Munich, and I don't recall it, but we knew there was a reason we never met our grandparents. If your Jews on Market Street went through a pogrom, it's no wonder they can't trust you. You're police. Where they come from, that means you can kill them like stray cats and no one will care."

Like runaway slaves, he thought, feeling bleak. Or the black Union soldiers at Fort Pillow in Tennessee, massacred by Johnny Rebs. People would do anything if they hated and feared enough. He knew that too well. The streets of Chicago had been their own kind of battlefield all his life and he a soldier in what he'd seen as a war against those who never gave a Mick a fair shake. Real war had taught him a different way to fight and broadened his ideas about what he was fighting for. But cruelty and prejudice still existed, here and everywhere, simmering beneath the surface. He saw hard evidence of it every day.

Three raps on the front door saved him from a reply. He sat feeling hollow inside while Ida excused herself and walked toward the front of the house.

"More tea?" Mam asked quietly.

"Thanks. Yes." When she set the cup in front of him, he added a splash of milk, a simple action that helped him collect himself. *Just in time*, he thought as he saw the two women who followed in Ida's wake.

The first was a stout matron somewhere past fifty, her companion a tall girl some thirty years younger. Both wore dresses and hats that would have cost Kate several weeks' wages. The younger one moved as if trying to be smaller, shoulders hunched and arms held tight to her body. She glanced around the room with timid interest, which vanished when she caught Hanley's eye. Cheeks pinking, she looked down at the toes of her elegant kid boots.

The matron eyed the kitchen and its occupants as if they had manure on their shoes. Nerves flicked raw by his talk with Ida, Hanley gripped his cup to keep from saying something he'd regret. These women were likely from the Aid Society. For Mam's sake, he couldn't afford to offend them.

He calmed himself by looking the matron over the way he might a suspect. The purple plume on her hat clashed with the navy-dyed straw beneath. Below the hat were muddy brown eyes, nearly lost in puffiness that spoke of frequent bouts of catarrh. Pursed lips made a splotch between a majestic nose and a chin that receded into a dewlapped neck. Pale lace ruffles down the bodice of the woman's navy dress made her look like a blueberry pie slice with too much whipped cream. Her poker-straight carriage seemed familiar, though he'd certainly never seen her down at the station. Well-off dowagers rarely turned up there.

She fished a paper out of her handbag, snapped it straight and squinted at it. "Which of you is Martha Rose Haney?"

"Hanley," Mam answered, a touch too sweetly. "Mary Rose. And whom might I have the pleasure of addressing?"

"Mrs. Josiah King," the matron announced. "And my niece, Miss Agnes Wentworth."

The sound of her name made Miss Wentworth fold even further in on herself. Her gaze shifted to a spot on the far wall. Hanley glanced over and saw one of Ida's iron fry-pans hanging on its hook. Agnes Wentworth stared at it, as if it were the most important thing in the room. Hanley felt a pang of sympathy. If he had to barge into strangers' houses in the company of Mrs. Josiah King, he'd spend a lot of time staring at fry-pans, too.

"Mrs. King." The lilt of recognition in Mam's voice was so subtle, Hanley almost missed it. "And Miss Wentworth. A pleasure to meet you."

"Please." Ida gestured toward the chairs. "Sit down."

Miss Wentworth hurried to pull out a chair, stumbled and caught herself on the table edge. She flicked her aunt an agonized glance and dropped her gaze back to her boots.

Mrs. King eyed the chair and her niece with equal disdain. She took the offered seat, perching on the edge as if to avoid soiling her skirt. She glanced at the dirty dishes and other remains of their meal, then pointedly looked away.

Suddenly Hanley knew who she was. Kate's Mrs. King, who'd hired her out of desperation, due to the shortage of experienced housemaids. Who still followed her around the house for half the morning unless there were callers to entertain. Kate had done a devastating impression of her after her first week on the job, reducing them all to aching ribs and wet eyes.

Mrs. King clearly was not pleased with the surroundings, or with Mam's less-than-humble attitude. "We are here to represent the Relief and Aid Society," she said, as if speaking of Almighty God. "We understand you have applied for…" She glanced at the paper again. "…a sewing machine?"

"This past October. Yes. How soon will it be arriving?"

Mrs. King folded the paper and replaced it in her handbag, from which she took a composition book and two pencils. "A decision has not been made on your case, Mrs. Haney," she said with a scowl. "This visit will determine that decision."

Mam sat and picked up her teacup. This time she didn't bother correcting Mrs. King's use of her name. "Then we'd best get started."

"Agnes!" Mrs. King barked. She took a folded sheet out of the composition book, then handed the book and one pencil to her niece. "Describe this house for the Relief Board. Don't leave anything out." She turned back to Mam, her own pencil poised over the paper. "Are you married, Mrs. Haney?"

"I was. To Francis James Hanley, the first of that name. He passed on some years back."

"Of what cause did he die? Drink?"

"Of the Great Hunger. In Ireland. Perhaps you recall reading of it in the papers. That was twenty-five years ago, of course."

Mrs. King glared. Her pencil moved in sharp strokes. "Have you been married since?"

"I have not."

"Nor lived with a man in a state of sin?"

Hanley's teacup rang against its saucer, beating Ida's by half a second. He drew in a breath, but Mam spoke first. She sounded remarkably calm. "Do people really answer that question?"

More pencil strokes, quick and hard. "How long have you resided at these premises?"

"Since the middle of November. Before that, we were at the Randolph Street barracks."

"And before that?"

"Number Twelve Maple Street."

The mention of Maple Street deepened the sour expression on Mrs. King's face. "And precisely where is that address?"

"Are you meaning which division?"

"I mean, what area of the division?"

"Why would that matter, seeing as we're not there anymore?"

"Mrs. Haney, were you a resident of the slum known as Conley's Patch?"

"My answer to that would make a difference, would it?"

"I don't see why," Hanley broke in. "Plenty of decent folks live in every part of this city. As a Chicago resident yourself, Mrs. King, I'm sure you know that."

"And who are you?"

"Frank Hanley. Detective." His pride in the title echoed through the kitchen.

She shot him another contemptuous look and returned to questioning his mother. "And what is your state of employment, Mrs. Haney?"

"I sew clothes. By hand, because I don't have a sewing machine. Makes for slow work and less money."

"And your level of income?"

"Very little. As I said, you can't make much with hand-sewing."

"Have you children of working age?"

"You've met my son." Mam gave Hanley a swift, proud smile. "I've a daughter as well. In service. Though the people she works for don't pay her much. Which is a surprise to me, because she works hard for them and they can well afford more than a dollar and a half a week." She shook her head. "They say greed is one of the seven deadly sins. Funny, how those who have the most seem to be more often beset with it."

Mrs. King gripped her pencil harder. "We are speaking of yourself, Mrs. Haney. Of your fitness to receive what has so generously been given by those who 'have the most.'"

"And by plenty who have too little for themselves, but gave of it anyway," Hanley cut in. "Generosity isn't limited to the wealthy, Mrs. King. Certainly not from my experience over these past few months, which has been considerable."

"Yes, I daresay you have plenty of experience with the worst sort of people. Drunkards and gamblers and cutthroats!"

"Aunt," Agnes said from the back of the room.

The hesitant word didn't stop Hanley, whose temper was up and running. "From whom I and my fellow officers daily protect you and yours, often at risk of our lives," he snapped. The touch of a brogue creeping into his voice, usually an embarrassment, now gave him a perverse pride in his Irishness. "And, for thanks, I get you coming round here three months after my mother made a simple enough request of your bloody Aid Society, looking at us like we're pig muck on your hem and asking my mam has she been living in sin since my father died. What'll you be asking next? How recently she gave up the demon whiskey? Or if she beat us when we were children?"

He had the brief, bitter satisfaction of watching Mrs. King's face turn strawberry red. Then she swept up her paper and stood. A cold feeling settled in the pit of his stomach.

"Agnes!" she snapped. Then she turned toward his mother. Each word she spoke was rimmed in ice. "I regret to say, Mrs. Haney, that your case does not look promising. You may expect a formal letter within two weeks from the director in charge of this aid district, who will give considerable weight to my report. Agnes—we're going!"

Her angry gaze found Ida next. The landlady looked straight through her and reached for the teapot. "You know your way out."

In the small silence left by the Aid ladies' departure, Mam scooped up a brandy snap and crumbled it to fragments.

"She deserved every word of it, Mam."

"We can't always afford to be giving people what they deserve. Haven't I taught you that yet, Frankie?"

"You weren't exactly the soul of politeness yourself!"

"No, I wasn't. But there are ways and ways. A fist to the head isn't the only way of keeping your pride. You're not fourteen now. You're near thirty, old enough to hold your temper and your tongue."

The rush of footsteps down the hall saved him from answering. Agnes Wentworth burst through the kitchen door and skidded to a halt in front of them.

"I told Aunt I forgot my gloves." She toyed with the small cloth purse that dangled from one wrist. "I just wanted to apologize. Aunt Augusta can be terrible." Her eyes sought Hanley's. "I didn't want you to think...I mean..."

"It's all right." Mam spoke gently. "We've heard worse."

Agnes's thin face flushed deeper. She dug in her purse and pulled out a calling card and a pencil stub. "The Second District's director is Harden Guthrie," she said, printing his name on the back of her card. "You can write to him if you want. Or come to me. I can find you that sewing machine." She held out the card to Hanley. "I volunteer at the district office. I'm there most afternoons until four o'clock."

He took the card, though he didn't yet trust himself to speak.

"I really am sorry." Agnes looked at them all, last and longest at him. Then she left.

Harden Guthrie. He recalled the name from somewhere. Someone of importance in the city, if they'd made him a district director. He turned the card over and read the address. 89 East Randolph Street. He knew the place. The McKee's Building, one of those in the area between Court House Square and the lakefront that was rebuilt in the first couple of months after the Fire.

He looked at Mam. "Can I keep this?"

"If you can keep your temper when you see him."

"I will. I promise." He would keep his word, no matter what the provocation. Harden Guthrie might be able to help him with much more than Mam's sewing machine.

EIGHT

Hanley had hoped to set off with Ida for Market Street right after lunch, but had to change his plans. "Today is Shabbos," Ida told him. "Even if they had not lost their rabbi, they will be in the synagogue for much of the day. Best to wait until after the burial. Better yet until after shiva, the seven days of mourning, which should last through next Sunday. The whole community will share in that to some degree."

Hanley couldn't wait that long to talk to the rabbi's people again. For today, however, he had little choice. He found that knowledge irritating, like a nagging ache he couldn't relieve. He needed to make progress, prove himself up to the job.

Agnes's card was in his pocket. He took it out and looked at it. The Second Relief District encompassed the Market Street area, along with Ida's section of the West Division. If any of Kelmansky's gifts had come from the Relief and Aid, Harden Guthrie's office might have a record of it. Workers at the Second District supply depot might even recall Kelmansky, though—remembering the chaos when he'd sought food and clothing back in October—Hanley knew he couldn't count on that.

Ida's wall clock told him it was near two in the afternoon. The supply depot was just a few blocks east and north, on the way to 89 East Randolph. With luck he could stop by there first and then catch Guthrie at the Aid office, if Guthrie was working on a Saturday afternoon.

The wind had picked up, sharp and cold. Hanley turned up his coat collar and jogged down the front steps. As he reached the bottom, a flicker of motion caught his eye. He turned toward it, half-expecting to see Mam or Ida watching after him out the parlor window. But the curtains were closed, the yard and the street beyond it empty. He lingered a moment, frowning, then hurried down the front walk.

The depot was a barn of a place on Desplaines near Washington, not far outside the burned district. Hanley had to use his badge to clear a way through the lines of people. Sad-eyed women nudged cranky children out of his path, while men in ragged coats stared at their feet rather than meet his gaze. Many of the children looked as if they hadn't eaten well in weeks. The exhaustion in all their faces felt like a weight in Hanley's chest.

As he'd half-expected, the harried clerks had no memory of Kelmansky. "Do you have any idea how many people we get here in a day? Still?" asked the sour-faced young woman who stood behind a table piled with donated clothing. She was the first employee Hanley managed to reach. "Hundreds," she went on. Her voice, thin and nasal, grated on his ears. "Half of them without the proper paperwork, or in the wrong place, or wanting more than they're entitled to. It's enough to drive you mad. All any of us wants at the end of the day is to forget all about it." She looked past Hanley to an elderly woman who clutched a piece of paper as if it were gold. "And what do *you* want?"

Hesitant, as if shamed, the old woman stepped up to the table. Hanley stayed close to her. "Whatever it is," he said, a hard smile fixed on his face as he tapped his badge on the tabletop, "I'm sure you'll see she gets it."

The clerk eyed the badge and pursed her lips, then took the old woman's paper with a grudging attempt at decent manners. Hanley lingered until the woman had received her due—a shawl to replace the near-rag she wore, a pair of mittens, and a woolen blanket—then nodded good-bye to her and walked away.

He did no better with anyone else confirming Kelmansky's presence at the depot, though several of the other workers at least had civil tongues in their heads. After a while, he left and walked over to Randolph, where he could catch an eastbound horsecar. He felt a little guilty at spending the nickel fare, but Moore would reimburse him from the detective squad's petty cash fund.

The stop was crowded, full of harried-looking women with shopping baskets and a handful of men. A young man of twenty or so boarded the car ahead of Hanley. His wide eyes and happy grin, as if he'd never ridden a horsecar before, marked him as fresh meat straight off the train. Hanley followed him to the last open bench in the car, with a notion of safeguarding him from any vultures who might be lurking. Someone pushed past Hanley as he reached the bench and nearly toppled him into the young man's lap. Hanley caught himself and drew breath to snap, but saw only the jostler's retreating back—skinny and slump-shouldered, flat cap pulled down over his hair. Hanley straightened his overcoat, apologized to the young man, and sat down. The horsecar lurched into traffic.

As they crossed the river into the burned district, Hanley smelled traces of smoke. Further down Randolph, half-finished commercial blocks shared the street with low-slung wooden structures that held small businesses—a locksmith's, a surveyors' office, a few eateries. Between them, Hanley saw empty lots where groups of workmen busily cleared away debris. Wooden signs proclaimed what the lots would become—"Future Home of Meller's Jewelry Store," "First Union Bank," "Bridgman's Business College." People moved with purpose here. Housewives with baskets, workmen leaving a tavern, two well-dressed men deep in conversation as they approached the surveyors' office.

As the horsecar went further east, foot traffic thinned and the office blocks gave way to small frame houses and shanties. Hanley felt himself tensing as they neared Randolph and LaSalle. Seeing the barracks there, its shadow covering the boardwalk, was bad enough. Worse were the dark gaps of foundation pits nearby, holes in the ground that held makeshift shelters of scrounged bricks, rough boards, and canvas. Most appeared empty, their inhabitants out seeking work or begging in some better-off neighborhood. From one pit came the glow of a campfire. Hanley glimpsed a woman and two children huddled around it, the woman toasting bread on a stick. Nearly four months after the Fire and people still lived like that. He wondered grimly how many froze to death in those pits overnight and whether anyone who could do something about it cared. A few dead poor folk here and there wouldn't make more than a one-line notice in the papers.

He turned away abruptly. On the right they were passing the Court House ruins. He was surprised to see so much of it still there. Bricks and chunks of heat-cracked marble from the Court House were among the most popular Fire souvenirs. After another block he got up and moved toward the rear exit, swaying slightly with the car's motion. The skinny fellow who'd shoved him was working his way to the door, but Hanley paid him scant attention. He got off the car at State Street and looked around for Red Jack. The jaunty little newspaper vendor was on the far corner selling papers to a pair of suit-clad young men, probably employees at one of the few office blocks built before winter set in. Hanley walked on toward the McKee's Building, east of State. A tobacconist's and a gentleman's haberdashery occupied part of the ground floor, flanking the main entrance. Hanley entered, found the directory, and walked up to the second floor.

Gilded lettering across the office door read *Relief and Aid Society—Administration, Second District*. Hanley went in and saw Agnes Wentworth filing papers in a set of pigeon-hole shelves against the wall. She turned as he entered, her cheeks still reddened from the cold outside, and gave him a hesitant smile.

"Miss Wentworth." Hanley nodded toward her. "Nice to see you again. Is Mr. Guthrie in?"

"Why, yes, he—" She halted, looking embarrassed. "I'm sorry. I'm supposed to ask if you have an appointment."

He smiled at her. "Do I need one? I won't take but a moment of his time."

"Let me ask if he'll see you." She tapped on an inner glass-fronted door and opened it slightly. "Mr. Guthrie? There's a gentleman here to see you. A—" She threw a questioning glance at Hanley.

He gave his full name and rank, which she relayed through the doorway. "Tell him to come in," a man's voice murmured in reply.

Agnes intercepted him as he approached Guthrie's door. "This might not be the best day to ask about the sewing machine. Mr. Guthrie's not been looking at all well. Something about investments. He's under terrible strain."

Hanley thanked her and stepped into the inner office. Guthrie sat at a large oak desk, an open ledger in front of him. A silver fountain pen rested in one hand. "What can I do for you, Detective?"

Hanley recognized him at once. Harden Guthrie had given a rousing stump speech in Ada Park back in late October just before the municipal elections, talking up fire-proofing regulations and promising reform if elected mayor. He'd lost to Joseph Medill, but had certainly known how to fire up a crowd. A big man, Hanley recalled, over six feet tall and seemingly oblivious to the autumn chill that had given him ruddy cheeks under his well-cut fair hair. He looked drained of color now, his broad shoulders slumped, as if he hadn't slept well in days.

Hanley nodded toward the ledger, where he could see rows of neat lettering and numbers. "Job a headache, is it?"

"I do the best I can." Guthrie said it as if putting the idea into words for the first time. He stared at the page before him, then shut the book. "How can I help you?"

"I'm tracing some items that may have come from your supply depot on Desplaines. They might relate to an investigation I'm pursuing. Several pieces of clothing, a twenty-pound sack of flour, a pair of child's shoes. They were given to a gentleman named Kelmansky. A Jewish gentleman, a rabbi."

Guthrie dropped the pen. It rolled off the desk and hit the floor. "I haven't been to the depot lately," he said, his voice muffled as he bent to pick up the pen.

"You must keep records, though. May I see them?"

"I…" Guthrie surfaced, pen in hand, then coughed as if he'd inhaled dust. "I'd need to know when the items were received. The right ledger might not be here."

Advent, Mira Pavlic had said. "Sometime in December. Before Christmas."

"Then I'm afraid I can't help you." Guthrie sounded more definite now. "December's books are at the Society's headquarters at 409 West

Washington. They won't let you see them without an exceptionally good reason."

"I have one. Rabbi Kelmansky turned up dead yesterday morning."

Guthrie blanched. "God." He stood and walked toward the window. "What a terrible thing."

"Yes." Hanley waited, but Guthrie said nothing more. He stared out the window, apparently absorbed in the view of the street.

He was taking the news more personally than Hanley would have expected. "Did you know him?"

"I did," Guthrie answered after a moment. "Not well. He came to me a couple of years back, looking for funds to build a Jewish boys' school. Henry Greenebaum, the banker, gave him my name. I wrote him a check for a hundred dollars." He rubbed a hand over his face. "What a terrible thing."

Guthrie was in shipping, Hanley recalled from news articles he'd read during the campaign. Rail and water. He'd have money like that to throw around. How much had he lost in the Fire? Several rail depots and riverside warehouses had gone up on that dreadful night and the deeds to countless others were lost when the Court House burned. No wonder the man was showing strain from money troubles.

A gentle knock interrupted Hanley's train of thought. Agnes poked her head through the doorway. "Mr. Guthrie? This week's manifest and receipts from Desplaines Street just arrived."

Guthrie turned toward Agnes and his bleak expression softened. He nodded toward his desk. "Put them there please, Miss Wentworth. And give the delivery boy a good tip."

"Yes, sir." She walked in, set a thick sheaf of papers and a receipt book on the corner of the desk and withdrew.

Guthrie glanced toward the papers. "If there's nothing else…"

"Who would I see at the head office about December's books?"

Guthrie went to his desk, picked up the manifest and glanced at it before replying. "Wirt Dexter. He's chairman of the executive committee. Though he's in New York on business until sometime next week."

"Who'd be next?"

Guthrie paused, as if to think. "The general superintendent. O. C. Gibbs."

It crossed Hanley's mind to ask about Mam's sewing machine, but then he remembered what Agnes had said and reconsidered. He thanked Guthrie for his help and left, with a friendly nod to Agnes on the way out.

The Relief and Aid's main office was too far away to visit that day. Hanley decided to go on Monday, then headed toward Market Street, even though he knew Kelmansky's people would all be in the synagogue. Their non-Jewish neighbors might know something about the items the rabbi had given them, or one of them might have seen him around on the last afternoon of his life.

He wondered briefly where Rivka was and what answers she might have found. If any.

◌ঽ

Rivka stayed close to Tanta Hannah as they walked home from the afternoon service. The sun was lower in the sky now. Sundown couldn't be more than an hour away. So short a time before Shabbos would end, and yet it stretched before her like the expanse of Lake Michigan. She felt restless, edgy. She wanted to cry or scream or run, or all three at once. Madwomen must feel this way, as if the world was out of joint and they couldn't put it right again.

The Nathans' daughters had walked ahead, within eyeshot of some of the younger men. They were all pretending not to sneak glances at each other. Tamar, Hannah's eldest, edged closer to Moishe Zalman and made a bold effort to catch his gaze. Just turned twenty, she carried herself with the confidence of someone who fit perfectly where she belonged. Moishe blushed and turned away.

Tanta Hannah sighed and Rivka knew she meant to go put a stop to things. Suddenly Rivka couldn't bear to walk alone. She gripped Hannah's arm and blurted out the first thing that came to mind. A bad habit, her mother used to say, though Papa had rarely minded. "Why did Onkl Jacob come to see Papa the other day?"

Hannah patted her hand. "Leave Jacob's business to Jacob."

"He was upset. They spent a long time in the study. He didn't tell you anything?"

"We'll be home soon. You can have a little rest before supper."

"Onkl Jacob always tells you things. You can't even guess?"

"Rivka. Enough."

Resentment flared as Hannah hurried them along. "Why am I not allowed to know anything? It's my father who…" The memory of his body sprawled by the bimah came to her, so vividly she couldn't go on. "I need to know why Onkl Jacob came. Where Papa went. Why he never came home."

"I said, enough." Hannah's voice hardened. They reached the Nathans' front door and she fumbled with the latch. "Those questions will not bring your father back."

Rivka caught her sleeve as the door swung open. "You know something. You must."

"I don't know anything that will help you properly remember your father." Hannah wouldn't look at her as they went in and Rivka saw a flush in her cheeks. "Which is the only thing that should concern you now."

NINE

The brief walk to the Market Street neighborhood was a welcome exertion, despite the cold. Hanley decided to try another of Mrs. Pavlic's neighbors—Murray? Murphy. The one with the donated winter coat. Received less than a week before Kelmansky's death, Mrs. Pavlic had said. Maybe Murphy knew something about where the coat had come from.

Pavlic's Bakery on Franklin shared its block with six one-story frame houses and some shops. Only a few vacant lots remained. The bakery wasn't the only place with marks of vandalism. Someone had splashed green paint across the front of Elway's Best Boots and Shoes and scrawled NO IRISH on it in black. As Hanley passed the shop, a stocky, round-faced man in a cobbler's apron came out with a bucket and sponge and started scrubbing at the paint.

Hanley continued to the bakery where he found Mrs. Pavlic and her little girl mixing dough. They looked startled to see him. He bought four fresh onion rolls to bring home for supper and noticed his purchase left very little still for sale. Did Harden Guthrie know about the Pavlics' situation? Was there a report filed somewhere in his office, written by Mrs. King or someone like her, describing Mira and Anton Pavlic as "an unpromising case"?

He swallowed his anger at the thought, not wanting it to show on his face. "Can you tell me which house is Mr. Murphy's?" he asked as he handed Mrs. Pavlic the money.

She gestured with her head as she dropped the pennies in the till. "Second from here, across the street. That way."

The woman who answered the door at the second house to the

north wore a water-stained calico blouse and a harried expression. Her carrot-colored hair trailed in a sloppy braid over one shoulder. "What d'you want with Jamie?" she growled when Hanley asked after Murphy. "It'd better be work. Tell me it's work or get out."

Hanley shrugged. "Job offers come face-to-face. Is he here?"

Her harsh laugh carried the odor of cheap whiskey. "Down the saloon. Callaghan's Grocery, the sign says. Jamie's there most hours of the day when he isn't plaguing me to go to bed. Go to Washington Street and turn east. You'll see the sign near the corner."

He knew where Callaghan's was. Tommy Callaghan had rebuilt on the same site his saloon had occupied before the Fire, though Hanley's promotion from beat cop to detective meant he personally hadn't been there in the past few months. His thanks were lost as the woman slammed the door. He thought about knocking again, to ask her what she might have seen or heard on Thursday, but decided to track down Jamie Murphy first.

The thought of going to Callaghan's made him itchy. He knew Charming Billy sometimes drank there. As always, the thought of Billy sparked fury in him. He breathed deep until it subsided. Billy was likely in jail again, for breaking the bones of some luckless whore or cracking the skull of whomever he'd most recently played cards with. Right now, Hanley had work to do.

As he neared the saloon, he saw signs of recent fighting—a broken pane in the front window, partly covered by heavy green blinds, and shards of brown glass from smashed liquor bottles. The sidewalk just outside sported stains that might have been spilled beer or whiskey, along with smears of what looked like dried blood. From the German boy who'd been beaten there a few nights before, most likely. There wasn't enough of it for a knife or gunshot wound. Thank God for small mercies. Assuming God was paying attention.

Hanley went in and stood still a moment, letting his eyes adjust to the dimness. Shelves against the back wall held boxes and canisters, the groceries Callaghan sold when he wasn't dispensing drink. A cashier's counter nearby did double service as a bar. Several barrels served as tables, with stools and chairs scattered around them, and a potbellied stove belched out heat. Today being Saturday, Callaghan could legally sell whatever he wanted. Hanley didn't anticipate much trouble talking to him or his customers—none of whom were Charming Billy just now, thank Heaven.

Callaghan, a potato-faced Irishman, built like the barrels that dotted the room, looked up from swabbing the counter. "Something I can get you?" His blue eyes showed no surprise at the sight of Hanley. Callaghan saw plenty and gave away little, except drinks to those who paid. Not chatty, either. Hanley had tried talking to him a time or three, hoping to enlist him as an informant, but had no luck.

He ambled up to the bar as if he'd no care in the world except to wet his throat. "Wouldn't say no to a beer."

"Lager or dark?"

"Dark."

While Callaghan drew the beer from beneath the counter, Hanley looked around the saloon. Two older men, sixtyish and in well-worn clothes, were playing cards on a potato barrel by the stove. Small glasses of brown liquor sat by each of their elbows. The only other customer was on the opposite side of the room. A rat-faced fellow of thirty or so, he sat slouched in a chair, nursing a beer. An overcoat draped across his chair back hung to the sawdust-covered floor.

The fellow looked familiar. Hanley nodded toward him as Callaghan plunked down the full beer mug. "That Jamie Murphy?"

Callaghan grinned. "Hey, Jamie! Molly's sent someone to fetch you again!"

Murphy tossed them a disgusted look. "Shut up, Tommy."

His whining tone, more suited to a bratty child than a grown man, jogged Hanley's memory. Murphy was a petty thief—or had been four years back when Hanley had run him in for stealing from Mr. Mahlon Ogden. A pair of gold cufflinks, if Hanley recalled right. Murphy had been living with another woman then, a maid at the Ogdens' northside mansion. He'd spent six months in jail. The maid had been fired.

Murphy watched, half sulky and half nervous, as Hanley walked over and pulled up a chair. His greasy dark hair flopped partway over his eyes. "If it's about those spoons, I didn't do it. So you can leave me alone, all right?"

Hanley sipped his beer, enjoying the rich malty flavor. Callaghan made a decent brew. "It's not about the spoons." Someone else could take care of that crime and likely was. Hanley set his beer on the cracker barrel that doubled as a table. "It's about your coat."

"What about it? You sayin' I stole it? Well, I didn't!"

"I know. I need to know where you got it."

"Why?"

Hanley sipped his beer and watched Murphy's face. He saw suspicion there, along with a hint of fear.

Murphy looked down at his drink. He drummed his fingers against the side of the glass. "Don't remember where I got it. Some do-gooder. Where else?"

"Some do-gooder from your neighborhood. About sixty. Black clothes. Beard. Any of that refresh your memory?"

He could see Murphy debating whether or not to keep lying. A stupid thing to lie about, not knowing where his coat had come from. Kelmansky would be a hard do-gooder to forget. Could Murphy have robbed the temple? He hardly looked strong enough to have wielded the menorah. Nor was brutal murder his style—or it hadn't been. Then again, prison could change a man.

"That Jew gave it to me," Murphy said finally.

"When?"

"'Bout a week ago."

Hanley waited. Murphy glanced at him, then stared back down at his beer. "Him and a couple others. One old fella with a beard—the shorter one, big arms—went into Pavlic's with a sack full of stuff. The other two went up and down the block. Taller old fella, not so square-shaped, and a skinny young one with specs. Left things at a few places. They gave me the coat." He shrugged. "Don't know why. Nothin' in it for them, is there?"

That matched Mrs. Pavlic's story. "You live pretty near the synagogue," Hanley said.

"The what?"

"Where they go to pray. The man who gave you that coat lives near it."

"So?" Murphy's fingers were tapping again, on his beer glass and the tabletop.

"Were you in the neighborhood Thursday? Afternoon or evening?"

"I was here." Murphy drained his beer and signaled for another. "Ask Tommy. I won a darts match that night. Olaf Johansson was the last man down but me. He's not here now. Shows up later, usually."

"What time did you get here?"

"After work."

"Work being…?"

"Down on State near Washington. Olaf got me a job clearing brick and scrap. There's a big bank building going up there come spring."

Hanley thought a moment. Murphy's likely route from State Street to Callaghan's would have taken him just short of the rabbi's immediate neighborhood. Unless Kelmansky had gone out of it, their paths wouldn't have crossed. Assuming Murphy was telling the truth. Talkative one moment and terse the next, the man acted nerved up about something. Murder? Robbery? Or the simple fact of being questioned by a cop?

Hanley sipped beer. Word around Lake Street said Callaghan was a fence. Plenty of saloon owners were. Knowing Charming Billy spent time there was enough to make Hanley wonder what other lines of business Callaghan might be involved in, and for whom—though he hadn't seen evidence of criminal activity yet, despite keeping an eye on the place. Callaghan was a careful sort. Maybe Murphy had come here to unload the spoons he'd denied stealing.

He made another stab at getting a time. "How late did you leave work? Before sundown? After?"

Murphy toyed with his empty glass. "Before. Heard the church bells ring three."

"You came straight here?"

Murphy nodded without looking up.

"Did you see the rabbi anywhere around?"

Murphy snorted. "Them people don't come in here. Bet they don't even drink."

"I meant on your way here. Did you see him on the street?"

"No."

"And you left here…?"

"God, man, I don't remember. Little too much whiskey, you know? Darts pay money when you win. Why not spend it, that's my motto."

The game must have paid well if Murphy had been able to afford whiskey. "Take a guess."

"Midnight, maybe? Olaf came in, we drank awhile, then we started playing. I stood him to a drink after I won. It was late, that's all I know. And cold." He patted the sleeve of the coat where it trailed across his seat. "Had to button this up to my eyebrows all the way home."

After the temperature drop, then. No chance of Murphy having made that frozen boot print in the synagogue yard. The print was on the large side for a scrawny bantam rooster like him anyway, if Hanley recalled right. He flicked some cracker crumbs to the floor and watched them fall, which gave him a few seconds to eyeball Murphy's feet.

Those are all wrong, was his first thought at the sight of the man's shoes. Murphy wore a pair of lace-up balmorals, cut from fine leather and looking scarcely worn. Shoes suited to a bank clerk or other professional man, not a workingman's brogans or boots. Either he'd gotten more than one lucky donation or he'd recently fenced some pricey items. Not likely the menorah and spice box, though. Even the best-connected thief couldn't have unloaded items like those and bought himself fancy shoes with the proceeds in barely over a day and a half.

Maybe Murphy worked as a bunco-steerer in addition to petty thievery. He certainly looked the part. And he'd need a fine outfit to play the well-heeled loser, drawing the farmers into rigged card or dice games and fleecing them of every penny they'd earned selling their crops in town. Hanley knew the racket well. Years ago, he'd run it damned near every night.

He drank more beer. Whatever the explanation for Murphy's shoes, those small, narrow feet definitely hadn't left the muddy boot print behind. The marks on the synagogue floor, though.... The shoe leather was too dark for a quick glance to show anything. Hanley wondered if Murphy had other footwear at home. Say, a pair of boots with bloodstains near the soles. "So where'd your shoes come from? The rabbi give you those, too?"

"Friend of mine." Murphy pulled his feet as far under his chair as he could manage.

"What friend? Where can I find him?"

"Here," Callaghan said as he set down a fresh beer by Murphy's elbow. Hanley hadn't seen him coming. "The shoes're my brother's. Left 'em behind when he went back to New York last month. Not my size, so...." He shrugged. "Freshen you up?"

"No, thanks."

"Suit yourself." Callaghan ambled away.

Hanley eased back in his seat, cradling his drink. Murphy's behavior was raising his hackles. Maybe the man needed a jolt to knock a little truth out of him. "The rabbi turned up dead yesterday morning. If you saw or heard anything Thursday night, now's the time to say so."

"I don't know anything about it." Murphy's voice had gone tight, his shoulders hunched as if warding off a blow. "I went straight from work to here and from here straight home to Molly. Didn't see anything, didn't hear anything."

From the way he looked, Hanley doubted it. He felt Callaghan watching them from across the room. If he tried to browbeat the truth out of Murphy, Callaghan might ask him to leave and Hanley didn't want a confrontation just now.

He went back to his original question. "Did Rabbi Kelmansky or his friends mention where they got your coat from?"

Murphy stared at him as if he'd lost his wits. "What's that got to do with anything?"

"Did they?"

"No." He gulped beer and wiped his mouth with his sleeve.

Hanley drained his own glass. He'd gotten enough out of Murphy for the time being. "If I need you again, will I find you here?"

Murphy muttered his answer into his drink. Hanley went to pay up.

"Jamie in trouble?" Callaghan asked, swabbing handprints off a beer glass.

"No more than usual." Hanley handed over a ten-cent piece.

"He got here at half past three on Thursday. Left just after midnight." Callaghan jerked his head toward a clock on the wall. "He never looks at that, but I did. Thought I'd let you know."

"Much obliged."

"Jamie's a steady customer. I like to keep those." Callaghan dropped the coin in the till, scratched a spot in his thinning dark hair, and picked up another dirty glass.

Hanley left the saloon. He wanted a chat with Molly. Also with Olaf Johansson, Jamie's darts opponent. He'd quite a bit to think about, starting with Murphy's coat and shoes—shoes too fine for him to own, let alone wear outside in the slop and wet. And ending with why Tommy Callaghan had seemed so eager to give his none too flush-looking "steady customer" an alibi.

TEN

James Connor Murphy, I swear you're the most—" Molly's tirade broke off as soon as she'd opened the door wide enough to see who was standing on her front stoop. "Oh, it's you. Did you find him, then?"

"I found him all right, thanks." Hanley gave Molly his most engaging smile. "We talked awhile about the job I've got to offer, and now I'd like to talk to you. If you don't mind?"

"Never a bit." She stepped back from the doorway, smoothing her hair with one hand. "Kitchen's that way. Just poured myself a cuppa if you'd like one." Her smile as he drew level with her might have been tempting were it not for the odor of drink on her breath. "Day like this takes it out of a man."

"It does that." He preceded her down the narrow hallway, rather startled that she'd invited him in so readily, and into a tiny, dank kitchen. Its single window overlooked a small yard of packed dirt with a scraggly tree off to one side. No fence marked off the yard from the back alley or the refuse pile that served as the neighborhood rubbish dump.

He glanced around the room as she fixed the tea. A large washtub and wooden washboard next to a giant wicker basket and a drying rack covered with dripping clothes told him how she made her living. The potbellied stove needed blacking and the smell of burnt toast lingered. He eased aside a bunched-up white shirt on one corner of the table and snagged a finger on the end of a sewing needle stuck through the fabric. He must have interrupted her mending. The sole touch of graciousness in the room was a polished wooden wall bracket holding a framed portrait of the Irish statesman Daniel O'Connell. The old man's dark eyes gazed out at them, as intense as though the sketch were a living thing.

On the far side of the laundry basket stood a pair of men's boots and a scrubbing brush. Tension shot through Hanley at the sight of them. Was he too late? But the leather looked dry. Maybe Molly hadn't cleaned them yet.

Molly brought him a cup of tea. Her own was likely laced with something more at home in a whiskey flask. He raised his cup to her by way of thanks and sipped. Nearly strong enough to stand a spoon in, the tea warmed him right down to his chilled feet. The cup was bone china, well made. Another unexpected touch of grace. He felt a sudden sadness and tried not to let it show. He'd known countless women like Molly in Conley's Patch well enough to know that anything like pity would only offend. And it wasn't in keeping with the role he needed to play. From what he'd seen at the saloon, Murphy was most likely still thieving and had taken up other criminal enterprises as well. If Molly knew anything of them, she'd say nothing to a cop.

"My mother's." Molly nodded at the teacup. "The only two left from a set of six. She had them as a wedding gift. My da said they pawned four during the first year of the Famine. Mam couldn't bear to part with the last ones." She took a swig of tea. "Da sent them with me when I came over. Good riddance to them, he told me." She stroked the pale china. "Didn't want the reminder, I guess. Myself, now…"

She trailed off, eyes fixed on the tree outside. Then she turned to Hanley and smiled again with obvious effort. "So, then? What did you want to talk about?"

"Jamie. Just a couple of questions." He cradled the teacup, making his posture friendly and unthreatening. He'd honed his skill at fakery in his younger days, when the right look or gesture could draw in the marks as surely as the wrong one would scare them off. It unsettled him sometimes how easy he found it, though that didn't stop him using his talents when the need arose. "I represent a building concern, and we're looking for workers. Mr. Murphy might suit. Does he have any experience in the building trades?"

"He worked some sites for a while right after the Fire. He's mostly been an odd-jobber since then." She glanced down at her tea, then back up at him. "What I said before…about him going to Callaghan's so much…he doesn't. Hardly ever. He's…he's celebrating today. Six years since he came to America. If it weren't for that, you'd not have found him in the place. He'd be fit for any honest work that's going."

Her stress on the word "honest" was slight but definite. Hanley wondered how much she suspected about Murphy's real business. Her fidgety hands against the teacup told him she was lying about the drinking. Floundering herself, yet hoping to save her man from trouble of his own making. This too was familiar. Hanley gulped tea. All he wanted here was information.

"So he's not much in drink? That's helpful. What work does he do now?"

"Meeting people off the trains, hauling luggage, clearing scrap, stocking cargo. Used to run messages for the downtown hotels. Got fancy clothes and all for that." A hint of pride crept into her voice. "Cleans up well, Jamie. You'd hardly know it to look at him some days, but—" She halted abruptly. "Don't mind a word of me. I'm babbling."

"Can you give me names of employers as references?"

She frowned in thought. "They're different every day or two. He just started as a regular messenger for Drake's Hotel. You could try there."

"They must pay well for him to have those fine shoes I saw him wearing." Hanley chuckled. "I may be in the wrong business."

"They gave him those when they hired him on after the Fire, he told me. He's working them off, but until then he needs every job he can get." She snorted. "D'you know what he did today? Threw out his work boots! Stuffed them into the rubbish heap as if they hadn't got plenty of wear left in them. As if we had plenty of money to buy new ones. Sometimes I don't know what he's thinking."

Tommy Callaghan had said the fancy shoes were his brother's. Why had he lied? The whiskey in the tea must be hitting Molly. She was growing indiscreet. Hanley nodded toward the boots by the washtub. "Those them?"

"None other. You can see they look fine."

"Good workmanship. I'm needing a new pair. Mind if I take a look?"

She smiled at him. "Suit yourself."

The boots were light brown leather, scuffed around the toes but otherwise in good condition. Where the upper met the sole on the left boot, Hanley saw a thin dark line. He made a show of examining the stitching there, as would be expected of a man checking for quality. The deep red-brown of the line was unmistakable. And only on the side of the one boot.

"These are excellent," Hanley said as he lined up his left foot toe-to-toe with Murphy's boot, gazing down as if imagining how a similar pair would look on his own feet. The boot-heel reached the same spot on his foot as the track on the synagogue floor.

So, then. Murphy *had* been there, a chance thief surprised into violence. Yet even as he thought it, that answer felt wrong. Murphy was a petty criminal, not a murderer. If he'd been surprised while stealing valuables, he'd more likely have run than attacked.

Still, the line of blood existed. Which meant Murphy either killed the rabbi or arrived just after someone else had. Minutes after at most, with the blood still wet and spreading. Hanley thought of the crime scene, doing his best to recall every detail. Something about it nagged at him, but he couldn't pinpoint what.

He put the boots back by the washtub. He needed to find the spice box and menorah. Were they in the house or had Murphy stashed them elsewhere? Or somehow found a fence this quickly? Callaghan, maybe. That might explain his lying for Murphy.

The rubbish dump caught his eye as he straightened up. This close to the back window he could also see the corner of a shed with a crescent-moon shape cut high in the door. Outhouse. Either one would make a good temporary hiding place. Keeping the things in the house was risky. Molly might find them, and Murphy's lie to her about his fancy clothes suggested he didn't want her to know too much about his criminal activities. Hanley suppressed a grimace. The outhouse or the garbage pile looked like his best choices.

"Mind if I…?" he said to Molly, with a sheepish grin and a nod of his head toward the outhouse.

"Not at all." From elsewhere in the house came a young child's fretful wail. Molly's face brightened as she turned toward the sound. She hurried out of the room. Hanley went to take care of business.

He eyed the tree as he passed it, but saw no signs of disturbed earth nearby and its spindly trunk contained no convenient hidey-hole. The outhouse stank. Hanley held the door open a crack to give himself air as well as more light, but saw nothing aside from a pile of torn-up squares of newsprint. No loose floorboards, no bits of sacking tucked in a corner. He wondered if Murphy had chucked the valuables down the privy hole, but dismissed the idea with a shudder. He couldn't see Murphy digging through crap if there was any less disgusting alternative.

The rubbish dump was one, though not by much. Hanley decided against exploring it now. Sundown was approaching, and he'd no excuse to offer should Molly look out the kitchen window and see him trolling through the neighborhood's garbage. Instead, he rinsed his hands with the water pail and dipper just outside the privy door and went back to Molly's kitchen.

He found her at the table, dunking bread into her tea and feeding it to a baby girl on her lap. Rusty curls covered the child's head and crumbs clung to her mouth. Hanley wasn't good at guessing babies' ages, but this one looked big enough to be around a year old. Sturdier than Mrs. Pavlic's baby and probably better fed.

The child made him realize he'd seen Molly before. At Lake Street Station back in October, the day of the Fire. Prostitution, first offense. The baby was with her, which had caught his attention. Murphy must have been off somewhere and she'd likely had no place to leave the child safely. "Thanks for the tea," he said. "Who made those boots? I might pay him a visit."

"Herrick Elway across the street. He gives me his washing when he can afford to." She frowned. "Poor man had a visit last night. Hooligans. They're all over since the army left—throwing paint and worse on people's doors, breaking windows, shouting and fighting at all hours. Next thing you know they'll be setting something afire and then where will we be?"

The thought of arson made Hanley shudder. He'd tip Schmidt to the trouble on his beat and let Moore know as well. "If there's anything for Jamie, we'll be in touch. Couple of days or so. Thanks again."

Outside, he turned north toward Lake Street. The smell of smoke seemed stronger—no, that was surely in his head. Distant church bells struck the half hour. The streets were nearly deserted. He found himself looking for toughs in the lengthening shadows, but the few rough men he saw slunk away without a challenge.

Schmidt would be over by Randolph about now, checking for disturbances in or near the barracks. Hanley decided to go tell him what Molly had said. He picked up his pace, thinking over what he'd learned. Callaghan had lied for Murphy. Was he holding the silver Murphy took from the synagogue? Callaghan might have some interesting connections—among the police, trading free drink for early warning of pending raids, or among the city's crime bosses, acting as a fence or informant in exchange for favors.

Moore would know. The chief of detectives kept an eye on Chicago's crime bosses and those known to work for them. The Fire, of course, had thrown things into disarray. Many a petty crook had snapped up free train tickets out of town, while a steady surge of newcomers replaced them. Still, Moore should know something useful about Callaghan and Murphy both.

The wind off the water ruffled his hair as he neared the river. If Murphy was a bunco man, he was on somebody's payroll. Callaghan might be also. Whose?

The thought of Sean Doyle crossed his mind, as if dropped into his brain by a passing gust. The outdoor chill settled in his stomach. Charming Billy drank at Callaghan's saloon. Now he remembered it, Hanley had seen a few other of Doyle's regulars stopping into Callaghan's as well. Not often, but enough to make him uneasy. They'd seemed to be there for no more than drink, but...

No use thinking that yet. Making more of Sean Doyle than he is. A jumped-up thug with a fancy card house and some brothels the Department won't raid no matter how many times I say. He's not behind every awful thing that happens in this city.

The barracks loomed in the fading light. From inside he heard a woman singing "The Rose of Tralee" in a rough, cracked voice. Schmidt was rounding the building's far corner, a distant figure in blue. Hanley raised a hand and hurried toward him.

ELEVEN

July 13, 1861

The Faheys' small barn smelled of cow and pig musk, overlaid with the sweetness of hay that made Hanley think of sunshine. He waited in the loft above the animal pens, heart drumming with excitement as he laid out and smoothed the blanket he'd brought to cover the dry, scratchy hay stalks. Everything had to be perfect. Everything *would* be perfect. He still could hardly believe she'd agreed to meet him here. Pegeen Sullivan, the prettiest girl in Conley's Patch. Laughing blue eyes that shone brighter whenever she saw him, slender curves that fit perfectly against him the first time he held her close and kissed her. He wanted to be holding her now, with not a thing between them.

The creak of the barn door sounded from below. Pegeen's voice floated up. "Francis?"

God in heaven, the sound of her was enough to send heat through him and tighten his loins. "Up here," he said, and moved toward the ladder that poked through the hayloft floor. "Climb on up. It's dead easy. Doesn't stink so much of cow and pig, either." *Idiot*, he thought, and clamped his mouth shut over the spate of babble.

He heard her feet on the rungs as she swiftly climbed, then saw her emerge through the gap. Skirt raised ankle-high, she picked her way toward him over the mounded hay, making it look graceful as only she could. When she reached him, he took her hands. Work-roughened and warm, they felt delicate in his grip.

"I've missed you since yesterday," she said.

He slid his hands up to her shoulders and let them rest there. She'd tied a pink ribbon around her dark curls. He fingered it, then stroked her cheek. "Sunday best," he said softly.

She blushed. "For you." She laid a palm flat against his shirt and laughed softly. "Your heart's pounding, Francis. Did you run here, then?"

"I'd run anywhere to be with you." He took an end of the ribbon in his fingers and tugged. It came loose and her dark curls tumbled down. He buried his hands in their softness, felt her breath against his neck as they stood close amid the hay. The need to hold her, skin to skin, surged through him—but he had a thing to say first and rushed ahead before he could lose his nerve. "When I can, when I've enough put by...we'll get married if you'll have me."

Her answer was one word breathed in his ear. "*Yes.*"

☙

Afterward, they couldn't stop laughing as they picked bits of hay from each other's hair and clothes and he tied up her curls in the pink ribbon. He made a ragged job of it, but she told him it was good enough. "I'm only after going to Doyle's," she said. Some of the lightness left her face as she spoke the name. "Better I don't look so well there."

He felt a flash of anger. "Sean's still pestering you? He's no bloody right. I told him before—"

She pressed her fingers to his lips. "Don't, now. I've said no, I can say it again, and there's an end." She moved toward the ladder, flicked up her skirt, and carefully started down. He followed her and they left the Faheys' yard together.

"I'll be there tonight," he told her as they reached the street and turned east toward the lake and Doyle's place, a ramshackle saloon by the lakeshore on the edge of Hell's Half Acre. "Keep him from bothering you." Or so he hoped, though unease spiked in him as he said it. Five years of working for Doyle, from stealing off the riverside docks all the way up to running the faro games that brought in packets of cash, had taught him how much Sean hated being thwarted. Still, he'd risk that friendship for Pegeen. Even if it cost him.

୧

"I don't know what you want with whoring, anyway," he said to Doyle later, as the pair of them sat nursing whiskeys during a lull in the faro games. Custom always dropped a bit around nine in the evening as the first wave of drinkers belatedly recalled their wives or sweethearts at home and skulked off, skint of whatever funds they'd walked in with a few hours earlier. "Don't we make enough with the faro and the dice and the drinks? Which we shouldn't water so much, by the way. Folk'll notice, especially on their first or second. You don't want people knowing you're cheating 'em, even if half of 'em are old-blood Yanks who deserve it." He despised them, the self-styled bluebloods who came slumming to places like Doyle's, bored with their own more genteel gaming establishments and wanting a walk in rougher territory. Not so much as Doyle loathed them, though. He watched the man toss back his whiskey in a single shot, thinking Sean did nothing by halves. When he liked you, you were golden. When he hated you, dead was preferable. Hanley felt lucky to be among the liked.

Lounging next to Doyle on a pulled-up stool, Billy Shaughnessy knocked back his own whiskey in direct imitation of his boss. Hanley snickered and ignored Billy's glare, which he knew would only infuriate him further. For all his size, Charming Billy couldn't hold his liquor half so well as he thought. Hanley looked forward to sobering him up later with a bucket of cold lake water to the face.

He grinned into his whiskey. A few years back, Billy had dared him to go to a brothel, boasted about the dozens of women he'd had there already. One of whom broke Billy's nose that night when he refused to pay her fee. "Real charmer, you are," Hanley'd said when he saw Billy's face covered in blood and snot. "Charming Billy." He'd lost no time spreading the story around, singing the little ditty everyone knew along with it. To Billy's impotent fury, the nickname stuck.

Charming Billy set down his empty glass and waved for another. At Pegeen, Hanley noted with a surge of irritation. On purpose, to bring her to Doyle's attention when she and Hanley both least wanted it. She came over, her expression carefully blank, and picked up Billy's glass. He grabbed her rump. Scorn flashed across her face as she eased out of his grasp and moved off.

Hanley's grip tightened around his own drink. He toyed with the notion of tossing it in Billy's face, but kept his composure. If Charming Billy wanted a fistfight, or worse, let him beg for it. *And then watch Sean shut him down.*

Doyle was gazing after Pegeen in a way that made Hanley's nerves itch. "Your girl's a fool," he said. "So are you, Frank. Looks like hers, she could make us a fortune."

"She's spoken for." He felt a rush of pride as he said it, remembering the *yes* she'd whispered in his ear just a few hours before. "It's a bad idea, anyway. I keep telling you. Half our custom comes from the Patch, and who're your fancy women but their sisters and cousins and sweethearts? As for the Yanks, is it really worth the money they pay to be giving them our women?" He knocked back the last of his whiskey, feeling bold as the liquor coursed down his throat. "Have more pride than that, Sean. No more whoring, just fleece 'em and be done with it."

Doyle gave him a look so piercing that, for a heartbeat, it chilled him. Then Doyle grinned and the unnerving moment was gone. "Maybe so," he said, with a nod toward the door of the saloon, where a few well-dressed young men were stumbling in. Hanley judged them with a practiced eye. A sheet or two to the wind already, sheep ripe for shearing. Sometimes his job was too easy.

Doyle clapped him on the shoulder. "Back to work with you. You too, Billy. You can handle four if things get unpleasant, can't you?"

Billy eyed Hanley. "Better than this boyo can."

"I do the thinking," Hanley shot back. "Breaking bones, that's your department."

Billy shoved his stool back. "You want a few broken now, that's fine with—"

Doyle held up a hand. The gesture silenced both of them. "Marks're waiting. Get to it."

"Sure." Hanley moved off toward the bluebloods, running through opening gambits in his head as he pasted a welcoming smile on his face. He threw a last glance over his shoulder toward Doyle. Pegeen was setting down a fresh round of beers at a table nearby. Doyle's gaze lingered on her, calculating as a butcher eying a steer's carcass.

A braying laugh from one of the bluebloods echoed across the saloon. Hesitating, Hanley glanced at the group of men. From the corner of his eye he saw Pegeen head for the counter where more drinks were poured and waiting.

Sean knows now. Nothing'll happen, he told himself and got down to business.

TWELVE

January 27, 1872

The deserted shul was blessedly silent. From a bench behind the curtain that marked off the women's section, Rivka savored the quiet. The evening service was over, everyone gone home to get a night's rest before the burial tomorrow morning. Fresh grief stabbed through her at the thought of Papa's body, empty of his spirit and waiting to be covered in cold earth. She wished she could cry. Apart from yesterday morning in front of Detective Hanley, she hadn't been able to. The pain of her father's death had hardened inside her like clay in fire. She felt as if she was choking on it.

She wasn't supposed to be here, of course. She was supposed to be in her room, having gone early to bed. She'd meant to sleep, but felt too restless. Her bedroom was too small, too close, too full of the fading smells of supper from downstairs. Unable to stand it any longer, she'd left. Out the window and onto the roof of the lean-to, then a long knee-jarring jump to the yard. Her brother Aaron had shown her how when she was twelve, the time she'd heard him sneaking into his own room next door after he'd stayed late at a rally for Abraham Lincoln.

She'd snuck out many times after that. No destination in mind, just the sweet freedom of being out in the night with no one to forbid her or demand to know where she was going. She went to the empty shul sometimes and sat in the men's section, where she could see the Ark. Or to a patch of nearby riverbank, between the docks and warehouses and lumberyards, where she could sit and think. Tonight she hadn't known where she was going until she saw the shul's roofline in the dark.

The shul had been Papa's place. His murder had left a ghost there, a fragment of his spirit that couldn't move on to reunion with Hashem. She needed to banish that ghost. To recapture a truer and better memory of her father, in the silence of this room that had always held the Holy Presence.

So she sat in the women's area, breathing the dust from the curtain folds, eyes shut, conjuring up the sound of Papa's voice—the singsong rhythm of the Hebrew as he chanted the words of the Torah. Anguish swept over her, leavened with anger she barely knew how to admit to, let alone express. She gripped her head, nails digging through her kerchief, and bit her lip until she tasted blood. "How did this happen?" she said in a strangled whisper. "I have no one now. Aaron is gone, Mameh is dead, and you…How could you leave me this way?" She couldn't say the word *murdered*. Instead, she listened to her racing heartbeat in the silence. Even here she could find no peace. Not until she knew the truth behind her father's death.

Onkl Jacob had come that day. In the middle of the afternoon, just when Papa was getting ready to go to the Nathans' for their weekly study session. They had practically run into each other on the doorstep. Rivka tucked her feet up on the bench, drawing her knees to her chin against the cold. She had heard them talking…they both sounded shaken. No words had reached her back in the kitchen where she'd been sorting through potatoes and carrots for supper. Only the tone of their voices and the door of Papa's study closing. Papa came to the kitchen then and asked her to make tea. "It seems we are studying here today," he'd said. When she brought the tea some time later, Papa took the tray at the door. She'd barely glimpsed Onkl Jacob, slumped in a chair with his head in his hands.

The door of the shul creaked. She caught her breath. Who would be coming here now? She twitched aside a curtain fold and looked through the narrow gap. The moonlight showed the bimah, the remaining menorah—mercifully cleaned and polished—and a stocky figure carrying a lantern, moving toward the pale gleam of the curtained Ark where the Torah scrolls were.

Onkl Jacob.

He set the lantern on the floor and reached inside the Ark. Then he withdrew his hand, curled shut around something. As he bent to pick up the lantern, Rivka saw that he had an empty satchel over one shoulder. He strode to the door, paused at the threshold and looked back at the bimah. "One last try, Rav," he murmured. Then he stepped out into the chilly night.

Rivka let the curtain fall. She sat for a few seconds in shock, watching her breath make white clouds. Onkl Jacob was *shomer*, the watcher over Papa's body. He had left that sacred duty to someone else and come here...for what? And where was he going now?

She rose and left the shul.

The ice-crusted mud in the yard made her shoes slip, but also muffled their sound. By the time she reached the boardwalk, Jacob was nearly half a block ahead of her. Moving as quickly as she dared, she followed him. After a few minutes she realized he was heading for the river...or perhaps the police station. Lake Street was only one block ahead. Was he going to see Detective Hanley? To tell him what? And why would he leave Papa's body to do it? She sped up, then slowed as he passed the intersection where the police station stood and turned toward South Water Street.

She followed him, keeping up as best she could without being seen. The sour reek of beer reached her as she passed a saloon. From inside she heard cursing and breaking glass. Next would come a brawl, fueled by liquor and anger, and someone would end up injured or dead. It happened nearly every day now. She shivered and hurried after Onkl Jacob, away from the sounds of violence.

Warehouses loomed black against the night sky, the outlines of docks barely visible against the dark water. A few street lamps lit the walkways that ran beside the warehouses. A watchman drowsed on a chair partway down the row of buildings. Farther off, she could see another guard walking past on patrol.

Onkl Jacob halted in the shadows, then hurried across the open ground between South Water Street and the riverbank. He stopped shy of the warehouses in another patch of darkness and waited. After a few moments the watchman slowly hauled himself upright. He was tall, with light hair, but too far away from the boardwalk for her to see any more detail. He picked up the lantern at his feet, glanced around, and walked off down the row of buildings.

Once he was gone, Jacob made his way to the small circle of light cast by the lantern over the entrance of the third warehouse down. He stood still a moment—unlocking the door, she guessed. The object he'd taken from the Ark must have been a key. Then he disappeared inside the warehouse, shutting the door behind him.

Rivka waited, heart pounding. She saw the watchman coming back and her throat closed so tightly she could hardly breathe. The man passed the warehouse and continued on.

Jacob re-emerged, the satchel slung over his back. He disappeared into a patch of shadow, then reappeared as he crossed the street, heading back east. Where could he be going? The satchel bulged with corners and curves. What had he taken? The outlines made her think of tea and cornmeal tins, coffee canisters, boxes of salt.

She followed him once more, head light and stomach hollow. She couldn't have seen what she thought she'd just seen. Onkl Jacob could not be stealing food.

But none of their neighbors owned a warehouse full of such things. Nor did they work for any company that owned one, where an employer might be giving food away. If anyone did, everyone would have known of it. And Onkl Jacob would not have to sneak past the watchman under cover of night. Whatever he had in that satchel, it didn't belong to him. Or to anyone from Market Street.

He turned onto LaSalle, heading south. Caught by surprise, Rivka hurried to catch up. Even with his load, he moved quickly. They covered one block, then two. Ahead of them loomed the Randolph Street barracks, its boxy outline visible in the moonlight amid the rebuilt storefronts and gaping holes of burned-out foundations around it. From somewhere inside one of the black pits came a small child's wail. Rivka shuddered with more than the cold and hurried after Jacob.

He was heading for the front door of the barracks. She hunkered against the side of a shed and watched him sling the satchel down. A brisk movement of one arm as he knocked. Then, before anyone could answer the door, he hurried around the side of the building and vanished into the darkness.

She waited, but he didn't reappear. The barracks door opened and a stout woman peered out. She spotted the satchel and hauled it indoors.

Rivka sagged against the rough wooden wall. Was this how Papa had gotten the things he gave away—the things she knew they didn't have? How many donations had come from that warehouse? The clothes for Mira Pavlic's children? The flour Mira baked into bread? How long had this been going on and Papa had not told her?

She pushed away from the wall and stumbled down the street. Onkl Jacob was nowhere in sight.

Detective Hanley should know about this. She would tell him when they met tomorrow. She huddled deeper into her shawl as she hurried on, plagued by sudden doubt. If she told, Onkl Jacob might be arrested. Jailed as a common thief, shamed before the community. Shamed on her word. Which made her *holchei rachil*, a talebearer. A murderer of reputations.

Could she even be sure they were stealing? Papa had many friends. Perhaps one of them owned the warehouse and knew all about the food deliveries.

Which is why Onkl Jacob left Papa to come here after dark and sneak past that watchman. And why Papa never asked me to help.

She reached Market Street and turned blindly onto it. How could she tell Detective Hanley that her father had been stealing—and that Onkl Jacob still was?

How could she not?

THIRTEEN

As always, Hanley went with Mam and Kate to eight o'clock Mass at Saint Pat's on Sunday morning. The spacious church was crowded. Turnout, always good, had nearly doubled since the Fire. He looked around for Jamie Murphy, but didn't see him. He felt mildly disappointed, though he hadn't really expected Murphy to show. Murphy probably spent his Sunday mornings worshipping beer at Callaghan's place.

Cloth rustled as they stood for final prayers and parish announcements and then started filing out of the pews. Hanley spotted Molly carrying her baby, but couldn't see whether Murphy was with them. He excused himself from his family and hurried to catch up to her. "Morning," he said as he reached her. "Is Jamie with—"

She rounded on him, her face set and angry under her plain straw bonnet. "Don't speak to me. Jamie told me what happened at Callaghan's. You're a filthy liar, and you'll go to Hell for it." She turned away and stalked off, holding tight to her child as she pushed through the slow-moving throng.

Hanley watched her go. He felt people staring, those within earshot who'd caught the exchange. His cheeks warmed. He did his best to ignore the looks as he moved along, keeping an eye out for Murphy.

"Spits like a cat, that one," a voice said from behind him. "I hear she's a handful between the sheets. Might be fun to teach her some manners."

Hanley's spine stiffened. It took an act of will to turn toward the speaker slowly instead of whirling around and smashing a fist into his face. "What do you want, Billy?"

Charming Billy Shaughnessy gave him a friendly grin. The sight of it made Hanley want to knock out his teeth, though not in the middle of Saint Pat's. His unkempt fair hair brushed his coat collar and he sported a fresh knife scar under one eye. "A drink and a talk over old times?"

"Not interested," Hanley said, jaw clenched, and turned away. Billy gripped his arm, but Hanley flung the man off hard enough that Billy had to side-step to keep his balance.

"Ah, now." Billy sounded aggrieved. "What's that for, when I'm tryin' to do you a good turn?"

The hell you are. "There's no good turn you could do me." Only the knowledge that he was in church kept him from lashing out with more than words. Then another thought struck him. "Why are you here? Doyle send you?"

Billy scratched his nose. Its misshapen bridge sported a new lump, as if someone had broken it again not too long ago. "If I said no, you'd say I was lyin'."

"Then get out of my way." Hanley started to push past him.

Billy blocked his path. "You need to listen to me. Honest to God, Frank. For your own good, I'm tellin' you."

"What are you talking about?"

"That old Jew, got himself killed." At Hanley's sharp look, Billy went on. "I know you're lookin' into it. I've seen you around the last couple of days. You and the other coppers, askin' questions and makin' a ruckus. Let me save you some trouble, all right? That old sheeney, he's dead because them Jews had things people wanted. Pretty things you can sell for cash. Somebody took 'em. Somebody pissed as hell 'cause he's got no food and no work and no hope of either. You're so smart, you always told me so. You'll figure it out. I'm just givin' you a tip."

Hanley watched Billy through narrowed eyes. "I don't need tips from you."

"Ah, God." Billy threw up his hands. "I'll make it simple. Stirrin' things up like you are, it's drawin' attention to them as don't want any. I shouldn't have to tell you. But I guess I do, 'cause you've forgot where you came from."

"Damned right I have." Hanley kept his voice low, but it held all the rage he felt. "And you—and Doyle—know bloody well why. So leave me the hell alone. And you can tell Doyle that as well."

Billy shook his head. "Just remember what I said, Frank." His gaze shifted over Hanley's shoulder. "Be better for everyone."

Hanley glanced back and saw Mam and Kate approaching, deep in conversation. Mam was being emphatic, Kate trying not to smile. Hanley felt a vein pounding in his forehead. "So help me, Billy, if you—"

The words died in his throat. Charming Billy was gone.

☙

Rivka sat on the edge of her bed. Her head was pounding, her stomach empty. Too distressed to eat, she'd scarcely touched anything at the meal of condolence a short while ago, except a little of the stewed beans with beef shank Sisel Klein had brought. She pressed her hands to her throbbing head and groaned softly. She had promised to meet Hanley today. The day of her father's burial. She hadn't thought of that. Hadn't thought of anything except her need to find the truth and not to be left out.

What could she say to him? *I saw Onkl Jacob last night, sneaking to the Randolph Street barracks with food, and I think he stole it?* She couldn't accuse Jacob of such a thing without proof.

A bitter laugh escaped her. Even *with* proof, she couldn't accuse him. Not directly. *Lashon hara,* she could hear Papa saying. *Gossip. To say bad things about someone kills a man's good name as surely as a stab to the heart kills his body.*

But what if a bad thing is true? she had asked him.

Even then we should keep silent, except to save a life. It is not for us to act as the means of Hashem's judgment. He will see to justice in His own time.

Her palms felt cool against her forehead, a small comfort in a sea of pain and confusion. The question she had not asked then was, *What if silence will permit a wrong to happen? What if the wrong thing only* might *happen?* Her fingernails caught in her hair as she curled her hands into fists. Now there was no one to ask. Papa was gone and Onkl Jacob too afraid to talk to her. Tanta Hannah wouldn't talk either, though Rivka was sure she knew something about Onkl Jacob's activities. If Aaron were here she would talk to him—they had always talked, about everything—but the war for the Union had drawn her brother away from home years ago. He had died fighting in it for all anyone knew. Suddenly she missed him so fiercely it made her throat hurt.

She straightened and stared out the bedroom window. She must say something. As long as there was any chance that what Onkl Jacob and Papa were doing had any connection to her father's death, she couldn't stay silent. Could she?

The children had troubled Papa most. Living on the streets, selling matches or melted lumps of souvenir iron from burned safes and wrought-iron fences. Children who received no help from anywhere because their mothers were in drink or their fathers had left or been jailed. Papa had wanted to do something about that. And Jacob would have followed him in anything.

She stood abruptly and fetched her warmest shawl from her wardrobe. She wouldn't be able to get her coat without being seen by the throng of shiva mourners in the parlor. At Lake Street Station she might find some answers to the questions swirling in her head. How much she would tell Hanley, she didn't yet know.

A light tap came at her door. "Rivka?" The voice was Tanta Hannah's. She opened the door and came in. Her eyes widened as she saw Rivka standing in the middle of the room, bundled up in her shawl. "Are you cold? Come downstairs and be with everyone. It's warmer, at least."

"I—" She had to get Hannah to leave. What would Hanley think if she never showed? "I want to be by myself. Maybe sleep a little. You go on back down."

"Nonsense." Tanta Hannah enveloped her in a warm hug, then led her to the bed. "You rest. I will sit with you until you're ready to come back to shiva."

☙

Snow was falling as Hanley emerged from the Lake Street tunnel and turned toward the station. His swift walk from Ida's had gotten his blood pumping. He felt brimful of energy and eager to see Rivka. They'd agreed to meet at one. It was nearly that now.

After Mass, he'd spent the rest of his morning enjoying a leisurely breakfast and a comfortable chat with his sister. She'd told him, laughing, of Mrs. King's return home after inspecting them on Saturday ("She'd a temper like a soaked cat! What did you say to her?") and hinted shyly at a new beau. He hadn't pressed her for more details about her young man. From her blushes and bright eyes, the thing was too new and delicate to be talked of much. He settled for her promise that she would bring the fellow to meet him soon, and trusted to Kate's good sense and Mrs. King's eagle eye for the rest.

He'd done a few outside chores for Ida as well, sweeping fresh snow off the steps and clearing a path to the boardwalk. Talk and activity had helped him keep the encounter with Billy out of his mind—though now, as he neared the stationhouse, he found himself thinking it over. Despite his show of friendly concern, Billy had no reason to stick his neck out for Hanley. Every reason not to, in fact. Nor should he care a damn about Rabbi Kelmansky's murder. The death of an old Jewish man would mean nothing to him. So what the hell was he doing at Saint Pat's?

The wind knifing off the river made Hanley's eyes tear. He blinked the moisture away and looked up in time to see two men leave the stationhouse. They were deep in conversation and didn't see him. He halted on the snowy boardwalk, scarcely breathing. One was a patrolman, spare and rangy in his blue uniform, his hair and mustache trimmed to military neatness—Officer Georg Reinhardt, Hanley's rival for promotion to the detective squad. The other was Sean Doyle.

They reached the street and turned eastward. Hanley followed them, his mind racing. What was Doyle doing at Lake Street? First Charming Billy at church, now this. And Reinhardt, talking with Doyle like the pair of them were old friends. Tension knotted his insides as he strode along the boardwalk as fast as he dared without attracting attention. He wanted to get close enough to hear what they were saying, but they'd spot him the minute he did.

They parted at Lake and Franklin, Reinhardt turning south and Doyle continuing eastward. Hanley watched Reinhardt just long enough to satisfy himself the patrolman was heading for his regular beat. Then he started after Doyle. Two blocks' walk took them to LaSalle Street, where Doyle hailed a passing hackney cab and got in. Frustrated, Hanley watched it rejoin the eastbound traffic flow. He'd no hope of following Doyle any further.

A single note from a church bell echoed through the air. Rivka would be at the station about now—probably nervous, maybe even frightened, with no notion of where he was or what to do next. He had to go back. He turned and hurried toward the stationhouse.

She wasn't there when he arrived. Nor had she been, according to the desk sergeant. "You plan to wait, I'll let you know if a girl turns up," the sergeant said with a sly grin. Hanley wanted to rearrange the man's teeth, but he kept hold of himself and thanked him as civilly as he could. *If Rivka doesn't come in the next ten minutes...* His thoughts ground to a halt. He had no idea what he ought to do. Go to her home, see how she was? Send a note by the afternoon post? Another thought struck him then that made him curse himself for a fool. They were burying her father today. She had other things to think about and had likely forgotten their plans to meet.

Ida had spoken of mourning time, he recalled. Shiva. A formal gathering that lasted several days, if he remembered right. Maybe Rivka *had* remembered but couldn't get away. Maybe she'd planned on sneaking out to meet him and something went wrong. Or she was too sunk in grief to do anything.

He needed to see her, make sure she was all right.

ᮋ

Ten minutes after leaving the station, Hanley halted at the intersection of Market and Washington. What was he doing, hurrying to Rivka's house like an anxious lover? Doyle's appearance, and Billy's, had spooked him and now he was acting crazy. He hadn't even thought about what kind of reception he was likely to get. Jacob Nathan hadn't wanted Rivka to speak to him at the synagogue on the morning after the murder. How would he—how would all of them—react to a Christian policeman bursting in on the very day they'd buried their rabbi, for no better reason than to see the dead man's daughter? What would Rivka think?

He didn't need to talk to her, he told himself. Not yet. He only wanted to make sure she was all right, not intrude on her grief. And he had other reasons to go there as well. The spice box, for one. Jacob Nathan could describe it in detail so Hanley would know precisely what he was looking for when he checked with fences he knew. He wanted to talk to Nathan again anyway, find out what had made him so edgy at the synagogue and the morgue.

He glanced down the road for traffic and saw a small general store. He could buy something for them—a tin of tea, a few potatoes. A funeral gift. Surely Jewish people would accept such things, even from an outsider.

He crossed the street toward the little shop.

FOURTEEN

The Kelmansky house stood near the middle of the block between Washington and Madison, nearly straight across the yard from the synagogue. With a tea tin and half a dozen potatoes tied up in brown paper and tucked in the crook of his arm, Hanley picked his way across the frozen mud toward the back door. It occurred to him as he went that he might not be allowed to see Rivka. They might even refuse him entry. He hoped not. He wanted to offer her some comfort if he could. But that was foolish. Surrounded by her own people, what need did she have for comfort from him?

He might see her briefly at least. Although, with a house full of mourners, she could hardly tell him what she'd learned. That meant he could concentrate on Nathan. He was sure Nathan knew where Rabbi Kelmansky had gone late on the day he died. The trick would be finding out without tipping his hand or causing irreparable offense.

Through the closed back door, he heard voices. A glance through the nearby window showed Nathan and Moishe Zalman talking together. Hannah stood near them, holding a platter of bread, her head swathed in a dark kerchief. As he watched, Nathan and his wife disappeared into a front room.

He tightened his grip on his packages and knocked. Zalman's startled face greeted him when the door opened. "Detective Francis Hanley," Hanley said. "I've something for Miss Kelmansky and I need to speak to Mr. Nathan."

Zalman's eyes widened even more behind his spectacles, emphasizing his owlish look. Had the man understood him? According to Jamie Murphy, Zalman had helped distribute relief items around the neighborhood. How much did he know about their source?

"May I come in? It's cold out here." Hanley stepped forward as he spoke and Zalman moved aside. Once inside the warm kitchen, Hanley set the tea and potatoes down on the scrubbed pinewood table. He didn't see Rivka. She must be elsewhere in the house. Zalman watched, looking bewildered, then ducked through an archway into the adjoining room.

Hanley followed, stopping just shy of the threshold. He caught an impression of black coats and trousers, sweeping black skirts and shawls, pale faces topped with kerchiefs or skullcaps. A crowd of people milled amid a jumble of furniture—bookshelves, a few cane chairs, a low table, a curve-backed sofa. Hannah Nathan was setting the bread on the end of a just-visible dining room table swathed in black crepe. Then someone moved aside and he saw Rivka sitting on the floor. She was shrouded in black. Her skirt pooled around her, nearly covering the cushion and rag rug beneath.

She looked up and saw him just as the room fell silent. She was pale, her eyes bruised-looking, as if she hadn't slept since Friday evening. Surprise flashed across her face and then vanished as she looked down again. Hanley felt confused. Why was she sitting on the floor? The apparent indignity of it shocked him. Hadn't anyone the decency to offer her a chair?

Then Jacob Nathan's stocky frame filled the archway, forcing Hanley farther back into the kitchen. "You should not be here," Nathan said. "A policeman should not be at this house, on this day of all days!"

He heard Rivka call Nathan's name, which Nathan ignored. Other feminine voices, all talking at once, drowned out the rest of her words. As he moved out of view, he glimpsed Hannah Nathan laying a hand on Rivka's shoulder, pressing her back down as she tried to rise. He wanted to intervene, but knowledge of his own ignorance forestalled him. Whatever was happening here, he didn't understand it, and right now he didn't need the distraction.

He gestured toward the packages on the table. "I brought these. I'm sorry for your loss."

Nathan looked at them. His anger ebbed, though not his obvious discomfort at Hanley's presence. "I thank you," he said with an effort. "Now if you will excuse us—"

"I need to talk to you first." Hanley kept his tone conversational. "The missing spice box...can you describe it for me in detail? That'll help me trace it."

Nathan held out one hand, thumb and fingers parted to make a rough six-inch gap. "About so long, a little less high. Two or three inches deep. It had etchings on the sides—Moses in the Nile, the burning bush, the parting of the Red Sea. The top is on a hinge, not separate." Nathan paused, resting his hands on either side of Hanley's purchases, his shoulders bowed. "The silversmith who made it is dead now. Murdered by soldiers of the Russian tsar. The work of his hands is all that remains."

I'm sorry, Hanley wanted to say, but knew it would mean nothing. Nathan seemed less on guard now, just as he'd hoped. "Miss Kelmansky told me her father said he was going to see a friend on the day he died. Do you know who it was, or where he went?"

A slight straightening of his spine betrayed Nathan's sudden tension. He picked at the knotted twine that held the potatoes in their paper. "He did not tell me."

"He didn't mention anything? Say, while you were studying?"

Nathan kept working at the knot. "When we study, we do not speak of anything other than Talmud."

Hanley wondered what Talmud was. He would ask Ida later. "So nothing was bothering him? Everything seemed as usual?"

"I have said." The first knot gave. Nathan moved on to the second without looking up.

The man was stonewalling him. "I think you know who the friend was," Hanley said softly. "I just wonder why you don't want to tell me."

Nathan went still for a moment. Then he resumed untying the knots. He was having trouble grasping the thin twine. Hanley waited, but said nothing.

Kelmansky might have known his attacker, Hanley thought. At the morgue, Nathan had reacted strongly when Will Rushton talked about the angle of the fatal blow and what that meant for the killer's height. Time of death could be late afternoon or evening. Three to nine o'clock was Rushton's estimate. And Rivka had said her father went to see a friend… Hanley felt a chill and a tautness of nerves, as if he'd taken a dip in the cold lake. "When exactly were you studying with the rabbi that day?"

Nathan pulled the second knot apart and began to unwrap the potatoes. "I have told you. In the afternoon."

"When? Two, three? Later?"

Nathan's eyes flicked toward the parlor. "Rivka was beginning to make supper while I was here. That would be later."

"Did you go to the synagogue?"

"We were here."

"And you left here when? Was the rabbi with you?"

Nathan picked up two potatoes as if slipping eggs from under a hen. He crossed to a basket by the wall and set them in it before he replied. "No. And I didn't look at the clock."

"You don't know when you left?"

"I have said. I didn't look at the clock."

Hanley tried another tack. "Where did you go when you left here?"

"To my shop. Then to shul for the evening minyan. Then home for supper." Nathan put the last two potatoes in the basket and picked up the tea tin. Hanley saw a subtle easing in him, though considerable tension remained. He walked across the kitchen, opened a cupboard and set the tea tin on a shelf.

If the minyan was at the synagogue, Hanley thought, then Nathan couldn't have killed the rabbi until after it was over. "What time was the evening minyan?"

"Sundown."

Which came about five o'clock this time of year. "So as far as you know, Rabbi Kelmansky was alive and well around five o'clock Thursday afternoon?"

"Yes." The cupboard door closed with a *thunk*. Nathan turned and began walking toward the parlor entrance. "I have been away from shiva long enough. Please excuse—"

"How long does a minyan last?" As he'd hoped, the question made

Nathan halt. "Our services at Saint Pat's take an hour or so. Are yours about the same?"

"The minyan, no." Nathan looked puzzled. "It is a small prayer service for perhaps half an hour. We give thanks to Hashem for bringing us through another day."

"And Rabbi Kelmansky was there?" A priest would have been at a church service, so presumably the rabbi should have been at the minyan.

Nathan closed his eyes briefly. "Forgive me," he said. "It is…difficult to speak of him."

"But he was there?"

"He had…something to attend to. Now please, I—"

"What was it? Where? With whom?"

Nathan moved abruptly toward the parlor. "Moishe!" he called out. Zalman appeared so swiftly, Hanley wondered if he'd been waiting for the summons. Nathan nodded toward Hanley. "I must go. Please show the detective out." Before Hanley could frame another question Nathan ducked through the doorway.

Hanley weighed his options. Blind impulse made him want to go after Nathan and demand answers, but that meant doing it in a room full of mourners, including Rivka. The last thing he wanted was to subject her to that kind of scene, today of all days. He could try to draw Nathan aside again, back to the kitchen or out into the yard. But Nathan was on home ground, surrounded by his own people. Hanley wasn't likely to get far under those circumstances.

He glanced at Moishe. The young man shifted his feet, his eyes on Hanley's face. "Please," he murmured, his voice thickly accented. "You will come now?"

His tone and manner reminded Hanley of a timid child. With a slight smile, he walked out the door. As he'd half-expected, Zalman followed him onto the porch. Clearly, his job was to make sure Hanley left.

With one foot on the top porch step, Hanley turned toward him. "Maybe you can help me, Mr. Zalman. Do you speak English?"

Zalman shrugged. "A little. Not good. In the shop—wool, cotton, linen. Stand, turn, please, thank you." He looked down at his fingers, twining them together, then back up at Hanley. "I want to say...thank you. For what you bring. For..." He trailed off and shrugged, as if the right words were beyond him.

"You're welcome. I'm sorry for your loss. You work with Mr. Nathan?"

Zalman nodded.

"Every day?"

Another nod, then a hesitant smile and a headshake. "But no work on Shabbos."

"Of course. You worked on Thursday?"

"Yes."

"And Mr. Nathan worked that day?"

"Yes." Zalman looked puzzled.

Hanley thought fast. He badly wanted to know where Kelmansky had been during the minyan, but Zalman might not know, or might clam up about it, just as Nathan had. "When did Mr. Nathan leave the shop?" Hanley asked instead.

Zalman's face went blank. "To study with the rabbi," Hanley elaborated.

Zalman's confusion deepened. He swallowed and moistened his lips.

Hanley kept silent, watching him. Had he run into the limits of Zalman's English, or was the young man playing dumb? "Mr. Nathan left work in the afternoon," he said. "What time?"

Understanding crossed Zalman's face. "One o'clock."

Considerably earlier than Nathan had implied. The tailor shop was mere minutes from Kelmansky's front door. What had Nathan been doing during that extra time? "Did he come back?"

Zalman nodded. "Before we close up. I think...four o'clock?" He shrugged. "Not five yet."

Could Nathan have gone somewhere other than the rabbi's house? Had he been to Kelmansky's at all? Hanley wondered how much Zalman might have seen from the tailor shop window. "Did you see Mr. Nathan before then? After he left, I mean. Did you see him or Rabbi Kelmansky?"

Zalman was looking confused again. Hanley paused to think through the language problem.

"One o'clock," he said. "Mr. Nathan leaves your shop." He continued when Zalman nodded. "He comes back around four." Another nod from Zalman. "Did you see him, or your rabbi, in between?"

Zalman frowned in concentration. Then his expression cleared. "Reb Nathan, no. Rav Kelmansky, yes."

"You saw the rabbi? Alone?"

"Yes." Zalman gestured up Market Street. "There. Walking."

"What time?"

"Four o'clock. Soon before Reb Nathan came."

He wanted to ask how precise Zalman's memory of the time was and why, but the question seemed beyond their halting level of conversation. Trying again with Ida along made better sense. For now, Hanley chose something simpler. In any case, he couldn't keep Zalman out here much longer. His absence would be noticed. "Which way did the rabbi go?"

Zalman walked halfway down the porch steps. As Hanley drew level with him, he pointed northward, toward Randolph Street.

"Did you see him turn off or…" Hanley fell silent at the bewilderment on Zalman's face. He dug out his sketchbook and pencil, flipped to a blank page, and drew a long vertical line. "Market Street," he said. Then he made three horizontal lines across it at different spots. "Madison, Washington, Randolph. Can you show me your shop?"

Hesitantly, Zalman took the pencil. He drew an "X" at the intersection of Market and Madison.

Good, Hanley thought. A corner lot meant a reasonable chance Zalman might have seen whether Kelmansky turned off Market Street. He pointed at the three cross-streets, one after the other. "Did the rabbi walk here? Or here? Or here?" He swept his finger down the length of Market Street. "Or keep walking here, down to the river?"

Zalman tapped the pencil against his lower lip, then used it to scratch beneath his scraggly reddish beard. Then he tapped the line for Randolph at a spot slightly to the right of the one for Market Street. "Here. That way."

East. Away from the river and the bridge, toward the lakefront.

Harden Guthrie's office was down that way. Maybe the rabbi had gone there. Maybe he'd used his acquaintance with Guthrie to acquire things to distribute to people in his neighborhood, people like the Pavlic family, who'd been cut off by the Relief and Aid.

A gust of wind made Zalman wrap his arms around his chest, with a questioning look at Hanley. Hanley reached for the pencil. "Thank you," he said as the young man dropped it into his outstretched hand. "I would like to talk more with you soon. It will be a great help."

Zalman blew on his fingers, then nodded. "We work tomorrow. You come then." He hurried up the steps and back inside.

Hanley tucked his sketchbook and pencil away. He'd learned a good deal today, but none of it fit anywhere. Not yet.

FIFTEEN

When Onkl Jacob came back to the parlor, Rivka tried to catch his eye, but he wouldn't look at her. He wouldn't look at anyone. He edged through the throng, murmuring apologies, until he reached the dining table with its single candle burning amid the plates of boiled eggs and stewed beans and roasted vegetables. She saw him stare at the candle as if he had never seen one before, as if its strangeness frightened him. He gazed at it for some time, hands in his pockets, shoulders slumped as if in utter exhaustion.

The sound of the back door closing, followed by footsteps, made him look up. Rivka followed his gaze toward the kitchen and saw Moishe Zalman returning to the parlor. Alone. Detective Hanley must have gone. He had looked so worried when he saw her. She wished she could have told him she was glad he came.

At the sight of Moishe, Jacob's fearful look eased a bit. Moishe joined a few other men from the burial society who were talking quietly near the bookshelves. Jacob started working his way toward them, or so Rivka thought. To her surprise, he passed them and continued into the kitchen.

Here was her chance to talk to him alone. But how? Hannah and the other women still crowded around her, chattering about Papa—what a wonderful rabbi he had been, how she must miss him. Then someone spoke of Aaron, how glad Rivka would surely be when her brother came home to take care of her. *If he comes home,* she wanted to snap. *If we can even find him.* They had tried after the end of the war. Letters went unanswered and no one they'd found from his regiment knew what had become of him. *If he still lives, I have no way to tell him Papa is dead.*

New grief hit her like a hammer blow. She clenched her fists until her nails bit skin and sought desperately for some distraction. Onkl Jacob was still in the kitchen. She wanted badly to find out what Hanley had said to him. Did Hanley know about the stolen food? Was that why he'd come here, and not to find out why she'd missed their appointment? Maybe he did know and Hashem had answered her prayers for guidance by taking the decision out of her hands. But how could he have found out in hardly more than a day? He had come for something, though, something more than to see her. He had spent too much time with Onkl Jacob for anything else to be true.

The women were still talking about Aaron. Lucky brother, able to leave this stifling place behind. He'd followed his conscience off to war to help end slavery, while she couldn't even get up off her cushion and leave this room. She had to stay here, seated on the floor to show herself struck down by her loss. Such was the custom at shiva. If she got up and left to talk to Jacob, people would be shocked. They would blame her, and Tanta Hannah and Onkl Jacob also, because their closeness to Papa made them nearest to family. Worst of all, they would blame Papa for not raising her properly after Mameh died. They wouldn't say it, but they would believe it in their hearts.

What would Hanley think? That she was brave, risking censure to find the truth? Or selfish, doing what she wanted without caring whom she hurt?

She rubbed a hand across her eyes. She was a bad daughter. Hashem had punished her by taking her father away. Or He had punished Papa— for teaching her Hebrew, for the afternoons they had spent sharing what they thought about the world.

For thieving, even with the best of reasons?

She shook her head, scarcely aware of the conversations that briefly halted around her. Hashem knew her father's heart. Jacob's as well. The One who loved them all would surely forgive anything that saved a life.

Hannah patted her hand and turned to the butcher's wife. "So, Sisel? How is the little one? It will be soon now, yes?"

Rivka scarcely heard her friend's soft reply. No one's presence was the comfort it should have been—not Sisel's, not Tanta Hannah's or Onkl

Jacob's, not even the girls she taught English to, whose open affection usually warmed her heart. She was so tired of sitting here, not allowed to do anything except wallow in her grief. Nothing to distract her from her memories and her pain, made fresh like bread with every story they told about Papa—how wise he had been, how good, how generous.

Nothing to distract her from what she'd seen Jacob do at the warehouse the night before.

Rivka hated it. She wanted to mourn in quiet by herself. And she wanted to find the truth, because there was no other way to get on with living. For no good reason, she thought of Hanley again. She'd seen in his face the concern he felt for her. She wished he were here to talk to. He had welcomed her help on Friday, listened to her as if her words mattered. As if she had a right to be a part of things. She would know what to tell him now if she could look into his eyes...

"Poor Rivkaleh." Tanta Hannah stroked her hair. "It will get better in time."

"Better." A bitter laugh escaped her. "Better than what?"

Tanta Hannah flinched and Rivka felt contrite. Hannah meant well. They all did. She pressed Hannah's fingers in mute apology.

The older woman's face cleared and she said, "Let me get you some challah. Your father would not want you to starve in his memory."

Rivka's throat closed. She couldn't stay here among these women, clucking and nattering about who had a new baby, whose husband had found work, whose daughter was giving her parents a terrible time. Onkl Jacob would come back to the parlor any moment and she would lose all hope of speaking with him. She swept her skirts out of the way and pushed herself upright against the sofa seat. Ignoring the shocked looks, she stepped past Hannah and headed toward the kitchen.

Onkl Jacob was dipping water from the bucket just inside the back door. His face wore the frozen look of someone trying not to think or feel. She watched his throat working as he swallowed. Then he dropped the dipper back in the bucket, turned and saw her.

Fear flashed in his eyes, swiftly replaced by anger. "What are you doing in here? Is this how you honor your father?"

His fierceness shocked her. She gripped her skirt to keep her hands from shaking. "What did Detective Hanley say? Why did he come here?"

"On this day you ask such a question?" He kept his voice low, but his words held the force of a shout.

Suddenly she was furious. "I am not a child! I have a right to know!"

"You *are* a child. A child who wants to grab what she should not have. You think you know better than anyone, even your poor father. What will you do now that you are free, Rivka? No father, no mother, no brother to command you. What will you do with your freedom?"

She gestured wildly around her, encompassing the kitchen, archway, and parlor full of mourners beyond. "You call this *free*?"

She held his gaze until he looked away. With his eyes no longer on her, the flash of anger evaporated, leaving behind a choking mass of hurt. Onkl Jacob had never spoken to her like that before. Always he had been gentle with her, even when scolding. She closed her eyes to keep back sudden tears.

A hesitant touch on her shoulder roused her. Onkl Jacob was looking down at her, his eyes wet. "Your father was a good man. Better than you know." His hand dropped and he moved away, walking like the old man he was for the first time she could remember.

She stayed in the kitchen. The only movement she could muster was to brace one hand against the table where she and Papa had shared breakfast and conversation for the past nine years. Whatever Jacob had talked about with Hanley, it frightened him. She'd seen it in his face just now, heard it while he spoke with Hanley, even though they were too far away to make out any words. She gripped the table with both hands. Maybe Hanley *did* know about the stolen items, though she couldn't imagine how.

She felt too spent to confront Onkl Jacob again today. Sooner or later, though, she would have to. He knew something about Papa's death. To do with the stealing, or where Papa had gone on the last day of his life. Whatever it was, she would find a way to make him tell.

SIXTEEN

That was some fine roast chicken, Mrs. Kirschner," Moore said. He looked over at Mam with a smile. "And the best boxty I've ever tasted. As usual."

Hanley, wiping his mouth with his napkin, had to agree. Ida, Mam, and Kate between them could lay out a Sunday dinner that would put Chicago's best hotels to shame. Not that boxty—a fried mashed-potato cake dotted with onions—would ever be on such a fashionable menu.

Mam returned Moore's warm look. "I'm glad you could share it with us, Tom." She and Kate rose to clear the plates, Mam waving at Ida to sit back down. "There's ginger cake for dessert. Then I'm sure you and Frank will want to talk shop." She gave Hanley a hopeful look. "You'll join us for a little music after? Perhaps Frank will play for us this time."

Cake eaten and tea drunk, the women cleared off to the parlor. Hanley caught Moore's eye and nodded toward the kitchen. "We can talk while we wash up."

Moore grinned. "While you wash up."

"You always say that." Hanley headed to the kitchen, knowing Moore would follow. Most men would find it odd that he still did the dishes, but he knew Moore was used to his quirks. Ever since boyhood, when Kate was so little and Mam needed his help, he'd found comfort in the feel of the water, the sense of accomplishment as each dish was rinsed and dried. When everything else lay beyond his control, at least he could manage clean plates.

He filled the dishpan with water from the rain barrel and placed it on the counter. As he worked, he brought his boss up to date. "Jamie Murphy's the one who left those bloody marks on the synagogue floor," he said, setting down a dripping plate. "He definitely robbed the synagogue. But I don't think he killed Kelmansky."

"Why not?"

"Position of the body's wrong." Hanley began scrubbing the next plate. "Something about the crime scene was bothering me, and I finally figured out what. Kelmansky's corpse was by that platform in the middle of the synagogue and it hadn't been moved. He got clubbed right there. But the spot where he fell is a good five feet further inside from the table where the stolen spice box and menorah were."

He rinsed the plate and stacked it, then grabbed some silverware and laid it out next to the dishpan. "Say this spoon is where the body was, and this knife over here is the door." Then he set a fork down between the other pieces of silverware, closer to the spoon. "And this is the table. Now, say Murphy's there stealing and Kelmansky walks in on him. If Murphy panicked and swung the menorah at him, Kelmansky would've fallen on the side of the table nearer the door." He snagged a chicken bone and set it between the fork and spoon. "Instead, he fell here, on the opposite side. So Kelmansky must have been there already, praying, when whoever killed him came in. I can't see Murphy looting the place if someone was already there. I remember him as an opportunist, not a brute killer. Unless you know something I don't?"

Moore leaned against the counter's edge. "Murphy's kept himself pretty clear of trouble over the past few years. Survives on odd jobs, mostly. I'm told he spends a lot of time around the rail depots and the downtown hotels…or he did until the Fire. All tricked out in fancy duds. He used to pick pockets, but he hasn't been arrested for that in months. I'd guess he's found a new line of work."

"Bunco-steerer?"

"Most like."

"Do you know who he works for?" He thought of Sean Doyle, but didn't say the name.

"Not yet. I've been more concerned with keeping track of the bully boys and panderers and thieves who like to rough up their victims. The gamblers and bunco men can wait."

Hanley picked up a glass, dunked, and scrubbed it. "There's also Tommy Callaghan. Saloon owner near Washington and Franklin. He lied to me about Murphy's fancy shoes—a lie he'd no reason to tell, unless there's something between them besides a seller of drink and his customer." He rinsed the glass and set it down. "Back when I walked that beat, I kept an eye on Callaghan's place as best I could. I never saw anything going on except the selling of drink, but I hoped you might know more. Is Callaghan a fence?"

"If he is, he's careful. No one's gotten him for it yet." To Hanley's surprise, Moore snagged a nearby dishtowel and began drying the glass with meticulous attention. "Though I'm told Charming Billy's been tipping back a few at Callaghan's in the past couple of weeks."

Hanley's gut clenched. "I saw Billy today. At Saint Pat's. Last I knew, he was in the old Armory jail. Someone must've let him out the night it burned down." A brief, harsh laugh escaped him. "Me, I'd have left him there."

"No, you wouldn't." The look Moore gave him held too much knowledge, sympathetic though it was. Hanley turned away from it. He grabbed a handful of forks and plunged them into the soapy dishwater, but even scrubbing fork tines couldn't keep the memory of Pegeen's dead body at bay. Dead because of Billy, on Doyle's word, and Hanley helpless to do a thing about it. Back then and now.

He gripped the clean forks hard enough to leave marks. "So is Callaghan Doyle's man? Or does he just serve them liquor?"

Moore eased the silverware out of Hanley's grasp. "I don't know. All I'm sure of is that Billy and a few others of Doyle's people go there. Some of them live in the neighborhood. I think Billy does. At best, Callaghan bears watching. But don't jump to conclusions."

Hanley scrubbed and rinsed the last fork. Water beads sparkled on the tines. "I used to know damned near everyone on Doyle's payroll. I even hired some of them. Now…"

"I told you then I could get you into the police department. Past associations be damned."

"I wasn't ready yet." Hanley washed a serving spoon. "And while I was off fighting Confederates, a lot of faces in Doyle's empire changed. Some I'd still recognize, but..."

"As I said, I'd not jump to conclusions."

"You know, he warned me?" Hanley dunked the carving knife into the water. "Billy. He talked about Kelmansky. Said he'd been killed for the silver in the synagogue and strongly hinted I should reach that conclusion."

Moore's eyes widened. "That's an interesting development."

"Isn't it?" Hanley worked on the knife blade. "And there's another one. Doyle turned up at Lake Street today. I saw him talking with Officer Reinhardt."

Moore looked concerned. "Do you know what about?"

Hanley shook his head. "Couldn't get close enough. Though I can't figure what it might have to do with my case. It's not as if Billy killed the rabbi. He's too tall, for one thing. And aside from that, I don't see Doyle's interest."

Moore picked up another wet glass and dried it. His face had the sober intensity of a man working out a puzzle. Hanley had the feeling he didn't much like the answer.

"Something I should know?" he asked.

Moore set the glass down. "Not yet. I'll tell you when I'm sure."

The knife was clean now and Hanley felt able to think more clearly. If Murphy stole things often, Callaghan could have lied for him to protect an income source. As for Billy and Doyle, they might have had their own reasons for turning up today. Billy might have meant exactly what he'd said and Doyle might have wanted to know about planned raids on his gaming hells. Plenty of crooked cops passed on such tips, for which they got money or a guarantee of free drink and a good night at the gaming tables.

His thoughts went back to Murphy. "I'm still not sure Murphy killed the rabbi," he said as he dried the knife blade. "But I am sure he saw something that night. Whatever happened, he doesn't want to talk about it. Or about anything to do with Kelmansky. He even tried to lie about Kelmansky giving him that coat." He frowned. "Which was spotless. If Murphy clubbed Kelmansky down, there should've been blood all over it. Spatter on his boots, too. But all I found was that thin stain around the edge of one sole. And the coat didn't look like it'd been washed recently."

"Any of the neighbors see or hear anything?"

"I haven't had much luck with that so far. Though I did learn something interesting—maybe to do with the relief supplies Kelmansky gave away." As he finished off the dishes, he told Moore about his visit to the Kelmansky house. "I bet Nathan knows who the rabbi went to see. And he doesn't feel like telling."

"You think they're connected—the relief supplies, that trip, and the murder?"

Hanley dried his hands. "I don't see how yet. But it's worth checking out."

They followed the sound of the piano to the front parlor. Ida was playing something classical Hanley couldn't place. Mam and Kate sat next to each other on the striped sofa, contentment on their faces. Hanley saw his fiddle case by Mam's feet and tensed. He still didn't feel like playing. Hadn't since the Fire. *Mam running back into their burning house, dragging the damned fiddle from under the bed, the wall going up in a curtain of flame behind her. Himself grabbing her and throwing them both to the floor as the window exploded, loud as an artillery shell, in a shower of hot glass...*

He shook off the memory with an effort. Ida finished her piece and looked up. "Ah, good. A full audience. What shall we have now?"

He saw Mam reach for the fiddle case and said the first thing that came to mind. "How about a song? Something we all know...'Buffalo Gals'?"

She smiled, nodded, and played the opening bars. Hanley made himself sing the first line, knowing it would help calm him down. The others joined in, Moore's airy tenor blending well with Hanley's dark baritone and the lighter voices of the women. As Mam took over Ida's place and they sang "Kathleen Mavourneen" and "Rocky Road to Dublin," he felt his tensions easing. Talk of Doyle and memories of the Fire had darkened his mood, but they were no match for the music.

The song ended and Mam glanced again toward the fiddle case. Before Hanley could respond, the parlor window exploded inward. He ducked flying glass, saw bright orange, smelled kerosene. Heard a rush of air as fire surged up the thin muslin curtains. The women screamed. Footsteps pounded out of the room.

Hanley threw himself at the window, grabbed the cloth just above the greedy flames, and yanked. The fabric tore away from the curtain rod. Fire licked his hands. He ignored the searing pain, hurled the burning cloth to the floor, and stomped on it. Moore rushed in then with the dishpan full of water and tossed it on the flames. Kate followed with the bucket they used to fill the bathtub. She emptied it on the smoldering heap of muslin. The smell of scorched, wet fabric filled the parlor.

"Your hands, Frankie!" Mam was suddenly next to him, her fingers gentle on his wrists as she turned his hands up to look at them. The skin on one palm was an angry red and fresh pain stabbed through it with every heartbeat. "Bacon grease," Mam muttered and hurried out.

A freezing gust blew through the shattered window. Hanley shivered, only partly from the cold. He looked around the parlor as his racing heart slowed. Broken glass covered the floor and the top of the piano. Ida had a cut on her forehead high up near the hairline. Kate was bleeding from a small gash on her cheek. "It's nothing much," she said as she met his gaze. "Barely even hurts."

Moore knelt to examine something a few feet from the window. He looked up, his face grim. "Rags around a brick," he said as he poked at a scrap of crisped fabric that clung to the blackened stone. "Soaked with kerosene. They must've been tied on."

"Not much chance of finding whoever threw it," Hanley said through teeth clenched against the pain.

"No." Moore stood. "But we'll see what we can find out." He turned to Ida. "Where do you keep a lantern?"

❧

Twenty minutes' search of the small front yard yielded no clues, not even footprints in the snow. Hanley stood on the walk he'd cleared that morning and eyed the distance to the parlor window. "He must've stood right here. Careful son of a bitch." His burned hand, smothered in grease and wrapped in old, soft sheet scraps, stung as if he held a handful of bees. "God damn Sean Doyle. And Billy, or whoever was sent to do this."

Rapidly approaching footsteps cut off Moore's reply. Hanley spun toward the sound, ready for a fight. Then he saw the approaching figure was a patrolman. "Detective Hanley," the man said. He paused, eyes widening as he took in Hanley's bandaged hand, the broken window, the lingering charred smell. "Officer Schmidt sent me for you."

"Officer Schmidt?" Rolf Schmidt's beat covered Market Street and the docks. Hanley's tension shot higher. "Why?"

"There's been trouble with your Market Street Jews. Someone tried to set fire to their temple."

SEVENTEEN

Hanley found Schmidt at the synagogue, along with Jacob Nathan. The odors of charred wood and kerosene hung in the air. Two men Hanley remembered from Friday morning were talking with Nathan in low voices, presumably about the broken window and the scorched section of wall they were examining.

"Incendiary device," Schmidt said as Hanley reached him. "Soaked rags around a brick. Lucky the son of a bitch don't know how to make it good. Last thing we need is another fire, *jah?*"

The idea made Hanley's skin crawl. "We got one like it through the front window where I live, about an hour ago. Any idea who threw this one?"

Schmidt looked shocked, then scowled and shook his head. "No. Ten people all in here to pray when that thing come in and no one saw nothing." He nodded toward Nathan. "I think that one knows something, but he won't tell me. Too scared. Don't know what of. Maybe you have better luck?"

Hanley hoped so. "Cross your fingers." He walked over to Nathan and his companions. They looked up at his approach. Then Nathan said something to his friends in what Hanley presumed was Yiddish and they walked off.

Nathan kept his eyes on the broken window. "I have told the officer all we know. I did not see who threw the bomb. You have wasted your time coming here."

"My time to waste." Hanley studied the charred boards. Two incendiaries on the same night, one at his home, the other against potential witnesses in his murder case. Whether there'd been time for the same

126

man—or men—to commit both acts, he wasn't yet sure, but it had to be more than random violence by street thugs. "Lucky you were here. Ten of you, Schmidt said. Do they all know as little as you?"

Nathan folded his arms. He was trying for defiance, but fear rolled off him like a wave. "Many have not the English to speak with you."

"I know someone who'll translate for me. I can come back tomorrow." He stepped forward to examine the window and waited.

"We put the fire out first." Nathan sounded weary. "By the time that was done, whoever did this had gone."

"Doesn't take ten men to put out a small fire. Somebody must have chased the scoundrel down, or tried to. Did they catch him?"

Nathan looked at the scorch marks. "No."

"Who chased him?"

Nathan shook his head. "Please understand. There have been...threats. Young men throwing stones as we carried our rabbi's body home. Muck from the privy on the door of our butcher's shop. It is safest if we keep to ourselves."

"If we know what he looks like, we can find him and jail him. End of threat."

"Until his friends throw another bomb. Or worse."

The man was immovable. Hanley squelched his frustration, knowing it would do no good to show it. Not that he could blame Nathan, considering his own terror when the incendiary device had hurtled through Ida's window. Maybe someone else would come forward...or maybe it was worth sending Schmidt to the butcher's about the muck-throwing incident. Schmidt could show sketches of known neighborhood toughs, see if the butcher recognized any. Maybe one of them threw this bomb, or both bombs. He thought of Billy, and Doyle, and made himself stop.

He beckoned Schmidt over and told him about the butcher. "Ask if he chased the bomb-thrower, too." Schmidt nodded and resumed his seat on a nearby bench. Hanley went back to Nathan. "So where was your rabbi going on the day he died? He went somewhere late in the afternoon. Heading east down Randolph Street. Right before you got back to work."

Nathan looked ill. He turned away from Hanley. "Rav Kelmansky did not tell me all his business."

"You said he had something to attend to that day. That's why he wasn't at your evening minyan." Hanley moved around so he could see Nathan's face. "Was that where he was going? To attend to something with the friend he went to see?"

Several seconds passed. Nathan's breathing sounded harsh in the silence.

"All right," Hanley said. "Tell me where *you* were."

"I was at the minyan."

"The others will confirm that?"

"Yes."

"What about earlier? Say, around one in the afternoon. After you left your shop."

Nathan opened his mouth, then closed it again. The look on his face reminded Hanley of a trapped dog.

He felt a twinge of pity that was swiftly overwhelmed by the thrill of the hunt. "You didn't go to Kelmansky's house to study. Not then, anyway. You weren't there until sometime after two or maybe three o'clock. So where were you?"

Nathan closed his eyes. When he opened them, his expression was carefully blank. "I went to the river. To a warehouse there."

"Which one? What for?"

"For relief supplies. Flour, cornmeal, coal, kerosene. Things people need."

The relief supplies again. Hanley was fairly certain none of the Market Street Jews owned riverfront warehouses full of food and other necessaries. He wondered who else might, and whether Nathan had a right to help himself from them. "Which warehouse?"

"I prefer not to say."

"You don't have that choice."

Nathan moistened his lips. "The man who owns it would not wish to be named. Mitzvot—good works—are best left anonymous. Does not your own scripture teach this?"

"Show me the place, then."

"It is late. I might get it wrong in the dark."

That was true enough. "Tomorrow, then. You'll be working?"

Reluctantly, Nathan nodded.

"Good." Hanley thought a moment. "Where did you bring the things after you got them?"

"To a storage room at my shop. I keep cloth there."

"So what did you bring back?"

Nathan looked away, then knelt and picked up a large shard of window glass. "I bring what people need."

"How do you know what people need? Did your rabbi find that out for you?"

Nathan set the shard down, then carefully moved another on top of it. He kept it up as he talked until he had a small pile. "It was our mitzvah. Rav Kelmansky went around the neighborhood talking to people. Finding out what they needed and if they were getting it. He wrote down what they told him. Then he made a list and I fetched what I could to give away later."

"Were the Pavlics on the list? Or Jamie Murphy?"

"We gave them things, yes. Someone had to."

"What about the Relief and Aid?"

A mirthless smile tugged at Nathan's mouth and he shook his head. Then he gasped and dropped the piece of glass he was holding. Hanley saw a bright line of blood on his finger.

He pulled out a crumpled handkerchief, checked to be sure it was clean, and laid it across his own bandaged hand as he grabbed Nathan's injured one. "Let me." Relying mostly on his good hand, he bound up the cut. "You'd best go wash that out. It doesn't look deep."

"Thank you." Nathan eyed Hanley's bandage and the reddened fingers poking out of it, but said nothing. He looked exhausted as Hanley helped him up.

Schmidt preceded them out the door and they walked together to the street. As they reached it, Nathan searched Hanley's face. He drew breath as if to speak, but then glanced toward Schmidt and looked down. "Good night," he murmured and walked away.

Hanley watched him go. "You'll talk to the butcher in the morning?" he asked Schmidt.

"*Ja*. If I don't see you, I leave a note." Schmidt nodded goodnight and walked off.

Hanley turned the opposite way toward the Madison Street Bridge. He hadn't gone more than a few steps when he stopped and headed back to the synagogue.

The yard was full of shadows. Spill from the streetlights scarcely reached it and thick clouds blocked the moon. Along with the ever-present hint of smoke, Hanley smelled the cold, wet tang of approaching snow. He picked his way over to the shattered window. Faint gaslight from Market Street glinted off the broken glass. The odor of kerosene reached him, stronger than it had been inside. As if someone had stood here just outside the building, spilling fuel while they soaked the rags.

The hair on his arms prickled and he had a sudden sense of someone near him in the darkness. "Who's there?"

No one answered. He turned toward the nearest patch of shadow. Too dark to see if anyone was in it. He stepped forward, bandaged hand in his pocket as if gripping a weapon. "I'm armed," he said. "You don't want to tangle with me."

His only warning was a rustle of cloth. Before he could move or put up a guard, a punch to the gut doubled him over. A second blow, this one to the jaw, sent him sprawling in the cold mud. He got only partway up before a booted foot to the ribs knocked him back down. He felt snow-crust cut his lip, tasted blood and grit. Another kick caught him behind the ear and made his head ring. He struggled to his hands and knees on the slick ground, fighting off the pain as he strained to see and hear in the darkness.

There. A movement in the shadows, the faint squelch of mud. Footsteps, moving fast. Away from him. Hanley dragged himself upright and stared after the fading sounds, but saw nothing. His assailant was gone into the night.

EIGHTEEN

Dawn light glimmered beneath low-hanging clouds as Rivka hurried, shivering, into her clothes. She fumbled with the buttons on her black wool dress, grateful for its warmth in the cold bedroom. She would have to hurry if she hoped to catch Onkl Jacob before he left for the tailor shop.

She halted briefly outside her room, listening for Tanta Hannah, who was staying over every night until shiva ended. She heard only silence from down the hall. She crept downstairs, snatched her coat from its hook, shrugged into it, and slipped outside.

Fresh snow lay on the ground, scarcely deep enough to cover the toes of her boots. She watched it scatter ahead of her as she walked next door to the Nathans'. She felt guilty wearing leather during shiva, but saw no alternative. Cloth shoes would leave her with frozen feet while she waited for Onkl Jacob. She'd decided against going inside and catching him at breakfast. Tamar or another of his daughters would surely prepare it for him, and she needed to speak with him alone.

He would come out soon. She stood near the front door to wait.

Her toes still had warmth in them when the door opened. She waited for him to latch it behind him before she spoke. "Onkl Jacob."

He turned, looking startled. "Rivka? What are you doing here?"

Now that the moment had come, her mouth felt dry. "What did you talk about with Detective Hanley yesterday?"

His face went blank. "That is not your concern."

"My father is dead. I have a right—"

"Go home, Rivka. Mourn your father as you should. Stop asking questions."

131

He started walking away. She strode after him and caught his sleeve. He turned, looking shocked. She forged on in spite of it. "You came to see Papa that day. You were upset. Not long after, Papa left. The next time I saw him, he was dead by the bimah in the dark and cold." She heard the quaver in her voice and did her best to control it. "Who did he go to see? Does Detective Hanley know? Is that why—"

"Enough!" His hand barely missed her as it slashed through the air, as if he meant to strike down the sound of her voice. The fear beneath his anger chilled her more than the cold. "Go home." He strode past her, half-running down the street.

She followed, calling out as he widened the gap between them. "What did you mean yesterday, Papa was a better man than I know?" Her voice sounded thin and shrill, a desperate child's cry. Not commanding enough to make him turn. Her steps slowed as she watched him shrink into the distance. There was no point following him to his shop. He had a hundred ways to evade her there. Besides, Tanta Hannah would soon be awake. Rivka could imagine her response to this morning's escapade...and in leather boots, too.

Brittle with frustration, she turned homeward and went in to build up the fire.

⁂

Head aching and bruises tender from last night's assault, Hanley started his Monday morning with a quick and angry search for Charming Billy. The man wasn't at any of his usual haunts and, after a while, Hanley gave up. He couldn't even be sure it was Billy who'd attacked him by the synagogue, let alone thrown the incendiaries. That Doyle was somehow behind it was the only thing he felt sure of. Exactly why, and who'd done the dirty work, he didn't yet know.

He took a horsecar into the South Division and got off on Clark Street by the United Hebrew Relief depot. Father Cavanaugh had suggested it when Hanley asked him after Mass about other sources of aid on which Kelmansky might have drawn. From the genial woman who oversaw the place, he learned that Kelmansky went there for help on November second, but hadn't received any of the items Hanley sought—the twenty-pound sack of flour, the overcoat given to Jamie Murphy, or the child's red shoes received by Mrs. Pavlic's daughter.

The November date—just three weeks after the Fire—stuck in Hanley's mind. In late October, Chicago's mayor had cut the City Council out of disbursing donations to the stricken city. The privately run Relief and Aid Society, composed of Chicago's leading businessmen, had gotten control over hundreds of thousands of dollars' worth of donated cash and goods from around the world. Had the change made relief harder to get for those deemed undeserving? If so, what exactly had Kelmansky done about it?

Another trip to Harden Guthrie's office was in order, as was a second try at the Relief and Aid headquarters on West Washington. The riverside warehouses probably belonged to people connected with the Relief and Aid. Guthrie or someone higher up should be able to tell him. Once he knew the location of the warehouse Nathan had mentioned, he could check what remained of Chicago's property deeds at the temporary city hall—though there was no guarantee any particular deed had survived the Fire.

First, though, Hanley had business closer by. A brief walk east and south brought him to the rough streets known as Hell's Half Acre, an ugly jumble of dingy groggeries, fleapit gambling dens, and low-rent whorehouses, of which several were panel shops—cheap bordellos where the walls slid back to let pickpockets rob occupied customers of whatever they'd unwisely left in their clothing. He passed by Peck Court without so much as a glance toward what used to be Doyle's saloon near the lakefront, where Hanley had run faro games and swigged whiskey and dreamt of a future as a rich man. Ten years on from what happened there and he still couldn't stand the sight, or even the thought, of the place.

The eastern edge of the neighborhood sported a slightly higher class of criminal establishments, among them the State Street pawnshop run by Original Andrews. Together with a couple of partners, Andrews did a thriving business in small valuables. After Hanley joined the police force, Andrews had acted as an informer when it suited his interest. Dealing with him always gave Hanley an odd turn—Andrews knew him from the old days and still saw him as the green kid bringing in his weekly take off the docks—but he was sharp-eyed with a mind to match, and mostly honest, so long as Hanley's questions didn't threaten his business.

"Can't say as I've seen 'em," Andrews said around the toothpick that stuck out from one side of his thin-lipped mouth. Scrawny and tough, he looked like an underfed rooster, despite the fact that he earned enough from pawned and stolen wares to dine on steak more often than not. He leaned his bony elbows on the short front counter which ran between the wood-and-glass display cases that filled his shop. "I'd remember stuff like that little silver box and that big candlestick. What'd you call it again? Never mind." He waved a skinny hand. "Whatever its name is, I ain't got it here. Ain't seen your man Murphy, neither."

"What about your place on Clark? Are they there?"

"Don't think so." He spat the toothpick into his hand, held it up, and inspected it. Hanley wondered what he could be looking for. "But I'll ask the fellas." He grinned. "For the usual consideration."

Hanley knew what he meant and had come prepared. "I'd appreciate it," he said as he placed a coin on the counter. "That oughta buy you a few drinks." Paying for information wasn't strictly legal, but the detective squad had wide latitude in how it did its job. "Tell your partners the department will be grateful for the items, if they have them, and their full cooperation."

While Andrews tucked the money away in his cash box, Hanley glanced around the shop. Andrews's place was well south of the burned district. From the look of it, he hadn't lost anything in the looting after the Fire, either. The Spencer rifle he kept propped near the back door that led to his storeroom had a lot to do with that, of course. The glass cases were full of jewelry, cigar boxes, silverware, whiskey flasks, and the like, though nothing Hanley could immediately identify as stolen. "Business ever slow down for you?"

Andrews laughed, a high-pitched bark like a small dog's. "Nope."

He nodded toward a whiskey flask etched with wheat stalks. "That there'd suit you fine if you're still a drinking man."

"Not so much these days." Not since the night he'd been three sheets and then some when he should have been looking out for Pegeen. He hadn't been able to stand hard liquor for a year after and he'd been sparing with all kinds of drink ever since. Even during the war he rarely got drunk. The smell of the whiskey rations doled out to the troops carried shame with it like an airborne disease.

"One more thing," he said, eager to turn his thoughts in another direction. "Ever hear of Tommy Callaghan, runs a saloon up by Washington and Franklin? I wondered if he's in your line of work."

Andrews fumbled in his trouser pocket and came up with a fresh toothpick. He eyeballed it as he spoke. "Haven't heard his name come up." He stuck the toothpick in his mouth and shrugged. "That's the best I can tell you."

His gaze had the rock-like steadiness of someone trying hard to be believed. "You're sure about that?" Hanley asked. "Think a minute. Maybe it'll come to you."

"Don't need to. I don't know the man. And I doubt you'll find anyone around here who does."

❧

Andrews was right, Hanley discovered, as he went to one dive after another looking for the stolen silver. He met flat denial everywhere—no silver, no Murphy, and no knowledge of Tommy Callaghan. The first two denials rang true. Callaghan's name drew an honest blank in some quarters, averted gazes and urgent distractions in others. Hanley strongly suspected why, with growing excitement and unease. *Doyle. It has to be.*

How to confirm a tie between them was the first question. The second was whether it meant anything with regard to the rabbi's murder. The more Hanley ran over it in his head, the more discouraged he felt. So what if he found proof Callaghan was a fence and moved a lot of merchandise for Doyle or was outright in his pay? What would that mean, except that Doyle protected his investments? It didn't make Doyle the killer or even tie him to the theft of the silver. Jamie Murphy might have done that on his own.

The aid supplies? Hanley felt renewed hope, but only for a moment. He was fairly sure now the supplies were stolen, but how on earth would Sean Doyle or any of his gang have gotten involved in a scheme apparently intended to help the poor? And what interest could Doyle have in a tiny sect of observant Jews with no money or clout?

Yet someone had bombed Ida's house and the synagogue, and assaulted him in the synagogue yard. Someone who'd waited there, and not for a potential robbery victim. For one of the Jews, to drive the warning home with a broken bone or two? For Officer Schmidt? For him?

He turned toward the Biler Avenue district, another tough neighborhood full of cheap saloons and groggeries, where tainted dealing got done in beer-reeking back rooms. He knew one place to go where someone could give him answers. There was no guarantee he'd find Paddy, of course, or that Paddy would talk to him. But they'd grown up next door to each other in Conley's Patch, dipped the same girls' braids into inkwells in grammar school, before Paddy dropped out to work. Gotten into, and out of, more boyhood scrapes together than Hanley could count. Paddy had been his friend before either of them knew Doyle. Maybe that would net him something.

He found Paddy in a back corner of the Skibbereen Club, named for a village in Ireland that lost nearly all its residents to the Famine in the 1840s. Paddy was playing cards with a scruffy pair of fellows Hanley didn't know. The place stank of beer and mildew, likely from several weeks' worth of spills into the moldy sawdust. The front window was thick with grime. Most of what light there was came from a kerosene lamp on each of the half dozen tables crammed into the room. It didn't help that the lamps were lit only at the three tables where people sat. A waste of money to light the others until more customers showed up.

Hanley grabbed a chair from an empty table, pulled it over next to Paddy, and sat down. "Deal me in?"

"Who the devil're you?" snarled the man to Hanley's left. His hair looked as if it hadn't seen soap in a month, and bits of soda cracker dotted his mustache. His brogue marked him as a son of County Galway. The other stranger, bulky and dough-faced, put down his cards and scratched under his arm. He paid no attention to Hanley or to his belligerent friend.

"I know him," Paddy said. Hanley nodded to him, then had to work at concealing his shock. Paddy's face was gaunt, his blue eyes too bright even in the dim groggery. He looked half the man he'd been the last time Hanley saw him, drinking beer and telling stories at the Irish Brigade reunion. What had happened to him?

Paddy was still eying him as if weighing what to say next. "Thought I'd come by to see you," Hanley said. "It's been a time. You keeping well, Paddy?"

"Tolerably." Paddy sipped the whiskey at his elbow. His face was relaxed, almost smiling. "How's your mam, then? And your sister?"

"Same as ever. Kate still asks after you." She'd always liked Paddy. He made her paper dolls and brought her peppermints she never knew were pilfered. Mam had banned him from the house once she found out he'd turned thief, but Hanley knew she'd regretted the need for it. Mam had liked him, too.

Paddy grinned. "He's all right, fellows. Give him some cards."

The game was five-card draw. Hanley tossed two bits into the pile of coins on the table and picked up his hand.

They played for nearly an hour before anyone spoke, other than as needed for the game. Hanley won more than he lost, but made sure he lost enough to keep things friendly. He could just about hold a beer mug in his burned hand, so he nursed one to be companionable, but drank little of it. The stuff was half water and as appetizing as skunk spray. At least there weren't any minnows in it. When the surly Irishman went outside to take a leak and his friend headed up for fresh drinks, Hanley took his chance for a private chat. "I need to know about someone. A saloon owner. Your gang on the East Branch of the river ever fence stuff through Tommy Callaghan?"

Paddy studied his cards. "Why're you asking?"

"I'm working a murder case. There's stolen silver involved." He paused as he framed the next bit of information for maximum shock value. It shamed him a bit, shading the truth for Paddy, but he saw no better way of persuading him to talk. "The victim was a man of the cloth."

"A priest?" Paddy blanched. "Good God. What's this city coming to when the collar won't protect a man?" He crossed himself, his cards forgotten. "Callaghan do him in?"

"Could be. Early days, though." Hanley hadn't yet considered it, but Paddy didn't need to know that. "So? Is he a fence?"

Paddy looked nervous. "I'd rather not say."

"Come on, Paddy. If you know, you know. You might as well tell me."

He fidgeted with his cards. "I've got three kids left to me and no way to make a living but off the docks. I talk too much, that's done. Or worse."

"He works for Doyle, doesn't he?"

"Don't ask me that." He darted Hanley an anxious glance. "A priest, you said?"

Hanley nodded. Not quite true, but close enough. "Hanging's too good for whoever killed him."

Silence fell. Hanley glanced at the back door that led outside, then up toward the bar. The man who'd gone for drinks was heading back. "Paddy..."

Paddy bolted the last of his whiskey. "If Callaghan killed your man... then we'll see."

03

Hanley left soon afterwards. The morning was gone and he needed to meet with Moishe Zalman at the tailor shop. Given the limits of Zalman's English, he'd need Ida, which meant a long trip home first. He fingered his winnings—a comfortable weight in his coat pocket, nearly balancing the cosh he carried on the other side.

He thought about Paddy's question as he walked—whether Callaghan killed the rabbi. He doubted it. Their paths weren't likely to have crossed. Unless Kelmansky gave things to Callaghan…but why would Callaghan kill him over that?

He was nearing the corner of Third Avenue when he heard footsteps behind him. Something heavy struck him on the back of the head. Dizzied, he staggered and groped for his cosh. More swift steps came from up ahead and a savage blow from a chunk of lumber swept his legs from under him. He landed hard on the muddy boardwalk, his cosh trapped underneath him. He swore as he scrabbled for purchase against the slick, cold wood. He caught a blurred glimpse of a burly man, no more than the body shape and the dull color of homespun clothes. The dough-faced man from the Skibbereen? A third blow came at his head. He raised an arm, too late. The blow connected and the world vanished in a blaze of white fire.

NINETEEN

When Hanley came to, his head was pounding and his left knee felt like someone had taken a hammer to it. His first breath sent fire down his side. At least one cracked rib, maybe worse. Hissing through his teeth, he raised himself partway up. His ribcage screamed, but he didn't feel the grating of broken bone. As he moved, small knots of pain flared everywhere on his body. Someone had worked him over and done a damned thorough job of it.

He tested his injured leg. It hurt like hell. When he tried to put weight on it, harsh new pain left him gasping. Had they broken his knee? Fear shot through him. An injury like that could cripple a man. He grabbed a nearby hitching-post and dragged himself upright, then tested his leg again. More than the barest hint of weight brought agony from ankle to hip. Forehead damp with cold sweat, he looked around for something, anything, he could use as a crutch. A splintered board half-buried in dirt-grayed snow a few feet away caught his eye. He hobbled over to it. Though rough and wet, it hadn't rotted yet. It was sturdy and just tall enough to hold him up.

He tucked one end under his arm and maneuvered himself around to face the street. Then he noticed how light his coat pocket felt. A quick check confirmed his fear. Whoever hit him had emptied it. Split the takings, probably. From the angles of attack, there'd been two of them.

A distant church bell began to toll. Hanley held onto the improvised crutch as he counted. Twelve times it sounded in the freezing air. Good. He hadn't been out that long. He hobbled away toward Clark Street. Fortunately his attackers hadn't found the few small coins in his trouser pocket, so he had enough to take a horsecar up to Madison and then could switch to one out to the boardinghouse. He'd have words with Paddy soon about his poor choice in card-players. Sore losers, those two, if they couldn't let him go without jumping him for his winnings.

Pain stabbed through his injured leg at every halting step. He felt it stiffening, as if the joint were swelling up. He hoped he wouldn't need a doctor. Along with the stiffness and pain came increasingly uneasy thoughts about who had jumped him and why. The men from the Skibbereen wanting their money back? He knew nothing about them. Or how Paddy knew them, come to that. Surely Paddy...no, he wouldn't think it. Paddy would never see him harmed.

One thing he knew—if Doyle or Billy had engineered this attack, or the ones on Sunday, thinking to scare him off, they'd just made a very bad move.

࠾

By the time Hanley reached the boardinghouse, his headache had ebbed to a dull throb. The dizziness was worse, though. He knew that was a bad sign. He hurt all over and his left knee had swollen to half again its normal size. He couldn't go to Market Street and talk to Moishe Zalman today. He needed rest and as much willow bark tea as he could pour down his throat. Probably more than that, but he didn't want to think about it now.

He struggled up the steps and made it inside just in time to hear the final chords of a familiar piano piece—slow, sweet, and wistful. It made a pleasant contrast to the faint burned smell that still hung in the air. The music soothed his aches of mind and body both. He heard no sour notes. Ida's student was coming along well.

Hanley leaned against the wall, savoring the warmth as the music died away. Voices murmured in the parlor, Ida's and her pupil's—Mr. Van Riis, who still spoke with the accent of his former home in Holland even after twenty years in America. Then the parlor door opened and van Riis walked out. Lanky and white-haired, he managed to look elegant, despite his worn trousers and well-mended shirt cuffs. He nodded to

Hanley, plucked his black bowler hat and patched overcoat from the nearby coat-tree, put them on, and bowed to Ida. "Until next Monday, Mrs. Kirschner. Your lessons are a pleasure, as always."

"The pleasure is mine," she said. "Next week we begin Bach. I think you are ready now."

His face glowed with pride. He tipped his hat to her and left.

"What are you doing over there?" Ida said as she saw Hanley. The amusement in her voice died as she got a better look at him. "You're hurt. What happened?"

"Had a little dust-up this morning."

"And it is none of my business."

He managed a faint grin. "True enough. Except I need some of your willow bark tea. Strong as you can make it. And then I need to sleep awhile."

☙

He slept all afternoon, waking long enough around sundown for Mam to fuss over him while he ate the light supper she'd brought. His sore jaw made it hard to chew the carrot slices that floated in the rich chicken broth. The willow bark tea tasted like stewed boot leather. He made a face as he swallowed it. He spied Kate hovering in the doorway, looking anxious, and forced himself to smile. "It's not so bad. I'll be fine with a good night's sleep."

She came into the room and straightened his blankets. "D'you know who hit you?"

He shook his head, then winced as his skull throbbed. "Didn't get a good enough look at either one before they knocked me out."

He yawned and Mam handed Kate the empty tea mug. "Let him sleep now. I'll be in to check on you, Frankie." She pressed a hand to his cheek, then herded Kate out.

The childhood nickname, usually irritating, was a comfort tonight. That thought made Hanley smile as he closed his eyes and drifted off.

He felt better the next morning, and his tightly bandaged left leg could bear enough weight to let him walk with a spare cane borrowed from a tenant down the hall. His burned hand felt almost normal. By ten he'd drunk another dose of willow bark, eaten a decent breakfast, and felt ready to face the day. "I need to see Moishe Zalman," he told Ida as he finished his toast. "When can you come with me?"

She gave him a long look as she cleared away his dishes. "Your color is better. If you think you are up to this."

"I was supposed to go yesterday. God knows what he'll think if I don't turn up today."

"Then I will come. I have no students this morning."

He followed her into the front hall, where she helped him on with his overcoat and then put on her own. "So?" she said as she wound a red woolen scarf around her throat. "When will you let me teach you piano?"

He answered as he always did. "I barely have time to practice fiddle tunes."

"You must play for me sometime." Ida pulled on her gloves. "As one musician to another, I insist."

"Maybe." He knew that answer wouldn't satisfy her, but it was all he wanted to give.

"How is your head?" she asked as he led the way outside.

"Hurts. But I can see straight."

Her glance was skeptical, but she said nothing.

TWENTY

They got off the horsecar just across from their destination. Jacob Nathan's shop was built of new lumber, with a tin roof and a plate-glass window that sparkled in the afternoon sun. Across the glass, gold-painted letters spelled out *Nathan and Zalman, Gentlemen's Tailors*. The light glinting off them sharpened Hanley's headache.

He saw Zalman swabbing down a corner of the window as he and Ida approached. It must need doing several times a day to keep ahead of the clouds of grit that still drifted from diggings throughout the burned city. Through the window Hanley spotted Nathan tending to a customer, his back to them. *Good*, Hanley thought. That would make it easier to talk to Zalman first.

Zalman looked wary as Hanley greeted him, in sharp contrast to the cautious friendliness of two days before. "Do you have a minute to talk?" Hanley asked. "Mrs. Kirschner—my landlady—speaks your language. She's very kindly agreed to help us out."

Zalman shook out his window-cleaning rag as if determined to dislodge every last particle of soot. "I have work. No time for talking."

"You told me to come," Hanley reminded him. "You said you'd help. Don't you want to?"

Zalman's hands stilled. Then he started folding the rag. Each fold seemed to take enormous care. "Reb Nathan said..." He trailed off, staring at the window as if scrutinizing every inch for dust specks.

The mention of Nathan's name told Hanley where the problem lay. "Mr. Nathan was a good friend to your rabbi," he said. "I spoke with him Sunday night. Surely he would want to help if he could. You can. Would he really want you not to?"

144

Ida, blessedly quick on the uptake, began translating almost before Hanley finished talking. He wondered how long they had before Nathan spotted them and what would happen when he did. He'd best convince Zalman to talk quickly.

"I have work." Zalman's hands knotted around the cloth. "Please."

"I know your rabbi asked for aid from other places," Hanley said. "And I know they didn't have much to give. So where did you get the things you handed out around the neighborhood—you and Mr. Nathan and Rabbi Kelmansky? Was it all from the warehouse where Mr. Nathan went?"

Zalman looked startled. He tucked his rag away in his coat pocket, muttering and shaking his head. Hanley glanced at Ida.

"He's wondering what is the right thing to do," she murmured. "Talk to the *goy*—the outsider—or not."

Nagging pain in his head and leg made him short-tempered. "Mr. Zalman, I will find out exactly where those items came from, sooner or later. You might as well tell me what you know about it. Less trouble for all concerned."

Zalman darted a glance at Hanley, then took his rag back out and swiped at nothing on the window glass.

"I have a thought," Ida murmured to Hanley. "If I may...?"

He nodded, then winced. Ida took a step toward Zalman and spoke in a gentle, motherly tone. He exhaled slowly and turned to look at her. His brief reply was bleak.

His tone and Ida's stunned expression told Hanley something was badly wrong. He hated not being able to understand. "What did he say?" he asked as calmly as he could manage.

"That he doesn't know what justice is anymore. I told him helping you would bring justice to the dead." Ida threw Zalman a compassionate glance. "That he would say such a thing..."

"He's protecting someone. Or he thinks he is." Most likely Nathan, and to do with that warehouse. Was it murder he thought Nathan guilty of, or a lesser crime, like theft? Had Kelmansky been involved—or whomever he'd gone to see?

"We have to know what happened," Hanley told him, calm but

insistent. "How can there be justice in a lie...or in silence that hides the truth?"

As Ida relayed his words, Hanley watched Zalman's face. Beneath the anxiety and confusion, he could see what he'd said taking hold. After a moment, Zalman looked at Hanley with new resolve. "So. Ask."

Relief flooded through him. "You saw Rabbi Kelmansky walking down Randolph Street the day he died. Did he go that way often? Or was this an unusual trip?"

A burst of speech from Zalman followed Ida's translation. The rabbi had walked that way many times since the Fire. Since the Thanksgiving holiday, in fact. Every week on Thursday afternoon, usually around half past two. Except for the last day. The lateness was unusual. On all the other days, he'd been on his way back by four o'clock or so.

"Do you know where he was going?"

Zalman shook his head.

"How did he look? Anxious, hopeful? Well dressed or not? Was he always alone?"

"He was always well dressed, and always alone," Zalman said. "Carrying a book. A thin black book, too thin and small for the *siddur*—"

"The book used at prayer services," Ida interjected.

"...or the Talmud. He looked..." Zalman paused as if to think. "Satisfied. Like a man who has accomplished something. Except for the last day." He grew somber. "That day, he looked like a man with many troubles on his shoulders."

So Kelmansky had kept records. Hanley wondered where the book was now. "Did he have the—"

"Moishe!"

Nathan's angry shout came from the shop doorway, where he stood with a face like a thundercloud. Hanley and Ida stared at him. Zalman looked stricken, but didn't move.

Nathan strode over to them, with a jerk of his head toward the shop. "Moishe. *Areyn*. Inside."

"Mr. Zalman is helping me," Hanley said. "He can go back to work when we're finished. Then you can show me the warehouse."

"He can help you how?" Nathan demanded. "This boy should know anything about our rabbi's murder? He knows nothing. Leave him alone." He turned to Zalman. "Go inside, Moishe. Customers are waiting."

Zalman stayed still and, for a moment, Hanley thought he'd hold his ground. But the habit of following his boss's orders proved too strong. With a mute look of apology at Hanley, Zalman trudged away.

Nathan moved to follow, but Hanley stepped in front of him. He saw Ida raise a hand, her mouth open as if to speak. Then her hand fell and she stayed silent. He wished she didn't have to watch this, but he couldn't afford niceties any more. "So tell me what you know, Mr. Nathan. About where the rabbi went on the day he died. And who owns that warehouse. Is the owner the person he went to see?"

"Let me pass."

"Not until you help me. Like I helped you at the morgue."

Nathan met his eyes at that. Hanley read anguish in his face. "You won't understand."

"Try me."

"I told him," Nathan muttered. "*Hashem in himmel,* but I told him."

"Told the rabbi? Told him what?" Hanley paused, but Nathan gave no response. He barely seemed to be breathing. "You weren't studying with him that day, were you?"

Nathan closed his eyes. When he opened them again, he kept them fixed on the shop window.

"Did you go to see him at all? Or did you get things from that warehouse and take them somewhere else? Maybe to sell them?"

"I did go see Rav Kelmansky." Nathan's voice was barely above a whisper.

"What about?"

"A matter of concern to me." Sounding a little stronger now, he emphasized the final word. "I can say nothing that will help you, Mr. Hanley. Except that I am no thief, stealing for my own profit."

The man was like a boulder. Hanley clenched a hand around his cane. "The things you helped Rabbi Kelmansky deliver...did they all come from the warehouse? And did you have any right to take them?"

Nathan folded his arms. "We did what was needed. Our rabbi was a good man. He had many friends. They were generous. This is wrong by you?"

"What about Mr. Harden Guthrie? He runs the Second Aid District. Was he a friend?"

Nathan's jaw clenched. "They had met."

"And?" Hanley waited. Nathan stayed silent. "That twenty-pound sack of flour you gave Mrs. Pavlic, things like that don't turn up every day. Did Mr. Guthrie give that to your rabbi? Does he own that warehouse?"

"I should know this?"

Already worn down by pain and fatigue, Hanley's patience snapped. "You do know it. You stole those things, didn't you? Is that what you've been talking around, telling me a pack of lies about anonymous good works…and where you went? Where Kelmansky went on that last day? Was he going to see your partner in crime?"

Nathan clenched his fists. "You will not insult my rabbi's memory this way!"

"What did you see him about the day he died? Where did he go afterward? Who owns that damned warehouse?"

"You need to go now." Nathan stepped around Hanley and stalked toward the shop. "I have work to do."

"I could arrest you," Hanley said. Behind him, he heard Ida gasp.

Nathan halted. He stood still as death.

"You've blocked me from the start," Hanley went on. "You've lied, you've evaded…and you're strong enough to have swung that menorah. He surely wouldn't have fought you. He'd never expect his good friend to kill him. You could have struck him down before he had time to react."

Slowly, Nathan turned to face him. When he spoke, there was no more anger in him, only a profound weariness. "If you think me guilty, then you must do what you must do."

"Take off your boot. The left one." The words left Hanley's mouth almost before he knew he was going to say them. He fished out his sketchbook and flipped to the page he needed.

Nathan pulled off his boot and held it out. Hanley took it and slowly set it down, ignoring sharp twinges from his ribs and damaged leg, then laid the sketch of the muddy print from the synagogue yard beside it.

The width was the same, but not the length. Nathan's boot heel ended a good two inches short of the heel in the drawing. Scrutinizing the sketch to be absolutely sure, Hanley noticed something he hadn't before. The swirl of tiny lines in the center of the heel formed a blurred pair of initials. A maker's mark. Nathan's boot heel had none.

Wordless, he straightened and handed the boot back. Nathan looked foolish standing on the damp boardwalk with one stockinged foot in the air, but Hanley felt no desire to laugh. He tucked the sketchbook away, thinking hard. Was he certain Kelmansky's killer had made the muddy print? If so, where did that leave him now?

He spared a glance at Ida, who looked shocked at what she'd witnessed. He'd warned her it might not be pleasant. Still, he regretted that she'd had to see him go this far.

"Are you going to arrest me?" Nathan asked.

"Not today." Hanley watched his words sink in. He and Ida stood, silent in the cold, as Nathan slowly went back inside his shop and closed the door.

TWENTY-ONE

Rivka stood by her bedroom door and listened to the fading sound of Tanta Hannah's footsteps. When she was sure Hannah had gone to join the other women downstairs, she crept to the window and eased it open. Cold blew through the gap and she wished she could get her coat without being seen.

Her heart pounded in her chest at what she was about to do. It would be a scandal if she were caught. She almost had been before. But she had to tell Hanley about Onkl Jacob and the warehouse. Jacob's fear Monday morning had only confirmed her own—that whatever scheme he and Papa had devised, it had led to murder. Knowing that, she couldn't stay silent. She had to help Hanley find the killer.

He might not be at Lake Street, of course—and what she had to tell, she didn't want to write down where anyone at the police station might read it. If Hanley was there today, she could tell him directly. If he wasn't, she could leave a note with a time and place to meet.

A last glance at the clock by her bed, then out the window and onto the lean-to roof. The rain barrel she'd moved into place Monday morning was still there. She had two hours, maybe a little more, before the men joined them for evening prayers. Tanta Hannah would expect her to rejoin shiva by then. She shivered, partly from the cold and partly from the risk she was taking. *Let him be there*, she prayed silently as she lowered herself from the roof to the rain barrel and then to the ground.

℞

Hanley saw Ida safely onto the westbound Madison Street horsecar before heading back north, his thoughts in a whirl. The muddy boot print appeared to exonerate Nathan—if he could be certain the killer had made it. The timing matched the weather changes on the night of the murder. After the rain, before the cold snap. Exactly within the time frame Will Rushton had mentioned. And right by the synagogue. Which meant the print belonged to either the killer or a witness.

He was nearing the Lind Block at the corner of Market and Randolph. He halted in its shadow, sheltered a bit from the wind, and flipped open his sketchbook. Moving stiffly, he placed the drawing of the muddy print on the boardwalk and lined up his own foot next to it.

"Long as mine," he muttered. The instep was wider, he noticed. Whoever left that print must be at least Hanley's own six-foot height, but probably broader built. Too tall to have struck the rabbi down.

He tucked the sketchbook away. What time had the rain ended that evening? Where was Kelmansky then? And who might have seen him near the synagogue?

He started east down Randolph, taking careful note of storefronts with a good view of the street. As he passed Franklin, someone called his name. "Detective Hanley!"

"Rivka?" Sheer surprise made her given name slip out. She was hurrying toward him, with only a shawl over her black dress to protect her from the cold. "Miss Kelmansky," he said, frowning with concern as she reached him. "You're shivering."

"It's nothing," she said, but he was already taking off his overcoat. His cane made it an awkward business, but he wrapped the coat around her as snugly as he could manage. Too long for her, it trailed on the fresh snow. She looked like a small girl playing dress-up in her father's clothes. For a moment he wanted to laugh, but the impulse died at the grave expression on her face. "You're hurt," she said. "What happened?"

"Long story." He wasn't ready to tell it, nor sure he should.

"I have something to tell you."

He glanced up the street, then back at her. "I know where we can go. It's not far."

CB

He took her to Lily's, half a block away from Lake Street Station. A dining room and enlarged kitchen tacked onto the little house owned by Lily Stemple, an officer's widow with four children to support and a knack for good cooking, the place was a favorite of Lake Street's patrolmen and local workers. Inside, he led her to one of the half-dozen small tables and pulled out a chair. "Would you like anything? I can get you a cup of coffee."

"No, thank you." She sat down, maneuvering as best she could in his coat. "I am not sure I could drink it anyway."

He stepped away to pour coffee for himself from the pot always kept on the cast-iron warming stove. He dropped a nickel in the canister at one end of the jerry-built counter where Lily's daughter took meal orders, then came back and sat across from Rivka. "You found something out?"

She drew a breath. "Saturday night...I saw..." She broke off and looked down at her lap. "I'm sorry. This is...difficult."

"Is it something to do with Mr. Nathan?"

She looked up at him, clearly surprised. "Yes. He—" Abruptly, she looked away at the falling snow outside the front window.

"You took a risk to come see me," Hanley said. "It's no easy thing to interrupt your mourning time, is it? I expect people will talk."

A thin smile crossed her face. "I am used to that."

"Then you might as well make it worth it."

She met his eyes then, as if coming to a decision. "I saw Onkl Jacob. He went to a warehouse by South Water Street. I followed him there."

Surprise made him sit back. Extraordinary that she'd gone out after dark, alone, in the bitter cold. Her bravery impressed him. "Why?"

"He was acting very strange. He left my father's body to come to the shul. He had an empty sack with him. He took a key from the place where we keep the Torah. And he spoke to my father. 'One last try, Rav.' That is what he said. As if Papa were there to hear him."

"He took things from a warehouse." Nathan had admitted as much on the night the synagogue was attacked.

She looked startled. "You know of this?"

"A bit. Did Mr. Nathan bring the items back to his shop?"

"No. I followed him from the warehouse to the barracks on Randolph Street. He left the sack there and went away." She stared down at her hands again. "I do not know that he did anything wrong." She looked up and he saw pleading in her eyes. "You understand? I am only telling you what I saw."

Hanley nodded. He could guess what it had cost her to speak up. Jacob Nathan was practically family from what he'd observed—and his actions were suspicious, which Rivka clearly knew, despite her disclaimer. Was this the first time he'd been to the Randolph Street barracks or had he brought things there before? Had Kelmansky?

He looked out at the weather, to give Rivka time to compose herself and to gauge how heavy the snow was. There wasn't much wind and the fat flakes came almost straight down. Their gleaming whiteness gave the street outside a deceptively clean look, though the muck on the ground would stain them soon enough. He would be able to manage with the cane. "Show me the warehouse."

ೞ

"There." Rivka pointed across South Water Street. "The third one west of LaSalle."

Hanley noted its location. "Was anyone on guard?"

"Yes. Onkl Jacob snuck past him."

"What did he look like?"

"I couldn't see much from across the street. He was taller than Onkl Jacob. Big. Fair hair—I saw it in the walkway lights."

He eyed the fellow leaning against the building. Likely the day guard from his position near the door. Short, slim build. "Not him you saw, I take it?"

She shook her head.

Hanley blinked snowflakes out of his eyes. The watchman might have an interesting story to tell. From what Nathan had let slip at the synagogue Sunday night, Hanley had gotten the impression that the supply pickups occurred during the day. If Nathan was stealing things, though, he'd have every reason to mislead Hanley into thinking his actions were legitimate. And every reason to fear getting caught. Clearly, the incendiary device hadn't been the only thing putting him on edge.

Rivka's kerchief was covered with snow. He wanted to brush it away, and the bleak look on her face along with it. If Nathan had been stealing aid, then her father had, too. That couldn't be easy knowledge to live with.

"Are you all right getting home on your own?" He wished he could spare the time to see her to her door. Still, so near her own street and in broad daylight, she ought to be safe enough.

"No. Please." The intensity of the need on her face startled him. "Let me come with you."

"I don't even know where I'm going yet." It was true, he realized. Rivka had brought him a gigantic piece of the puzzle and he'd had little time to consider how it fit. "And I'm sure you're not supposed to be out with me." *Especially alone.*

"I don't care. Besides, they won't miss me for a little while yet." Her brief defiance faded and she watched the falling snow a moment before going on. "I cannot stand it…just sitting there, thinking of Papa, doing nothing. It makes me want to scream, or…or break something."

He knew those feelings as well as he knew his own name. His sympathy for her was so sharp it caught his breath. "All right," he said when he could trust his voice. "Let's go visit the Randolph Street barracks."

TWENTY-TWO

The city barracks at Randolph and LaSalle took up the entire northwest corner of the intersection. The area around it was a patchwork of Chicago's fitful recovery from the Fire—pine-board shops and saloons, scattered empty lots, dark gaps of cellar pits dotted with jerry-built shelters. A thin layer of fresh snow covered everything with a patina of white. The five-story brick bulk of the Brigg's House hotel, a lucky survivor of the Fire, loomed on the western edge of the same block. The air smelled of smoke and bad drains and boiled cabbage.

Hanley glanced at Rivka as they approached the barracks. She was taking everything in, her face drawn with fatigue and sorrow and a hint of anger. She saw him looking at her and gestured toward one of the holes in the ground. In the west corner, where the day's light would hit first, scavenged boards and a swath of dirty canvas made a crude lean-to. No one appeared to be home. The shelter's inhabitants were no doubt scrounging for work and enough food to get through the day. "Why do they live like that? Is there no room for them even here, where they would at least be out of the snow?"

"The barracks aren't much better." He didn't know how to describe it, or even if he should. A few square feet to lie down in and a turn at the cook-stoves twice a day. People fighting for space away from the walls, where every crack and knothole let the wind through. One man, he recalled, had been stabbed over it. The smell was the worst—hundreds of unwashed bodies all crammed together, with only two outhouse pits hastily dug a few feet from the back door. "But you're right. It's shameful."

"My father tried to help," she said in a low voice as she joined him by the barracks door. "He and Onkl Jacob. That's why..."

155

"I thought as much," he said gently. He wished he could take her hand, offer some comfort deeper than words. But there was none to give.

A length of rope dangled by the front door. Hanley tugged on it and heard the muffled jangle of brass bells. Next to him, Rivka stirred.

"You don't have to do this," he said.

Her jaw set. "Yes, I do."

The door was opened by a stout middle-aged woman in a dark blue dress. Beyond her Hanley saw a jumble of people, some sitting, others lying down. He heard the rattle of dice on floorboards, the low hum of conversation, the cries of a small child. "There's no room—" the woman started to say.

"We're not looking for shelter," Hanley said. "I'm with the police. I need to ask you a few questions."

The inside of the barracks was as grim as he remembered, drafty and stinking and too full of people with nowhere else to go. The lucky ones clustered around four fat iron stoves, breathing in coal dust but grateful for the heat. The rest huddled wherever they'd found room, passing the time by any means they could. Mothers tended children, fathers dandled babies, and young women darned socks, while young men threw dice and children played whatever games they could invent that didn't need too much space. Hanley turned away from them toward the woman in blue. Seeing the people brought back too much of his own first days after the Fire.

"You look familiar," the woman said, as Hanley tried to recall her name. "You lived here, didn't you? A few months back? With your mother and sister. Doing better for yourselves now, I hope."

"Yes." He had the name now. Mrs. Lewis. A no-nonsense woman with a difficult job, but kind beneath her brisk outward manner. "Detective Frank Hanley. I need to know about some aid donations you've gotten recently."

Mrs. Lewis was willing to talk. Clearly, it hadn't occurred to her that Jacob Nathan's supply drop-offs were anything but legitimate. "Four deliveries, from late November to early January," she said. "Food, clothes, soft coal, and kerosene. Two times, Mr. Nathan came with Mr. Kelmansky, then twice more with Mr. Zalman." Hanley saw Rivka's eyes widen at Zalman's name, but Mrs. Lewis didn't seem to notice. "They're very generous," she went on. "We're grateful. Lord knows we need everything we can get. The Relief and Aid directors have no idea…"

Too true, Hanley thought. He went on with his questioning. All deliveries were made by day, she told him. No, no one acted the least bit furtive. "And why should they? Aren't they doing the Lord's work? Those are good men, Detective. I hope you're not suggesting any different."

"Just finding things out." He was sharply aware of Rivka, who was looking around the barracks, absorbing everything. "Were you surprised to see Mr. Nathan last Saturday night?"

"I didn't actually see him." Her frown showed worry rather than annoyance. "We heard the bell, went to the door, and there were the things. I assume Mr. Nathan brought them. Or Mr. Zalman, or Mr. Kelmansky."

"Not Kelmansky." Hanley glanced toward Rivka as he spoke her father's name. She'd moved a few feet away and was watching a little girl draw on a slate. "I'm afraid he's dead."

"Poor man." Mrs. Lewis crossed herself. "Was he ill? He never looked it."

"It was sudden." Hanley watched Rivka kneel by the girl with a friendly smile and a soft word. The child pointed to her slate and spoke. Rivka responded, though Hanley couldn't hear what they said. A gust of wind shook the walls and ruffled the little girl's tangled dark hair. Hanley saw her shiver. With some difficulty, Rivka worked her shawl out from beneath his overcoat and wrapped it around the girl. The child looked up, disbelief on her face. Rivka brushed her cheek. Then she stood and came back toward Hanley. As she reached him, he saw she was close to tears.

He should take her away from here. He'd learned what he needed to, anyway. "Thank you," he said to Mrs. Lewis and gently shepherded Rivka back outside.

❦

"I cannot believe Moishe Zalman was part of this." Rivka sounded stunned as they left the barracks behind. "For him to risk…" She frowned as if in thought. "Then again, he and Onkl Jacob are very close. He would do anything Onkl Jacob asked."

She seemed to have recovered somewhat, though he sensed her distress like a coiled spring beneath her outward calm. "How much would Mr. Nathan tell him about what they were doing?"

"I don't know."

The snow was falling thickly now. Hanley did his best to ignore the fat flakes melting against his shirt as he thought over what they'd learned. If Nathan and Kelmansky had stolen the things they brought, why come in daytime when anyone might see them—at the warehouse as well as the barracks? Surely the day guard would have noticed. But if the deliveries were legitimate, why make the last one at night and with obvious subterfuge?

Something still didn't add up. Hanley needed more information and he thought he knew where to get it. Whether to bring Rivka with him was another question. If she was supposed to be in mourning, sooner or later she'd be missed. Reluctantly, he decided he couldn't ask her to risk getting caught any more than she already was.

His shirt, thoroughly damp now, felt clammy against his skin. He suppressed a sneeze. Rivka looked over at him. "You are freezing," she said and began to unwrap herself from his coat. "Please…take this back. You need it more than I do."

"I'm fine." He sneezed violently.

She slid the coat off and held it out to him. "Take it. Don't be foolish."

"I'll take it when we reach your house."

A troubled look crossed her face. "I don't want to go back." She came close to him and reached upward in an awkward attempt to drape his coat around him.

He grabbed it to keep it from falling. Their hands brushed. Her fingers felt warmer than he'd expected. Slowly he put his coat on. She didn't want to go, and he didn't want to see her leave. Foolish, both of them. "You'll be all right?" he made himself say.

"Yes." Her voice was subdued. She looked down at the snow-covered boardwalk.

He reached out to her, then let his hand fall. "Listen," he said. She looked up. He spoke quickly, worried about her without even her shawl in the biting wind. "Your father carried a book when he went out on Thursday afternoons. A thin, black book. Do you remember it?"

"Yes." She blinked snow from her lashes. Long and thick, they deepened the gray of her eyes.

"Did he have it with him that last day?"

Her expression turned thoughtful. "Not when he came to tell me he was leaving. I was scrubbing carrots for soup. I can't say if he picked it up on his way out."

"Then it may still be in the house. Can you look for it?"

She nodded. "And if I find it?"

"Bring it to Lake Street Station. Day after tomorrow? That'll give you some time to search. Can you come by at, say, one in the afternoon?"

Her expression lightened. "I will be there." She lingered briefly, as if to say more, then turned and hurried away through the snow.

TWENTY-THREE

Hanley watched Rivka until she turned the corner, then retraced his steps to Randolph Street. He was sure Kelmansky had gone to Guthrie's office on the day he died. He walked east down Randolph, making quick stops at a few places to ask about the rabbi. A clerk in a surveyors' office at LaSalle recalled a bearded man dressed all in black passing by regularly on Thursday afternoons. A saloon owner near Dearborn, a big German who looked as if he personally handled his rougher customers, thought he might have seen Kelmansky late last Thursday afternoon, but couldn't be sure because a fight had broken out and he'd had to "go tend to things."

Hanley left the saloon. Randolph and State lay not far ahead. He knew one person who surely would have seen Kelmansky if he'd gone to visit Harden Guthrie.

Sure as taxes and watered whiskey, there was Red Jack standing at the northeast corner of Randolph and State, blowing on his hands next to a stack of the *Chicago Gazette*. An informant of Hanley's ever since he'd first walked a patrolman's beat in the area, Red Jack paid attention to everything and everyone. Hanley found him invaluable and considered him a friend as well.

"Paper, Mr. Hanley?" Jack said, as Hanley approached. He stood as high as Hanley's shoulder. Years of sunshine and windburn had browned his face to the shade of old shoe leather and he sported untidy white hair under his dark red cap. He gave Hanley the jaunty smile of a practiced salesman. "Alderman C. P. Holden is at it again, him and his bummers down in city hall. Best scheme they come up with yet. You won't find a better three cents' worth of entertainment, I'm tellin' you honest."

160

"I'm sure." As always, Jack's enthusiasm warmed Hanley. He dug out a nickel and took a paper. "Been out here a lot the past few days?"

"Never miss," Jack said. Then he frowned. "'Cept for three weeks ago when I had an awful cold on Sunday. But I been here all last week, and the week 'fore that. Even the Fire couldn't keep me away. Soon's it cooled down enough to walk around, I'se right back out here." He handed Hanley two cents change from a small leather sack at his belt. "Givin' out the news is a callin'. Ain't fer any of your soft types."

"You out here last Thursday afternoon?"

"Sure was. Made near four dollars 'fore lunch. Winter thaw days go like that. They bring everybody out."

Hanley tucked the *Gazette* under his arm. "I'm looking for someone who came by here that day, sometime after four in the afternoon. A Jewish man around your age. About my height, black suit, well-trimmed gray beard." He did his best to conjure up Kelmansky's face based on the half that hadn't been shattered. "Long face, square-ish, strong bones. He might have been carrying a book."

Even before Hanley finished, Red Jack started nodding. "I saw him, yeah. Fella come by here every week. Bought papers off me, which most of them black-hat people don't. They mostly read their own papers, in some funny language. This fella bought mine. Thanked me real nice every time, too." He paused. "Didn't buy a paper last Thursday, though. Came by later—near half past four. Seemed in a hurry. Don't remember no book. Coulda had one, though. Not like I'se lookin' for it."

"Which way did he go?"

Jack gestured down Randolph, further east. "Thataway."

Toward the McKee's Building. "Did you see if he went into McKee's?"

Jack shook his head. "Banker-type fella came up then, wanted a paper. Lots of 'em work around here, in them big stone office blocks they been puttin' up since the burn." He patted the coin sack at his belt. "Sure am glad them buildin's went up so quick. Otherwise I'd still be livin' in that damned barracks up west."

Hanley, recalling his own miserable weeks in the stinking, crowded barn on Randolph Street, nodded agreement. "I don't suppose you saw which building he came out of?"

To his surprise, Jack pointed southward down State. "Saw 'im comin' outta Muskie's. This was awhile later, mind. I went into Jimmy Hardy's Tavern over there 'round five, for a warm-up and a bite of supper. Jimmy's wife makes the best potato soup I ever ate. I'd been hearin' thunder, of all the damnfool things, and the clouds looked like they'se gonna let loose with more 'n spit-drizzle. Saw yer man again after the hard rain stopped and I came back out, musta been around six." His face wrinkled in thought. "Yep, 'cause I remember the church bells struck 'most right after that."

Hanley tensed. "Muskie's Chop House? You're sure?"

"Ain't no other place with that green stripey canopy over the door." Jack cleared his throat, then spat into the nearby snow. "Looks danged silly, but it keeps the drizzle off. Plus, folks comin' outta there sometimes buy papers. I passed yer fella on my way over."

Hanley looked down the street toward the chop house. Sean Doyle had lost no time rebuilding his most profitable gaming-hall. Muskie's was a respectable restaurant on its first floor, a favorite among businessmen and bankers and the occasional politician. The clientele for the two floors above it were much the same as when Hanley was part of that world—wealthy men who wanted a discreet place to gamble or indulge in worse vices. Hanley had pushed to raid it more than once since late November, but Doyle had pull with the police force. He thought of Doyle's appearance at Lake Street Station on Sunday and the bombings that same night. A queasy feeling roiled his gut. What in the name of God could have brought Kelmansky to Doyle's place?

"You all right, Mr. Hanley?"

"Fine. Which way did the man go after he came out of Muskie's?"

"Turned on Washington. Headed west."

Homeward to Market Street. Where he'd gone into his synagogue, knelt to pray, and been struck down by someone he knew. Or by someone he hadn't expected, so fast he'd had no time to react.

"Did you see anyone else headed that way? Say, within five minutes afterward or so."

"There was a fella in a mighty hurry," Jack said. "Near knocked me down comin' out the door. I'd got under the canopy by then. Big fella, light hair, black overcoat. Couldn't see much else, he was goin' so fast."

The size and light hair made Hanley think of Guthrie—but surely, if he and Kelmansky had gone to Muskie's for a bite to eat, they'd have left the place together. Hanley wasn't even certain Guthrie had left his office, though he was sure Kelmansky went there.

"'Nother fella come out a couple minutes after him," Red Jack went on. "Short as me, skinny, dark hair all slicked down. Face like if you crossed a weasel with a huntin' dog. He was movin' pretty quick, too. Like he was tryin' to catch up with the first guy." He scratched under his cap. "Skinny fella works at Muskie's, I think. I see 'im go in there most every day, always between four and five. Always got a carpetbag with 'im. Didn't have it on his way out that night, though."

Hanley's heart jumped into his throat. He pulled out his sketchbook and swiftly drew Jamie Murphy's face. Then he showed the sketch to Jack. "This him?"

"Yep." Jack grinned. "That's somethin', how you do that. I still got that picture you made of me that one time. Good as a mirror."

Hanley put the sketchbook away, his mind racing. Murphy had followed the rabbi from Muskie's. Or he'd followed the big blond man—who might have left the muddy footprint. Had Murphy killed Kelmansky after all? Could he have been told to rough the rabbi up and things got out of hand?

Hanley tugged at his hair. Murphy was a bunco man and petty thief, not a bully boy. And who would have told him to harm the rabbi? Doyle? But that made no sense. If Doyle wanted Kelmansky roughed up, he'd have sent Charming Billy—but Billy, at six foot plus, couldn't have crushed the skull of a man kneeling at prayer. Not with a straight-on blow. Come to that, why would Doyle have ordered Kelmansky hurt? What conceivable link could exist between an apparently saintly rabbi and Chicago's most vicious gambling prince?

If there was a link, Hanley realized with a sinking feeling, Rivka would learn about it. So would all of the Market Street Jews. There was no way to prevent that. He hoped there wasn't any link—or if there was, that the rabbi was just another blameless Doyle victim.

Murphy was at least the right height to have struck Kelmansky. He'd spent six months in jail since the last time Hanley dealt with him. Half a year of prison time could change a man. And Callaghan, the saloon owner, had lied for him—about the shoes and about where he'd been late Thursday afternoon. There seemed no reason for that last one, since Kelmansky was alive at the time. Unless Callaghan meant to hide Murphy's mode of employment and thereby his employer as well.

Which brought things back to Doyle. And there was that bruise on the dead man's temple. The right size and shape for a cosh, a weapon most criminals carried for their own protection.

Hanley clapped Jack on the shoulder. "Thanks. I may be back."

He strode off down Randolph, determined to find out who the big blond man was. He reached the McKee's Building in time to meet Guthrie walking out of it. Guthrie looked startled at the sight of him. "I was just coming to see you," Hanley said. "Can we have a word in your office?"

TWENTY-FOUR

Detective." Guthrie took a moment to collect himself. "Hanley, isn't it? Your mother requested a sewing machine, if I recall rightly."

"Yes." The unexpected question rattled Hanley somewhat, but he recovered quickly. "Can I ask how likely it is she'll get one?"

"I haven't read Mrs. King's report yet." Guthrie's half-smile couldn't hide the weariness in his face. "But Miss Wentworth told me enough that I'd like a second look."

"Thank you," Hanley said and meant it. "I have other questions for you, related to Rabbi Kelmansky's death. If we could talk in your office—"

"I'd rather not." Guthrie sounded abrupt. "It's a small place and Miss Wentworth might be distressed if she overheard. As it happens, I've an appointment. Some other time—"

"This won't take long. I was told Kelmansky came to see you late last Thursday afternoon. Is that true?"

Guthrie turned up his coat collar and began walking toward State Street. "Yes. Though I'm afraid I can't discuss it. I'm due at the Desplaines Street depot for inspection, so I can write up my report for the executive committee."

"I'll walk with you." Hanley fell into step beside him. Guthrie glanced at Hanley's cane and slowed his pace a fraction. They passed Red Jack, who waved, and continued west along Randolph toward the nearest horsecar stop. "How long was he with you? Do you recall?"

"Not long." Guthrie walked faster, dodging occasional pedestrians without appearing to see them. "Really, Detective, I don't have time—"

Hanley kept up, though it took effort. "What did you talk about?"

"He asked for help for some neighbors of his. I said I'd consider it."

"A friend of Kelmansky's told me he regularly got supplies from a riverside warehouse near Market Street. South Water west of LaSalle, in fact. Is that warehouse being used by the Relief and Aid? And would you know who owns it?"

Guthrie cleared his throat. "A lot of the deeds to those properties went up in the Fire. Left quite a mess to sort out."

"I was outside the Court House when it went. Part of the bucket brigade." Hanley recalled it vividly—the long line of men, and some women, passing boxes and file drawers stuffed with legal papers to safety while the fire roared through the building. They'd fled only when the heat grew fierce enough to explode the stone façade. The nerve-shattering roar and the rain of marble fragments had reminded him of artillery fire from the massed guns at Gettysburg. At the time, the only thing stronger than his terror was an overwhelming desire not to sully his badge by being the first to break ranks. "So you don't own the warehouse by South Water and LaSalle?"

From up ahead came a child's voice, sharp with the effort to be louder than the wagons that rattled down the street. "Souvenirs! Pieces of the Fire you can hold in your hand! Penny a piece, your choice. Sooo-vuh-neeers!" In the gap left by a passing matron, Hanley saw the souvenir-seller—a scrap of a girl in a linsey skirt and a flannel shirt several sizes too large. A length of rope belted the shirt around her skinny waist. Red curls in need of a comb tumbled from beneath a knitted hat. Beside her was a small wooden wagon full of odds and ends, all melted or charred.

Guthrie went toward her. Hanley followed as swiftly as he could manage. The girl grinned at them as they drew closer. Beneath the grin, Hanley read the bone-deep exhaustion of nights spent sleeping in cold churches or cellar holes and never enough breakfast in the morning. He groped through what little change he carried, searching by feel for a penny.

She shook the wagon handle, making the contents rattle. "Want one, misters? Best you'll find in the whole division. Promise."

"Well, now," Guthrie said. He looked over the things in the wagon, as if considering the finest merchandise at Field, Leiter & Company. "I am looking for a gift, as it happens. For a young lady I work with. What would you recommend, miss?"

"Is it her birthday?"

"You know, I've never asked her when her birthday is." Guthrie smiled at the girl. "But I suppose I can save it till then, if it's past."

The girl sorted through her collection—several scorched porcelain doorknobs, some bricks likely from the Court House, a half-melted key. The oddest thing was a pair of scissors with one intact handle shaped like a stork's head. The other handle and the blades were virtually gone, reduced to a hardened trickle of silver like some bizarre icicle. "Is she pretty?" she asked.

"Yes." Guthrie flushed faintly as he spoke.

The girl pointed to the scissors. "I'd want that one if I was her. Something pretty as me."

"I'll take it." Guthrie dug a few coins from his pocket and handed them over.

The girl gave him the scissors, then scowled at her payment. "One penny, mister. That's my price. I didn't ask for three."

"The other two are for helping me." Gently, he closed her hand around them. "One for pointing out this fine specimen and the other for reminding me about the lady's birthday."

The girl chewed her lip. Watching her brought Hanley a sudden, vivid memory of his own boyhood—selling papers and sweeping street crossings, near desperate for what a few extra coins could buy, yet fiercely proud enough to despise any thought of charity. Guthrie, he realized, knew that. Knew it well enough to give the girl an out.

"Fair enough," she said finally, as she pocketed the change. "Nice doing business with you."

"Likewise," Guthrie answered and shook her hand.

Hanley bought a lump of iron and they walked on. The horsecar stop was just ahead. Hanley saw a westbound car approaching. "About that warehouse," he said.

"The warehouse. Yes." Guthrie's gaze was fixed on the horsecar. "I'm happy to find out who owns it for you. I have to complete my inspection today so I can make my report. Another day, though..."

The car arrived with a jangling of bells. The horse that pulled it snorted loudly, its breath making clouds in the cold air. As Guthrie moved toward the car, Hanley followed. "Did you and Kelmansky go to Muskie's Chop House last Thursday?"

Guthrie called back over his shoulder as he stepped aboard. "I'm sorry, Detective, I—" Two more men and a woman pushed past Hanley to board in Guthrie's wake and the nearly full car pulled away before Guthrie could complete his sentence.

TWENTY-FIVE

anley watched the horsecar with Guthrie aboard leave, then turned back toward State Street. The church bells hadn't rung four yet. Agnes Wentworth might still be at work. Maybe she'd seen Kelmansky leaving last Thursday, with or without Guthrie. He'd have gotten there after her usual departure time, but she might have run late that day or passed him on the street.

He reached the McKee's Building and went up to the second floor where he found Agnes seated at her desk nibbling on a half-wrapped sandwich. At the sight of him she put down her meal and grabbed a nearby handful of papers. "Mr. Hanley! I wasn't expecting anybody...that is..." She saw the cane and concern crossed her face. "What happ—I'm sorry. It's none of my business."

He gave her his warmest smile. "No, *I'm* sorry. I didn't mean to interrupt your snack."

She blushed deeper and dropped two of the papers. They drifted to the floor. Hanley picked them up and saw they were forms, with names and addresses penciled in, followed by written paragraphs. One of the latter looked lengthy. The other took four lines. "Would it break a rule if I put these away for you?"

"N-no...no, I suppose not." Her cheeks stayed pink, but he saw relief in her face. Likely that he wasn't laughing at her. He resolved to be as sweet to her as possible.

She pointed toward a bank of pigeonhole shelves against the wall. "They go in there," she said. "Fourth from the top, five in from the left."

He put them where she'd indicated. He couldn't help reading a bit of the shorter paragraph before tucking the form away. *Mrs. McGinty should receive nothing whatsoever from this office. The condition of her home is deplorable, and the 'missing' husband is likely to be found haunting the local saloon. Enough of these shanty Irish have abused this city's hospitality. Let us not add to their numbers.*

He resisted an urge to crumple the form and cram it into the pigeonhole. Agnes Wentworth didn't deserve to catch the raw edge of his temper. Instead, he conjured up another smile for her.

Her sandwich put away and decorum restored, Agnes had recovered her composure. "Did you come about your mother? Mr. Guthrie probably won't be back today…he hasn't been looking well. He'll likely be in tomorrow, though."

"Ah, now, that's a shame. But that doesn't mean you can't help me. Not about Mam and the sewing machine." Recalling what Guthrie had said of Agnes, he made a swift decision not to mention the murder. "I'm looking for someone who came here last Thursday afternoon. How long were you here that day?"

"Till half past four." She blushed again. "I stayed late because… because I didn't want to go home. I did go home, because I had to, but…" She grabbed more papers from her desk. Looking at them instead of at Hanley, she continued. "Who are you looking for?"

He described Kelmansky. "Did you see him before you left?"

"Yes." She put down the papers. "He used to come here every Thursday. He had a standing appointment at three. He didn't talk much, but he always smiled at me. Is he a friend of yours?"

"Just someone I know," Hanley said, covering his surprise. So Kelmansky had come here on his weekly walks from Market Street. An observant Jewish rabbi, meeting regularly with the Christian director of the Second Relief District. Yet, from what Guthrie had said a few days before, the two men barely knew each other. "What time did he get here last Thursday?"

"Right as I was leaving. I was surprised to see him. He'd missed his usual time, and I wondered if he was ill. He didn't look well when he came."

"Did he talk to Mr. Guthrie?"

"Yes. He did that every week. Not for long. I think he was working with Mr. Guthrie and a Jewish relief agency. They have their own, you know. But that's only my guess. I never asked."

Not a Jewish relief agency, Hanley thought, buoyed by the thrill of discovery. Rabbi Kelmansky had worked for himself and his neighbors. Until something went wrong. "And last Thursday?"

"I know they talked. I'm not certain for how long." She looked embarrassed again. "I glanced into Mr. Guthrie's office right before I left. Aunt Augusta was having one of her musical evenings, and she'd invited him, and I…" She picked up another paper and began fiddling with it. "I asked him not to come. Aunt Augusta always wants me to sing, and I'm not very good. It's bad enough to make a fool of myself in front of people's tiresome sons and nephews, but I couldn't bear looking silly in front of Mr. Guthrie." She dropped the paper and twined her fingers together. "He had his ledger book out. I knew he could use work as an excuse so Aunt Augusta wouldn't feel insulted if he didn't show. He's kind like that."

He was, Hanley thought, remembering the souvenir girl. He felt a sudden, sharp pity for Agnes. "So you don't know what time either of them left? Or if they left together?"

"I'm afraid not. Though Mr. Guthrie didn't come to Aunt Augusta's."

Hanley looked around the office. Bookcases and pigeonhole shelves took up most of it, all crammed with ledgers, receipt books, and papers. Records upon records, determining people's daily lives. Who needed what and got it. Or didn't. "How much does the Relief and Aid take in? Plenty, I'd bet."

"That's true." Agnes relaxed. "People all over the world have been so generous. Last week we received a bank draft for ten thousand francs from four little villages in the Loire Valley in France. Farmers, mostly. They all got together and raised whatever they could spare."

"So what do *you* do for the Aid?"

She shrugged. "I keep track of the paperwork, mostly. There's so much to do, and never enough volunteers."

He leaned against the desk and gave her his warmest smile. He felt a little guilty using her shy interest in him to charm her, but he needed to know how things worked here, and what role Guthrie had surely played in the apparent theft of aid supplies from the riverside warehouse. "It would set my mind at ease if you could tell me a bit about how the Aid Society does things. What happens after someone like my Mam sends a letter requesting relief? There's a home visit, and then what? Someone decides yes or no right away?"

"Well." She walked back to the desk and shuffled the remaining papers on it into a neat stack. "First we get the letter and Mr. Guthrie checks the sender's name against our master list. If it's someone we've already given things to, or marked down as having gotten a job ticket, it goes into the 'Claim Denied' box. Otherwise Mr. Guthrie sorts it for immediate relief or home visit. Mrs. Hanley was put down for a home visit." Her skin pinked. "Then the visitors write their recommendations. Mr. Guthrie reads them and decides. Sometimes, if he's not satisfied, he'll go see the claimant himself."

"Might we be expecting him?" Hanley asked over a cold lump in his innards. She'd warned him, Mam had.

Agnes gave him a hesitant glance. "I'm sure so."

Hanley looked down. His scuffed boots stood out against the polished hardwood floor. Shanty Irish, he and Mam and Kate. That's what Mrs. King would call them. Good for nothing but to be sat on by their betters. Though Guthrie had sounded as though Mrs. King wouldn't have the last word. "And Mr. Guthrie's decision is final?"

She bit her lip and nodded. "He's very generous. He gives things to lots of people that the home visitors wouldn't have. I've known him to do it plenty of times."

"And if he doesn't?" Hanley forced himself to sound casual. "What then? Does a claimant get a second chance?"

"No." She gazed at the hem of her dress. "Their names go on the master list, too. To make sure aid only goes to the truly deserving, Aunt Augusta says."

"So if you're turned down once, that's it?"

Her silence told him the answer. He straightened abruptly, not wanting to frighten her but unable to keep his body as still as his tongue.

One person's judgment, two at the most, to determine permanently who would be found worthy of food to keep from starving, building materials for a roof over their heads, the tools they needed to make whatever living they'd lost. All from a single visit of no more than half an hour.

The callousness of it appalled him. From what he read in the papers, the Aid Society controlled most of the donated cash and goods that had poured into the stricken city since mid-October. Surely they had plenty to offer everyone in need. What in the name of God were they doing with it all?

He thought of Mira Pavlic, turned down by the Relief and Aid, despite having three young mouths to feed. Kelmansky had known of her plight and of many others in the area around Market Street. He'd surely come here for aid, openly received or otherwise. How had he gotten it from a system like this? Had Guthrie known where the aid would end up, or had Kelmansky and Nathan duped him? "So you keep lists. Who got what, who's been offered work, who's been barred. Are there lists of what's been donated as well?"

"Oh, yes. We keep track of everything." She sounded eager to get past the painful subject of his own family's fate. "Most donations come in by train, so there's someone at the stations to note down what we get. From there things go to the district supply depots or into storage, to be given out as needed. Mr. Guthrie loaned the Society one of his own warehouses when they made him Second District director."

The warehouse Nathan had gone to, Hanley guessed. The one Guthrie hadn't admitted to owning. "So who decides what goes where? Do workers at the supply depots send requests? They keep track of things they give out, I imagine."

She nodded. "The depot workers have people sign receipts for everything they give away. Our office gets those every week and Mr. Guthrie enters them into that month's ledger. If they need more of something, they notify us and Mr. Guthrie authorizes it for distribution."

Hanley recalled the receipt book and manifests from his earlier visit. "So if someone applies for aid and gets it, they have to go to a supply depot? Anything get handed out anywhere else?"

Agnes looked uncomfortable. "Our volunteers sometimes pick things up for people. For the Special Relief."

"Special relief?"

"For..." Pink was creeping back into her face. "For people who aren't as accustomed to...difficulties. People who might not be able to bring themselves to go down to the depots and—"

"Wait in line," Hanley finished for her. He felt anger rising again, though not toward Agnes. "These would be better-off applicants, I take it? Do they get home visits too?"

She shook her head. "They just write or get word to us through someone they know. I saw one letter from Aunt Augusta's dressmaker. She'd opened up a new shop with insurance money. She and her husband were living over the shop and they wanted lumber for a house. They got money for that right away." The look she turned toward him was troubled. "I know we help a lot of poorer people, too—the ones still living in barracks and...and worse places. I see them sometimes on my way here. But I wondered why Mr. and Mrs. DeTappan got money for lumber when other people still don't have a decent place to sleep. Aunt Augusta says I'm too soft-hearted to judge who deserves help. I suppose she's right. But it doesn't seem fair."

"It's not," Hanley said. "And don't you let your aunt tell you any different."

They shared a look, before she glanced down and tugged at a crease in her skirt. He leaned against the desk once more. "Do Special Relief distributions get recorded as well?"

"Oh, yes. Everything taken from storage is listed. We get those lists here every week along with the depot records." She brightened as she went on. "Mr. Guthrie goes over the books very carefully to make sure the numbers match—what we took in versus what went out and what's still being stored. He wants to make sure everything goes to the needy and nothing gets wasted."

"You said the dressmaker got money. The Society gives out cash, too?"

"Checks, actually. For rent payments or large purchases like the lumber for the DeTappans' house. The district office does the buying for that sort of thing. That's mainly how we use cash donations. The money goes into the bank and the Society draws on it. Mr. Guthrie wrote a check to the lumber dealer and gave it to the DeTappans along with a voucher for how much they could purchase."

"And those get recorded also?"

"Yes. Mr. Guthrie writes out a receipt saying how much a check is for and who it went to. If someone buys something with it, the seller sends us a copy of the purchase receipt."

Guthrie seemed to do an awful lot and keep unusually quiet about it. And he'd lied about the warehouse, if only by omission. Hanley was sure of it. Maybe he wasn't only helping the poor. He didn't like the thought, but he couldn't dismiss it. "So who does Mr. Guthrie report to? He mentioned an executive committee."

"Oh, yes. City leaders and such. Not aldermen. Important people, like Mr. Wirt Dexter and Mr. O. C. Gibbs."

"Leading citizens. Of course."

The sarcasm in his tone bypassed Agnes, or else she was generous enough to ignore it. "Mr. Guthrie sees them every week with the books. The committee wants to know exactly what goes where. They take their responsibilities quite seriously."

Hanley moved away from the desk. He needed to see that December ledger and any records of checks or purchase vouchers Guthrie'd written over the past couple of months. If it took a judge's order, so be it. In the meantime he wanted a quick look around Guthrie's inner office. "Would Mr. Guthrie still have the ledger for January? I'd like to see it."

Agnes looked doubtful. "That's confidential information. I shouldn't."

He lowered his voice. "I probably shouldn't tell you this, but I'm in the middle of an investigation that may concern donations going astray. I don't need names, just the clearest picture I can get of how things work here."

"I'm sorry." She was blushing again. "I can't let you see it."

"Not even to help Mr. Guthrie? Surely he'd want to know if relief supplies are ending up somewhere they shouldn't."

She was wavering. He could see it in her face. "There are people in this city who may be getting their hands on aid items to resell them," he continued. "At a shocking profit. Surely you and Mr. Guthrie would want to stop that." Another lie, but how did he know it wasn't happening? Especially if Guthrie was doing more than helping poor people. He thought of Sean Doyle, then caught himself. He'd no evidence yet that Harden Guthrie knew Doyle, or that Nathan, or even Kelmansky, did. The rabbi could just have gone to Muskie's for a bite to eat.

After a moment, she nodded. "All right. As long as I come with you."

The ledger was on a bookshelf behind Guthrie's desk. Hanley opened it and saw columns of names, dates, and notations. He glanced over a few pages, looking for one item.

There it was. A man's heavy woolen overcoat, size small, given to Mr. Andrew Osgood of 210 West Washington Street, on January 19th. Not to Jamie Murphy of 100 South Franklin, who was likely on the master list under "Claim Denied."

He replaced the ledger and looked around the room. Guthrie's desk held a book of blank receipts and a folded copy of the *Chicago Tribune*, dated January 19th. Hanley picked it up. Why would Guthrie keep a week-and-a-half old newspaper in his office? "May I take this?"

"Is it a clue?"

"I don't know yet."

"I can't see as Mr. Guthrie would mind."

He nodded toward the receipt book. "That for checks?"

"Yes."

"Where do those receipts end up?"

"At the main office. Mr. Guthrie brings them along with the ledger at the end of the month."

January's receipts didn't appear to be lying around. Guthrie probably kept them in a desk drawer. A warrant might get Hanley back in to search more thoroughly, but just now he couldn't think up a convincing excuse to do so. Part of him felt glad to put it off. He wasn't sure he wanted to know what the receipts might tell him.

When they returned to the outer room, Agnes stopped by her desk, ruffled through a stack of papers, unearthed one, and held it toward Hanley. "Here. You should have this."

He took it just long enough to see it was a form with Mam's name across the top. "Miss Wentworth...I can't. You'll get into trouble."

"No, I won't. I'll tell them I lost it. I do that sometimes. Aunt Augusta says I'm hopeless. For once maybe that'll do some good. I only have this position as a favor to her. Or so she keeps reminding me."

"But—"

"You come back and see Mr. Guthrie. Tell him about your mother. Your being a policeman should help. He admires the police force. Aunt Augusta was completely unfair. And I'm getting tired of it."

Relief that Mam might still get her sewing machine warred with shame at the thought of accepting charity. He also felt guilty. Here he was, benefiting his family through personal connections. Just like Mrs. King's dressmaker and others who got extra help because of who they knew.

But Agnes was so sincere in her desire to make things right. How could he throw that back in her face and ruin his mother's chance to regain her livelihood for no more than his own pride?

He managed to thank her, then slowly folded the form and tucked it in his coat pocket.

TWENTY-SIX

By the time Hanley reached Lake Street Station Wednesday morning, he felt chilled through. In the wake of yesterday's snow, temperatures were falling again. His leg ached even after the brief walk from the horsecar stop. Maybe he shouldn't have left the cane at home. He checked with the desk sergeant, learned that Moore was in, and headed upstairs.

He found his boss going over paperwork. Moore set down the report he was holding and nodded toward the fireplace. "Warm yourself, Frank. New developments?"

"Plenty. Only I'm not sure what to make of them." Hanley went and stood near the fire, grateful for the warmth against his legs. He'd thought long and hard last night about what he'd learned from Agnes Wentworth and what Red Jack had told him. He wanted Moore to hear it, find out if his sergeant thought he was right or only seeing an answer he wanted to see. "I think Sean Doyle's involved in this. But I'm damned if I know how. The things Kelmansky gave away? I'm dead certain they came from Harden Guthrie. Without the blessing of the almighty Relief and Aid. The two of them and Jacob Nathan had a scheme going to get aid to people who'd been cut off for no good reason. Kelmansky found out who needed what, Guthrie made sure he got it and cooked the books afterward. Nathan was the errand boy."

"Robin Hood in Chicago," Moore said.

Hanley nodded. "Only it doesn't seem worth killing over, not by itself. Guthrie's bosses on the executive committee wouldn't be too happy with him conniving at theft. But, in the end, the three of them were doing a decent thing. That'd be obvious if it ever came out. So something else must have been going on. Something Kelmansky stumbled on that posed a threat to someone."

"Doyle?"

"Yes." Hanley wished he could pace, but doubted his leg could take it. He moved to lean against the wall nearby and related what he'd learned from Red Jack about Murphy and the other man who'd left Muskie's Chop House within minutes of Kelmansky the night he died. "Jack saw both of them go the same way the rabbi did. Like they were following him home."

"You think one of them caught up with him at the synagogue?"

"Murphy. Kelmansky was killed at prayer, so whoever hit him couldn't have stood more than five and a half feet. And Murphy was definitely there right after the killing."

"You're certain he works for Sean Doyle?"

"Red Jack's seen him go into Muskie's with a carpetbag every day since the place was rebuilt and stay quite a while. Murphy looked pretty down and out when I found him at Callaghan's saloon on Saturday. I'm sure he can't afford to gamble or buy himself whores, so he has to be an employee. Probably as a bunco-steerer like we thought, given those fancy duds he shouldn't own."

"So why would Doyle send Murphy after the rabbi? What's his interest?"

Hanley took a moment to frame his thoughts. That he found them distasteful made it harder to say them. "What if Guthrie wasn't only slipping relief supplies to Kelmansky and Nathan? What if he was slipping things to Doyle as well? Goods to sell for cash…or cash itself. Or both. The Relief and Aid writes checks and purchase orders. Guthrie had charge of that for the Second District. Easy enough to falsify a check receipt or a voucher for a purchase no one ever made. If the people Guthrie reports to ever try to match the names on the receipts with bank records, he'd get caught…but maybe they don't. Maybe they're satisfied as long as the numbers add up."

"So Harden Guthrie gives Doyle money, Kelmansky finds out about it, talks to Guthrie, and then confronts Doyle?"

"That would explain his coming out of Muskie's. And why Guthrie followed him, if he did. Guthrie'd have been desperate to keep him quiet. He has a reputation as a businessman to protect...and there's the mayoral election as well. He lost last November, but not by much. What if that wasn't his final try for office? Embezzling aid for the poor is one thing, plenty of people might forgive that. But stealing for a gambling prince and brothel owner? Especially the kinds of places Doyle runs? Guthrie'd never be able to hold up his head in public again."

"So Red Jack saw Kelmansky alive around six. Then what?"

"He'd have gotten back to Market Street around half past. Jack saw him turn onto Washington. There's no horsecar line on that street, so he likely walked home. Maybe to save the fare. Even walking fast, it'd take him a good half hour to reach the synagogue. Their minyan—their prayer service—would've been over by then. Nobody there."

"Did he go straight to the synagogue or did he stop anywhere first? At home?"

"Rivka...Miss Kelmansky didn't say so." He paused to recall her exact words that past Friday evening as he'd walked her home. "She said he went out that afternoon and never came back."

"Anyone in the neighborhood see Murphy around? Or your big blond man?"

Hanley shook his head. "No one admits to seeing or hearing anything that night. I do know it wasn't Jacob Nathan who left that boot print in the mud near the synagogue, though." He described their confrontation at the tailor shop. "The big fellow Red Jack saw—he could've made that print. Whoever he is, Guthrie or someone else, he must have seen something. I need to find him." Hanley paused. "Miss Wentworth said Guthrie and Kelmansky had met weekly at his office since late November. Yet Guthrie didn't mention it when I told him Kelmansky'd been killed. He also claimed not to know who owns the warehouse, but I can't believe it belongs to anyone else."

Moore steepled his fingers. "What if Guthrie invited the rabbi to Muskie's?"

"Sounds like you're asking that for a reason."

"I don't know anything concrete," Moore said slowly. "I voted for Guthrie in the election and I wouldn't have if I'd known anything to his detriment. But not long after that—a month or so after his appointment with the Relief and Aid was announced—I heard Doyle paid Guthrie a visit. What they talked about, or even if they talked, my informant didn't know. But the visit took place at Guthrie's home. Not at his business or the relief office."

"They know each other," Hanley murmured. The realization chilled him. Sean Doyle with his claws into Guthrie, who'd seemed like such a decent man. Or maybe Hanley's judgment was so flawed that he'd mistaken a few outward shows of kindness for the real thing. Which would mean he could no longer trust himself. "How well?"

"I don't suppose you recall Doyle mentioning anything about him all those years back?"

Hanley scowled. "Sean Doyle never told anybody anything unless it suited some scheme of his. Including me, for all we were meant to be friends back then. That stone-hearted bastard never knew the meaning of the word." He paced away from the wall. Despite the dull ache it raised, the motion helped discharge some of the anger that always came with thoughts of Doyle. "If Kelmansky went to Muskie's to confront him...I'm asking myself how he'd know who Doyle was. Respectable people don't know men like him by sight. How does a rabbi from a poor section of town cross paths with him?"

"One of his congregants might have a gambling habit or a taste for whores. Kelmansky might've tried to help."

"Maybe it's Nathan. They were close friends. And there's something huge he's not telling me. Maybe the Robin Hood scheme, maybe more. Even being threatened with arrest didn't budge him." He felt reluctant to speak his next thought, but honesty compelled him to. "Or maybe Kelmansky was the one with the problem. Though the man seems to have been a saint and I've no reason to think otherwise."

"So who are your suspects at this point?"

Hanley ticked them off on his fingers. "Murphy, obviously. Jacob Nathan—he's around the right height, and Kelmansky wouldn't have expected an assault from him. Maybe he wasn't only playing Robin Hood. Maybe he was selling on the side."

"What about the daughter?"

Hanley shook his head. "I can't see her battering her father's head in with a holy object and then going home, changing her clothes, ditching the bloody ones, coming back out to the synagogue, and sitting with the corpse the whole freezing night. Or at least enough of the morning for Jacob Nathan to find her there. Plus, I don't see a motive. She seems to have loved her father. She's devastated by his death." He sighed. "And then there's Tommy Callaghan, the saloon owner. No one'll tell me if he's a fence, let alone whether he's close to Doyle. He has to be Doyle's man, though—that's the only way his lying for Jamie Murphy makes any sense. He's local, so if Murphy needed to get rid of the stolen silver fast, Callaghan'd likely be his first choice. I'm going to get a warrant for his saloon, see if I get lucky."

Moore nodded. "Follow up wherever you need to. Let me know how it goes."

03

Downstairs, Hanley got a complaint form from the warrant officer and started to fill it out. He'd just written out Callaghan's name and address when the lobby doors opened and Captain Michael Hickey strode in.

Hanley's jaw clenched. It had been two years since his transfer to the Second Precinct, away from the constant lash of Captain Hickey's sharp tongue, yet anger rose in him at the mere sight of the man. Anger and unease. The West Division's overall commander rarely came by Lake Street Station. He spent most of his time running the Armory stationhouse, where the jail was, and sucking up to crooked politicians. And engaging in some racket or other. He'd been notorious for that ever since the war. What was he doing here?

He caught sight of Hanley and a look of contempt came over his face. He still looked and moved like a prizefighter despite the extra belly padding he'd developed. "Where's your captain? Go tell him I need to speak to him."

Hanley didn't move. "He's in his office. I'm guessing you know the way."

Anger flashed in Captain Hickey's eyes, swiftly quenched by calculation. The sudden change deepened Hanley's unease. Captain Hickey walked over to the warrant officer's desk and nodded toward the complaint form. "What's that?"

"Complaint for a search warrant." Hanley shifted to block his view, but not fast enough. Captain Hickey eyed the form and scowled.

"You want a warrant for Tommy Callaghan's grocery store? Why? Mr. Callaghan is an upstanding citizen hereabouts, and—"

"He runs a saloon." Hanley kept his temper with an effort. "There may be gambling going on there and other illegal activities as well."

"Nonsense." Captain Hickey snatched the complaint form. "Don't go harassing law-abiding people just to make a name for yourself on your first case."

"Make a—" The charge was so absurd Hanley couldn't even repeat it.

Captain Hickey tore the form in two. "Stay away from Callaghan. I've read your case notes. He'd no reason to rob that synagogue. Your job is to find out who did and bring a murderer to justice. If you can't do it, I'll see that this case is given to someone who can."

TWENTY-SEVEN

H ave a little bread, Rivka." Tanta Hannah knelt next to her, holding out a slice of challah.

"Go on, take it," another woman said, patting Rivka's shoulder. Sarah Cohen, mother of Aviva and Rachel, the only pair of twins in the children's English class Rivka taught. She wished fiercely she were there now, sweeping the floor and setting out the primers. Knowing Papa would be here with his pipe and his books when she finished her morning class and came home for the midday meal.

The women, a dozen of them, had been here since eight, coming to keep shiva after seeing their husbands and sons off to work and school. Coming also just to be together. They were all pretending not to be afraid, but who could help it after the incendiary device was thrown into the shul? Rivka shuddered as she remembered the sound of glass breaking and the sudden, stronger odor of smoke in the darkness. If the fire hadn't been so small... Was it only another act of violence brought on by envy of what little her people still had? Or was it connected with Papa's murder?

Hanley should know about it if he didn't already. She would see him tomorrow at Lake Street Station if she could get away, hopefully with Papa's black book. He was counting on her to find it. That he needed her help—had asked for it—gave her a small, warm glow of pride. Onkl Jacob never would, nor would any of the men she knew. Her concerns should be at home, nothing to do with theirs or with the world outside her door. What kind of women was Hanley used to? Were Irish girls so much bolder, so much more a part of things? For no sensible reason, she wondered what kind of girl Hanley expected to marry. Her cheeks warmed. *For all I know, he's married already.*

Tanta Hannah pressed her hand. "Perhaps you'll want it later." She turned and spoke to Mrs. Cohen. Rivka lost track of what they said. Her friend Sisel Klein would have been nice to talk to, but Sisel had stayed home with a chill today. Rivka hoped it wouldn't affect the baby.

Her thoughts circled around to Papa's black book. She wondered what was in it and where he might have left it. Had it been with him when he died?

She grabbed the sofa and pulled herself upright. "I need to…" She nodded toward the rear of the house.

Hannah looked sharply at her. "You don't look well, Rivkaleh. Do you want me to come with you?"

"No. Thank you."

She left by the back door, then hurried around to the front. The latch made a soft click when she raised it and she held her breath. After an eternity, she eased the door open. The hinges made no sound and the gentle voices of the women carried to her from the parlor. No one seemed aware of anything amiss.

Quickly and quietly, she went to Papa's study. If he had come home before he went to the shul, without her knowing it, surely he would have left his book in this room he'd loved best.

The sight of the study made her vision blur and brought a hard lump to her throat. Writing desk, bookshelf, polished oak table with the leather-bound volume of Talmud on it that Papa had been studying. On the dreadful night of the Fire, Onkl Jacob and others had helped them save the table and the Talmud books, throwing them in the butcher's delivery wagon. Papa had built a new desk and bookshelf afterward with scraps of lumber bought cheaply at the re-opened yards. She remembered watching him shape the wood, bringing beauty out of it with a carpenter's plane, and the skill of his hands while she held the nails and gave them to him one by one. Almost, she could hear his voice. *I made things like this when I was young, Rivkaleh. Before I went to yeshiva. My father taught me. Your grandfather, Baruch Hashem. He would have marveled at this city where we live. Rebuilding so fast, as if no calamity can break its spirit.*

Like us, she had said. *We don't break either, do we? No matter what happens.*

He'd smiled and agreed, and they finished their task in companionable silence. All for nothing, she thought now. He would never use his study again.

Impatient, she dashed her tears away. A call of nature could only take so long before Tanta Hannah got worried and came in search of her. She didn't have much time.

⊂ঽ

Callaghan's Grocery was nearly empty, the day's drinking not yet begun. A middle-aged woman in a worn coat was buying a box of salt and half a dozen potatoes. While she finished up, Hanley looked around. There were a hundred places to hide the menorah and spice box. Inside an empty barrel, tucked behind the counter, even under one of the sawdust-covered floorboards. Without a warrant and some help, he had little chance of finding them. *Damn Captain Hickey.*

The woman took her groceries and left. Hanley approached Callaghan, who stood behind the back counter. An open crate sat at one end of it. Callaghan saw him and nodded as he took a tin from the crate. "I'm not selling drink yet. Day's brew'll be ready in an hour or so if you'd like to come back."

"Now suits me fine." Hanley looked Callaghan over, estimating his height. Five-ten, he guessed. A good four inches too tall to have bashed the rabbi's head in. He felt a twinge of disappointment, but he hadn't really expected Callaghan to be his man. He leaned against the counter and peered over it. The lower shelves—the only area in his view—held flour and sugar sacks, all of them unopened. Nothing stuck out from behind them. "I know you lied for Jamie Murphy the other day," he said. "How long has he been a bunco-steerer?"

Callaghan picked up a box of crackers. "I don't ask how a man makes his living. I just serve him drink."

"You do more than that." Hanley pushed away from the counter and ambled around the near end of it. There was nothing beneath it but several crates of liquor bottles and two cans of kerosene. "How long have you been fencing stolen goods?"

Callaghan put the crackers on a shelf. "I run a saloon and I sell groceries. You think different, you're welcome to prove it. But I'd watch yourself. You don't want to be harassing a legitimate businessman. Especially nowadays, with folks on edge like they are."

"I could shut you down." Pure bluff, but Callaghan couldn't know that. "I saw card-playing here the other day. Looked like more than a friendly no-wager game. I tell that to the right people and you'll lose a week's income, easy."

Callaghan's affable expression didn't change. "As I said, you're welcome to prove it. But unless you can, I've no more to say." He took two boxes of salt from the crate and shelved them. "And until you can, I'll thank you not to come by here. I don't need cops bothering my customers."

"Like Jamie Murphy?"

There was no reaction from Callaghan, who continued working. He must be one hell of a poker player. He'd given nothing away, not so much as a twitch. And Hanley had nothing to use as leverage.

He stepped away as if to leave, then turned back. "Did you ever get anything from Rabbi Kelmansky?"

Callaghan turned around. "Who? What're you talking about?"

"Rabbi Kelmansky. And some friends of his. Jews from Market Street. Not far from here. They were going around the neighborhood, giving away food and clothes. They give you anything?"

"Kelmansky," Callaghan said. "That old fellow who got murdered last week. Is that what you're fishing for? You're wondering did I kill him?" He chuckled and shook his head. "The answer's no. You can ask anyone who was here last Thursday. I'll give you their names if you like."

Ω

Rivka paced around the study, frustrated and anxious. No black book in the desk or on the bookshelves. Could Papa have left it in his bedroom? But no, she would have heard him come up before he went to the shul. Where else could he have put it?

She heard footsteps in the hall, along with Tanta Hannah's voice. "...make sure she's all right." Hannah's steps receded toward the rear of the house.

A moment's agonized indecision. Could she get out and around the back in time to meet Tanta Hannah where she should be? Then Rivka moved. She walked into the hallway and stood just shy of the parlor door.

A minute later Tanta Hannah came back inside. "I can't find her, she's not—" She caught sight of Rivka and halted. "You came back in already? Why didn't you—"

"I was in Papa's study," Rivka said. "I wanted to see it...I needed..." She let her voice trail off as if helpless to explain the impulse that had led her there.

Hannah's surprise gave way to motherly concern. She came to Rivka, took her hand, and led her back into the parlor.

ଔ

Hanley's next stop was the East Branch docks, where he hoped to find Paddy at work. Paddy could confirm that Callaghan fenced stolen goods and Hanley hoped to persuade him to swear out a complaint at the Twelfth Street sub-station near his home in Hell's Half Acre. By the time anyone made a stink about it, Hanley would have searched the saloon and found whatever there was to find.

No one had seen Paddy since late Monday afternoon. "He's not been well lately," said a carrot-haired lad of fourteen or so, whose freckled, good-natured face would take him far as a thief. "Might be home sick. Or taking a day's rest."

Hanley thanked him and headed south toward Hell's Half Acre.

Paddy lived on the second floor of one of the better tenements, a three-story brick building near the eastern edge where the poorer streets gave way to slightly more prosperous ones. No one answered when he knocked and he remembered Paddy's youngest girl was still at school. The two older children were likely out working.

The latch was easy to jimmy. Hanley went inside, calling for Paddy. No one answered. He pushed aside the striped calico curtains that divided the large front room and found two sleeping alcoves, both empty. Dresses on wall hooks and a smiling rag doll on one of the beds told him which alcove belonged to Paddy's daughters. The one used by Paddy and his son smelled of unwashed clothes and something medicinal. On a small table that held a plain china washbasin and pitcher, Hanley saw a brown bottle half full of laudanum and a glass with a quarter inch of whiskey in it.

He checked the kitchen, but found no sign of Paddy. Maybe he'd gone to the Skibbereen Club. If he could drag himself out of bed, he'd be there having a drink and playing cards.

The contrast between the dank, stinking Skibbereen and Tommy Callaghan's well-kept saloon hit Hanley as soon as he walked through the door. The next thing that hit him was the emptiness of the place. It was just past midday. A few drinkers should be here by now. But Hanley saw no one, not Paddy, not even the barman.

The hairs on his neck prickled. Another glance around the empty room told him nothing. He checked the storeroom, a ramshackle lean-to on one side of the building whose rickety shelves held beer barrels and crates of cheap whiskey. No one was there, either. He went through the saloon toward the door that led to the rear yard.

Something large and dark lay sprawled in the snow a little distance away, near the outhouse. Hanley hurried over to it, heart racing. He saw splayed legs, an arm bent at the elbow, a face mottled red with blue eyes open and staring.

He dropped to one knee beside the body and breathed Paddy's name, barely aware of fresh pain flaring in his bad leg and the cold snow beneath him. Paddy's shirt and thin jacket were drenched in darkening blood. Hanley steeled himself and touched it. Still wet. From that and the color, Paddy hadn't been dead long. Likely no more than an hour. He peered at the red mess of Paddy's throat and saw what looked like a small, ragged hole.

He staggered up and stumbled out of the yard, heading toward the signal box at the corner of Third and Polk.

TWENTY-EIGHT

July 14, 1861

Midnight had long since passed and the last of the gamblers gone home, as sobered up as the loss of their stakes could make them. Hanley and Doyle sat at their usual table, glasses of whiskey by their elbows as they counted up the night's take. A record, especially from the faro games. Hanley felt jubilant. Not even Charming Billy cracking his usual jokes about Hanley's skill with a pen—"Look at His Ladyship, with fancy writin' and all"—could dent his sense of pride. He knew he'd done well for them tonight. Doyle's calculating glances at Pegeen and his comments about her prospects, earlier in the evening, would be forgiven and forgotten. And Billy could suck eggs.

Doyle grabbed the whiskey bottle—his private stash, smooth and smoky without a drop of water in it—and refilled Hanley's glass. "Just you wait, boyo," he said, clapping Hanley's shoulder. "With that honest face of yours drawing the suckers in, we'll be printing money. Your mam and your pretty sister, they'll have all the fine dresses a woman'd ever want. A fine house, too. And their own coach to take them to the Tremont Hotel for daily lunch if they've a mind." Up went Doyle's own glass. "Here's to us. The best team of sharpers in Chicago. You stick with me, we'll take this city in five years or less. Guaranteed."

"So we will, Sean. So we will. " Hanley downed his whiskey in a gulp and wrote a final number in the book. Harder to grip the pen now. He glanced over and saw his glass was full again. When had that happened?

He set the pen down and rubbed the bridge of his nose. He'd best slow down on the drink, he was losing his sense of things.

"Drink up." Doyle's eyes glittered at Hanley in the lamplight. "It's not gone three yet. We've more celebrating to do."

Three? God, it was late. Pegeen would be waiting for him to walk her home. Bleary-eyed, he looked around the saloon. She wasn't there. She must be waiting outside. Billy, he saw with relief, was skulking in a corner, a look on him like he'd tried cheating at cards and lost. Pig-faced ugly bastard, sniffing after Pegeen like a tomcat in heat. As if she'd so much as grace him with a single smile.

Hanley stood up. The room swayed and he braced himself against the table. "Got to go," he said. "A great night, Sean. Great night."

Doyle's gaze didn't leave Hanley's. "Billy," he murmured with a nod toward the saloon's front door.

Billy left, his sulky look giving way to a feral grin that turned Hanley's insides cold. As Hanley moved to follow, booted footsteps swiftly crossed the floor. Next thing he knew, two pairs of hands gripped his arms. "Wha…" he muttered, too dazed with drink to resist.

From outside he heard Pegeen's cry. "Let go of me, I *won't*—" and the crack of an open-handed slap. Then scuffling and shrieks as Billy manhandled her back inside the saloon and across the floor toward the staircase.

Terror cut through Hanley's whiskey haze. He fought to free himself, to reach Pegeen and Billy, but his strength had gone and his limbs wouldn't obey him. The more he strained against the bully boys' grip, the harder they held on.

Doyle stood and sauntered toward Hanley. His hard-edged smile promised hurt. "A great night, it is," he said. "And it's just beginning."

TWENTY-NINE

January 31, 1872

Hanley braced himself against the side of the police wagon as it rattled through the streets toward the morgue. Paddy's body lay on the floor, wrapped in a length of canvas. Hanley did his best to keep it from rolling with the wagon's motion. In death at least, Paddy Moroney deserved a little dignity.

The patrol squad from Twelfth Street had come and gone from the Skibbereen Club, leaving just one officer to accompany the body. The squad leader had raised no objection to Hanley going too, especially once he knew Hanley was a detective. "Don't know how much there'll be to investigate, though," he'd said, with the weariness of someone who'd seen too much for too damned long. "Man knifed at a place like that? Be a strange thing if it *didn't* happen. Hardly a week goes by that someone around here's not stabbed, beaten, or shot. Usually over a game where somebody with as much liquor as blood in him didn't like the outcome. You think there's more to it, good luck finding out."

The wagon pulled up outside the City Hospital. Hanley climbed awkwardly down and helped the officer carry Paddy's body along the back corridors to the morgue. Through the numbness that still gripped him, he saw Will Rushton and felt a glimmer of hope. If anything in the autopsy could point toward Paddy's killer, Rushton would find it. Then Hanley would have something to work with.

Rushton helped them lift Paddy onto an examining table. As he unwrapped the canvas and carefully stripped the body, laying Paddy's worn clothing aside, Hanley went to the sink and filled a glass of water. He gulped some and spat, rinsing bile out of his mouth. He heard the Twelfth Street officer talking with Rushton, but paid scant attention. The numbness was giving way to pain, guilt, and a smoldering rage. He heard footsteps receding down the hall, then Rushton's quiet voice. "The officer said you found him. Tell me about it."

Hanley swallowed more water and took a steadying breath. Then he told Rushton everything—Paddy's absence from the docks, the empty Skibbereen Club, Paddy's body splayed in the rear yard like a pile of discarded rags. "The snow in the yard was disturbed. Footprints all over, like there'd been a scuffle. Different sizes, too. He was attacked by at least two men. And I saw blood—not just from his throat, but smears here and there in places not too far from him." He couldn't bring himself to call Paddy *the victim*. "He fought them, whoever they were."

"Could you tell if there were more than two?"

"No." He sagged against the wall.

Rushton laid a hand on his shoulder. The sympathy in his face was too much to bear and Hanley shut his eyes. "How well did you know him?" Rushton asked.

"Since we were kids in Conley's Patch." Hanley breathed slowly, hoping it would steady him, despite the stink of carbolic and death. It didn't help much. Paddy had fought for him when they were younger, then taught him how to fight for himself. Given him his first job on the riverside docks. And now he was here, naked and dead on a morgue slab because Hanley had asked him the wrong question.

He opened his eyes again. "He was an informant as well as a friend. I'm guessing someone didn't like something he told me."

"I'll take you to the inquest room if you want. You can sit down there."

Hanley shook his head. "I'm staying." He pushed away from the wall and walked toward the examining table, where he made himself look at Paddy's corpse. Naked, Paddy was scarcely more than skin and bone. His lower body was unmarked. Hanley had a sudden sense of him close by, bewildered by his violent death and counting on Hanley to punish his killer. Morbid fancy, but he couldn't shake it. "Let's get started."

He felt Rushton watching him and did his best to look as if he'd pulled himself together. Rushton fetched his autopsy kit and a record book. Then, with a damp cloth, he gently swabbed the dried blood away from Paddy's neck and torso. The cloth reddened as he worked. Paddy's throat, pale skin dotted with dark beard stubble, clearly showed the fatal wound at its base. As Hanley had thought, it wasn't large. No bowie knife had done this. Something smaller and narrower.

Rushton set the cloth aside and examined the wound. "Carotid artery," he murmured. "He died in seconds." He reached inside the kit and brought out something that looked like an oversized pair of tweezers. "Artery forceps," he said, then paused with the instrument held up. The forceps gleamed in the late afternoon light. "You don't have to watch."

"I'm fine. Let's get on with it." He swallowed more bile as Rushton used the forceps to poke around inside the wound.

"Carotid severed," Rushton said and wrote in the record book. "Wound immediately fatal." With the tip of the instrument he traced the edges of the hole in Paddy's throat. "Inch wide, maybe a little more." He took a folding ruler from his apron pocket and measured the wound from top to bottom and end to end. "Inch and a half across, not even an eighth of an inch thick. Now let's see how long it was. Can you help me roll him onto his side?"

Hanley nodded. He slid his arms under Paddy's lower back and gently lifted. Rushton pushed aside Paddy's unkempt hair and examined the back of his neck. "Smooth as my palm. No pierce mark."

Rushton took a length of string from his pocket and laid it against Paddy's neck from nape to the front of his throat. He marked both spots and set the string against the ruler. "Four inches. So the murder weapon's shorter. Push knife, I'd say. Wielded by someone who knew exactly where to strike. We'll turn him back over now."

Doyle carried a push knife, or he had back in the old days. Plenty of gamblers did. Hanley wasn't sure about Charming Billy. The men from Twelfth Street Station thought Paddy's death was the result of a dispute over a card game, but Hanley didn't believe it. Not a mere two days after he'd talked to Paddy at the Skibbereen Club about Tommy Callaghan, the simple saloon owner no one wanted to admit knowing anything about. He recalled the assault he'd suffered right after he left the place. A warning he hadn't heeded? Was Paddy another? The latest one, starting with the bombings on Sunday night?

"He was definitely beaten before he was killed," Rushton said. "Cracked cheekbone, torn lip, multiple bruises to the face and chest...here's something interesting." He pointed to a vivid bruise on the lower left side of Paddy's jaw. Hanley saw two purpling ridges close together with a shallower mark between them. "See how close the ridges are? Something small and thin and hard left those, and it hit our victim flat on. I'd guess a fist blow from someone wearing a ring. No stone in it. A stone would've left scratches." He paused, frowning at the bruise. Then he went and fetched a small kerosene lamp, lit it, and held it close to Paddy's head.

Hanley fumbled for his sketchbook and pencil. He peered at the jaw bruise. Between the ridges he made out two faint wavy lines, intertwined. "Pattern on the ring. That's what it is."

"I think you're right. Whoever hit him was right-handed."

He knew the ring, or thought he did, and felt the thrill of the hunt stirring beneath the grief and anger. "Can you tell if the knife wound was also made by a right-handed man?"

Rushton shook his head. "I can't say."

"Doesn't matter. That ring should be enough." There'd be no witnesses, Hanley knew, if Doyle was involved. Anyone who'd seen anything would develop swift and deep forgetfulness about the incident. *I should find Doyle and take care of him myself.*

He forced his attention back to Rushton, who was scraping with the flat of a scalpel blade under Paddy's fingernails. Each scraping went onto a small glass rectangle from a stack by Rushton's elbow. "He fought back, all right," Rushton said. "Trauma marks all over his hands—abrasions, split skin on the knuckles. That's where some of your blood smears came from, that and his torn lip. He might have snagged a coat sleeve well enough to pull a thread or caught a strand of hair. I'll see what it looks like under the microscope. Should take me half an hour or so if you want to wait."

⚘

The half hour felt like ten. Unable to stay in the examining room, Hanley went out into the hall. His mind spun like a wheel on an upended wagon with thoughts about Doyle and Paddy, and whoever else had beaten Paddy up in the Skibbereen yard. Charming Billy was the most likely. Doyle trusted him more than anyone, kept him close at hand whenever there was bodily harm to be done. Why had they beaten Paddy? Just to make the lesson more vivid for anyone around to witness it…or did they want to know how much Paddy had said about Tommy Callaghan? He gave a bitter laugh. If that was it, Paddy had died for no damned reason except Sean Doyle's need to punish whoever crossed him.

Rushton's voice calling his name was a welcome relief. He went back into the examining room. Still seated near the microscope, Rushton beckoned him over. "Here's something. Take a look."

Hanley bent and looked where Rushton indicated. At first he couldn't make sense of what he was seeing—a circle of brightness crossed by a ragged smudge, in the middle of which a thin line stood out. Then his eye adjusted and the line's color leapt out at him. Rust red, like a fox's coat.

"Hair," Rushton said. "Human, not animal. Animal hair is thicker and coarser. I found two strands—one under a fingernail, the other on his shirt. Paddy's no redhead, so they're not his. They came from whoever he fought with."

A throbbing ache started at the base of Hanley's skull. He straightened and gripped the sides of the table on which the microscope sat. "I know whose hair it is." Gut-sick and hot with fury, he also felt a breath of exhilaration. He had Doyle now. Maybe. If the hair and the ring mark on Paddy's cheek were enough.

Rushton opened a small wooden box and took something out of it. Hanley stepped aside and watched him as he swapped the glass slide they'd been looking at for another. "I found this on your dead rabbi," Rushton said. "Stuck to his coat sleeve. I sent a note to Lake Street Station, but I guess you haven't been there much in the past few days. It's definitely human. No guarantee it came from whoever killed him, but it's likely."

Rushton made a minor adjustment to the microscope. Hanley looked into it again. This time, the thin line across the bright circle shone pale gold.

ca

Rivka watched the daylight fade outside the parlor window. The soft murmur of women's voices blended with Tanta Hannah's footsteps as she walked around the room setting out siddurs for the evening prayers. The men would arrive soon.

She turned away from the dying sunset and stared at the toes of her slippers where they peeped out from under her skirt. She had found no black book in Papa's bedroom, hastily searched earlier that afternoon. Slipping away from the women long enough to search the shul had so far proved impossible. Had he left the book there or somewhere else entirely—perhaps with whomever he'd gone to see that afternoon? Discouragement settled on her like a weight. If that was it, then the book was out of her reach. Unless she made Jacob tell her where Papa had gone. But, so far, she'd failed at every attempt to do that.

Would Moishe know anything? Maybe she could make him talk. She was still astonished by his involvement in the thefts. She hadn't known he had such boldness in him. That thought recalled her trip to the barracks with Hanley. His face came to mind, sober and full of concern for her. He knew how much she feared having nothing to do but mourn and wait. That was why he'd given her this important task. An outsider, a goy...yet it was oddly comforting that he understood her so well.

A knock came at the door. Rivka listened as Tanta Hannah went to answer it. Her shoulders sagged when she heard the voice that greeted Hannah. It belonged to Lazar Klein, the butcher. He entered the parlor and nodded to her, then picked up a siddur and sat down.

Tanta Hannah's steps receded toward the kitchen. The scent of bean soup grew stronger. She must be checking on their supper. Rivka shifted on her cushion, easing cramped leg muscles. She felt guilty looking forward to the end of shiva, when she would once again be allowed to sit in a chair. Moishe and Onkl Jacob would surely be here soon. She had to find a way to talk to Moishe alone.

The front door opened again and she heard Jacob's voice, sharp and urgent. "Is Moishe here?"

"No. What's wrong? Is Moishe all right?"

"I don't know. I don't know where he is."

He sounded afraid. Rivka gripped the edges of her cushion. Moishe's absence felt like a bad omen. Where had he gone?

♣

"It's my fault." Hanley sat in Moore's office, staring out the window at the gathering darkness. The trip back to Lake Street had been long, tiring, and cold. The office fire was slowly warming his body, but it couldn't touch the chill within. His hard-edged thrill at the prospect of jailing Doyle had faded, replaced by guilt and weary knowledge of the markers Doyle could call in if he needed to. What hope was there against that?

"No, it isn't." Moore sounded impatient, almost angry. "If you and Rushton are right about his findings, Doyle's to blame. If you're wrong, it has nothing to do with you or the Kelmansky case. Either way, you're in no fit state to chase it down now." His voice gentled. "Go home, Frank. Get some rest. Start fresh in the morning."

"They think I'm cracked," Hanley said. "The men from Twelfth Street. They're sure one petty criminal killed another for his winnings. Or because he thought Paddy cheated. Paddy's nobody to them. They don't care."

Moore leaned across his desk. "I'll open a case. You've told me enough to justify it. There's plenty on the detective squad who'd like to see Sean Doyle brought down."

"I want the case. I want to get that bastard. I want—"

"You have a case already." Moore's voice didn't waver. "Whoever this one goes to will get Doyle, if he's responsible."

"You think he's not?"

"I think he is," Moore said. "But we need to make sure any case sticks. We can't give Doyle a chance to persuade a judge that murder charges against him stem from a personal feud with the charging officer."

"And we certainly don't want to parade my past associations." Hanley heard the bitter sarcasm in his tone, but felt too tired to moderate it. "If things even get that far." Slowly, he hauled himself out of the chair. "I thought I'd left Doyle behind me. I'd even made my peace with not killing him and Billy after what they did to Pegeen. And now…" He paused, searching for words. "What are Paddy's children going to do? How do they keep a roof over their heads and food in their mouths? The youngest one's seven. A little girl. I can guess where she'll end up, especially if Doyle gets hold of her." He remembered Molly Murphy, feeding softened bread to her baby daughter. Billy's words about her came back to him—*I hear she's a handful between the sheets*—and fresh anger flared inside. "What a message to the next person who thinks of so much as inconveniencing him. Not only are you dead, your family suffers as well. I can't let him go on, but I don't know how to stop him. Except in the way that'll end with me twisting on the hangman's rope."

"Go home, Frank," Moore said again. "Have a decent meal. Get some sleep. And then get back on the Kelmansky case. You said you think Doyle's involved in that, too. One way or another, we'll get him."

"I hope so. Because, otherwise, I can't answer for what happens next."

☙

"Fella here to see you, Detective," the desk sergeant called as Hanley trudged downstairs. "Been waitin' awhile."

Hanley looked toward the visitors' bench just inside the stationhouse doors. Standing in front of it, a determined look on his face, was Moishe Zalman.

THIRTY

The entryway at Ida's house smelled of pan-fried onions and fresh-baked rye bread. Hanley took a deep breath of the homey scents and felt the chill inside him thaw a little. As he and Zalman wiped their feet and removed their coats, Mam came to meet them. "Ida's just dishing up." She gave Zalman a curious look, but included him in her smile. "Come on back. We'll make room for your friend."

They went to the kitchen and Ida spoke kindly to Zalman in his own tongue as she gave him a set of dishes from a different cupboard than the usual one. His relieved look as he took them puzzled Hanley, but he let it lie. "Where's Kate?" he asked as he pulled out his chair.

Mam handed him a soup spoon. "Out with her young man. He's taking her to supper. I told her to be home by eight."

"You've met him, then?"

Mam nodded. "He came by around eleven and had tea with me. Declan, his name is. Well-spoken, keen to make something of himself. He's going to night school, wants to work in a bank."

That sounded all right. Hanley ate and gradually felt better. The hearty lentil soup and bread warmed him, as did the cheerful talk of everyday things. Paddy's death remained an ache he couldn't banish, but he welcomed the distractions of supper and chat. Still, he couldn't help listening for Kate at the front door.

After the meal, Ida led Hanley and Zalman to the parlor. She lit the lamps and motioned for them to sit. The new window, still bare of curtains, was a blank rectangle of darkness. Hanley turned his body so he wouldn't have to look at it. At least he knew what Zalman wanted to talk about. Their stilted conversation at Lake Street Station had gotten him that much. "So. Tell me what happened last Thursday afternoon."

Ida translated the question. Zalman replied at length, his voice soft and halting. Ida also spoke softly, as she turned his answers into English. "Reb Nathan left the shop at one o'clock. Every Thursday since late November, he is gone between one and two. I take care of things while he is absent. It makes good training for when I will run the business one day." Zalman twisted his fingers in his lap.

So Moishe expected to take over the tailor shop. Hanley tucked that fact away. "Go on."

Zalman moistened his lips. "Reb Nathan took his peddler's cart with him," he said. "He always brought it to the river, to the warehouse I told you of. Things are stored there—food, clothes, coal, kerosene." He leaned forward, locking eyes with Hanley. "Things given so others can live. Things that belong to those who need them. Things we gave to those who could get nothing any other way. A mitzvah, Rav Kelmansky said, to care for those who suffer, when those who should do it will not."

Robin Hood in Chicago, as Moore had put it. It clearly mattered to Zalman that Hanley accept the moral virtue of what they'd been doing. "And Rav Kelmansky? What did he do in all this?"

"He would come to our shop with his book. They would go to the cloth room...where the things were stored. A little later the rabbi would go on his walk."

"To Randolph Street? Taking the book with him?"

Zalman nodded.

"What was in it? Do you know?"

"Numbers. Some writing. I only saw it once, a little. Not enough to know what it said."

"Where's the book now?"

Zalman shrugged. "I don't know."

Maybe Rivka had found it. Hanley hoped so. "So what happened last Thursday?"

Sudden pounding at the front door forestalled Zalman's reply. A jolt of nerves sent Hanley to his feet. "Excuse me," he said and went into the hall.

He opened the door and Kate stumbled inside. He caught her instinctively. Her hair was falling down, half covering her face, and she was shaking. "You're home," she said and began to cry. "Declan didn't...nobody..."

"Declan?" Hanley heard the rough edge of fear in his voice. He forced the feeling down so as not to upset Kate further. "Your Declan? What's he done to you?"

Kate shuddered. "He came to the Kings'. Said he had a message for me. From you. I went outside with him...just for a minute. He shoved me against the wall and put a knife to my throat and tore my dress and—"

"Kate?" Mam's voice behind them, sharp and afraid. She hurried over. "Dear God. What's happened to you?"

"Declan," Hanley said grimly as he handed Kate over. She clutched her coat tight around her, he noticed, and moved as if in pain. He wanted to hit something, go find Declan what's-his-name and bash his skull to pieces. "Your well-spoken young man. He attacked her." He couldn't put the worst of it into words. If the worst had happened. He knew he should ask, but he couldn't face it. Not right now.

Mam shut her eyes and for a moment she looked old. Then she drew a slow breath and herded Kate toward the staircase. "Go make some chamomile tea, Frank. And dish up some soup."

At the base of the stairs, Kate turned and locked eyes with Hanley. "Declan told me...when he had hold of me..." Grim satisfaction flitted across her face. "Before I kicked him where it hurts most. Like you taught me. He let go then and ran off, good riddance to him."

A glimmer of relief broke through his anger. "Good girl. What'd that bastard say?"

Her gaze didn't waver. "He said, 'Tell your brother to back off. Last warning.'"

He knew whose words those were, even though she didn't say the name. Fresh rage drove him across the hallway, where he halted with fists clenched, trembling with the effort not to punch the wall. *God damn you, Sean bloody Doyle. God damn you straight to hell.*

THIRTY-ONE

Zalman looked anxious when Hanley returned to the parlor, but waited patiently while Ida brewed tea and fixed a tray. Hanley envied his ability to sit there, eyes closed, murmuring in his strange language. Praying, probably. Hanley felt too on edge to sit down. He prowled the room until the throbbing in his injured knee made him stop. He wished he had something to tear up or break. Somewhere to go, someone to hurt. First Declan what's-his-name, then Sean Doyle. There'd been a Declan in the old days...Coyne, was it? Declan Coyne. Handsome enough, but somehow rat-like beneath his easy charm. A cousin of Charming Billy's, a hanger-on. Fifteen or so then, too young to catch Doyle's attention for all his trying. *Guess that's changed.*

The parlor door opened and Ida rejoined them. "She's better. Not much harmed, thank goodness. Only some bruising on the throat. She should be all right with food and sleep."

Hanley sank onto the sofa next to Zalman. He wanted to be with Kate, but forced his mind back to business. "Tell me about last Thursday afternoon."

Zalman swallowed, then spoke. Ida resumed her translation. "Reb Nathan did not come back for a long time. I was worried. So I went to find him." Zalman paused, as if steeling himself to go on. "I went to the docks. I did not meet Reb Nathan on the way. When I reached the warehouse, I saw men coming out. One was the foreman. I knew him. So I went to ask where Reb Nathan was." He halted again and seemed to shrink. Whatever came next, it frightened him.

"How many men? What did they look like?"

"Three men. Two were very tall. Like you, but bigger in the shoulders.

Yellow hair." He closed his eyes briefly, as if recalling their appearance. "I had seen one before. His face on walls, before the election. An honest face. But afraid at the warehouse. Afraid of the others."

Guthrie? "Afraid of the other blond man?"

"Yes. Of him and the third man who was with them. A fox-faced man, that one. With hard eyes. I think…" He paused. "I think they were all afraid of him. I was."

"You spoke with him?"

Zalman shook his head. "He asked me my name. Before I could say it, the first blond man—the one I recognized—said I was an acquaintance of his from outside the neighborhood. Then he urged me to leave. 'This is not a good day for Special Relief,' he said. 'I can let you know when would be better.' I did not know why he said that."

"Describe the other two men for me."

"Hard faces, both of them. The blond one's nose was misshapen, it looked like someone had broken it. Wide in the body. Big hands." He paused and, when he resumed, Hanley heard anger in his voice. "He laughed at me. Said, 'Look, another Jew come to play.' Like you would say, 'Look, another rat.' So at least I knew Reb Nathan had come there."

"And the fox-faced man?"

"Not so tall, but broad across the shoulder and hip. A square man. Red hair. Eyes like yours. Fine clothes, good wool. A rich man." He shivered. "He looked at me the way a cat looks at a bird it is thinking of killing."

Hanley's nerves felt taut as fiddle strings. "Did he wear a silver ring?"

Zalman nodded.

Doyle. And Charming Billy. Did Billy work at Muskie's? Had he been there Thursday night?

"What was the man with the broken nose wearing?"

"Trousers…ordinary ones, not fine broadcloth like the fox-faced man. Work boots. A black overcoat." He made a face. "Cheap wool. With a button missing, here." He touched his shirt collar.

Hanley blessed Zalman's eye for detail. It must come with being a tailor. Billy had been wearing a black coat with a missing upper button at

Saint Pat's on Sunday morning. Hanley recalled it vividly once Zalman's story brought it to mind. His description matched the tall blond man who'd left Muskie's right before Jamie Murphy. The man Hanley had thought might be Harden Guthrie. He found himself recalling the strand of blond hair Rushton had found on the dead rabbi's coat. Guthrie's or Billy's? No way to tell. "What happened next?"

"The fox-faced man told me the Special Relief was finished and I should not come back. He told Broken Nose to see that I left. Then he and the first blond man walked away." He wet his lips. "Broken Nose came toward me. I knew he meant me harm. So I ran." He hung his head, his voice dropping to a whisper. "What else could I do? When they come for you, you run. Because that way, maybe you live." He looked up, his eyes moist.

Hanley clasped his shoulder and asked gently, "Did you go back to the tailor shop?"

Zalman nodded. "By then it was three o'clock. My hands were shaking so, I could not work on the suit I was making. So I went to the cloth room and counted things until I felt calmer. After a time, Reb Nathan came back. His cart was broken. Empty, too. He was very shaken. He dropped things as we cleared up for the day—spools of thread, a pair of shears that barely missed his foot. He wouldn't tell me what happened. 'It is not your concern, Moishe. Better you should not know.' That is all he would say. I did not tell him I had gone looking for him. I thought he would be angry that I left the shop empty."

Hanley sat back. Nathan had refused to talk about where he'd spent the afternoon on the day the rabbi died, aside from grudgingly admitting his trip to the warehouse and insisting that he went to see Kelmansky. He shifted his weight, easing a mild muscle cramp. For now, he would take Zalman's account as accurate. "And after that?"

"After that, the minyan. Rav Kelmansky was not there. Reb Nathan told us he had urgent business. Then we went home together for dinner."

"To the Nathans'?"

Zalman nodded, his eyes brightening. "Reb Nathan invites me often. Fray Nathan made chicken with kasha and onions." His mournful expression returned. "Reb Nathan hardly ate anything, even after the Rav came."

Hanley sat up straighter. "Kelmansky came to the Nathans'? What time was this?"

Zalman frowned as if in thought. "Half past six, maybe a little later. Just before Fraylin Tamar—Reb Nathan's daughter—brought out cake."

"Did the rabbi join you?"

"No. Reb Nathan answered the door and he stayed there with Rav Kelmansky. I recognized the Rav's voice when they were talking."

"Did you hear what they said?"

"Only a little. Reb Nathan said, 'And if he doesn't?', and Rav Kelmansky said, '…safe, I promise you.' I don't know what they meant. Then the Rav said something about shul and told Reb Nathan goodnight. Reb Nathan came back into the dining room. He looked as if someone had died. He took a slice of cake, but didn't eat it. He just sat there, shredding it in his fingers."

"When he came back…how much time had gone by, would you guess?"

"Ten minutes, maybe? Long enough to drink a little tea."

"What time did you leave after dinner?"

"Seven o'clock. We left together."

"Mr. Nathan left his house? Where did he go?"

"To the warehouse. He didn't take the cart. I said I would come with him, to help carry things, but he said better I should go home. I walked to Madison Street and over the bridge. My mother and I live just on the other side."

Hannah Nathan or her daughters might confirm when both men left the house, Hanley thought, and if Kelmansky had come there. Maybe Ida could approach them. They might not talk to a strange man, especially a police detective. Nathan could have doubled back to the synagogue—though if Nathan had struck Kelmansky down, the question was why. It sounded as if he'd gotten the same reception Zalman had from Doyle and Billy. If he was in league with them, stealing things and getting paid for it, then something must have gone wrong. Had he asked for a larger cut or wanted to stop? Or maybe Kelmansky learned of the scheme and threatened to expose him.

Hanley shifted again, suddenly itching to get up and pace. Now there might be a motive for Zalman to shade the truth. His descriptions of Doyle and Billy were so detailed, Hanley had no doubt he'd gone to the warehouse and seen them. But maybe he and Nathan were both stealing for Doyle on the side and Zalman was feeling greedy. If Nathan landed in jail, Zalman would presumably get all the gains…and he'd inherit the tailor shop that much faster. Though he'd need to keep his own part in the scheme quiet or he'd be jailed as well. How could he hope to accomplish that if Nathan had nothing more to lose?

Still, the young man was tall enough to have left the muddy footprint in the synagogue yard. Hanley sat back. "Mr. Zalman, would you hand me your left boot?"

C3

After Zalman left, Hanley found it hard to settle. He paced around his bedroom, ignoring twinges from his leg, restless as a skittish horse. His idea of Zalman as murder witness had turned out to be wrong. The young man's feet were narrower than the muddy print and his boots had no maker's mark. Maybe he'd told the simple truth.

He thought of Nathan's boots. They'd showed no trace of blood and, if he'd bludgeoned his rabbi to death, blood would have spattered all over him. Clothing was easy enough to take care of. Leather work boots were another matter. Could Nathan afford to own more than one pair, given what it must have cost to rebuild and restock his shop after the Fire? Hanley doubted it. Maybe Nathan *had* gone back to the warehouse that night—presumably to get whatever he'd failed to get on his afternoon visit.

Hanley walked to the window and stared out at the dark street below. What had happened to Nathan at the warehouse that Thursday? Why was Guthrie there with Doyle? And where was the rabbi's black book? He'd bet a week's wages Nathan at least had some idea.

He pressed a hand against the cold glass. He wanted that book. If Doyle had used the Robin Hood scheme for his own benefit, the rabbi's records might show some interesting discrepancies. But if Murphy had followed and killed the man on Doyle's order, he might have been told to take the book along with the silver. Assuming Doyle knew the book existed. If so, it was gone, and with it a key piece of evidence for taking Doyle down.

He swore and turned away from the window. His eyes fell on his fiddle case, a stark black shape propped against the white wall. Playing sometimes helped him think. But not tonight. Not when the sight of the fiddle brought with it the smell of smoke and the sound of exploding glass.

He went to check on Kate. She was sleeping, curled up like a baby rabbit beneath her quilt. He eased her door shut and went downstairs to the parlor. Ida and Mam were drinking tea, Mam sitting nearest the lamp with her workbasket at her feet. She'd taken nothing out of it and still looked shaken from the evening's events. Hanley glanced toward the teapot. "Enough for three?"

Ida nodded. "Help yourself."

He fetched a cup, poured tea, and sat on the sofa's edge. The tea's warmth seeped into his fingers. He turned the cup slowly, watching the liquid swirl inside it.

"Kate'll be all right," Mam said after a time. She sounded like she wanted to convince herself. He nodded, but didn't trust himself to speak.

"Are you troubled about Mr. Zalman?" Ida asked.

"No. I'm satisfied he told me the truth." Hanley sipped his tea. "It's something else. A reliable witness says he saw Rabbi Kelmansky coming out of Muskie's Chop House Thursday evening." At questioning looks from both women, he explained. "Muskie's is a gambling den, famous among those who like to play for high stakes. Not the kind of place a man like Kelmansky ought to know of, let alone be seen at." He shrugged and drank more tea. "The place pretends to be a respectable restaurant. If you're not a gambler, that's what you'd know it as. Maybe he didn't know any different, but…"

Ida looked sharply at him. "Not a kosher restaurant, I take it?"

"Kosher? What's that?"

"A place where observant Jews would go to eat. There are dietary laws they must follow and the laws matter very much. An observant rabbi like your Kelmansky would be very careful not to eat anywhere that didn't follow such laws or that even *might* not. He would make sure."

Hanley gave a hollow laugh. "I doubt Muskie's gets many observant Jewish patrons. Or that anyone there knows what kosher is."

"Then your rabbi would not eat there."

Thinking of Harden Guthrie, Hanley asked, "What if someone invited him?"

"It would depend on the circumstances. He might go if it was important enough, but he wouldn't eat anything."

Hanley gulped tea. So much for the rabbi's bite to eat. What had Kelmansky told Nathan afterward? He closed his eyes and tried to recall the bits of their conversation Zalman had overheard. *"And if he doesn't?"* *"Safe, I promise you."* Kelmansky had made Nathan a promise. Of safety? For whom, or *from* whom? Why?

THIRTY-TWO

Late Thursday morning, Hanley strode into Lake Street Station and headed for the stairs. He needed warrants for Callaghan's saloon and Jamie Murphy's house, and for Guthrie's recent ledgers and other records. Sean Doyle was guilty—either of simple embezzlement or of ordering Kelmansky killed—and Hanley meant to prove it. That would pay for Paddy as well, if nothing else did. And for what happened to Kate. Moore would know which judge to point him toward.

Raised voices brought him up short outside Moore's office. Shocked, he recognized one of them as Captain Hickey's. "You'll do as you're damned well told, Sergeant. You've been allowed to run this department your way because you got results. But when your hand-picked man starts chasing down wild ideas, harassing law-abiding people, instead of doing his job—"

"Detective Hanley *is* doing his job," Moore shot back. "Or is it now the policy of the department not to follow leads whenever people don't like it?"

"This is a simple robbery gone bad. Hanley's own notes make it obvious." Captain Hickey's voice dripped scorn. "Too bad he hasn't got the sense to follow them. Your captain tells me there was a break-in on Prairie Avenue last night. A silver tea service was stolen. Put Hanley on that. If he can handle it."

"Detective Hanley has my full—" Moore began, but Hanley had heard enough. He rapped on the office door.

"Come in," Moore said.

Hanley entered. Moore was behind his desk, arms braced against it as he leaned toward Captain Hickey. "Sir," Hanley said, snapping the word off as if he were back in the Union army. "I came to report on the progress of my investigation."

"This ought to be good," Hickey said with a sneer.

Hanley bit back a sharp retort. Given Captain Hickey's rank, an ill-timed loss of control would cost Hanley and Moore both. He looked back at his boss. "May I speak, sir?"

"One moment." Moore looked past him. "Are we finished, Captain? My detective and I have business to tend to."

Dull red crept up Captain Hickey's bull-like neck. "Your detective is off this case," he growled. "I warned him to leave Mr. Callaghan alone. Reinhardt will take over. Officer Hanley can chase down silver teapots until I decide what to do with him."

"I will *not*—" Moore began.

"Captain—" Hanley said at the same moment.

Captain Hickey ignored them both and stalked out.

Hanley stared after him. He felt Moore's gaze on him, but was too much in shock to turn around. *Officer* Hanley. And Reinhardt...Captain Hickey had backed Reinhardt for the promotion Hanley had gotten. Reinhardt had seemed so friendly with Doyle when Hanley saw them together on Sunday.

"He can't put you back on the beat," Moore said. "The superintendent will listen to me." He didn't mention Lake Street's captain. They both knew the man was rarely sober and hung onto his job because it suited Captain Hickey to have no trouble from him. Hanley heard Moore move around his desk, then a faint creak as he leaned on its front corner in his favorite listening pose. "So? What else do you have to tell me?"

Slowly, Hanley turned to face his boss. "I'm off the case because Tommy Callaghan complained? A grocery seller and saloon owner?"

"Now we know he's better connected than we thought." Moore gave Hanley an inquiring look. "We don't have a lot of time. Fill me in?"

Quickly and concisely, Hanley recounted everything he'd learned the previous night and that morning. He'd had trouble sleeping and had set out not long after sunup for the bank construction site at State and Washington in order to find Olaf Johansson, Murphy's supposed companion at darts on the night of the murder. "Murphy was at Callaghan's Thursday night, but nine in the evening is as early as I can put him there. He played darts with some Swedes who got there around then. Kelmansky left Jacob Nathan's house around six-thirty, six-forty. That leaves near two and a half hours unaccounted for."

"So Murphy had plenty of time to kill the rabbi, rob the synagogue and hide his takings until he could fence them."

Hanley nodded. "But none of the fences I know admitted to seeing the spice box or the menorah—or Murphy, for that matter—as of Monday. Four days after the murder. He's taking his time to unload his swag. And it's not as if he doesn't need the cash." He thought briefly of Molly. *Does Murphy know what his wife is doing to keep their baby fed? Surely not or he wouldn't bother lying to her about his own criminal activities. The pair of them lying to each other, all just to survive the only way they can.* "Hear anything from Schmidt about Callaghan?"

"Not yet." After Captain Hickey warned him off, Hanley had asked Rolf Schmidt to keep an eye on Callaghan's Grocery, watching for evidence of trafficking in stolen goods. Though Schmidt hadn't had time yet to learn much.

Moore nodded and Hanley continued. "Then there's Murphy's clothes. If he struck that blow, he'd have gotten blood all over his coat and likely his bunco suit as well. The trousers, at least. What happened to them? He had on everyday clothes at Callaghan's saloon. They looked clean and dry according to Olaf Johansson, the fellow he played darts with. His coat, too—which I saw when I spoke with him on Saturday." Hanley drew a breath. "I did the heavy washing for Mam when I was a boy. I know what a thick wool coat looks like after it's been dragged across a washboard. And how long it takes to dry in cold weather. Murphy's coat was clean and hadn't been washed in at least three days. Maybe four. I'd swear to that. But he was wearing it when he left Muskie's. His bunco suit, too. I checked with Red Jack, the newspaper vendor. He saw the trousers that night."

"The murder weapon's another problem. If he followed Kelmansky home, intending to kill him, why not bring a weapon along? Snag a knife from the kitchen, or borrow a cosh from one of the bully boys. Hell, he probably has his own. Why not use it? Or maybe he did use it. That bruise on Kelmansky's right temple...the same height as where the menorah hit and definitely the right shape for a cosh. Only, why hit him with the menorah as well? A weapon grabbed up on the spur of the moment and tossed away in a corner?" He sighed. "Maybe Rushton's right and Kelmansky got that bruise when his head hit the floor. Either way, there's more going on here than Murphy robbing the place and getting caught at it. There has to be."

"You think Doyle sent him after the rabbi?"

"Could be." Hanley began to pace. "The way I figure it, Kelmansky threatened to tell the Aid Society about some scheme between Guthrie and Doyle. He found out about it through Nathan, maybe...that afternoon. Or Guthrie might even have told him. Especially if Guthrie wasn't helping Doyle willingly. I can't see Kelmansky revealing the Robin Hood plan, given how many people depended on it. Not unless he knew of something connected to it that was a lot worse."

Moore frowned. "If you're right, was Murphy meant to kill him? Or just frighten him, and something went wrong?"

"I don't know." Hanley ran a hand through his hair. Again, he thought of the blond hair on the rabbi's coat. "And it might not be Murphy. Though if it isn't, I'd love to know why he followed Kelmansky to Market Street. Jacob Nathan's still a suspect too, if only because he was close by and he's the right height. All I'm sure of is that the simple explanation of a robbery gone bad doesn't add up, whatever Captain Hickey thinks."

"What if Kelmansky is your link to Doyle? Maybe through one of his congregants?"

"I doubt it. Moishe Zalman saw Doyle and Guthrie at the warehouse, and Doyle was definitely in charge. It's possible Nathan had a side deal going to steal for him...maybe as payment for a gambling debt? Though how he could afford to gamble in the first place..."

"Does Guthrie own the warehouse?"

"I'm sure he does. I can confirm it at the courthouse if the deed survived the Fire. If not, the Relief and Aid can confirm it." Hanley began to pace again. "I need leverage to make Guthrie talk. I think he's a good man in a bad situation. Maybe I can offer him a way out. If he's got everyone fooled and is Doyle's willing partner, I can use him to get both of them. But only if I've got proof of what's going on. I'll need a warrant for records at the Relief and Aid. They have pull and I'm just a Mick policeman. The records for December are at the main office. Ledgers, aid vouchers, check receipts. Maybe for January as well. I already saw that month's ledger at Guthrie's office, but who knows where the other paperwork is. I'd best have a warrant for Murphy's house too, with Captain Hickey on the warpath about 'harassing law-abiding folk.' I want to try Callaghan's place again, too." He didn't have to ask whether Moore would help him.

Moore straightened a stack of papers on his desk. "Try Judge Carruthers. He went to school with my brother. I know him well and he trusts my judgment." He left unspoken the rest of that statement— *As I trust yours.*

Words were inadequate to express Hanley's gratitude. The best way would be to prove his instincts right.

"You won't have much time before word gets around," Moore went on. "I can probably save your job, but the superintendent may not overrule Captain Hickey about the case. He'll need something pretty convincing before he takes political heat for implicating someone like Harden Guthrie in a fraud scheme."

"I know." Chicago was no place to tangle with wealthy men, on either side of the law. The thought of risking his livelihood—especially what it would mean for Mam and Kate—made Hanley go cold inside. Then he remembered Kate's near-rape and Paddy's corpse sprawled in the snow behind the Skibbereen Club, and knew it could get worse. But he couldn't back down now. Not with Sean Doyle in his sights. One way or another he'd make the bastard pay for Paddy. And Kate. And Rivka, who'd lost her father because of Doyle's scheming. And Pegeen at long last. "That's why I need your help."

"Can you prove what you need to with a look at those records?"

"I'm sure I can. If any of this was aboveboard, the ledger for December should have Kelmansky's name in it, or Nathan's, or Zalman's, as recipients of that flour sack and those little red shoes and whatever else they gave away. They weren't in January's, from what I saw…not for Murphy's overcoat, anyway. I can trace what names I do find. If they're fake, that makes Guthrie guilty of fraud, since he's the only one who could falsify those books. Same for purchase orders and check receipts. The names on them will be false if the money went to Doyle. All I need is a few names to do it. Enough to make the Relief and Aid launch its own investigation."

Moore glanced down at his desk. His narrow fingers traced a paperweight, a water-smoothed hunk of reddish rock dug out of Lake Michigan's sands. "You'll be careful."

"I know. Hickey's political backers—"

"It's more than that." Moore paused as if gathering his thoughts. "Mike Hickey is Doyle's man. I can't prove it yet, but I've good reason to think so."

The chill settled in the pit of Hanley's stomach. It was an open secret on the force that Captain Hickey had criminal ties to match his political connections, though the stories varied as to which vice king's pocket he was in. If Moore said it was Doyle, Hanley believed him.

"Be careful," Moore repeated.

"As careful as I can."

og

The warrant officer downstairs knew nothing of the change in Hanley's assignment and cheerfully handed over the necessary complaint forms. Hanley wrote out the specifics for each and the warrant officer signed them. As Hanley thanked him and turned to leave, the station door opened. Rivka walked in, her coat and dark kerchief flecked with snow.

THIRTY-THREE

Miss Kelmansky." Surprise made Hanley stumble over her name. She was near three hours early for their meeting, and she looked pale and nervous. "What's happened?"

"Someone broke into Onkl Jacob's shop last night. He found the window shattered this morning with three bricks on the floor inside. When he came and told Tanta Hannah, he said they robbed him and slashed everything they could to pieces—bolts of cloth, all the shirts and suits he was making." She reached a hand toward him in appeal. "You must come. I know this has something to do with my father's death—"

"I can't." He hated himself for saying it, hated seeing the dismay in her eyes, but he had no choice. He needed those warrants before anyone knew he'd been thrown off the case. "I have to get to city hall, now." A familiar figure in blue passed by and he felt a surge of hope. "But I know someone who can go to Market Street. Schmidt!"

Officer Schmidt turned with a questioning look. "*Ja?*"

"Can you go with Miss Kelmansky to Market and Madison? Someone vandalized a tailor shop there. It could have to do with my case. I'll need a description of the crime scene and as many statements as you can get." He turned to Rivka. "Could you translate?"

"I…" She took a deep breath. "I shouldn't even be here. If I go back with a policeman…an outsider…I don't think they will tell him anything."

Damn. He turned to Schmidt. "Try Jacob Nathan, then. It's his shop. He should be happy to help."

As Schmidt left the station, Hanley turned to Rivka. The need to be gone on his errand made him edgy. "So, then. What are we going to do with you?"

SHALL WE NOT REVENGE

Rivka gazed out the window of the horsecar as it rattled down Clark Street, on the way to the temporary courthouse. Everywhere amid the cleared lots and foundation pits she saw signs of rebuilding that only the winter's cold had halted—half constructed walls of red brick and pale stone, meant to house banks, hotels, and even a theater. Solid and invincible, they gleamed in the sunlight. A promise, she thought. Of permanence, of hope, of the reality that life went on.

She glanced at Hanley, who sat near the edge of the wooden bench across from her. He was staring out the window as well, seemingly absorbed in the passing landscape. He must have felt her scrutiny because he looked up and gave her a small, tired smile. "Just two more stops. Not long now."

"Thank you for letting me come with you." Her words conveyed so little of what she felt—surprised, grateful, determined to meet his expectations of her.

"I'm hoping you'll be of help. You can look at some names and tell me if you recognize them." His smile faded as he looked out the window again.

The horsecar jounced over a crack between the roughened blocks of concrete that made up the street. Rivka watched Hanley brace his feet against the floor and did the same. The car slowed, then stopped. An elderly man got off and two smartly dressed young women got on. They sat three rows behind Rivka and Hanley, chattering like squirrels. Rivka caught the words "Marshall Field's" and "new muslins" amid scattered giggles. She snuck a glance at Hanley to see his reaction—were they typical of Gentile girls?—but he appeared unaware of everything save his own thoughts, which he seemed to find a burden.

Amazed at her own daring, she leaned forward. "Tell me what's troubling you."

He blinked like a man startled awake and shook his head. "Nothing to concern yourself with. I was just..." He fell silent. The grief in his face made her throat catch. "A friend of mine died yesterday. I was thinking of him."

217

"I'm sorry." She wished she dared take his hand. "Was he a good man?"

"Not as the world would judge. But he was good to me. And he'd help out most anyone he knew who asked him."

"Then Hashem will forgive," she said.

He met her eyes and his expression lightened a touch. She felt a happy flutter, for no good reason at all.

ଓ

The horsecar pulled up to the curb. Hanley let Rivka precede him to the exit, steadying her with a hand on her elbow as the car swayed to a halt. She looked startled, then glanced away with murmured thanks and flushed cheeks as she stepped down onto the street. He wondered, embarrassed, if he'd done wrong to touch her—but he couldn't very well have let her fall.

Once on the boardwalk, he recovered his composure and gestured southward. "The courthouse is that way. You'll be all right waiting in the lobby while I talk to the judge."

"And then?"

"Then we go to the Relief and Aid's main office." He'd go to Murphy's house afterward to look for blood-stained clothes and the silver, then to Callaghan's saloon if necessary. If he still could. Reinhardt would need his own warrant for Murphy's home in taking over the case, which meant he'd need to make the same journey Hanley had. That would take time. If they were quick, Hanley could get the names at the Relief and Aid and have Rivka look at them on the way back to Market Street. Then he'd persuade her to go home. She couldn't tag along on a search of a suspect's house. Letting her come with him at all was irregular enough.

He watched her now as she marched beside him, a slender figure in dark colors against the whiteness of the fresh falling snow. So much courage in that slight frame, that strong-boned face too full of feeling for prettiness. Away from the world and the people she knew, walking toward a truth that was sure to be painful. Yet, she sought it, no matter if it cost her peace of mind and the regard of those she loved. He vowed then and there that he would see this case through, no matter how high the obstacles placed in his way. Not just to bring Doyle down, but for Rivka too. She deserved no less.

Luck was with Hanley when they reached the courthouse. Judge Carruthers proved obliging and the deed to the warehouse still existed. As he'd thought, it belonged to Harden Guthrie.

And so they took yet another horsecar, this time out Madison Street to the Relief and Aid Society headquarters. They spoke little on their way. Hanley regretted what he knew he'd have to do—report the theft of the aid supplies and shut down the scheme that had become a lifeline for so many. Guthrie and Nathan might even face charges if the Relief and Aid decided to make an example of them. Zalman too. And he still wasn't certain how Doyle figured into things. Had he ordered the rabbi's death or simply wanted him followed? Intimidated? Spied on, to see where he went and who he spoke to?

Hanley tensed at that thought. If Murphy was Doyle's spy, the attacks on the synagogue and Nathan's shop might be more than random acts of ill will. Anyone close to Kelmansky could be in danger. Nathan, Zalman, and Rivka, as well.

⟨ℬ

Committee Chairman O. C. Gibbs was out when they arrived. Gibbs's secretary, a sour-faced angular fellow somewhere past fifty, took his time examining Hanley's warrant. The secretary reminded him of a strict schoolteacher looking for spelling errors and inkblots. Hanley chafed at the delay. Rivka's presence was some comfort at least. Knowing she was there made him feel steadier. "This seems to be in order," the secretary said finally, as if he wanted to say the opposite. "I'll bring you the ledger, Officer."

"Detective." He quashed an uneasy pang at the use of his rank, wondering how long he would keep it. "The warrant covers check and voucher receipts as well, for December and January." He stepped past the secretary to the door of Gibbs's office. "If you'll just show me where they are?"

The ledger was in a small bookcase next to Gibbs's desk. The desk held filled-in receipt books neatly stacked, a few letters from the previous evening's post, and a pair of wooden trays marked "Checks Received" and "Checks Disbursed." Several slips of paper were in the "Received" tray. The other was empty.

"Are these for January?" Hanley asked.

The secretary's scowl deepened. "I'll see." He sorted through the paper slips one by one while Hanley skimmed the ledger and tried not to show his rising frustration. He caught a glimpse of Rivka in the outer room, pacing as if anxious, and his frustration increased. Was the damned fellow being slow on purpose?

He caught Rivka's eye and gave her what he hoped was a reassuring nod. Then he went down the lists as fast as he could manage. No names looked familiar, but he found some of the items he sought five pages in—a twenty-pound sack of flour delivered to Mary L. Boothe of South Franklin Street on December 4th, several clothing items and a pair of child's red shoes to the same place ten days later. He marked Mary L. Boothe's name and address along with three more between the flour sack and the clothing—Aloysius Frasier, Geraldine Willems, and Daisy S. Price. Each had received donations during Advent and all had addresses in the Market Street area. He looked for Molly Murphy, but didn't find her. If any Aid ladies had visited the Murphy household, Molly and Jamie had likely been cut off, just like the Pavlic family.

The thought of Molly reminded him of his next destination. He tucked the ledger under his arm. "I'll take those receipts now. And the ones for December."

The secretary held the papers close to his chest. "These are confidential records. They do not leave these premises. Mr. Gibbs would not allow it. You may view them here."

Hanley held out a hand for them. "The warrant permits me to search for and seize the items in question. They'll be safe with the police department and will be returned as soon as we've finished with them."

The man stiffened further. "Mr. Gibbs—"

"Is not here," Hanley said. "Time is essential. There are penalties for impeding an investigation. I'm sure you don't want to be guilty of that." The word *guilty* made him flinch inside, but he kept it from showing. If Mr. Whatever-the-Name found out Hanley had no right to demand these documents, that he'd gotten his warrant under false pretenses... He suppressed a shudder. O. C. Gibbs would have his head and that would be just the start. He could be accused of harassment, insubordination, even criminal intent. God knew if Sergeant Moore could help him against all that. But this was his best shot at proving Doyle guilty of embezzlement, maybe more. His best shot at making sure Doyle answered for the suffering and deaths he'd caused.

He glanced at Rivka and their eyes met. He saw her anxiety fade, replaced by determination. She was ready to help, waiting only for word from him.

Lips pursed, the secretary reached into a desk drawer, fished out two large India-rubber bands, and wrapped them around the receipts. "I shall inform Mr. Gibbs of your conduct," he snapped as he handed the small bundles over. "If he complains, it'll cost you your job."

It just might, Hanley thought. He took the receipts and rejoined Rivka, caught between fear and a fragile sense of hope.

CB

"I don't know any of these names." Rivka read them as they rode back toward Market Street. "None of them are Jewish."

"What about neighbors who aren't Jewish?"

Rivka frowned at the ledger. "This is not right. Mary L. Boothe... that address is next to Pavlic's Bakery. A wheelwright's before the Fire. It's empty now. No one has rebuilt there yet."

She handed the ledger back. Hanley had thought Mary Boothe's address might be the Pavlics', though he couldn't recall the bakery's exact number. He wondered if the other addresses would turn out to be empty lots as well and whether the names were former owners or had come from another source. Ida had a city directory that might be some help even though it was a rushed job put out right after the Fire. Property deeds might even exist for a few sites, though Hanley knew he couldn't count on it.

They got off the horsecar at Randolph and Franklin. "Where do we go now?" Rivka asked.

She wouldn't like what came next, but he had to say it. "You need to go home. You've helped all you can for the moment."

"But—"

He held up a hand. "I'm going to execute another search warrant. You can't help this time and, if I find anything, your being there could cause trouble later on." He didn't tell her how legally suspect the search of Murphy's house was likely to be, given his suspension from the case. He hoped that he and Moore, between them, would be able to convince a judge the warrants had been executed before his replacement was fully briefed and, therefore, constituted Hanley's final legitimate actions as the investigating officer of record.

Rivka was gearing up for further protest. He could see it in her face. "Have you found your father's book yet?"

The question brought her up short. "No."

"We need it. It could help put some bad people in jail."

"Including my father's killer?"

"I'm sure of it." He dug out his sketchbook, scribbled Ida's address, tore out the page, and handed it to her. "When you find it, send me a note here. We'll figure out how to meet some way that won't cause you too much trouble."

She tucked the paper into her coat pocket. "There is trouble enough, Detective Hanley, everywhere I turn."

THIRTY-FOUR

Hanley had scarcely knocked on Molly's door when it was flung open. Her fierce glare gave way to surprise as she saw him. Then she launched herself at him, fists raised. "You lying bastard! He's gone because of you!"

Hanley caught her arm before her blow could connect. He staggered under her weight. She folded in his arms, fury giving way to tears. "Jamie didn't kill anyone. And you won't find a damned thing in this house. But you don't care. Lying bastards, the lot of you." She tore herself out of his grasp, propelled by renewed anger. "Go ahead. Search all you like. There's nothing in this house that doesn't belong to us. Not one blessed thing!"

Hanley walked inside. Molly followed, slamming the door behind them. "You'll not be keeping him in jail. I'll get bail money somehow. I'll—"

"Jamie's in jail?"

She stared at Hanley as if he'd lost his wits. "Didn't your friends take him away to the Armory not more than an hour ago? Didn't they send you back here with some paper or other, gives you the right to snoop round as you please? I know how you work. You've all decided he's guilty and you're here to make sure of it. But I won't let you. Whatever you say, I'll say different. There's no stolen goods here and my Jamie didn't kill anyone. All your lies can't make it so."

Hanley felt his nerves go taut. Captain Hickey had lost no time setting things in motion. "The officers who came here...what did they say? Exactly?"

Confusion crossed her face. "What're you asking me that for?"

"Please. Just tell me what they said when they took Jamie."

"Said he was under arrest for theft and murder, didn't they? That Mr. Kelmansky. That kind old man." Molly's voice shook as she spoke of him. "Then they said they'd be back to search my house and I shouldn't touch anything."

"And then they left you?"

"Then they left me."

He heard the baby's voice from the kitchen, a wordless babble just shy of a wail. Molly glanced toward the sound, then back at Hanley. He pulled his own search warrant out of his pocket. "I do have a right to search this house. For what is in here." He held the paper toward her. "I didn't know about Jamie being arrested. Who came for him? What did they look like?"

She stared at the warrant. "How do I know what this says?"

The baby's calls grew louder. Hanley closed his eyes against a creeping headache. Molly couldn't read. "Two items were stolen from the Jewish temple near here. A silver candelabra and a small silver box. Kelmansky was murdered the night they were taken and I know Jamie was there. Whether he killed Kelmansky remains to be proved. But if there are no stolen items here, that makes it more likely Jamie's innocent." He didn't mention bloody clothing. "Please. Tell me who took him."

She folded the warrant closed, but kept hold of it. "You lied before. Why should I believe you now?"

"I don't have an answer for that." He waited, willing her to trust him.

"There were two of them," she said finally. "One a bit shorter than you, looked like a bully boy in a fancy copper's uniform. Dark hair and a hard face. The other one called him 'Captain.'"

Hanley's tension rose another notch. That sounded like Mike Hickey, personally handling an arrest in Lake Street's jurisdiction. Had Doyle asked him to? "And the other man?"

"Tall as you, but bigger 'round the middle. Younger, I'd be guessing. Looked German. I've seen him around walking the streets."

Schmidt, most likely, Hanley thought. This area was his beat. Reinhardt must have gone for the search warrant while Schmidt and Captain

Hickey took care of the arrest. Why wasn't Schmidt on guard here until Reinhardt came? "Did they give you any names?"

She shook her head.

"And they told you they were coming back to search the place?"

She nodded. "I followed them as far as I could. I kept telling them, 'It's not Jamie, it's not Jamie, you've made a mistake,' but they wouldn't listen. Told me to go home and wait for them, and not disturb anything. In my own house!"

Hanley shifted his feet. There wasn't enough room in the narrow hallway to pace. If Murphy had been taken off more than an hour ago, then Reinhardt must have headed straight to the courthouse with a complaint. Which meant Reinhardt, and Captain Hickey, probably knew he'd already done the same thing. He didn't have much time before Reinhardt showed up.

"I believe you," he said to Molly with all the sincerity he could muster. He was inclined to—not that the stolen items weren't here, or that Murphy hadn't taken them, but at least that she thought so. Which also meant that, either she hadn't seen any bloody clothes, or there weren't any. He wasn't yet ready to deal with the implications of that.

"I'm going to look through your house," he said. "You can watch. I need to do it before the other men come back."

Her grip tightened on the warrant. "Will you help Jamie?" Tears brimmed over. "That poor old man. He gave us a box of food once when we hadn't a blessed thing to eat and I'd come back empty from the Aid. Them people wouldn't give us a thing, said we were on the 'Denied' list. He gave Jamie that fine coat, too. Jamie'd not have hurt him for the world."

"If Jamie's truly innocent of murder, I'll do everything I can for him." That was the most he could promise her.

She handed the warrant back. "Look wherever you like."

His first stop was the cramped bedroom which held a cheap pine wardrobe, a bedstead, a blanket-stuffed crate where the baby clearly slept, and a battered-looking washstand. Molly hung in the doorway, holding the baby, her face drawn with anxiety. He opened the wardrobe doors and halted in surprise. Next to a pair of calico dresses hung a man's suit—trousers and jacket of brown broadcloth and a wool-fronted vest with a silk back. Beside the suit was an evening shirt with button cuffs. The buttons were pearly ovals about the size of a fingernail.

He remembered that same shirt on one side of the kitchen table, a cuff button half sewn on, the needle threaded through the cloth just above. Molly had been mending it on Saturday when Hanley asked her about Murphy's boots. He took it out and examined it. Under the left cuff button, he felt a nubbin of bunched thread. The fabric around the right button was completely smooth.

He put the shirt back. There was no trace of blood on it. Nor had there been on Saturday afternoon. Bloodstains were hard to get out. They almost always left some mark behind.

He took a deep breath, then looked through the wardrobe again. The spice box and menorah weren't there, nor was there any suitable hiding-place for them. He went to the bedstead next and lifted the fat straw ticking. He found nothing underneath. The ticking smelled musty and the rucked-up sheets had been patched several times. Wherever Murphy spent his bunco-steering wages, it wasn't on his household. Before leaving the room, Hanley looked in the crib and tested the floorboards. None were loose, not even under the bedstead.

His search of the kitchen proved equally fruitless. He rolled his shoulders, working out the kinks from shifting the meager furniture, then headed outside toward the rubbish dump. The cold at least kept it from stinking much. He paced around it, trying to work out how Murphy might have marked the spot if he'd hidden his swag amid the garbage.

The swag would be near the edge, he decided, where Murphy wouldn't have to dig too far in. Wrapped up, surely, against any telltale glint. The final clue would be some distinctive piece of rubbish easy to spot amid the snow-covered vegetable peelings, apple cores, and dirty rag scraps too small for re-use. That bright blue half of a broken bowl to his right, maybe. Or the dented brass spittoon a few feet to his left. Or the tattered rag doll with one yarn braid torn off and a button eye missing.

He took off his overcoat and laid it on the dirt, then rolled up his sleeves and plunged in.

Ten minutes' careful search netted him nothing. He even looked inside old tea tins and half-crumpled salt cartons—any container large enough to hold the spice box. Nothing. He straightened, breathing shallowly against the odor of rotting food that clung to his arms.

Molly's voice carried across the yard. "I've told you and told you, my Jamie's done nothing. You'll not find what you're looking for here, and that's that."

Hanley shrugged into his coat, eyes on the house. Reinhardt had arrived. Maybe Captain Hickey as well. He thought of nipping away down the alley, but decided against it. Flight would only prove he knew he wasn't supposed to be here. Better to brazen it out if he wanted his search—and its interesting lack of results—to stand. Had Murphy fenced the stolen goods since Monday? Or was Molly right and they'd never been here? If they weren't here and they hadn't been fenced, where were they—at Callaghan's? Had they been there since the night of the murder?

He reached the back door just as Reinhardt stepped out of it. Detective Reinhardt now, he supposed, at least for the moment. Only Hanley's quick step backward saved them from colliding.

"Hanley." Reinhardt's contempt showed plain on his pinched face. "Isn't Prairie Avenue a long way from here?"

"My next stop, as a matter of fact." Hanley stepped past him into the kitchen. He wondered where Schmidt was—or Captain Hickey—come to that. "I thought to save you some work before you take over."

"Your warrant is invalid," Reinhardt said. "You got it under false pretenses. Captain Hickey has been notified."

Hanley didn't drop his gaze. "I acted in good faith. Up until two minutes ago, as far as I knew, I was still the officer of record. Now that you're ready to work the case, I'm happy to give it to you."

Molly stepped toward him. "But—"

He held up a hand to forestall her, then continued talking to Reinhardt. "You do have a valid warrant to search this house?"

"House and property," Reinhardt answered coldly.

"I'd like to see it."

"You've no standing to see it."

"I want him to read it for me," Molly broke in.

Bless the woman, she was quick. Reinhardt looked as if he'd bitten something rancid. He shrugged and handed the paper over.

Hanley took his time reading it. The warrant mentioned only the spice box and menorah—no clothing. Heart hammering in his chest, he gave it back with a glance at Molly. "The warrant allows this officer to search this parcel of land and all buildings on it. That means your house, yard, and outhouse. Just as I would've done."

She held his gaze a moment, as if taking in what he'd said, and nodded. "Then he'd best do what he came for."

THIRTY-FIVE

Standing in the snow, a few feet from the rain barrel, Rivka's nerve failed her. She had been gone too long to simply climb back in through her bedroom window and pretend she'd never left. Tanta Hannah must have gone up at least once to check on her. *Where can I say I've been all this time, that she'd believe?*

Falling snow brushed her face. Its touch felt like a kiss from her father. *You will forgive me*, she thought, *even if Tanta Hannah doesn't.* She smoothed her kerchief, tucked a wisp of hair beneath it, and started toward the rear steps.

The back door opened. Tanta Hannah came out, her face dark with anger. "Good of you to come home," she said, her voice low but fierce. "I have watched for you for hours. People were starting to talk, wondering where you were. Wondering how long a headache could possibly last." She stood halfway down the back steps, arms folded, breath coming out in rapid white puffs. "Where have you been?"

"I was with Detective Hanley." Anger of her own made Rivka match Hannah's glare. "Helping him find out who killed Papa."

"That is not your place."

"Isn't it?" She strode up the steps until she and Tanta Hannah stood level. "I know so little, I can do almost nothing. But what I can do, I will. Which is more than I can say for others."

Hannah blanched. "What do you mean?"

"I saw Onkl Jacob Saturday night." A memory came to her as she spoke—Tanta Hannah after services on Saturday afternoon, shutting her out when she asked why Onkl Jacob came to see Papa the day he died. Then on Sunday, insisting on staying with her until she felt able to come down for shiva. As if she'd guessed, and feared, what Rivka meant to do that day. "How long have you known Papa and Onkl Jacob were stealing the things they gave away? You of all people should have known we didn't have those things to give—you, who have acted as our *rebbetzin* in the years since my mother died. Everyone tells everything to the rabbi's wife. She watches out for everyone, makes certain no one is in need or in pain, without the rabbi and other leaders knowing it. You filled that place because I couldn't. Where did you think all those things were coming from?"

"Rivka—" Tanta Hannah began, but Rivka overrode her.

"Onkl Jacob loves and trusts you beyond all people, even my father. I can't believe he didn't confide in you."

Hannah's face paled. She reached out and gripped the stair railing. "He did not tell me. Because I never asked him to."

Rivka sagged against the rail. The tensions of the day were catching up with her. "You should have told Detective Hanley. You and Onkl Jacob together."

"A policeman? A goy? Tell him we were stealing. . .we Jews were stealing from good Christians because they failed to care for their own? What do you think your policeman would have done, Rivka? Thanked us for our honesty and given us a reward? You can't be such a child as that. Jacob would have ended up in jail. Or worse."

Rivka's head snapped up. "Detective Hanley isn't like that. We're not in the old country now. We can trust him to—"

"Trust him? Trust him to let us break the law, as they see it? Trust him not to think Jacob is a killer as well as a thief, who murdered your father in some dispute over their scheme?" She paused for breath, then continued more gently. "And even if we could trust your Hanley, what about those he works for? How much would he. . .or could he. . .keep secret from them? And what would happen to Jacob then? To all of us?"

Confusion swamped Rivka. Too many questions, not enough answers. Tanta Hannah was wrong, she felt it in her bones, but couldn't come up with the words to say why. Bewilderment made her latch onto the one thing Hannah had said that she felt up to dealing with. "Why do you call him 'my' Hanley?"

"Oh, Rivkaleh." Tanta Hannah's hand cupped her cheek, a brief and welcome warmth. She sounded as if she might cry. "You know already. You just haven't told yourself yet."

⊗

Hanley hurried over the rough boardwalk toward Market Street. Prairie Avenue lay a long distance south and east of Jamie Murphy's house and he had no intention of going all that way. He couldn't go to Callaghan's either, now that Reinhardt had caught up with him. That search warrant was useless. Instead, he headed toward the synagogue.

He didn't know what he expected to find there. But the search at Murphy's hadn't gone as he'd thought it would and he harbored a hope that another look at the crime scene might jog something in his memory. As long as he was in the neighborhood he might as well try it.

The synagogue was empty, as he'd expected at mid-afternoon on a weekday. Some things weren't all that different between synagogue and church. He walked toward the spot where Kelmansky's body had lain, pulled out his sketchbook, and turned to the drawings he'd made.

The bloodstains had been scrubbed away. Not a trace remained of the boot prints Jamie Murphy had left or the pooled blood around the dead man's head. Other than that, every detail was exactly as he remembered. He looked around, but nothing new leapt out at him.

Discouraged, he found himself focusing on trivialities—the plain glass in the windows, the unadorned wooden benches. The pews at Saint Pat's had padded kneelers for comfort during prayer, but there were no kneelers here. The Jews of Market Street seemed not to believe in comfort during worship. Or he might simply be failing to understand yet another thing about these people and this case.

As he turned to leave, the door swung open. Rivka stepped inside, saw him, and halted. She looked startled by his presence. The sight of her lifted Hanley's spirits. Then, abruptly, he felt awkward, as if he were sixteen again and a mere tenant in his own lanky frame. "I'm sorry, I just came to…never mind. I'll leave you in peace if you want to pray."

"I don't know what I want. I just needed to come here." Her own words seemed to surprise her, as if they'd spilled out before she could stop them. She came further in, hesitant as a deer edging out of the woods. "Did you learn anything in your search?"

He nodded. "Quite a bit. Though I'm not sure what to make of it yet." He wished he could pour it all out to her, see what she thought. Share with her the puzzle of it, which only got more tangled the more he discovered. It had felt good to have her with him before, a friend among these wary people who remained such strangers to him. But he'd have to explain too much, including things no decent young woman should know of. Would she despise him if she knew about his past? Or would she see he'd left that Frank Hanley behind? "I should go," he said, but didn't move.

"What is your church like?" she asked.

"It's big. Full of light. It's called Saint Patrick's. They say he drove all the snakes out of Ireland." He felt himself relaxing as he talked. "There's stained glass in the windows, colored pictures of saints and of Jesus preaching to the people." He nodded toward the benches. "The pews aren't much different than those, though we've got kneelers in front with padding." He grinned. "Hard to keep your mind on prayer when your knees are half-killing you."

"It sounds beautiful. And different." Her voice held a wistful note. Then curiosity crossed her face. "Why do you kneel down to pray?"

"Don't you?"

She shook her head. "We stand. Papa says—" She broke off, then continued. The look on her face, loving memory blended with grief, made Hanley's throat catch. "Papa said we are Hashem's children, and children don't kneel to the Father who loves them."

It took a moment for her words to sink in. When they did, Hanley felt robbed of breath. "Your father was standing while he prayed."

"Yes." She looked confused, as if wondering why it mattered.

A thousand words tumbled through his mind, not one of them adequate to say what he felt. He settled on, "Thank you," his voice taut with excitement. Then he bolted out the door.

THIRTY-SIX

anley got off the horsecar and hurried south toward Harrison Street. Wagons and coaches rattled past and he heard a train whistle shriek as it approached the Rock Island depot several blocks away. The sound added to his sense of urgency. He wasn't sure how much time he had left for what he needed to do.

Twenty minutes' walk took him past busy commercial blocks and storefronts, through gradually thinning crowds of shoppers and workers. As he neared Harrison and the rough-edged Biler Avenue district, foot traffic dropped off sharply and the occasional friendly nod gave way to the blank faces and hurried steps of people wishing to be gone before something happened. Up ahead, the shadow of the new Armory jail darkened the boardwalk. Part police station and part prison, the ramshackle wooden structure had been a schoolhouse until the police department took it over as a temporary replacement for the original armory—a squat, forbidding pile near the city center that hadn't survived the Fire.

Bits and pieces had been added to the new armory in the months since October—holding cells, an extra room for storing paperwork saved from the burned-out station, and more work space, as the number of officers assigned to the First Precinct expanded. The place now looked like half a dozen schoolhouses all jumbled together by a squad of blind carpenters.

Some things about the Armory hadn't changed. It was still a depressing place, a way station toward hard time in the county or state lockup. And it was still commanded by Mike Hickey.

Please God, let me not run into Captain Hickey today. If I see him, I might deck him, and then there'll be real trouble.

Hanley walked through the doors as if he had every right to be there. Like its predecessor, the new Armory smelled of coal dust and sweat and the sour stink of fear. He did his best to ignore the atmosphere. With luck he could bluff his way to the prison cells, before Captain Hickey got wind of it, and have a quick chat with Jamie Murphy. The sole eyewitness to Kelmansky's murder.

That thought, fully formed for the first time, gave Hanley a sudden qualm. If Murphy talked to him and Doyle found out, was he signing the man's death warrant? *Suspect died in custody, Your Honor…shanked in a prison fight. You know how crowded those basement cells get, half-a-dozen men fighting over the same cup of water.* Followed by a posthumous conviction, most likely, with everyone breathing a sigh of relief that a violent criminal had met a well-deserved end. Except that Murphy wasn't one and didn't deserve any such thing. Thanks to Rivka, Hanley knew that now.

Not this time, he vowed as he approached the desk sergeant. In his mind's eye he saw Paddy's slashed throat, and Kelmansky's battered head, and then Pegeen with her torn clothes and swollen mouth and sightless upward gaze. He suppressed a shudder. *Not another death because of Doyle.* Somehow he'd find a way to keep Murphy safe.

He gave the desk sergeant Murphy's name and the particulars of his arrest. The sergeant's chubby face was unshaven and he looked as if sleep came hard these days. Hanley wondered how many duty shifts in a row he'd pulled lately. The department was still sorting itself out in the wake of the Fire, which might play to his advantage. "Lemme check for the paperwork," the sergeant said. "What'd you say your name was?"

"Hanley!" The angry shout cut across the lobby.

Hanley stiffened, then turned. "Captain Hickey," he said as coolly as he could muster.

"What the hell are you doing here?" The man's tone could have frozen hot coffee. "I heard about your little stunt earlier today. You want to keep that badge, *Officer,* you get yourself down to Prairie Avenue, talk to the robbery victims, and don't do one damned other thing unless your captain at Lake Street orders you to. You got me?" He raised his voice to carry, making sure every uniform within earshot could hear him. "I want everyone paying attention. This man up here right now, Officer Francis Hanley, is not to be permitted within the walls of this stationhouse. He is not to go near Jamie Murphy of Franklin Street, the suspect brought into custody today for robbery and murder. He no longer has any authority in that case and will not be allowed to interfere with it." He shot Hanley a viciously triumphant look. "If you see him here again, arrest him."

Shock robbed Hanley of speech. The desk sergeant's expression mirrored his own. He looked around the room and saw varying degrees of surprise, even dismay and, on some faces, cold calculation. Some of those were men he knew, had worked with before he transferred out. He thought he'd earned their respect by doing his job well. That they would accept—even seem to back—Captain Hickey's extraordinary statement rocked him like a gut punch.

"Now get out," Captain Hickey barked.

Fury shot through Hanley. He felt his muscles lock with the effort to keep from smashing a fist into the man's sneering face. It took all the willpower he had to turn and go without a word. He felt Hickey's eyes burning into him as he left.

He reached the boardwalk and headed down the street, consumed by frustration so intense that he barely noticed where he was going. How was he going to get to Murphy? Captain Hickey had every right to bar him from the Armory, at least until Hanley's appeal of his removal from the Kelmansky case reached the superintendent. The arrest threat was excessive, but even there Captain Hickey could claim Hanley's insubordination made it necessary. How much time did he have left to find out what Murphy knew? Would Doyle want Murphy alive long enough for a trial or had Hanley just made him too much of a liability? *Like Paddy*, he thought, and fought back a surge of guilt.

He shoved his hands in his pockets and touched folded paper. The search warrants. He'd gotten them just a few hours ago, but felt as if he'd lived a week since.

He turned up his coat collar and hurried toward East Randolph Street.

 C8

Guthrie was out on inspections according to Agnes Wentworth. It took some persuading and a mention of the Relief and Aid's head office, but Hanley finally left with the January ledger. After stopping at Lake Street to leave it with Moore, Hanley made his way all the way down to the burgled house on Prairie Avenue. Its residents weren't pleased to have been kept waiting for the attention of the Chicago Police Department, but Hanley put on his best manners as he asked about their stolen tea set and got out as soon as he could. He took a long horsecar ride up State Street, then headed back to Lake Street, to transfer his notes to the proper paperwork in scrupulous detail. Let Captain Hickey chew on that. He would also talk with Moore about the Relief and Aid records. By now, Moore should have had time to look them over.

THIRTY-SEVEN

Mary L. Boothe isn't in the latest city directory," Moore said when Hanley reached his office. "She's in the previous one. On Madison west of Clark. I found the three other names you marked, but none of their addresses match, either. Mrs. Willems lives all the way up north on Schiller Street, the German neighborhood. Mr. Fraser's not far from you on West Monroe. Miss Price lives on Ewing just off Jefferson."

"What about Andrew Osgood? His name was down for Jamie Murphy's overcoat."

"I found him, too. 635 West Carroll Avenue, just across the river."

"So the names are real, but the addresses aren't."

Moore nodded. "I'd guess they're all empty lots."

"What about the check receipts? Those names in the directory, too?"

Moore glanced down at the slips of paper on his desk. When he answered, he sounded strained. "I found some of them. Joseph Doherty, carpenter, thirty dollars for tools. Liam O'Mara, no occupation, twenty dollars for lumber. Rose Meredith, seamstress, forty dollars for a sewing machine. William Alder, cabinetmaker, sixty dollars for two doors and some windows." He gave Hanley a sober look. "One name I couldn't find in the directory. Pegeen Sullivan. Serving girl."

Hanley stiffened. "Let me see that one."

Moore dug through the receipts and handed one over. The black ink showed stark against the thin white paper. *Pegeen Sullivan, eighty dollars.* Dated December 23rd. In Harden Guthrie's slanting hand with his initials in the corner.

"I don't suppose it's another Pegeen Sullivan?" Hanley asked. His mouth felt dry, his gut tight, as if someone had wrapped an iron band around it.

Moore shook his head. "I found thirty female Sullivans in the directories. No Pegeen, no Peggy, no Margaret. Not anything close."

Clumsily, Hanley folded the receipt. His mind went back more than ten years...holding his dead sweetheart in the upstairs room at Sean Doyle's first saloon. Abruptly he thought of Kate, of the bruises on her throat left behind by Declan Coyne. A shudder rippled through him. She'd been luckier than Pegeen. She might not be again.

He tossed the receipt down. "Some kind of sick joke, was it, using her name? Using her to get money for himself. Like he meant to back then, only Billy killed her first. Who but Doyle would know it's the name of a dead woman?" The sound of his words sparked a thought that made bitter memory loosen its grip. "Dead people," he said. "Guthrie had an old paper in his office. *Chicago Tribune*, January nineteenth." He grabbed the January ledger and flipped pages. "There. Andrew Osgood—meaning Jamie Murphy—got his coat on the same day."

"Osgood's address isn't far from here," Moore said.

Hanley gave him a wolf's grin. "Care to go with me?"

ᚳᚱ

Osgood's house had black crepe on the door and windows. Straw blanketed the street in front. Mr. Osgood, a moderately prosperous family man in his middle sixties, had succumbed to pneumonia on January fifteenth. "He took a bad chill right after Christmas," Osgood's daughter told them, tearing up. "My father never had the strongest constitution, and this winter has been so terribly cold...he simply never got better." She dabbed her eyes with a lace-edged handkerchief that bore signs of mending. "The *Tribune* published his obituary four days afterward. He had a friend on the staff who saw to it." She blinked at them, her blue eyes still wet. "How did you say his name came up again?"

ᚳᚱ

"So there's your proof," Moore said as they left Carroll Street behind. "Dead people's names for both schemes."

Hanley scowled. "But I'm no closer to Kelmansky's killer. I only know it's not Jamie Murphy. And I can't get to him, not after Captain Hickey's show at the Armory today. Hell, Doyle's probably pulled strings to have Jamie arraigned by now. They'll bring him back there after, of course, but for how long until trial?"

"Doyle's not your killer either," Moore said. "He's near a head too short."

"He could've done Paddy, though. He was there. He left the mark of his ring on Paddy's jaw and a couple of hairs on him as well."

"Chamberlain's following up on that. He's one of our best men."

"I know, but if you'd just let me—"

"We've been through this. I've made my decision."

"I don't have to like it," Hanley snapped.

They walked on in silence until Moore spoke again. "So who are your suspects now?"

Hanley made an effort to answer as calmly as Moore had asked. "Charming Billy, for one. I'm dead sure he's the thug Zalman met at the warehouse. Zalman said he was wearing a black overcoat, and Rushton found a blond hair stuck to Kelmansky's collar. Billy could be the big fellow with blond hair and a black coat who followed the rabbi out of Muskie's that night." Hanley's anger ebbed as he talked. "Maybe Doyle sent him to shut Kelmansky up. Permanently."

"What about Murphy, then? Why was he following Kelmansky? Doyle'd hardly have sent two people after him within minutes of each other."

"I know." Hanley walked faster, thinking out loud. "Murphy came out after the blond man. Molly said..." He paused to remember her exact words. "She said Kelmansky helped them. Her and Jamie and their baby. Gave them food and clothes. What if Murphy saw whatever happened inside Muskie's, saw Kelmansky leave with Billy on his tail, and tried to warn him? Only he didn't catch up in time."

"Then why steal from the synagogue? If he left Muskie's to try to prevent a killing, why rob the dead man's holy place?"

Hanley shook his head. "That doesn't make sense either."

They'd reached Lake Street. Moore turned and then stopped as Hanley failed to follow. "Frank?"

"I need to talk to Murphy," Hanley said. "And find a way to keep him safe until this is done."

THIRTY-EIGHT

July 17, 1861

anley stood at the graveside, head bowed in the dripping wet. The warm summer rain had soaked him through, a minor misery that seemed fitting. He'd tried to pray all through the short interment service, and before that during the funeral mass at Saint Pat's, but the words wouldn't come. No decent God, he thought, would have let this happen. A decent God would have struck Billy down before he dared touch Pegeen. Struck Doyle down too, for putting him up to it.

Struck me down for not stopping them.

He dug his fingernails into his palms, creating a new set of half-moon bruises to match the ones he'd already made. As before, the physical pain did nothing to lessen the searing ache in his heart.

Beside him, his mother laid a hand on his arm. "Frankie. Come along now. They'll be having a little something at the Sullivans'. We should go."

He kept his gaze on the filled-in grave. The thought of Pegeen's body under all that wet dirt made him shivering sick despite the day's warmth. "They won't want me there. It was my fault, what happened to her." The mound of fresh earth wavered before his eyes. He'd had everything he wanted, he thought. In his grasp, then gone in the half second it took for the expression on Doyle's face to change. A bitter laugh escaped him. He'd thought himself safe from Doyle's ruthless streak. The good friend, the indispensable right-hand man. Right up to the moment it all went wrong.

He swallowed hard and lifted his head. Beyond Mam, his sister wandered amid the tombstones, reading inscriptions, heedless of the rain. "You and Kate go on," he said. "I've a thing to take care of."

☙

He looked for Billy first, spent an hour in a fruitless search before giving up and moving on. He found Doyle in a back room at the Shamrock Tavern on 14th Place, drinking and tossing dice, a smirk on his face that said he'd been winning for a while. The smirk maddened Hanley further. Pegeen was dead, Hanley's life in ruins, and Sean fucking Doyle had not a care in the world except amusing himself and pouring drink down his throat. As if he weren't as guilty of Pegeen's murder as Billy fucking Shaughnessy was.

Doyle looked up as Hanley barreled through the crowd of drinkers toward him. "Well. Didn't think you'd be showing your face around today—"

Hanley swept out an arm and knocked Doyle to the floor. The man landed hard, sat up, spat sawdust. "You goddamned fool, think you can take *me* on?"

Hanley hurled himself forward. Every punch, every kick, was balm for his raging soul. Through the mad exhilaration that gripped him, he was dimly aware of shouts from the throng, Doyle landing his own blows, flashes of pain from gut and ribcage and chest. He ignored them. *Pin him down. Wipe off that smirk. Take your punishment, you stone-hearted bastard.* His fist connected with Doyle's mouth, tore his lip, drew blood. Hanley rejoiced at it. He struck again, a hard punch to the throat. Doyle blocked it with one arm and scrabbled near his own hip with the other. Metal glinted in his hand. The sight of it sent sudden fear through Hanley. *Push knife.*

He threw himself backward as Doyle swung at him. Hot pain scored across his ribs. Panic fueling his fury, he grabbed Doyle's wrist and slammed his knife hand against the floor. Doyle twisted in his grip, but Hanley held on. Another slam. Another. The knife dropped and skittered away. Doyle was flat on his back now, eyes glittering with hate. Hanley drove a fist into his face. He heard bones crunch, saw blood spurt from Doyle's nose. Behind him the shouting grew louder.

Doyle bucked, throwing Hanley off balance. He swung wildly at Doyle's jaw, barely aware of a flurry in the crowd. Then someone grabbed his arms and hauled him off his prey. "Stop! Stop it, you'll kill him!"

He knew the voice. Tom Moore, a cop from the Patch. Mam must have found him and sent him looking for Hanley. He strained against Moore's hold. "I *want* to kill him. He killed her…him and Billy…they *deserve* it—"

A few of the drinkers were helping Doyle to his feet. Hanley recognized a pair of them as Doyle's bully boys from the night Pegeen died. No chance of getting through them even if he could throw Moore off. His ribs ached where the push knife had cut. Miniature bonfires of pain were flaring across his body. "Let me go, damn you, let me finish him—"

Forcibly, Moore turned him toward the door. "Not this way, Frank. There's a better one. I promise you."

THIRTY-NINE

February 1, 1872

The evening's service had ended, the mourners all gone home. Onkl Jacob had taken the siddurs back to the shul. Rivka, huddled near Tanta Hannah's feet, silently battled rising frustration and anxiety. She had felt so hopeful after leaving Hanley, so certain of finding Papa's book after all. What if it was gone? Would that mean Hanley couldn't prove his case?

He had left her so abruptly at the shul. Remembering his face, her cheeks grew warm. He'd looked at her as if at a priceless gift, when all she'd said was that her father had stood to pray. She wanted to see that look again.

The thought made her restless. She shouldn't have thoughts like that, especially not about Hanley. A goy, an Irish police detective whose only part in her life was to solve her father's murder. Sudden grief made her eyes sting. Papa was dead and her mind was full of the man she never would have met were it not for that terrible reality. She couldn't make sense of it, or of herself. An all too familiar sensation, worse now because of everything that had happened over the past several days. *What is wrong with me?*

She glanced at Tanta Hannah, who sat mending a blouse by lantern-light. Hannah looked calm, but Rivka knew she was listening for the creak of the door that would tell them Onkl Jacob had returned. He'd been gone longer than needed to put the siddurs back. Or was that merely her own jangled feelings distorting her sense of time?

She rested her head on her knees, thinking again of Hanley. And of what he had asked her to do. Papa hadn't left his book behind or she'd have found it. He must have brought it with him. If no one else had taken it, where might he have left it?

Propelled by sudden urgency, she pulled herself upright. Tanta Hannah glanced up. In the silence, Rivka's heart gave four strong, slow beats.

"Good night, Rivkaleh," Tanta Hannah said. "Rest well." She bowed her head again over her stitching.

"Good night," Rivka whispered and left the room.

⊗

The moon gave enough light to see by, even without the lantern in Rivka's hand. Faint light gleamed from the windows of the shul, even the papered-over broken one. Onkl Jacob must still be there.

She found him sitting on a bench near the bimah, his own lantern next to him, his head in his hands. He didn't look up at the sound of her footsteps.

"It has been a long day," he said. Rivka wasn't sure if he was speaking to her or to himself. "A very long, very difficult day. No wonder I am so tired. Have you ever felt so tired, Hannah, that even your heart scarcely had the strength to beat?"

Rivka set her lantern down nearby and knelt to look into his face. "Tanta Hannah is waiting at the house. But I need to ask you something before you go."

At the sound of her voice, he opened his eyes. Surprise gave way to resignation. His attempt at a smile wavered and his eyes glistened in the lantern light. "Again with questions," he said. "You were always the persistent one...even as a little girl. If you wanted something, you didn't stop. You kept asking and asking and asking..."

She leaned forward. "Papa kept a book. A record of what you gave away. Is it here? Do you have it?"

He looked away from her, around the shadowed room. "Your father didn't raise a foolish child. I will grant him that."

"Onkl Jacob." She touched his knee, hoping to anchor him to the here-and-now. "If Papa were here and could see us both...what would he want you to do?"

Silence fell. Rivka waited, scarcely breathing. Jacob sat very still, as if blood no longer flowed in his veins nor breath into his lungs. *Like a golem, a clay man,* Rivka thought, and shivered. That old tale had always terrified her, the relentless creature with no self or thought or feeling. Nothing but blind obedience, endlessly carrying out whatever command it was given, even if it destroyed things in the process.

Onkl Jacob stood abruptly and walked away from the bench, then halted. Rivka's heart pounded in the silence, so loudly she half-expected him to hear it too.

Slowly, he went to the small table by the door where the prayer books were stacked. He set several aside and picked one up—a slimmer book than the rest, but otherwise hard to distinguish. "We meant to do good. There were so many in such need. Only it went so terribly wrong."

She stood as he came back toward her. He stopped in front of her and hesitated. One hand caressed the book as if it were a living thing. Then he held it out to her.

Her fingers closed over the cold, smooth leather. Thin as it was, it felt heavy in her hands. She ran her fingers across it, then opened the cover. Numbers and words jumped out at her—*overcoat 1, flour 20 pounds, cornmeal 5 pounds. Murphy, Pavlic, Heller.* Mr. Heller, she recalled, had been the wheelwright next to the bakery. After the Fire, he and his family had vanished. Papa must have found them in dire circumstances somewhere nearby. Maybe living in a cellar-pit with a length of canvas for a roof.

She looked at Onkl Jacob, who hadn't moved. Papa's death had aged him ten years in a week. Rivka felt a decade older as well. "Tanta Hannah is waiting," she said as she closed the book and picked up her lantern. With a gentle touch on his arm, she steered him toward the door. He went, docile as a tired child. Watching him made her want to cry.

She would take the book to Hanley in the morning. Beneath her sorrow for Onkl Jacob, she felt her heart flutter at the thought of seeing the detective again.

ભ

Partway down the street from the Armory, Hanley loitered in the shadow of a half-built store as he watched the sparse traffic pass by. A patrol wagon, the harsh rattle of its iron wheels drowning out the horses' hooves, came around the corner of Pacific Avenue and pulled up near the station. Uniformed policemen manhandled three drunks and a fourth man, who appeared sober, around the side of the building and through the entrance nearest the lockup. One drunk was singing "The Minstrel Boy" off-key at an impressive volume. The closing of the door cut him off in mid-note.

Hanley silently counted to a hundred and eighty, then left his hiding place and sprinted toward the lockup entrance. The heavy padlock, opened by the patrolmen, hung crookedly on its hasp. He eased the door open and stepped inside.

He stood a moment in the shadows and got his bearings. Ahead of him stretched a dim hallway lit by a pair of gas lamps. About a hundred feet further in was a cross-corridor packed with jail cells, from which he could hear shouts, jeers, and more of "The Minstrel Boy." A dull thwack, an abrupt end to the song, and the clang of a cell door swinging shut told him he needed a hiding place, fast. He spotted a closed door a few feet away, dashed for it, and slipped inside. The smell of black powder and metal oil told him he was in the gun room.

He waited for what felt like an eternity while the patrolmen's voices and footsteps came closer, passed, and died away. The outside door thudded shut. Hanley counted to a hundred, listening for sounds in the hallway. He heard nothing. He stepped out of the gun room and eased the door closed.

The duty roster for the First Precinct, perused in Moore's office, listed Hiram Wallace as the night-shift officer in charge of recording arrests. He was a recent hire, just two months on the job, and didn't know Hanley by sight. Hanley was counting on that. He took a deep breath to steady himself and headed down the hallway, out of the shadows that had kept him concealed from the cells up ahead.

He approached the barred window of the small office where arrests were taken down. Officer Wallace, balding and short in his blue uniform, looked up from the *Chicago Times* he was reading. "Yeah?"

"Detective Reinhardt," Hanley lied, mimicking Reinhardt's slight accent. "Here to see Jamie Murphy."

Wallace put down his paper and waddled to the window. "You the arresting officer?"

"Yes."

Wallace studied Hanley's face. Hanley kept his own expression neutral, feigning a hint of bored impatience at the scrutiny. Moore had helped trim his hair to Reinhardt's squared-off neatness and loaned him his new-looking coat and muffler, which matched Reinhardt's garments better than Hanley's shabbier ones. That, plus the fact that Wallace hadn't been on duty in the Armory that afternoon, would have to be enough.

Looking satisfied, Wallace slid a sign-in book and a pencil under the window. "Putcher name down here. Ya got fifteen minutes. S'posed to be lights-out."

Hanley scribbled Reinhardt's name. Wallace reclaimed the book and jerked his head toward the far end of the hallway. "Third one on the right."

"Thanks."

He walked down the line of cells, ignoring shouts and catcalls. A skinny youth of maybe sixteen whined for a bottle of whiskey. Another man, dark haired and pockmarked, made fun of Hanley's posh clothes. Hanley kept going.

He found Murphy huddled in the corner of his cell furthest from the bars. The only other occupant was a bean pole of a man with a forgettable face sitting a few feet from Murphy and flipping greasy playing cards into a pile on the floor. Hanley eyed him warily and called Murphy's name. "Get up and come over here."

Murphy stirred, looked toward Hanley, and slowly hauled himself up. As he made his way over, Hanley worked out his options. "Officer," he called as Murphy reached the bars. "Your help, please."

Bean Pole was watching them now. Hanley kept half his attention on the man as Officer Wallace came out of his office. "Mr. Murphy and I need to have a private conversation," he said as Wallace reached the cell. He jerked his head toward a spot down the hall, out of earshot of Murphy's cellmate but within sight of Wallace's duty station. "Over there. A few minutes."

Wallace frowned. "Not the usual thing."

"Not the usual case. As you've surely been told."

Wallace looked hesitant. "My captain assured me there would be no trouble," Hanley said. "I believe he spoke to Captain Hickey about it."

The name did the trick. Wallace nodded and reached for his keys.

03

"I didn't kill him," Murphy said. Panic made his whisper harsh. He gripped his elbows, shivering as much from fear as from the chill in the corridor. "Swear to God."

"I believe you." Hanley wanted to buck him up with a handclasp to the shoulder, but that didn't fit the role he was playing. "But you were there that night. I know you saw something. Tell me what happened. We don't have much time."

"He's got people here, I know it," Murphy said. Hanley didn't need to ask who he meant. "They'll kill me if I talk to you."

"Your cellmate? Is he one of Doyle's?"

Murphy pressed against the wall, as if trying to burrow into it. "I dunno. I only know for sure the ones who work at Muskie's."

Hanley propped a hand against the wall near Murphy's shoulder, looming over him. "Listen. If you die before trial, that's as good as a shout from the rooftops that Kelmansky wasn't killed in a robbery gone wrong. Doyle knows that. His best hope is to get me out of the way, frame you, and let things take their course. You tell me what really happened that night and I can prove he's lying. Him and every crooked cop working for him. And you'll walk out of court a free man."

Murphy gave him a look halfway between hope and fear. "Sure of that, are you?"

Hanley resisted the temptation to lie. "That he'll let you live long enough for trial? Yes. That you'll go free? No. But I'm the best chance you've got."

He waited, counting heartbeats, while Murphy wavered. Then Murphy licked his lips. "You'll keep Molly safe? And our girl?"

"All of you. With money for train tickets out of here the minute this is over if you want." He had no idea how he'd make good on that promise, but he'd manage somehow. The important thing now was that Murphy believe it. "Did you see who killed Rabbi Kelmansky?"

Murphy nodded. "That fella of Doyle's." The words sent a surge of excitement through Hanley, which died as Murphy continued, his lips pinched in scorn. "Ran for mayor awhile back, promised to rebuild Chicago so we'd all get a fair shake in her. Mister Harden Guthrie."

FORTY

Mr. *Harden Guthrie*. Hanley hadn't expected to hear that, though as it sank in, it made a terrible kind of sense. He didn't want it to. He wanted Doyle to be responsible for Kelmansky's murder, sending Billy to do his killing for him, as well as for blackmailing Guthrie. He'd been so sure Doyle gave the order that cost Kelmansky his life. So sure Billy, not Guthrie, was the big blond man who'd left Muskie's after the rabbi. So sure of finding a way to prove it and take Doyle down, even if Paddy's case went nowhere because people higher up than Moore didn't give a damn who cut the throat of a card-playing thief. Instead, this.

He knew how faint his hope was of Murphy being mistaken even as he asked the obvious question. Guthrie had run for mayor less than three months before. Anyone who paid any attention to politics would remember his likeness from a poster or handbill, or would have seen him at a public speech. "You're sure it was him?"

Murphy nodded. "Hit him with one of them big candlesticks." He shivered. "Poor old fella didn't have a chance."

Suddenly, Hanley felt angry. He'd liked Guthrie, thought him at worst an easy mark for wolves like Doyle. Not the kind who'd murder an old man who trusted him. He crushed the feeling as one he couldn't afford right now. "And where were you?"

Murphy's chin shot up. "You sayin' I should've stopped him? How'm I going to do that from outside in the cold wet, lookin' in through the church window? Or whatever they call the place. I'm supposed to what…jump through the glass and throw myself across the room at a fella twice my size?"

"That's not what I meant. I need to know how you saw—" Hanley broke off as something Murphy had said came back to him. "Why did you call him 'that fella of Doyle's'?"

"'Cause he's around, isn't he? Has been for a month and a bit now. Couple nights a week he comes to Muskie's. Not to gamble and I haven't seen him eat much. Just seen him with Doyle."

More than a month, less than two. That fit with the timing of everything else Hanley had learned about the blackmail scheme— Guthrie's appointment as district director, Doyle's visit to his home, the dates on the check receipts. "Do you know what they talk about?"

Murphy snorted. "Doyle don't tell me his business. Guthrie's rich, though. Got to be something to do with money."

Hanley wondered what Doyle's leverage was. No use asking Murphy. He wasn't important enough to know. "Tell me how you ended up at the synagogue."

"Followed him there, didn't I?"

"Guthrie? Or Kelmansky?"

"Kelmansky." Murphy swallowed, looking sick. "If I'd known what your fella meant to do...but all I could think was not to let anyone see me."

"Why'd you go after Kelmansky?"

"To warn him. About Doyle."

"What d'you mean?"

"He saw them at Muskie's. Together. Kelmansky and Guthrie. Havin' a private chat, him not included. And it was my fault."

Hanley waited while Murphy got a grip on himself, wrapping his arms around his thin chest as if a tight hold could give him courage. "Doyle was in the back office," he said. "There was a fella upstairs havin' a long run of luck and I needed to know what to do about it. So I came down from the gaming room to ask him, and I saw Kelmansky sitting with Guthrie. I knew Kelmansky from when he brought us food right before Christmas. Whatever they were talking about, it was bad. They both looked like grim death."

"And where was Doyle?"

"He came out of the office after me. Saw them and stopped. Asked me who the old man was. I told him." He stared at his feet. "I didn't know what would come of it."

"Did they see him?"

Murphy shook his head. "Kelmansky stayed stuck on Guthrie, like Guthrie was the only person in the whole place. Guthrie barely looked at the old man. Kept playing with stuff on the table…his water glass, silverware, a piece of bread he tore to bits. Never saw Doyle far as I know."

"So Doyle saw them. Then what?"

"Told me to get back upstairs, then went and sat himself down close by them and listened. I stayed too. Couldn't move, you know? Way Doyle looked at the pair of them, I knew something was going bad somehow. I had to see it out."

"How long did Doyle listen in?"

Murphy shrugged. "Minute or two. Then Kelmansky said something that made Guthrie freeze up. Doyle too. After that, Kelmansky left."

"What did Doyle do?"

"Watched him a second. Then he went straight up to the gaming room to take care of Mister Lucky. Me, I'm shaking scared for that old man. Whatever Doyle's thinkin', it can't be good for Kelmansky. Not the way he was lookin' after him." He looked Hanley full in the face, and Hanley was surprised to see anguish there. "I owe the old fella, you know? And he's got no idea what a mess he's in. I don't know for certain either, but I know Doyle. And that's enough.

"I duck upstairs for my boots and coat and I'm out the door. I've got to warn him. On my way back down I can see Guthrie's gone. Outside, I don't see Kelmansky at first. He's too far ahead. I see Guthrie, though. Half a block away or so, damned near running. Can't mistake him, big as he is with that light hair and black overcoat. Must've left right before me. Right then, Kelmansky walks under a gas lamp a ways ahead of us both. He goes up Washington and I figure he's heading home. I'm thinking to catch him before he gets too far, but Guthrie has the same idea."

"So you followed them to Market Street. Then what?"

"Kelmansky knocks on someone's door. I'm still a ways down the street when the old man goes in. I wait around a bit 'cause I don't know if it's Kelmansky's own house or not. Don't know if I should go knock on the door myself or what. Guthrie's waiting too. I saw him duck into the shadows when I come 'round the corner.

"Little while later, Kelmansky comes out. Walks around the back of the house in the dark. Guthrie follows him. I don't know what to do. I don't want Guthrie to see me, but I can't just head back to Muskie's without doing what I came for. So after a bit I go too.

"There's moonlight, so I can see all right, except when the clouds go past. I can see their—what'd you call it, synagogue?—across the yard. Nobody's around, so I figure they went in there. I go to the nearest window for a look.

"Inside, there's pews and a pisspot-sized altar in the wrong place. Off to the side. Guthrie's standing right by it. Only way I can even tell what it is, is the big candlesticks on the altar cloth. Kelmansky's there, got a shawl draped over him. Him and Guthrie have words. Guthrie looks so piss-scared he's not even sane. Kelmansky just looks sad. Like Guthrie's drownin' and he'd give anything to save him, but he can't swim and he's fresh out of things to hold onto. He shakes his head and Guthrie grabs him by the collar. Shawl and all. Kelmansky gets mad then. He knocks Guthrie's arms away. Guthrie falls back a bit, right by the table with them candlesticks. Then—"

The sound of footsteps approaching cut him off. Not Wallace, whose duty station was behind them. Hanley shifted position as best he could to hide his face. His back muscles crawled as if awaiting a knife thrust.

"What's Murphy doing out of his cell? And who the hell are you?"

He knew the voice. Eddie Norris, who'd taken over Hanley's old beat in Conley's Patch. His breath quickened as he waited for disaster.

"Detective Reinhardt said he needed—" Wallace, stepping out from his post, sounded breathless and anxious.

"That's not Reinhardt." Norris's steps echoed off the walls as he circled around to look Hanley in the face. "Evening, Frank."

FORTY-ONE

Hanley met Norris's eyes. "He's innocent, Eddie. I can prove it."

"Captain said otherwise." Norris folded his arms across his chest. "And you're trespassing."

"I won't be if you let me walk out of here."

"Take Murphy back to his cell," Norris told Wallace. Then he looked at Hanley. "Those weren't our orders."

"Eddie, come on." The urgency he felt spilled into Hanley's voice. "This case isn't what Captain Hickey says it is. But I can't prove that if you do what he wants and put me in there." He jerked his head toward the nearest cell, just as the door of Murphy's own cell slammed shut. "You've got to let me go or a killer walks free…and Jamie Murphy hangs for a murder he didn't commit."

Wallace was hurrying back, as if determined not to miss another word. Norris noticed and his face hardened. "Fed you a line, did he? They're all innocent in here, Frank. You know that."

"What makes you so sure he's guilty, Eddie? What makes Captain Hickey so sure?" The man damned well knew otherwise, Hanley was certain, but he wanted to know what story the captain was giving out.

"Not for me to tell you." Norris's tone gentled. "You're not on that case anymore."

"Have you asked yourself why? You know how Captain Hickey was with me. You saw it when I worked here. Go ahead, ask me why."

Norris looked away. "Don't do this, Hanley."

The gesture chilled him. Norris had trusted him, even stood up for him—one of the first men in this precinct to do so. Or so Hanley had thought. Had he been wrong?

255

"Eddie, if you're at all the decent cop I remember you as, at least hear me out. And then—" He heard the desperate edge in his voice and squelched it. "Then decide whether to toss me behind bars or let me go finish my job."

He watched the struggle play out across Norris's face—past regard, even friendship, battling skepticism and fear—and his heart sank as he knew he'd lost. "More than my job's worth to buck the Captain," Norris said finally, looking regretful as he nodded to Wallace. "Put Hanley in Cell Five. I'll let Captain Hickey know."

 C3

It was cold in the cell. At least Eddie hadn't taken his overcoat along with his pencil and loose change. Hanley sagged against the least chilly of the walls and pulled the coat tighter around him. He thought of the week he'd spent just before transferring out of the Armory, walking Eddie through his old beat. Telling him everything he needed to know about the streets where Hanley grew up. Sharing drinks a time or three before that. He felt betrayed and angry, and more frightened than he wanted to admit.

He shoved himself away from the wall. With three other men sharing the same small space, he had little room for pacing. He reached the bars and slammed a hand against them. The echoing impact prompted a muttered curse from one of his cellmates, the pockmarked man who'd laughed at his clothes. Hanley stared him down, but wondered whether there was more to that look. Did Captain Hickey—or Doyle—intend to let him survive the night? Or was he the one due to be knifed over the water cup?

Fear gripped him, mixed with pain and rage as he thought of Paddy bleeding his life out into the snow. He could almost see the push knife as it sank into Paddy's throat. He pressed his forehead against the bars until it hurt. Doyle wouldn't kill him. Not now. *A dead cop raises all kinds of questions. That's the last thing he wants.*

Doyle could cripple him, though. Have someone beat him so badly he'd be no good for the rest of his days. Or go after his family again, this time succeeding at rape. Or murder. He spun away from the bars, breathing hard to keep his stomach under control. Maybe they'd just settle for kicking him off the force. Render him powerless and leave him knowing it. Captain Hickey would be happy to take his badge and make sure he never got it back.

He gripped the bars until his knuckles whitened. If Doyle harmed his family again, he'd kill him and damn the consequences. Then the futility of it hit him and he pushed away from the bars. He couldn't break out of here. Even if he succeeded, it would do him no good to make himself a fugitive. He'd be discredited, disgraced, thrown off the force. No power to arrest Guthrie or make anything stick to Doyle. Rivka would despise him for failing her...or worse, pity him. And Jamie Murphy would hang for murder. For being poor and a thief, and a petty criminal whose gambling-prince boss had decided he was more valuable as a scapegoat.

He peered across the hall. He could just see Murphy hunkered down, apparently asleep. Or maybe wide awake but pretending not to be, in hopes it would all go away. At least Murphy was still alive. His cellmate seemed to be asleep too. Bean Pole didn't look familiar, though that didn't mean anything. Doyle had hired on plenty of new people since Hanley's time. *No way to know. No way to stop anything, either. If anything happens.*

A footstep close behind made him turn. He saw a blade glint as the pockmarked man swung at him. Faster than thought, he blocked the blow with one arm and drove his fist into the man's face. Pockmark staggered backward. The weapon flew out of his hand. Hanley heard it land, but didn't see where. Riding a wave of fury and fear, he grabbed his attacker by the collar and slugged him under the jaw. Pockmark went limp.

Hanley let him drop to the cold dirt and straightened, breathing hard. He looked around and saw the blade just outside the cell. A shank, a sharpened piece of metal. A thing no prisoner should have had on him. Hanley's blood pounded in his ears, shockingly loud in the silence. Not a sound from Officer Wallace down the hall, nor any sign of him coming to check out the commotion.

The other men in his cell looked away when he glared at them. No threat there, Hanley judged. He looked across at Murphy. The man was huddled up tight, head on his knees as if to shut out everything around him. Softly, Hanley called his name. Murphy stayed still. Hanley tried again. And again, until Murphy lifted his head.

"So you're still alive," he said. "But for how long?"

"We're neither of us dead yet." Hanley pressed closer to the bars. "You know what'll happen if you leave it like this."

"And you're going to do what? Float out of here through the walls like a ghost?" He gave a barking laugh. "Take me with you, then. I'm that sick of the place."

"They'll throw me out of here come morning." As he said it, Hanley hoped it was true. Doyle's, or maybe Captain Hickey's, attempt to kill him had failed. He didn't see how they could make another tonight. "Once I'm out, I've people to go to. People I can trust. People others can trust. But right now I need you to trust me. Without that, nothing can happen."

"Haven't I told you enough already? What more do you want?"

"I want to get Doyle. And anyone else who helped put you here. Don't tell me you don't want that too."

"I don't know what—" Murphy went quiet at a rustle of cloth. Hanley saw Bean Pole shift in his slouch against the wall. He watched the man breathe, eyed the line of his back and legs. Was he really asleep or awake and listening to every word they said?

Hanley gripped the bars again, eyes on Bean Pole. Murphy stayed motionless as well. Seconds crawled by. Bean Pole didn't move. Hanley waited some more, counting slowly in his head.

Bean Pole let out a snort. He shifted again and smacked his lips, but didn't open his eyes. He looked relaxed, his body limp as a sleeping child's.

Murphy stared at Bean Pole and Hanley saw uncertainty slowly displace the fear in his face. He had to risk it. He must know he'd gone too far not to. "All right, Jamie," Hanley said. "Tell me what you did with the silver you stole."

FORTY-TWO

The door to the three-flat was oak, polished to glowing warmth. The brass knocker, a horse's head, shone in the early morning sun. Rivka loitered on the stoop, clutching her father's black book in one arm. In her other hand she held Hanley's scrawled note with his landlady's name and address. *Ida Kirschner, 240 West Monroe Street.* Rivka read it over for the tenth time since getting off the horsecar. A Jewish name, Kirschner. A scrap of reassurance to cling to in the madness of this journey. Would Hanley even be here? What time did he leave for work? It might have made more sense to go to Lake Street Station, even though he hadn't said to. For the first time she wondered why.

Not that she would have done the sensible thing, she admitted to herself. She wanted to see where Hanley lived, where he spent his time when he wasn't doing his job. Who he lived with and what they were like. She wanted to learn as much about him as he'd learned about her. Tanta Hannah's remark about him—*your Hanley*—had rarely left her mind. Nor, since their unexpected meeting at the shul, had Hanley himself. He shouldn't be so much in her thoughts, but she couldn't help it—and didn't want to.

She tucked the paper away, smoothed her kerchief, grasped the knocker and gave three sharp raps, then counted heartbeats in the silence. Muffled footsteps sounded from inside. Lighter steps than Hanley would have made. A bolt shot back and the door opened. Rivka saw a woman somewhat older than Tanta Hannah, with warm brown eyes behind gold-rimmed spectacles. She wore no kerchief or shaytel over her silver hair, but was otherwise clothed modestly in a high-necked everyday dress of dark blue wool.

She looked surprised, as if she'd been expecting someone else. Then she schooled her expression to politeness. *"Gut morgen. Kumt ir kuken tsimer?* Have you come about a room?"

Rivka shook her head. *"Nein tsimer,"* she managed to say. No room. *"Bitte... iz* Detective Hanley *hier?"*

Concern darkened the woman's eyes. *"Kum areyn,"* she said, stepping back from the doorway and beckoning Rivka inside.

∞

Hanley woke abruptly, stiff-necked and chilled through. It took him a moment to work out why, and what he was doing on a packed-dirt floor. Then he remembered he'd spent the night in a jail cell. He looked across the hall and felt his gut clench. Murphy was gone.

He stood up too quickly and paid for it with cramps in his stiffened legs. The few steps it took him to reach the bars did little to relieve his discomfort. "Officer Wallace!" he shouted, though after last night he doubted the man would respond even if he were still on duty. He noticed the shank had disappeared and fought down a jolt of nerves. He couldn't tell what time it was, but the empty feeling in his stomach suggested several hours had passed.

"Food's coming," someone shouted back. Not Wallace. "Till then, shut the hell up."

He glanced around for the pockmarked man and spotted him slumped against the back wall. His jaw was turning purple where Hanley had hit him. "Better move quick when the grub comes, you want any," Pockmark said with a malignant grin. "Cold mornin' like this, might even be beans. I like beans. 'Specially with a few maggots in 'em. Stick to yer ribs, they do."

Hanley turned away from him. He spent the next small space of time tearing blank sheets from his sketchpad and folding them into boats, while his thoughts went around and around about the stolen silver and Harden Guthrie. Soon enough, sound and scent announced the arrival of a turnkey with breakfast—beans with salt pork. God knew what it would taste like, but Hanley's mouth watered in spite of his doubts. He'd missed supper and his body craved food.

Then he saw who followed in the turnkey's wake. Eddie Norris continued down the hall to Hanley's cell. His eyes looked smudged from fatigue and Hanley guessed he was near the end of his shift. He could barely look Hanley in the face, which made Hanley uneasy. How much did Eddie know about the attack last night?

"Captain wants to see you," Eddie said.

Hanley gestured toward the turnkey, who'd begun dishing up bowls of beans. "At least let me have some breakfast."

Norris shook his head. "He said now."

Cß

Captain Hickey was reading the *Chicago Tribune*, feet propped on his desk, when Norris and Hanley reached his office. He must have heard them enter, but didn't look up from the paper until the second time Norris cleared his throat. "I've brought Hanley, sir."

"Good man." Captain Hickey closed the paper and glanced at him. "Your shift's almost over, isn't it? Why don't you take off a little early?"

"Yes, sir. Thank you, sir." Norris left without a look in Hanley's direction.

Slowly, as if savoring Hanley's silent tension, Captain Hickey lowered his feet, folded the paper into a neat rectangle, and set it down. Only when he was finished did he look Hanley in the eye. "I should thank you, Francis." His smug grin made Hanley want to wipe it off his face. "You've made my job easy. Impersonating a fellow officer, violating orders from a superior—"

"You're not my superior," Hanley shot back. "You haven't been for two years."

"And when did you earn captain's rank?" Captain Hickey's grin widened. "Violating a direct order from a superior. Obstructing justice. Maybe aiding a murderer. Quite a list of charges you've saddled yourself with."

Hanley forced skepticism into his voice. "And you know how to make them all stick. Especially those last two. I'd say they apply to you more than me. Along with attempted murder last night in my cell."

Captain Hickey laughed. "Nice play, Francis. But you've got a bad hand. You're off the force, for one thing. Your badge was gone the minute you set foot in this station last night. Passing yourself off as Reinhardt…even worse. And you did it to meddle in a case that was taken from you. I make it three charges out of four so far."

He'd expected it, but the words *off the force* still hit him like a blow to the stomach. It took everything he had not to let it show. He was damned if he'd give Hickey the satisfaction.

"As to conspiracy…" Captain Hickey shrugged. "I might let that one pass. If I feel like it."

No reaction to the attempted-murder charge, though Hanley was nearly certain Captain Hickey had set up the attack. Not that he could prove it. He gave the man a cold smile. "Where's Murphy?"

"On his way to court. They should start picking a jury by three this afternoon."

Hanley felt his face stiffen. Captain Hickey kept talking, clearly enjoying his discomfiture. "Things are moving fast, but the killing was brutal. The evidence of guilt is clear. Once people see that play out, the city calms down. That's what everyone wants."

"What evidence?" The bloody boot marks, they knew about. He'd put them in his case notes. From what Murphy had told him, the silver surely came into it as well. He needed to know where they'd found it and how it got there. Not that he expected Captain Hickey to tell him.

The captain stayed quiet a moment. Then he shoved the paper across his desk. "Page two, column five."

Startled, Hanley took the paper. The column headline read, *Stolen Silver Key Evidence in Market Street Murder.* He skimmed the article, picking up details: *silver spice box…back corner of wardrobe at suspect's abode…statement of Detective Georg Reinhardt.* Mention of the menorah came near the bottom. *Original Andrews, known dealer in stolen goods, is prepared to testify that the silver menorah came into his possession through one*

James Murphy of South Franklin Street, a petty thief with whom he has had numerous past dealings.

Hanley dropped the paper back on the desk. They'd gotten to Andrews. Why had Captain Hickey shown him the article? "Sounds like you've got him dead to rights."

The man's look said, *And there's not a damned thing you can do about it.* "Get out of here, Hanley. I'll see you at your disciplinary hearing. If you're fool enough to ask for one."

FORTY-THREE

After the cold outside, the warmth of the kitchen made Rivka's nose and cheeks burn. She held tight to Papa's book, her anchor in an unfamiliar sea. She smelled toast browning, saw iron and copper pots against white walls and pale wooden cabinets and shelves.

The woman in blue spoke to Rivka in Yiddish. "Please come sit and have a little tea to warm you. Then we'll talk. I am Ida Kirschner, Detective Hanley's landlady, and this is his mother, Mrs. Hanley." She gestured toward a woman sitting at the table in the center of the room, who pulled out a chair for Rivka.

Rivka sat, feeling like a stranger in her own body. She watched Ida pour tea from the blue-and-white china pot and only then shyly looked over at the woman seated beside her. Fray Hanley was staring at her, eyes bright and intense. Like Detective Hanley's eyes, slate gray with a touch of blue. The mother's face was all angles, capped by gray hair that looked hastily brushed and pinned. Her fingers moved restlessly against the curve of her own full cup of tea. She glanced away as Rivka's eyes met hers. She picked up the slice of toast on her plate and then set it down again.

"Eat something, Mary Rose," Ida told her gently. "None of us will be any use if we're starving." She looked at Rivka and switched back to Yiddish. "What is it you wanted to see Detective Hanley about?"

"I am Rivka," Rivka said, in English, so Hanley's mother would understand. "Rivka Kelmansky."

"Kelmansky?" Fray Hanley dropped her toast onto its plate. "That's Frankie's case." She gripped Rivka's wrist. "Do you know where he is? Did he send you here?"

Gently, Rivka laid down the book and covered the anxious woman's hand with her own. "I came to bring him this. My father had it with him the night he was killed. Detective Hanley asked me to find it. I thought he would be here."

"We don't know where he is," Ida said.

Rivka's heart lurched. "He's in trouble, isn't he? That's why he said to bring the book here instead of Lake Street Station."

Fray Hanley closed her eyes. "Ah, Frankie. What've you got yourself into now?"

Ida fetched the fresh toast and set it down in front of them. "First we eat. Then we talk."

☙

Hanley loitered on the far side of Lake Street, trying to ignore his rumbling stomach. Time enough to head home for a meal after he'd talked to Moore. He was close enough to Lily Stemple's to smell boiled coffee and frying ham, but hadn't a penny to bless himself with, let alone buy breakfast. A cop he didn't recognize—a patrolman, from the blue cap pulled low on his head—passed him and headed toward Lily's. His coat collar was turned up against the cold and covered half his face. He looked skinny enough to put away two of Lily's hearty breakfasts. Hanley envied him.

He moved away from the distracting scents and turned his thoughts to the problem at hand—how to get to Moore without anyone from Lake Street spotting him. He'd tried Moore's house first, but Moore had already left. He'd likely heard by now about the escapade at the Armory and its consequences. Still, what Hanley had learned was worth it—if they could find a way to act on it.

He knew the silver spice box hadn't been in Murphy's wardrobe, and he knew Original Andrews had told the truth on Monday when he'd claimed neither sight nor knowledge of Murphy since the murder. Murphy couldn't have fenced a damned thing through Andrews. He hadn't had the silver anymore.

"Left it with Callaghan, didn't I?" Murphy had said, his voice soft but clear in the chill dimness of the Armory jail. "Went there for a whiskey to clear my head. I needed it, after…" He'd shuddered and fallen briefly silent before going on. "So I left the things with him. He said he'd take care of them." His tone turned bitter. "I guess he did, seein' as I'm in here for theft along with murder."

Knowing he was right about Callaghan brought Hanley no joy. "Why'd you steal the stuff in the first place?"

"Because it was there." He looked away from Hanley as he said it, shoulders hunching as if he felt ashamed. "It was just *there*, right in front of me…and I knew we'd be needin' more food soon and the rent on the house…and poor Kelmansky wasn't going to be helpin' us out of that again, was he? So why not?"

"I take it Callaghan never fenced them?" *Ah Paddy, you should've told me. I could've found the silver, shut him down, done Doyle some hurt. Maybe in time to do you some good…*

Murphy snorted. "Never give me a damned penny. Should've told him I promised a cut to Doyle after he asked me where I'd gone Thursday night. Doyle wasn't too happy with me leaving Muskie's during workin' hours. I figured a little money'd sweeten him. He took to the idea right enough, or at least I thought so then."

"Doyle knew you took the spice box and menorah? And where you left them?"

Murphy nodded. "Callaghan handles all kinds of stuff for Doyle's boys, from the depots and the docks and suchlike. Has done ever since he married Doyle's sister three years ago. I figured he'd be safe as houses."

Hanley let out a breath. So Callaghan was Doyle's brother-in-law. He ran a hand through his hair. Doyle knew where the silver was. And could get his hands on it to set up Jamie Murphy as the killer in Harden Guthrie's place. Evidence tampering and obstruction of justice to go along with blackmail. But how to prove it? He couldn't let himself think about Paddy. Aside from a punch to the jaw and the strands of red hair, they'd nothing to tie Doyle beyond doubt to that murder. Not even the knife wound. Plenty of criminals carried push knives, and who was to say which blade left that hole in Paddy's throat?

The rest of Murphy's tale matched what Hanley already knew or had guessed. He'd tell Rolf Schmidt about Callaghan first chance he got. Assuming Schmidt was still watching Callaghan's place, that Captain Hickey hadn't gotten word of it somehow and told Lake Street's captain to order him off.

A sharp gust of wind struck Hanley in the face and sun glinting off the snow made him squint. He shaded his eyes and peered across the road. A few hardy souls were out, braving the bitter cold to shop for food, head for work, or hunt down what few jobs existed. He thought of the people living in cellar pits and shivered. How cold did it get down there, with frozen earth for walls and no sunlight reaching in until hours past dawn?

Movement caught his eye—a boy trudging up the boardwalk, dragging a cart behind him. He wore a homespun jacket, but no hat over his mop of curls. As he drew closer, Hanley saw his sleeves were several inches too short. He looked hardly older than eight or an underfed ten. His cart rattled over the boardwalk, the items in it rolling and bumping. As he drew closer, Hanley could see a few of them—a sooty porcelain doll's head, a half-melted brass knocker. Souvenirs from the Fire, scrounged for sale to anyone who might part with a penny or two. He thought of the girl he and Guthrie had met, with her wagonload of similar finds, and wondered if Agnes Wentworth ever got the scissors.

He knew the boy, he realized. He'd seen that wild hair and too-small jacket before. Last Friday afternoon, in the muddy yard, through the back window of Pavlic's Bakery. The boy looked tired and hungry. Hanley wished he could buy something from him.

An idea struck him. He fished out his sketchbook and the pencil he'd persuaded the Armory desk sergeant to return to him, scribbled a note, and approached the boy.

The boy looked up as Hanley reached him. Smudges under his eyes spoke of too little sleep. He'd be a handsome lad with more weight on him. Hanley searched his memory for the boy's name. "Anton?"

"*Ano.*" It took Hanley a moment to recognize the Bohemian word for *yes*. Then the boy switched to English. "You want souvenir, mister?"

"No, thanks. But there is something you can do for me." Hanley held out the folded note. "Can you take this paper in there?" He nodded toward the stationhouse. "Give it to Sergeant Moore. Tell him Hanley sent you. He'll pay you. Then come back and tell me what he says. How about it?"

Anton looked skeptical. "How much?"

"A quarter-dollar." A large sum for a small errand, but one look at Anton's scrawny frame and Moore would surely give it.

Anton's eyes widened. He grabbed the note. "You watch my cart, okay? I go quick!"

Very shortly he was back. A wide grin made his face look more like it belonged on a child and his fist was clenched tight around his payment.

"Good man," Hanley said as the boy reached him.

Anton dropped the quarter into a trouser pocket and patted it. "He said go to Lily's. He be there. Ten minutes."

"Thanks." Hanley picked up the cart handle. "How about you come, too, and we'll buy you breakfast?"

◌ঙ

While they waited for Moore, Anton put away a plateful of scrambled eggs, bacon, and fried potatoes. The skinny patrolman was still there, one of three other customers in the place, working his way through a stack of johnnycakes at a table by the window, his attention on the newspaper in front of him. Hanley made himself a sandwich from a slab of ham and thick slices of toast and washed it down with Lily's strong coffee. He'd pay Moore back for both meals out of his salary once he was reinstated. If he was reinstated.

That uncomfortable thought gave rise to others. Suddenly nervous, Hanley surveyed the room as unobtrusively as he could. A shop girl sat talking in low tones with a patrolman Hanley recognized as a night-shift man from Lake Street. Another man, jowly and sixtyish, slurped coffee and read the *Chicago Times*. None of them looked likely to be spies for Captain Hickey, or Sean Doyle, though Hanley had to assume they'd keep tabs on him somehow. He would in their place, especially after the failed attempt to kill him. Would they try again? Or was it enough that he'd no badge, no job, no power against them?

He stared at his ham and toast. Maybe they wouldn't try again, or even bother to keep track of him. Maybe they thought they'd beaten him. Off the force with charges pending, nearly knifed in jail, knowing Paddy was dead for talking to him, Ida's house bombed, and Kate damned near raped as warnings. He set his sandwich down and grabbed his coffee, gripping the mug as if its heat could banish the frightening images that rushed through his brain. The boardinghouse door broken in, Mam or Kate or Ida beaten and left for dead. Rivka attacked on her way to Lake Street. *I've seen you around*, Charming Billy had said on Sunday. If he'd seen Hanley with Rivka since, he knew what she looked like. And that she was helping him. They'd already gone after Kate. Would they harm Rivka next?

He took a scalding gulp of coffee. If he dropped the case now, what then? Would anyone he cared about be safe? And Murphy—he'd be dead for a crime he didn't commit. Hanley's livelihood would be gone too, and God knew how they'd keep themselves without his wages.

Slowly, he set the coffee down and picked up his sandwich. The only way to stop Doyle was to see the case through. He'd need his strength for that.

The door opened. Sergeant Moore walked in, saw them, and came over. He nodded to Anton, who stuffed a last scrap of potato into his mouth and got up. "I go now?" Anton said.

"You go now, yes." Hanley shook the boy's hand. "Thank you for your help."

Anton fetched his cart from the corner where he'd left it and maneuvered himself outside. Moore watched him go and then turned toward Hanley. He eyed the emptied plates. "What's the damage?"

"Dollar and a half. They hustled me out of the Armory before breakfast."

"I hope it was worth it."

"I think so. So did someone else. Mike Hickey or Doyle, I'm not sure which. I nearly got shanked last night in my cell."

Moore's eyes widened. As he stepped away briefly to order, Hanley sipped coffee. When Moore returned some minutes later with his own steaming mug and full plate, Hanley was ready.

"I know who killed Kelmansky," he said. "But we'll have to move fast to keep Jamie Murphy from swinging for it."

FORTY-FOUR

T he thing is," Hanley said as he swirled the dregs of his coffee, "we can't directly implicate Doyle. Not yet. The check receipts aren't in his name and the only signature on them is Harden Guthrie's. Moishe Zalman, and probably Jacob Nathan, can swear to seeing Doyle at the warehouse and to how he acted there, but they were both stealing aid supplies along with the murder victim. That they did it to help desperate people won't outweigh the plain fact of theft."

"The warehouse foreman?" Moore took a bite of fried egg.

"Was in on the Robin Hood scheme, too. Had to have been for the records to match up."

"And Guthrie is a thief, embezzler, and murderer. A man with every reason to lie."

Hanley slugged back the remains of his coffee, which had turned bitter as it cooled. "Doyle set up this situation. I'm certain he blackmailed Guthrie—I'd give a month's pay to know over what—and because of that the man went straight out after Kelmansky that night in a hell of a state. I know the law won't see it that way, but Doyle's as responsible for Kelmansky's death as Guthrie is. And if Murphy ends up hanged for it, Doyle will have murdered again. This time using the police to do his dirty work." His grip tightened on the mug. "Any word about Paddy's murder? Did Chamberlain at least bring the bastard in or search his house for the push knife?"

Moore sighed. "Two respectable citizens swear they saw Doyle at Muskie's on Wednesday, right around the time Paddy was being attacked in Hell's Half Acre. Eating, chatting with patrons, keeping an eye on things. They probably gamble there, and for pretty high stakes if they're

271

willing to lie for Doyle, but proving they lied takes time. Chamberlain went for a warrant yesterday, but got turned down. Could be bad luck, but I'm guessing Captain Hickey called in a marker on Doyle's behalf." He speared a chunk of egg. "What concerns me most with your case is that Reinhardt found the spice box in Murphy's house."

"Reinhardt lied. It wasn't there when I searched the place and he searched right after me."

"Not quite. I saw the news article this morning and asked him about it. After you left, he parked himself in the kitchen with Molly Murphy, until Officer Schmidt returned several minutes later from getting Murphy booked. He made his search with Schmidt in tow. Schmidt saw him find the box in the wardrobe. Molly Murphy did too."

"He wanted a witness," Hanley said slowly. "Someone better than the wife of the accused. Someone a jury would see as above reproach. He must have had the box with him, then."

"Or Schmidt brought it."

Hanley stared at him. "Rolf Schmidt's a good cop. I'd swear…" He trailed off. He'd asked Schmidt to watch Callaghan's saloon, but how sure could he be that Schmidt wouldn't tip Callaghan off instead? Or what might he do short of that to help out a fellow German officer? Ethnic loyalties were as strong among the police as anywhere and sometimes they led good men astray.

"I'd swear it too," Moore said. "But we just don't know."

Hanley toyed with his empty mug. One of Lily's daughters set a fresh pot of coffee on the warming-stove and the skinny patrolman got up for a refill. Hanley considered doing the same, but felt too unsettled for more. "Whoever brought the box had to get it from somewhere. Murphy left it with Callaghan. I can't see that man giving it over to anyone else until Doyle told him to. Who was around Callaghan's place the day of the search?"

"That's easily checked." Moore ate the bite of egg. "The trickier bit is the blackmail money. How did Doyle get his hands on the cash? The receipts are all drawn on one bank. First Illinois State, on Randolph out by Union Street. He couldn't have turned up there multiple times using different names without someone remembering his face, even if they didn't recognize it from the *Police Gazette*."

"I've given that some thought." Hanley snagged a chunk of potato from Moore's plate. "Guthrie's signature is the thing that lets the bank know the receipt is valid and they can give out the money. I'm guessing Doyle picks people who work for him—probably the same people who steal things off the docks and the trains, or pick pockets in his panel-shop whorehouses—and sends them to cash the checks. They bring the money somewhere—Muskie's, maybe, or Callaghan's Grocery—for Doyle to collect."

"So if we catch one of them…"

"We have Doyle. Solid proof he blackmailed Harden Guthrie and set Kelmansky's murder in motion."

ೞ

Back outside in the sunlight, Hanley watched Moore hurry toward Lake Street Station. He'd looked eager as a dog after a bone at the thought of staking out the bank. He must be itching to get back into action. Hanley grinned at the thought.

The skinny cop came out of Lily's and passed him, heading east down Lake, collar turned up against the biting wind. It was warmer inside than out here. He should go back in, Hanley thought, scratch out a note for Mam in decent comfort while he waited for Moore to return with the things they'd need at the bank. Instead he found himself turning south along Market Street. He should have a good quarter hour before Moore came back. He wanted badly to see Rivka, make sure she was all right. Maybe she'd found her father's book by now. He could get to her house and back in time if he hurried.

Her face came to mind, the way she'd looked with snow on her lashes, and on the shining, dark hair just visible beneath her kerchief. He walked faster. A barrel-laden cart approached, too fast for the slippery pavement. The horse shied as its footing slipped. Two barrels fell off, landed hard in the street, and burst, spilling beer in all directions. Hanley jumped back out of the path of a skidding stave and saw a man loitering near the dry-goods store he'd just passed. The man ducked around the building when he saw Hanley looking at him.

Hanley strode toward the spot where the man had disappeared. He turned the corner onto Randolph and stopped. The block ahead of him was deserted.

He looked around for anyplace the man might have gone. Nearest him stood a small frame house with an empty lot between it and the dry-goods store. He glanced at the house, then hurried to the lot. It gave him a clear view across the yard, which was as empty of people as the street had been. He saw an outhouse at the near end, the neighborhood rubbish heap, and farther away a cluster of small homes and empty lots. No sign of anyone around.

He spotted fresh boot prints near the boardwalk, but they were soon lost in the crisscrossing tracks that led from nearby buildings to the outhouse. He clenched his fists, then strode to the outhouse and threw the door open.

Even blunted by the cold, the smell made him flinch. No one was there. He let the door swing shut and stood in the churned-up snow, oblivious to his freezing feet as cold fear crept up his spine. They were watching him. He'd likely been followed all the way from the Armory. By the skinny patrolman who'd been at Lily Stemple's? Something about the patrolman nagged at him, but he couldn't place it. Was he Captain Hickey's man or Doyle's?

He headed back toward Lily's. He didn't have time to see Rivka now and he wouldn't risk leading danger to her door.

03

The stone pillar he'd parked himself against offered some shelter from the stiff breeze, for which Hanley felt grateful. The slouch hat and muffler Moore had brought him, along with a worn army blanket to throw around his shoulders, could only do so much against the cold. The horsecar ride to Union Street had at least kept them out of the wind, but the chill remained. For a moment he envied Moore, who'd taken up a position inside First Illinois State Bank. Between them they should have the place pretty well covered.

He hoped they'd figured the dates correctly and Doyle would send someone here today with a Relief and Aid check to cash. Someone who hopefully wouldn't spot him despite his attempt at disguise. Doubt gnawed at him. What if Doyle sent a person neither of them recognized? Even Moore didn't know everyone on Doyle's payroll. Doyle's errand boy—or girl—might waltz right past them, in with the check and out with the money, and they'd never know it.

His hand went to his hair, but was blocked by the hat. Annoyed, he scratched under it. The bank was their best shot at catching Doyle red-handed. Just the pair of them could hardly hope to follow every likely looking suspect who came out of Callaghan's Grocery or Muskie's Chop House. Anyone cashing illicit checks for Doyle would have to come to First Illinois State, which at least narrowed the field enough that they'd have some chance of success.

He gritted his teeth. They had to succeed. With Captain Hickey playing games on Doyle's behalf, Doyle might never pay for the deaths he'd caused. Including Jamie Murphy's if Hanley couldn't prove his innocence.

"Spare a penny, sir?" he murmured to the next person who approached the bank—a natty-looking businessman with a derby hat and sideburns. "Penny for a Union soldier?"

The businessman scowled, but fished a penny from his coat pocket and dropped it into Hanley's tin cup. Hanley thanked him and sank back against the pillar, looking up and down the street. Plenty of people out today, enjoying the sun despite the wicked cold. So far, though, none of Doyle's people, at least not those he knew by sight. None also, he hoped, who'd been told to follow him. He and Moore had kept an eye out for tails, but hadn't spotted any.

His nose was dripping. He wiped away the moisture with his hand. When he looked up again, someone else was approaching the bank. As the new arrival drew closer, Hanley stiffened. *Tommy Callaghan.*

He blew his nose gently on a corner of the army blanket as Callaghan passed him. Doyle's brother-in-law, a respectable grocery and saloon owner, made the perfect courier. He followed Callaghan into the bank, where the sudden warmth made him shiver in reaction. He held the blanket closed and looked around for Moore. The chief of detectives, his everyday suit and greatcoat embellished with a pristine derby and a gray muffler of fine merino wool, was filling out a slip of paper at a long counter to one side of the tellers. His fourth try, to judge from the three crumpled paper balls by his elbow. Hanley noticed he'd placed himself so he could glance around the lobby as he worked without drawing attention.

Callaghan had joined the shortest of the teller lines. Three people stood in front of him. Hanley noted his position and headed toward Moore.

"You! What's your business here?" A bank guard, barrel-chested and muscular, blocked his way. Silently, Hanley swore. With the blanket around him and the scruffy hat and muffler, he looked like a street bum. Not like the kind of person who had any business in an elegant bank lobby.

"Saw a fella," he mumbled as he tried to sidle past the guard. He shook his tin cup. Moore was looking straight at them both. The guard held up a warning hand. Hanley jerked his head toward the line where Callaghan stood. "Over there," he said, more loudly this time. "Saw a guy I know. Cap'n Tom. Hey, Cap!"

He stepped closer to the line, knowing the guard would block him. From the corner of his eye he saw Moore gather up his deposit slip and join the line behind Callaghan.

The guard threw out a meaty arm, halting Hanley's advance. His other hand moved to the truncheon on his hip. "Get on out of here. No begging on the premises."

"Okay, okay, I'm goin'," Hanley muttered as he turned and left the building.

Just out of sight of the lobby windows, he took off the blanket and dropped it on the boardwalk. Some lucky soul would snatch it up within minutes, but the department could spare it. He tucked the muffler beneath his coat and squashed the hat into his pocket. He smoothed his hair, checked his reflection in a window, and hurried back inside the bank. The guard gave him a bored glance and looked away.

Only one person—a weedy-looking youth in a worn plaid suit— stood now between Callaghan and the teller. Moore stood just behind him. Hanley grabbed a deposit slip and scrawled on it, then hastily got in line behind Moore.

The teller handed a sheaf of bills to the young man in plaid, who moved off. The teller opened a drawer, put some papers in it, closed it, opened another drawer, took out a stack of forms, tapped them against his counter, and set them down. He took off his spectacles, blew on them, polished them on a sleeve, put them back on, and adjusted the armband around the other sleeve. Hanley wanted to shout, grab Callaghan, do anything besides stand and wait with his nerves jangling like fire bells. He could see Callaghan shifting his feet as if he, too, felt restless at the delay.

"Next, please!" the teller called.

Callaghan reached into his coat and set a folded check down in front of the teller. "I'd like to cash this." Hanley craned his neck, trying to read it, but the writing wasn't legible from where he stood. He could feel Moore's sudden alertness, like a hawk waiting to strike.

"William Alder, isn't it?" A hank of pomaded hair fell over the teller's right eye. He shook it back as he pulled the check toward him and eyed the signature. "This looks in order. For more wood? Good to see someone doing well."

The name sent a shock through Hanley. He started to move, but Moore was faster. The chief of detectives clamped one hand around Callaghan's brawny arm and pulled out his badge.

"This isn't William Alder," he said, flashing his detective's star at the teller as Hanley moved into position on Callaghan's other side. "His name is Tommy Callaghan and he's under arrest."

FORTY-FIVE

Where to?" Hanley asked, keeping his grip on Callaghan's arm vise tight.

Moore nodded toward the nearest intersection. "That way." They began to move toward Union Street.

"Long way in the cold to the Armory," Callaghan said, as if he, Hanley, and Moore were three friends heading out for a chat and a beer.

"We're not going to the Armory."

Callaghan looked puzzled, then regained his casual pose. "Just as well. I don't much care for the lockup."

They were near the intersection now. Hanley could feel Callaghan's body tensing as his gaze darted around. He gripped the man's arm tighter and spoke in a low growl. "I'm faster than you are and I don't much give a damn what happens to me right now, as long as I get you and your slug of a brother-in-law. You break for it and I catch you, you'll regret it. And if by some miracle I don't catch you, we'll have every decent cop in Chicago hunting you down."

Something flashed through Callaghan's eyes—a wariness just shy of fear. Then his affable poker face returned. "Seems like a lot of effort for a man trying to help out a friend. Is that a crime these days?"

"Shut up."

"You're making a mistake," Callaghan said. Tired of the game, Hanley ignored him.

They reached Union Street. Hanley followed Moore's lead and steered Callaghan southward. He knew where they were going now. Not the Armory jail, but the police court at Union Street Station. Moore must have friends there or at least a captain he could trust.

Moore caught his eye as they neared the stationhouse. Hanley tightened his grip on Callaghan and with his other hand pulled the muffler up over his chin and nose. Callaghan gave him a curious look, but said nothing. He hoped the man wasn't astute enough to guess at the fact of, or the reason for, his disguise. Word of his disgrace would have gotten round by now. If he walked into the station with Moore, bold as brass, it could undercut everything they hoped to achieve.

They booked Callaghan without incident and marched him to a small room in the station's basement near the holding cells. In the room were four straight-backed chairs and a scratched wooden table. The grime on the single window, which only rose halfway above street level, blunted what little sunlight leaked in.

Moore and Hanley sat Callaghan in a chair and then seated themselves across from him. "So," Hanley said. "You want to tell us why you tried to cash a check under another man's name?"

"I told you. Helping out a friend." Callaghan leaned back, as easy as if in his own saloon. "Can I go now?"

"You do that well," Hanley said. "That friendly, innocent act. You think we'll take your word for what happened at the bank?"

"Why shouldn't you?"

Moore tossed the check on the table. "Because William Alder died three weeks ago. Why were you using his name and who's the money for?"

"We don't need to ask him that," Hanley said. "We know already. His sainted brother-in-law, Sean Doyle." He picked up the check and waved it. "How big a cut were you supposed to get from this, Tommy? Enough to buy your wife something pretty or were you planning to spend it all on yourself? You might want to check with Doyle first. Get his approval. He'd want a say in your plans, I'm sure. Not a good idea to cross him."

"How much has he paid you already?" Moore asked. "The teller called you William Alder before you gave him that check. How often have you done this and for how much?"

"Good point." Hanley folded the check in half, then in half again. Silent, Callaghan watched him. "Any time now," Hanley said. "We can wait all afternoon."

"Then you'll be waiting awhile."

Hanley tossed Moore a glance. "He thinks we can't touch him."

"Because he's got connections."

Hanley stood and leaned across the table, arms braced. "Thing is, Tommy, we're not at the Armory. Mike Hickey doesn't run this station and he won't get word of your arrest for a while. So if my sergeant"—he nodded toward Moore—"asks for the loan of a few trustworthy men to, say, raid your grocery store…he'll get them. Now I'm asking myself, what'll they find at your place? Today's take from the East Branch docks?" He forced back thoughts of Paddy, who'd run the dockside gang. "Or other stolen goods you're holding until Doyle tells you what to do with them—like you held the things Murphy took from the synagogue on Market Street?"

"I don't know what you're talking about." Callaghan's voice was smooth as butter, his expression unchanged.

Moore got up. "I'll find Captain Miller. Half a dozen men ought to be plenty." He went to the door, then stopped and gave Callaghan a chilly smile. "I'll ask them to take care, of course. But things get broken in these searches sometimes, and we'll need to be thorough."

"You're making a mistake." Callaghan's affability had vanished. His big hands opened and closed against his knees. "I'm an honest businessman—"

Hanley's snort of laughter cut him off. "An honest businessman tied at the hip to a gambling prince and brothel owner. Who lies to cops and depends on a few dirty ones to make sure he never gets held to account. Who tried to cash a check for a dead man not an hour ago. Can't you do better than that?"

Callaghan looked past him to Moore. "You're still here." The anger on his face gave way to calculation. "If you could do what you said, you'd be doing it. But you're not."

Moore gave him a measuring look. Then he left the room. The door thudded shut behind him.

Silence fell. Callaghan looked uneasy, though he was trying not to show it. Hanley sauntered back to his chair, turned it around, and sat astride it, as if it was a horse. He picked up the check and unfolded it. "Can't have been a very big cut. Eighty dollars is a fair amount of money, but Doyle always likes to keep the lion's share. Doesn't matter of what." He dropped the check on the table. "So what makes it worth getting involved in embezzlement and murder?"

"If you're talking about that old man—" Callaghan sneered.

"I'm talking about Paddy Moroney." Hanley's voice hardened. "He was a friend of mine. Doyle killed him. That's two murders down to your prince of a brother-in-law. What if we charge you as an accessory?"

"You can't."

"I can. And I will." He saw Callaghan blanch. The man didn't know Hanley had lost his badge. "While I'm at it, I'm sure I can think of a few other things to charge you with. There've been some violent incidents in your neighborhood recently—fueled by drink and gambling, no doubt. Fights, broken windows, even a bombing. Your saloon'll be shut down while we sort it all out—" He halted, caught by the jolt of fear that flashed across Callaghan's face. He'd gotten that look before. *When he was thinking to break for it, and I said we'd have every decent cop in the city hunting him.*

"You did something," Hanley said slowly. "Something you might actually go to jail for, and that your well-placed friends can't bail you out of. Or won't. What was it, Tommy? Did you beat someone up? Knife someone?" He rose from his chair and loomed over Callaghan. "Were you in Hell's Half Acre late on Wednesday morning?"

Callaghan held his stare. Incredibly, Hanley saw his fear give way to relief and then scorn. "I'm done talking."

Hanley grabbed his shirt front and hauled him up. "The hell you are." He threw Callaghan back down in his chair. It toppled with a clatter. As Callaghan regained his feet, Hanley grabbed him again and twisted his collar tight around his neck. "Where were you Wednesday? And where was Sean fucking Doyle?"

Callaghan's breathing was ragged. He grabbed Hanley's arms and yanked, but Hanley didn't loosen his grip. Callaghan threw his weight sideways. Hanley followed the move, twisting the shirt tighter.

Callaghan scrabbled at Hanley's hands. He was trying to shake his head and Hanley saw panic in his eyes.

Abruptly disgusted at his loss of control, he shoved Callaghan backward into the nearest wall. He heard the door open, turned, and saw Moore walk in. Moore looked from him to Callaghan, who had fallen to his knees and was tugging at his collar.

Callaghan coughed and shot Hanley a glare. "You're crazy. I was nowhere near Hell's Half Acre Wednesday morning and I've a dozen customers who'll swear to it."

ᘓ

"That got us nowhere." Hanley wrapped the muffler back around his throat for the trip upstairs, cursing himself for losing his temper. Callaghan'd done something other than lie about the damned check. But what? "We have to make him talk."

Moore looked as discouraged as Hanley felt. "Maybe we can get something out of Guthrie, along with a confession. That's just about the only thing that'll convict him, anyway."

Hanley knew how a jury would see their evidence for Harden Guthrie as a murderer—the sworn testimony of a rogue cop and a thief arrested for the same crime. The angle of the fatal blow and what that meant for the killer's height would prove Murphy wasn't guilty, but not that Guthrie was. And, without cooperation from Guthrie or Callaghan, they were as far as ever from bringing down Sean Doyle.

Moore cleared his throat. "You should also know…your disciplinary hearing's been scheduled. It'll be Monday." He made a sour face. "Captain Hickey's note arrived just before I came to meet you this morning. I'll go make sure our friend is safe here for the night." He headed away up the stairs.

Hanley pulled out his crushed hat and glared at it. He glanced down the hall toward the holding cells where they'd deposited Callaghan after their interrogation session. Then he jammed the hat on his head and started up. He passed Moore, who was talking to the desk sergeant, and went outside to wait for him.

A patrolman was coming up the steps. Hanley recognized Schmidt and wondered what he was doing here. Maybe he'd come to testify at the police court. *Or he's with Reinhardt and Hickey, and they sent him to check up on me.*

He told himself not to start at shadows like a high-strung horse. Schmidt had reached the top of the steps. Hanley badly wanted to ask him if he'd seen Reinhardt anywhere near Callaghan's saloon on the day they'd arrested Jamie Murphy. Or if he'd gone there himself. He might not get a better chance to do it without other cops around.

"Rolf!" He pushed the muffler down as he strode over. Schmidt looked surprised to see him, then uneasy. Hanley's heart sank. He thought fast. "Did you ever find out about the incendiary device at Market Street? Anyone who saw the bomber?" No one knew anything about the incident at Ida's house. So far the police hadn't found a single witness.

Relief crossed Schmidt's face as he answered. Hanley had the impression he'd been expecting a different question. "I talk to the butcher. Didn't get much, though. Can't talk their language and I think they don't like me. He didn't go after the bomber. Someone else did. Scrawny fellow like a telegraph pole, name of Zalman. Only he won't say what the bomber looked like. Or can't say." He shrugged, then looked uneasy again. "It's true what I hear? You get fired?"

"By Mike Hickey." Hanley couldn't keep the bitterness out of his voice. "I'll have a hearing in a few days."

"Sorry about that. You're good cop. Don't matter who you used to be. I tell them so if you want."

A spark of warmth flared inside Hanley. Maybe he could trust Schmidt after all. "I don't want to drag you into this. But thanks just the same." He paused, trying to think how to bring up what he really wanted to know.

"He ask me to watch you," Schmidt said abruptly. Hanley stiffened, thinking he meant Captain Hickey. "Reinhardt," Schmidt went on. "Back when you get to be detective, he don't like it. Then that rabbi turned up dead and Reinhardt says I should keep an eye on you. Make sure you do the job right. With the city like it is now, everybody ready to kill everybody else over a card game or bad look, we have to be sure everything goes right. And he says—" He broke off, his ears turning pink. "He says maybe you can't handle it. Maybe you find out some old mate of yours did it and you let him go. Arrest someone else, make trouble."

Hanley felt sudden anger. "You've been spying on me?"

"No." Schmidt looked awkward. "A little. Just enough to know you doing OK." He shifted his weight. "Then, yesterday, I see Reinhardt coming out of Callaghan's. He don't go to Irish saloons. When I see him later, searching Murphy's house, he won't tell me why he went to Callaghan's. Says it's not my job to know."

"He was at Callaghan's right before you searched Murphy's house?"

Schmidt nodded. "Wouldn't think nothing of it, he didn't shut me down like that. If he's there because he thinks Callaghan's a fence, like you think, he'd tell me. No reason not. Why's he there right then, anyways? Captain said he's at the courthouse getting the warrant. Why's he stop off at a saloon? Don't make sense." He shook his head. "Don't none of this make sense."

"How much did you tell Reinhardt about me?"

"Not much. About you going to Murphy's couple times on Saturday, Callaghan's in between. The stuff you ask that guy, Nathan, on Sunday."

Hanley felt cold. "Did you mention the warehouse where Nathan said he got relief supplies?"

Looking uncomfortable, Schmidt nodded.

Moore came out then, greeted Schmidt, and spoke to Hanley. "All set. Let's go."

"We may have Reinhardt," Hanley murmured as they moved off. "Schmidt had some interesting things to tell me. I'll fill you in on the way."

"Can we trust him?"

"I think so. They've been using him and he just figured it out."

Moore looked down the road toward the distant jingle of bells from the Madison Street horsecar. "Let's hope we get as lucky with Harden Guthrie."

FORTY-SIX

A t least have some tea before you go out again." Mam kept tight hold of Hanley's hand as they stood in the boardinghouse foyer. "It's brewed and still hot."

"We've no time, Mam." Hanley squeezed her hand gently, then disengaged his own. They'd only stopped because Ida's place was on the way to Guthrie's home, where they hoped to find him. And because Hanley wanted a weapon, in case anyone who might still be following him decided to make trouble.

She gave him a shrewd look. "And you've no time to tell me what's happened since yesterday afternoon, either. Or why you told Miss Kelmansky to come here instead of Lake Street."

"Rivka?" He was staggered. "You spoke to her?"

He saw her then, walking down the hallway with Ida, as if the sound of her name had conjured her up. She carried a slim black book. He watched her approach, not quite able to believe she was there in front of him. She held the book out. "It was in the shul."

Their fingers brushed as he took it. The touch sent a rush of emotions through him—relief that he had another piece of evidence, amazement that Rivka had traveled alone across the city to bring it to him, pride in her courage, fear for the consequences she might face. Her people knew she was gone by now, must have known for hours. And what about Doyle? Had she made herself a target by coming here today, guaranteed he would try to do her harm?

A million words rushed through his head, but he couldn't say any of them. He could only stand there and look at her as he turned the book in his hands.

Mam broke the silence. "Anyway, you can't go back out in that cold without something to warm you. Won't take but a minute." She went down the hallway toward the kitchen and Hanley heard the distant clink of china. After a moment, Rivka followed.

He watched her go and then paged through the book, noting the neat rows of names, items, and numbers. For this, the brief stop home had been worth it. She must have known how valuable it was to bring it all this way. How much had that journey cost her? "She's in trouble, isn't she?" he asked Ida. "For leaving home when she's meant to be mourning. For staying away so long."

"Yes. But I think she does not care as long as she can be of some help to you."

That answer brought a warm glow, like a hearth fire on a cold night. He remembered Rivka in the synagogue, standing near enough to touch, her face alive with love and grief at the memory of her father. Something stirred in him that hadn't in years—a sense of yearning, a desire for a connection. The feeling thrilled and troubled him. He didn't know what to do with it.

Ida nodded toward the book, her expression troubled. "She told us a bit about that. Will it be necessary to bring out everything Rabbi Kelmansky was doing? He and those who helped him?"

"I don't see any way around it," Moore said. He sounded resigned. Ida's shoulders sagged.

"Maybe we'll find one," Hanley said.

"I know you will try. That will have to be enough."

"Their synagogue was bombed last Sunday an hour or two before we were. That might earn them some sympathy."

Ida shook her head. "I have never known that kind of violence toward Jews in this city. Not even with the Fire. Elsewhere, but…"

Mam and Rivka returned with mugs of tea. Mam placed one in Hanley's hands. "Have they caught the fellow who did it?"

He sipped to please her, then took a larger swig as the warmth hit him. He'd needed it more than he realized. "We can't even get a description," he said, sounding weary to his own ears. "Moishe Zalman saw the man, but won't talk about it to the beat cop. They're nervous of him down there. Probably since he threatened to throw some of them in jail, when they wouldn't let him take their rabbi's body to the morgue."

"Could the bombings have to do with the murder?" Ida asked.

Hanley froze with the tea mug halfway back to his mouth. "Say that again."

She did. He looked at Moore. "My God. That's it." He related what had happened at the police station while Moore was out of the room—how Callaghan looked and what both of them had said. "He was frightened of something he'd done that he thought I knew about. Something bad enough that no friends in high places could save him. If he threw those incendiary devices—or even just the one on Market Street..."

Moore set down his tea on the hall table. "Only one way to find out."

Hanley ran a hand through his hair. "We can't go all the way down there now. Zalman barely has enough English to make it worth our while." He saw Rivka exchange glances with Mam and Ida, and his throat went tight. "*No*," he said, and grasped at the first practical objection he could think of. "What if he won't talk to you? Observant Jewish men don't talk to women. Ida said so. And you're in a lot of trouble at home—"

Rivka smiled. "He will talk to me. Especially if I have a little help."

03

Harden Guthrie's home was pale gray clapboard, easily four times the size of the little frame houses in which most Chicagoans lived. It stood on a quiet block of Ada Street, just off Fulton. Two small trees flanked the flagstone walk that led to the front steps. Gold from the sinking sun painted the windows, making it impossible to tell if the gaslights were on or not.

Hanley stamped his feet to bring feeling back into them. His nerves felt taut. Rivka, Mam, and Ida would be nearing Market Street by now. He forced himself to stop thinking about them and focus on the task at hand. "What if he's not here?"

"Then we wait," Moore said. "He'll have to come home sometime."

Hanley wondered if Guthrie was at Muskie's now, getting new amounts from Doyle for the next batch of checks. Or if he'd buried himself in work, staying late at the office in an effort to keep at bay the reality of what he'd done. He'd looked ill when Hanley saw him just two days after the murder. How close to cracking was he now? And what would Doyle do about it, if he thought Guthrie might give way?

Hanley fingered the leaded cosh in his pocket. He hadn't seen the skinny cop who'd been tailing him earlier, nor anyone else who acted like a shadower. He'd mostly healed up from the beating last Monday. He and Moore together should be able to handle anyone who might come after Guthrie. His fears for Guthrie's physical safety seemed overblown the more he thought about them. Surely Doyle wouldn't kill his golden goose unless he had no alternative. And he couldn't know yet whether that was true. Anyone who might still be following Hanley hadn't had time to go tell Doyle anything.

Moore started up the walk toward the front door. Once more, Hanley eyed their surroundings. Ada Street, with its large graceful houses, set back stables, and a small park across the way, was nearly empty. A stout woman with a basket, likely someone's cook carrying groceries, walked around toward the rear entrance three houses down. Across the street near the park a man halted in the middle of the walk and dug in his coat pockets. Hanley watched him a moment. From a distance in the fading light, it was hard to make out much beyond his outer garments and lanky build. The man abruptly stopped his hunt and hurried up the steps of a white clapboard house. Hanley dismissed him from thought and followed Moore.

The chief of detectives raised the brass knocker and gave three sharp raps. Hanley listened as they faded into silence. The silence lengthened, gained weight.

"Gave his housekeeper the evening off?" Hanley asked.

Moore shrugged and tried again. Hanley snuck a look over his shoulder, but saw no one on the street aside from a passing carriage. The silence in its wake was so profound he could hear faint hoofbeats and bells from the horsecar line on West Lake Street a block away.

"Nobody home." Moore turned to Hanley. "Let's try his office."

"Maybe he's just not answering." Hanley grasped the knocker and rapped. If this didn't work, he'd force the door just to be sure the house was empty before they left. "Mr. Guthrie? It's Detective Frank Hanley. We met the other day." He paused to compose his next words. "I think I can help you. But you've got to talk to me."

Silence fell again. Hanley could hear his own heartbeat in counterpoint to the distant clopping of hooves. He eyed the door, trying to gauge how heavy it was. Then he heard muffled footsteps from inside and a click as the bolt shot back.

FORTY-SEVEN

Harden Guthrie stared at them from the doorway. He looked exhausted, with an unhealthy pallor and deep shadows under his eyes. The sight of him shocked Hanley. During the war, he'd seen men with yellow fever who'd looked better.

"You'll want your coat, Mr. Guthrie," Hanley said gently. "We'll be taking you to Union Street Station."

Guthrie blinked at them. When he spoke, his voice sounded brittle. "What for?"

"The murder of Rabbi Asher Kelmansky."

Guthrie sagged against the doorframe. "So he did it, then."

"Who?"

"Doyle." Slowly, Guthrie focused on Hanley's face. "Kelmansky was alive when I left him. But God help me if I know how to prove it."

ʚ

Ida Kirschner wore a shaytel now, a beautifully made wig that matched the natural silver of her hair. Rivka had seen her put it on before they left her house. "Your shul was bombed last Sunday," Ida said in Yiddish from her place next to Tanta Hannah on the sofa. Beside her sat Hanley's mother, her hair covered by a length of black lace. She seemed to be listening intently, as if sheer force of will could help her understand Ida's words. "No great harm came of it, *Baruch Hashem*," Ida went on, "but it may have some bearing on your rabbi's death. We must find out who the bomber is and let the police know. Otherwise there may be a grave miscarriage of justice."

"What have the police to do with justice?" The sharp voice was Fray

Zalman's. "Years ago I lost a husband and two sons because the police got drunk after their Good Friday mass. My Moishe is the only one left to me. Where is the justice in that?"

"I know the officer on this case," Ida said. "He is an honorable man and so is the sergeant he works for. They will do what is right, if we help them."

"I heard a man was arrested for murdering our rabbi." Hannah spoke through stiffened lips, as if she were cold despite the room's warmth. "Mr. James Murphy. An Irishman and a common thief."

"Detective Hanley does not believe him guilty," Ida said.

"Why not? Because he is Irish too?"

Confusion and a glimmer of anger crossed Fray Hanley's face. Rivka wondered how much she had understood. Fray Hanley drew breath as if to speak, but Ida touched her arm and she kept silent.

"Tanta Hannah." Rivka laid a hand on Hannah's knee. "Detective Hanley knows about Onkl Jacob."

"How?"

"I told him."

Hannah's face crumpled. She stood abruptly and stalked into the front hallway.

The sounds of footsteps and male voices outside stifled whatever Rivka might have thought to say. She took refuge in the obvious. "The men are here from the minyan," she told Ida and Fray Hanley. "Moishe will be with them."

∛

The gloom in Guthrie's house felt thick enough to touch. Hanley and Moore followed him into a front parlor, where he halted just inside the doorway and turned on the gaslight with a shaking hand.

The sudden glow revealed a comfortably appointed room, with a small divan and several chairs upholstered in tan velvet. A Turkey carpet in brick red and deep blue covered the floor. Well-stocked bookshelves stood on either side of a fireplace that looked as if it hadn't seen use for days. On a small round table within reach of the divan Hanley spotted a glass tumbler containing a finger's width of whiskey. Although the nearby bottle was only half full, Guthrie didn't smell drunk. Maybe he hadn't gotten beyond his first glassful.

Guthrie shuffled to the table and picked up the whiskey, but didn't drink it. He stared out the front window at the gathering dusk. "I didn't kill him. But I might as well have. I told him to leave it, go home, forget everything that happened at the goddamned warehouse. He didn't listen. I should've made him."

"You followed him from Muskie's that night," Hanley said. "You followed him all the way to Market Street and into the synagogue, where you argued with him and then killed him. In his own holy place. How does a man like you do something like that?"

Guthrie met Hanley's eyes, his face gone even whiter. "I didn't follow him," he said. "I went to his home to talk to him. Or I meant to. But I saw him coming out of another house, and then he went around behind it. I knew he was going to their temple. So I went too. To talk to him one more time."

"About his threat to expose you," Moore said.

Guthrie glanced away. "Yes."

"How did you know the temple was there?" Hanley asked.

"We went there the one time I visited the neighborhood. To see what the Relief and Aid wouldn't, that was how Kelmansky put it." The ghost of a smile flitted across Guthrie's face. "He could be very persuasive."

"So you went in and found him. And the two of you argued and you killed him."

"No!" Guthrie's grip tightened on the whiskey glass. "We had words. I grabbed him. He pushed me away. That was the only time I touched him." He knocked back half the whiskey and wiped his mouth. "I was half-crazed with fear. Doyle saw us at Muskie's, overheard everything we said there. He knew who Kelmansky was, knew he was planning to tell everything to the Relief and Aid executive committee. Doyle meant to go after him. I had to make him understand that." He sank down onto the divan. "I failed."

Hanley gave him a long look as he turned Guthrie's story over in his mind. So far it matched Jamie Murphy's, except for Guthrie's insistence that he hadn't actually followed Kelmansky to Market Street. Just gone there on his own. Though Hanley couldn't see much difference. The shoving match at least explained the odd bruising on Kelmansky's wrists. Not a real fight, just a single moment of impact when the rabbi broke Guthrie's hold.

What had Murphy said happened right after the shoving match? Hanley recalled their conversation as best he could. The last thing Murphy described was Kelmansky breaking Guthrie's grip, pushing him backward toward the table with the menorahs on it. At that point in his telling of the story, Eddie Norris had interrupted them. Murphy never had described the actual murder. Hanley realized that he'd simply assumed Murphy had seen it along with everything else.

He glanced at Moore, who shrugged. Could Murphy have been mistaken? Heard someone coming and run off, then come back to find Kelmansky dead and reached the obvious conclusion? But if Guthrie hadn't swung that menorah, who had?

He thought of the bruise on the rabbi's temple, roughly opposite the fatal head wound. The right size and shape for a cosh. He walked over and sat next to Guthrie. "How did you get to Market Street that night?"

Guthrie looked up. "You believe me, then?"

"Just answer the question."

"I went over to Randolph Street and caught a horsecar." His voice grew anguished. "Only it broke down before we'd gone a block, so I had to walk. I thought I'd reached him in time. I thought..." He shuddered. "I never should have left him alone."

Hanley got up and started to pace. "The horsecar driver. What'd he look like?"

"Short. Round face, mutton-chop whiskers. He got annoyed when I dropped my fare. I remember him swearing at the horses after the wheel came off."

Hanley looked at Moore. They could check the horsecar company's roster, find the driver. Which left one question—if Guthrie was telling the truth, who had Murphy and Red Jack seen following Kelmansky to

Market Street—and who left that muddy boot print in the synagogue yard?

A carriage rattled by outside. The front window was a wall of dark. Hanley stared at it, uneasy. He shook off the feeling. "Do you own boots, Mr. Guthrie? I want to see them. Every pair you've got."

ᴄჳ

"Yes, I saw the man who threw the bomb," Moishe said. "He ran fast, but I was faster. Not that it did much good."

"Tell us what he looked like," Rivka said.

Moishe glanced at Onkl Jacob, who gave him a slight nod. "Taller than Reb Nathan. Not so tall as your father. Big chest. Extra weight around the middle." He rubbed his jaw. "Strong like an ox. He hit me so hard, my head rang."

"Did you see his face?" Ida asked.

Moishe nodded. "Round like a potato. Blue eyes, dark brown hair going thin on top. No beard or mustache." Faint satisfaction crossed his face. "I gave him a nosebleed when I tackled him. I tried to hit him, but—" A pink flush crept up his neck. "He kicked me—" The blush deepened. "He made me let go. Then he hit me and ran off. By the time I could get up again, he was gone." He paused. "He smelled like kerosene. Also like liquor, on his breath and his hands. Like the slivovitz we had at Purim last spring."

"You will tell this to Detective Hanley?" Rivka said.

Moishe looked at Onkl Jacob again. Seconds passed. Then, shoulders slumping, Jacob nodded and left the parlor. To find Tanta Hannah, Rivka realized. Her throat felt tight as she turned to Ida and Fray Hanley. "Is it the same man? The one Hanley thinks it is?"

Ida shrugged. "I don't know. But we will tell him as soon as he comes home."

FORTY-EIGHT

Guthrie's dressing room held a wardrobe, dressing table, shirt stand, and a chair, all of solid dark wood. Hanley and Moore watched him take two pairs of boots out of his wardrobe. After he'd finished, Hanley looked the interior up and down. He saw three dress shirts, two sack suits, some folded trousers, and a fitted black suit with a cutaway jacket. He couldn't tell how recently any of them had been washed.

He examined the boots. One pair was fine black leather suitable for horseback riding, the other well-made walking boots. Neither bore a maker's mark, though that alone didn't prove anything. Guthrie could have tossed out the boots he'd worn that night or given them away. If he'd thought of it.

If he killed Kelmansky.

Hanley told him to take off his left shoe, then found his drawing of the muddy footprint and set it on the floor. "Put your foot here. Toe to toe."

Guthrie did so. Hanley knelt for a close look. What he saw made him ease back on his haunches, his thoughts narrowing to a single point. Guthrie's stockinged foot completely covered the pencil lines.

"That'll do," Hanley said. Guthrie lifted his foot and reached for his shoe. Hanley stood and handed the drawing to Moore, but he was certain of what he'd seen. Guthrie's feet were too big to have left the muddy footprint behind.

"You believe me now," Guthrie said.

Hanley wanted to, so badly he wasn't sure he could trust himself. If Guthrie had told the truth, then Hanley knew what must have happened that night. Yet it all rested on the shape of a single footprint. And there were other things that didn't fit. Like the menorah. That was the kind of thing a man like Guthrie would grab and swing in the grip of terror and rage. Not the choice of a habitual violent criminal who'd carry his own weapon. *Like Billy Shaughnessy.*

He thought of Kelmansky's shattered skull. No question the menorah blow had killed him. He fished out his sketchbook and found the drawing of the wound. Kelmansky's dead face stared up at him from the page. Hanley traced the outline of the bruise on the temple. *Two blows*, he thought. One with a cosh that struck Kelmansky down and a second, fatal one with the menorah as he lay unconscious on the floor. The menorah was heavy, he recalled, much heavier than a chunk of leaded wood. Heavy enough to kill for sure. For Doyle, Billy would have made sure.

The crackle of paper sounded loud in the stillness. Hanley glanced over and saw Moore folding up the drawing of the footprint. Only one piece of the puzzle remained and Hanley prayed Guthrie had more than words to back it up.

"What I want to know," he said, "is exactly what Doyle had on our friend here." He looked at Guthrie. "We know Kelmansky threatened to expose something you were doing. Can't have been your little Robin-Hood aid scheme, because Kelmansky himself was neck deep in that, and it was helping people in need. He wouldn't have wanted to shut that down. Not unless he found out about something bad enough to make it necessary. And for Doyle to have him killed."

Guthrie stood still while Hanley ignored the plea in his eyes. He glanced at Moore next, who shrugged. Then he went to the dressing table, took something out of a drawer, and handed it to Hanley. A book, bound in brown leather and small enough to fit in a coat pocket. Hanley opened it and saw rows of numbers and names in Guthrie's handwriting. Some numbers were dates, others dollar amounts. The first half-dozen entries matched those he and Moore had found on the falsified check receipts from the Relief and Aid. There were sixteen names in all with dates spaced two and three days between them.

"I was giving Doyle money," Guthrie said. "He told me how much he wanted every few days and who he'd be sending to the bank to get it. Not their names, just whether they were men or women. So I could pick names that fit from obituaries."

"We'd guessed as much," Moore said. "Kelmansky knew?"

Guthrie nodded. "I told him. That night. I didn't want to. But he wouldn't leave it. Everything I said to make him go away just made him more determined to get answers out of me."

"And he was going to tell the Relief and Aid," Hanley said.

"Yes." Guthrie slumped into the chair. "Only about what he and I and Jacob Nathan were doing—but that would've made the executive committee take a closer look at my books. They'd have found out about the money as well."

"So what was it between you and Doyle to make you pay him blackmail?"

Somewhere downstairs a door creaked. Guthrie stiffened. Dread crept over his face.

The ensuing silence pressed against Hanley's ears. Then he heard footsteps, stealthy and soft. Two people at least, moving slowly through the house.

He reached into his back pocket for his cosh.

FORTY-NINE

G od help me," Guthrie whispered. He gripped the chair arms so hard Hanley half-expected to hear the wood crack.

Hanley leaned toward him. "Is there a back staircase?"

"Just off the kitchen."

"Front's closer," Moore said softly.

"Stay here," Hanley told Guthrie. He and Moore left the dressing room.

Out in the hall, Moore cocked a thumb toward the rear of the house, then moved in that direction. Hanley nodded. Cosh in hand, he crept toward the front staircase.

Voices floated up from below, whispers he couldn't make out. They seemed to be coming from the parlor. The fifth stair down creaked, Hanley recalled from their earlier trip upstairs. He avoided it and kept his gaze on the spill of light from the half-open parlor door.

The door opened wider and someone came through it. Tall and broad-shouldered, the gaslight behind him glinting off his blond hair. *Charming Billy.*

Hanley pressed against the wall, then launched himself forward as Billy turned toward the staircase. They collided with bruising force and fell against the base of the steps. Hanley raised his cosh, but Billy threw him off. Hanley's lower back slammed into the stair railing. He grabbed the rail with his free hand to keep himself from going over. "Where is he, Billy? Where's Doyle?"

Charming Billy swore and charged him, his own cosh raised. Hanley sidestepped and swung his weapon at Billy's head. The glancing blow made Billy stagger, but he didn't go down.

From the back of the house came grunts, curses, and the sound of blows. Moore must have run into Doyle, or maybe another bully boy. Or both. Hanley had no doubt Doyle was here—but where? Then Billy rushed him again and he had no time to think of anything else.

He ducked around Billy, away from the staircase. Billy swung at him. Leaded wood struck Hanley in the ribs, shooting fire through his side. It took everything he had not to double over. He turned in time to meet Billy's second charge, which sent them both crashing through the parlor doorway.

Hanley landed on his back, Billy half on top of him. The weight sent new agony rippling through his injured ribs. As Billy shoved himself up on all fours, cosh raised, Hanley kicked upward as hard as he could. His right foot caught Billy's wrist. Billy's weapon flew out of his hand. He yelled and jerked away.

Hanley rolled to his feet and hurled himself forward. Billy swung wildly at him, but Hanley blocked the blow with his forearm and rammed a fist into Billy's jaw. Billy crashed into the little table. The whiskey bottle on it hit the floor and shattered. Hanley smelled the sharp tang of spilled alcohol. His back hurt and his ribcage screamed, but he kept moving. Billy was on his knees, shaking his head. Hanley staggered over to him and slammed his cosh against Billy's thigh. Billy howled and fell to the floor. Hanley hit him again, this time on the knee. He heard a bone snap as Billy screamed, then merciful silence as the pain took him.

Hanley sank to the floor, breathing hard. His left knee throbbed, its injury aggravated by the fight. From the rear of the house he could still hear grunts and blows. *Just another second*, he promised himself. In just another second he would get up and go help Moore—

"Didn't think you still had it in you." The voice, drawling and amused, belonged to Sean Doyle.

Hanley turned. Doyle was leaning against the archway between parlor and dining room, a derringer in his hand. As Hanley's eyes met his, he aimed the gun at Hanley's chest.

A hurtling body slammed into Doyle, throwing him off balance. His shot buried itself in the ceiling plaster. Hanley lurched up and ran toward the archway, where Harden Guthrie grappled with Doyle for the gun. *The damned fool.* Hanley threw himself at Doyle. All three of them staggered backward. From the kitchen came a gigantic crash and a thud as a body hit the floor. Then silence.

His hand closed over the derringer. Doyle had one shot left before he'd need to reload. He could feel Doyle's fingers, every muscle and tendon taut as he fought Hanley's grip. Doyle threw his weight sideways, taking Hanley and Guthrie with him in a grotesque mockery of a boxer's move. No one let go.

"Drop it," Hanley hissed in Doyle's face.

"Go to hell." One finger inched toward the trigger.

Hanley braced his feet and held fast with both hands, fighting to keep the derringer pointed down and away. The effort sent fire through his damaged knee, but he ignored it. "I should've sent you there long ago."

The second shot cracked through the air and dug a hole low in the wall. Doyle dropped the empty gun and shoved Hanley backward. "You first, boyo." He raised a foot and stomped down. Guthrie cried out and loosened his grip. With a half turn and a hard shove, Doyle threw him off. Guthrie crashed into the sideboard and slid down it, one hand clutching his side. Hanley saw blood seeping through his fingers.

Push knife, Hanley realized as Doyle swung the three-inch blade toward him. He moved to block the blow, but he'd miscalculated. The knife scored across his arm near the elbow.

White-hot pain made him gasp. Doyle laughed. He felt the man's hot breath against his cheek. Violent images flashed through his brain—finger-shaped bruises on Kate's face, fire hurtling through the boardinghouse window. A shank blade coming toward him in the dim Armory cell. The bloody gash in Paddy's throat. Kelmansky's staved-in skull. Pegeen, empty eyes unblinking over her bruised and swollen mouth. He was all fear and rage and pain, seeing death and knowing it was either Doyle or him.

Doyle swung again. Hanley gritted his teeth and grabbed the blade. Braced against a fresh wave of dizzying pain, he pulled it from Doyle's grip and backhanded the knife hilt into his face.

Doyle grunted and staggered, then recovered his balance and headbutted him in the chest. They crashed against the parlor archway. Hanley dropped the push knife. As Doyle dove for it, Hanley braced himself on his good leg and rammed his injured knee into Doyle's chin. The impact made him gasp. Doyle *whuffed* and went down. Hanley plunged after him, rolled him over, grabbed his coat collar, and slammed the back of his head against the floor.

Doyle grabbed Hanley's wrists and bucked, but couldn't shake him off. Hanley slammed his head again. Doyle grunted in pain. Hanley took joy in the sound. Fury had him in its grip and wasn't letting go. "You're done, Sean bloody Doyle." *Slam.* "Boyo." *Slam.* "You're done!"

He was dimly aware of Doyle's hold slackening, Doyle's voice begging him to stop. Soft and weak and full of pain. Other voices too. Moore, saying his name. And a third voice, one he'd thought not to hear again. Guthrie. "Don't," Guthrie was saying. "Don't."

He blinked and glanced toward the sideboard where he'd seen Guthrie fall. Moore knelt by the man, pressing a wadded-up handkerchief to his ribcage. Guthrie's face was a mask of pain.

"Don't kill him," he said. He sagged back, pale and sweating. "Been enough of that."

Hanley looked down. He saw fear mingled with the loathing in Doyle's eyes. He tightened his grip on Doyle's coat and lifted his head and shoulders a few inches. Doyle looked terrified.

Slowly, Hanley lowered him back down. "*We're* done," he said and belted Doyle across the jaw.

○3

"He needs a doctor." Moore looked pale and tense as he held the handkerchief against Guthrie's stab wound. "You, too."

"I'm all right." Hanley barely recognized his own voice. He felt like he'd been through a cannon barrage followed by a bayonet charge. His cut fingers burned and his arm and ribcage throbbed. His left leg could barely hold him up. "Where's the nearest fire-box?"

"South…end of the block," Guthrie said. He sounded weak and thready. "Doctor…" He closed his eyes. "Three doors down. This side. Should be home."

The handkerchief was mostly red. With his good hand Hanley dug out his own handkerchief and gave it to Moore. "Tell the firehouse to send to Union Street," Moore said as he took it. "Make sure they talk to Captain Miller."

☙

Captain Miller came himself, along with four handpicked officers. While the doctor saw Guthrie safely loaded into an ambulance, Miller and his men hauled Doyle, Billy, and the man Moore had fought with up off the floor and cuffed them. When the Union Street officers marched Moore's attacker outside Hanley recognized him as the skinny cop from Lily Stemple's. Captain Hickey must have set him to shadow Hanley after his release from the Armory jail.

Hanley followed them out. He needed to see Doyle thrown in the paddy wagon and the barred doors close on him. Needed to know he'd finally put Doyle—and Billy—where they belonged. Where they couldn't hurt Kate, or Rivka, or anyone, anymore. Too late for Paddy and for Rivka's father. Ten years too late for Pegeen. Still, it was worth something.

"You're making a mistake," Doyle said through gritted teeth, as the Union Street captain hauled him around the back of the wagon. He jerked his head toward Hanley, but managed to avoid meeting his eyes. "That one's lost his badge. Had no right to be here. Captain Hickey will—"

"Shut up," Miller said. He shoved Doyle into the wagon, slammed the doors, and dusted off his hands.

"He's right, you know." Hanley felt like he could sleep for a month, if only he could ignore the dull ache in his ribs and leg and the sharper pain in his injured arm and hand. "I'm not much in favor with some powerful people at the moment."

"Sergeant Moore'll vouch for you. So will I." Miller glanced back at the paddy wagon. "I've wanted Doyle ever since one of his guns got my brother killed back in '62. Blew his hand clean off. I looked into things, after, and found out who sent that damned gun." Miller looked bleak. "Poor Matt never even got to fight for the Union. Because of Sean fucking Doyle." He gripped Hanley's good arm and gave it a gentle shake. "Far as I'm concerned, you did right bringing Doyle down. And I'll say so to anyone who asks."

FIFTY

February 27, 1872

S unlight flooded through the horsecar as it jounced down Madison Street. A late February thaw day, warm enough to melt the remaining snow and turn the streets glistening damp. A welcome change from the bitter cold during most of the past three weeks. Hanley shifted in his seat, settling his just-healed arm as comfortably as he could, and wished his mood matched the weather. He had plenty to celebrate—the successful end of the Kelmansky case and his reinstatement after a hearing. But he couldn't give himself over to it.

Billy and Doyle were behind bars, awaiting trial. Billy's boots, taken in lockup at Union Street Station, had only confirmed what Hanley already knew. Any mud and blood from the night of the rabbi's murder had long since been scrubbed away, but nothing could remove the incriminating size, shape, and maker's mark. By rights Billy should hang for killing Rabbi Kelmansky, though certain arrangements—unfortunately necessary, given Doyle's clout—would spare his miserable life. Doyle might yet swing for Paddy, though. The red hairs, plus traces of blood in the design on his ring, tied him to the beating beyond doubt. Will Rushton had hopes of finding similar traces on Doyle's push knife. Near the hilt, maybe, where Guthrie's blood might not have obscured it completely.

Guthrie would be jailed too, for embezzlement and theft, as soon as he recovered. That was part of what weighed on him, Hanley realized.

The thought of Guthrie in prison seemed wrong, even though he deserved it. And the theft charges weren't confined to Doyle's blackmail money. They included the stolen aid supplies as well. True to the word he'd given Hanley, Guthrie had tried to shield Jacob Nathan and Moishe Zalman from full culpability. How successful he'd be was anyone's guess.

Hanley leaned against the hard wooden bench and closed his eyes. Just a few more stops till Market Street. He needed to have some idea of what to say by then. How to explain to Rivka why her father had died.

03

"I had a chance to buy stock in a railway," Guthrie'd said from his hospital bed when Hanley had demanded answers about his entanglements with Doyle. "The Pittsburgh, Fort Wayne, and Chicago was going bankrupt. It needed buyers to reorganize. I wanted in for as much as I could get. But I needed money and I was stretched to my limit."

"You couldn't go to the banks?"

"Wouldn't give me the time of day. And I couldn't lose the opportunity. So I went to a friend who usually had money to play with. This time he didn't...but *his* good friend, Sean Doyle, did."

"Doyle gave you a loan?"

"He bought in with me. I got my railway stock, and a fat government contract just a few months later. Then another and another. We were making money so fast we might as well have been printing greenbacks. And then Doyle started making even more money by sending shoddy uniforms and bad food and poorly made guns to the front lines. He knew people—patrons of his gambling hells, I'd guess—who cut corners to pad their contracts. They paid extra to ship the things with no questions asked."

"Jesus." Vivid memories had sent Hanley out of his chair to pace across the room. Long marches in ill-made boots that gave him stinging blisters, stomach cramps sharp as stab wounds from camp stew made with tainted pork. Men crippled or killed when their guns exploded in their hands. "What in hell possessed you to partner up with a crime boss?"

305

"I didn't *know!*" Guthrie gripped the blankets. "He told me he was a businessman. And I..." He looked down. "I needed the money. I wanted the chance."

"So you, what? Helped him out? Went along for the ride?"

"Neither." The word came out in a gravelly whisper. "I found out what he'd been doing when I started getting complaints. That was my job, keeping track of things like that. I went to him. I thought he'd be shocked. He laughed at me." His voice rose a notch. "Called me a chump, asked me where in the name of God's bleeding heaven I'd thought our profits were coming from. I got angry. I told him I'd go to the War Office. And he said—" Guthrie turned his head toward the window, as if the pale winter sunlight could give him strength to go on. "He said I was welcome to. That he'd have his own story and it'd be a damned sight more convincing."

"So you let him get away with it."

"I got out." Guthrie stared out the window. "Too lily-livered to buck him. But I couldn't keep taking the money, knowing. I came back to Chicago, poured what I had left into lake and river shipping. I should've gone elsewhere, I guess—started over someplace Doyle wasn't—but I'd lost so much, I needed every contact I had to rebuild. Months went by, then a year, with no word from him. I thought I was safe, that he'd moved on to larger targets."

"Until he came to see you last December."

"Before that, actually." Guthrie fidgeted with the bedclothes. "Four years ago, when I'd made good my losses and was expanding into rail again, Doyle made me take him on as a silent partner. I guessed later he needed my business to launder money for political influence. I let him. I didn't think I had a choice."

A horrible thought struck Hanley. "Your mayoral campaign? Was that Doyle's idea too?"

Guthrie shook his head. "He was all for it when he found out, though. If I'd won, he'd have had a mayor in his pocket. Instead, he had to settle for the cash I could slip him once I became district director. He wanted money to rebuild what he'd lost in the Fire. I thought...I hoped...the

Fire'd ruined him. Sent him away from the city like so many others, looking for opportunities back East. Or further west. I should've known better." A huff of air escaped him. "Poor Agnes Wentworth. She thinks she's been working for a saint."

The waste of it appalled Hanley, all the more because he'd liked Guthrie. He seemed to give a damn about people, to want to do good where he had a chance. An honest man too inclined to trust that others were as well. Doyle's favorite kind to chew up and spit out.

He opened his eyes. They were approaching Market Street. He pulled the cord and got to his feet.

☙

When Hannah Nathan opened the door and saw him, her startled look swiftly turned wary. Hanley felt a pang of guilt, along with doubt about the wisdom of coming here. Of course Rivka wouldn't be on her own, and Hannah Nathan was the person least likely to let him in. He squared his shoulders and plunged ahead. "Good afternoon, Mrs. Nathan. Is Miss Kelmansky at home?"

"If you have a message, I will give it." Her voice was low and tightly controlled.

"Who is it, Tanta Hannah?" Rivka appeared in the hall, just visible over Hannah's shoulder, wiping her hands on her apron. Framed by her dark kerchief and the collar of her mourning dress, her face was a pale oval marked by lack of sleep. His heart jumped at the sight of her.

She saw him and halted. Surely he hadn't imagined the flash of gladness in her face? "I won't take but a few minutes," he said. "I promised to tell her what happened to her father."

His heart was hammering so hard it seemed Hannah must hear it. She stepped back, leaving space for him to pass. "You may talk in the parlor."

The warmth within was a welcome change from the damp outdoor chill. Hannah stepped out, but left the parlor door half open. Hanley watched her go and then looked at Rivka. A few wisps of hair clung to her cheek. A desire to gently stroke them back made his hands tingle.

Suddenly he felt awkward, unsure of what might come out of his mouth. Buying time to cover his feelings, he glanced around the little parlor. Against the back wall stood a narrow bookcase of dark wood, a heavy-looking thing likely saved from the Fire. He moved in for a closer look at the volumes it held. Foreign lettering stood out in gold against their dark spines. He glanced up and saw similar lettering on the room's sole piece of artwork—a gilt-framed rectangle with words he couldn't read forming an intricate, colored design around a central block of text.

"It is Hebrew," Rivka said from behind him. "My parents' *ketubah*— their marriage contract."

He kept his eyes on the alien letters as if they could tell him what to say. He felt nervous of even turning toward her, and yet the only place he wanted to be was here. "Jamie Murphy's home," he said finally.

"He was not guilty, then. Just as Fray Kirschner said." She glanced down at her hands, which were bound up in her apron. It struck him suddenly that she also didn't know what to say or do. "If...if you would like some tea..." she began.

"I came to tell you about your father." The words came out in a rush. "He tried to save a friend. That's why he died. I'm sorry I didn't come sooner, but I wanted to make sure the case was closed first."

The rest of it poured out of him then, as if a locked gate had been shoved open. He told her about Billy and Doyle. And about Guthrie. "He'll go to prison. Over the money. God knows if he'll survive it. And Doyle—we've got him now, but he could still buy his way out at trial if he taps the right judge. Make Billy take all the punishment for your father and my friend Paddy. Even after everything. Wasn't Doyle who killed your father, after all. I'm sure he did for Paddy, but we may not be able to make that stick." He ran a hand through his hair. "You don't need to hear all that. Forgive me."

"This man Doyle," she said. "He is in prison now?"

Hanley nodded. "Thanks to you, and Ida, and my mother. If you hadn't found out Callaghan was the bomber, we'd never have gotten him to turn on Doyle." He smiled a little, remembering. He'd finally dragged himself home that night, his thoughts veering between grim satisfaction and fear that Doyle might yet walk free, to hear from Ida the truth that would make it well-nigh impossible. Early the next morning, Hanley and Moore had gone to pick Callaghan up.

Callaghan's kinship with Doyle hadn't withstood his terror at the threat of being publicly identified as an incendiary. Anyone suspected of attempted arson in the wake of the Great Fire would have been hanged from the nearest street lamp and Callaghan knew it. His testimony along with Guthrie's had gotten Doyle indicted for blackmail, while Billy ensured he'd pay for murder as well. At least Hanley hoped so. In exchange for his sworn evidence about Paddy and Doyle's order to kill Kelmansky, Charming Billy would get life in prison, instead of the rope, for carrying it out. "He's at Union Street Station." Not the Armory. Moore had insisted on that. "Which he won't be getting out of any time soon, even with a fat bribe. With the Relief and Aid involved, the case is front-page news now. The papers'd be all over it, if nothing else."

"Then whatever happens next is a trouble for another day."

He smiled wider at that. "You sound like Mam. She keeps telling me the world's not meant for me to fix all by myself." He sobered abruptly. "I only wish I could."

She took a step toward him. Light from the window gave her face a soft glow. "We have an old story—that Hashem has not sent another Great Flood because forty righteous men are working to heal the world. For their sake He lets us all live out our imperfect lives." She paused as if searching for words. "We were strangers, but you did your best for us. Risked your livelihood, even your life. Not many would have done that for poor Jews. Especially now. You are a righteous man, Frank Hanley."

Without planning to, he took her hand. He wanted to do more. Hold her close, feel her slender warmth in his arms, her heart beating against his.

Surprise flashed across her face. He dropped her hand as if burned and turned away. What in the name of God was he doing? Not daring to look at her, he moved toward the door. "That's all I came to say. I'll go now."

"Frank!"

He turned at the sound of his given name on her lips. Her eyes were overbright, her cheeks flushed, one hand raised toward him as if to draw him back. "Thank you. For everything."

He hardly dared believe the tenderness in her face. Then Hannah came in and all he could say was goodbye.

⁂

Rivka stood at the front window, watching Hanley walk away. With every step he took, she felt her heart contracting. She hadn't wanted him to leave, but had no words to make him stay. *Because I should not want him to.*

Still she watched him, unwilling to sacrifice even these last few seconds of their acquaintance. If he knew what she felt...if she had the courage to tell him...would he turn back? Even just to look at her one last time?

Her breath caught as he stopped a little way down Market Street and turned toward the house. Could he see her? She moved closer to the window. He did see her. He must—he was lifting a hand in farewell.

She raised her own hand and pressed it to the glass.

⁂

Later that night, Hanley sat on the edge of his bed and took off his boots. He heard Kate singing "Green Grow the Rushes" in the next room as she brushed out her hair. She hadn't sung since the night she was attacked. The sound made him happier than he'd felt in days. He leaned back and stretched, and his gaze fell on his fiddle case.

The fiddle felt unfamiliar after nearly five months of neglect. He cradled it and rested his fingertips on the polished wood. Kate had stopped singing and he heard her cross the room toward her bed. He plucked a string, then another. They were only a little out of tune.

He tightened the frog and rosined the bow, ignoring twinges of pain from the barely healed knife cuts on his fingers and forearm, and settled the fiddle on his shoulder. Then he realized he had no idea what to play. He thought of Rivka, watching him out the window as he walked away down Market Street.

His fingers knew his heart better than he did. He began to play a familiar tune, wistful and bittersweet—"If Ever You Were Mine." Each note fell like rain into the quiet night.

ACKNOWLEDGMENTS

An author never writes a book alone, and this book would not be what it is without the contributions of many people. I owe enormous thanks to literary agent Danielle Egan-Miller and her wonderful staff at Browne & Miller Literary Associates, for running *Shall We Not Revenge* through their collective brain trust and offering copious notes that helped give my story greater depth and higher stakes. Similar thanks go to my publisher and editor, Emily Victorson, who prodded me to bring out more vividly some pivotal pieces of Detective Hanley's past. My writers' group, the Red Herrings—Libby Hellmann, David J. Walker, Michael Allan Dymmoch, Mary Harris, Irene Reed, and Jerry Silbert—all asked excellent questions and gave the most useful critiques an author could desire. Thanks to each and every one of you for your time, expertise, and friendship.

Thanks also to my mother, Alice Piron, for Hanley family stories that stuck in my head—I'm sure there's more than a little of Nana Hanley in the character of Mam. My father-in-law, Phil Gelman, served as my Yiddish consultant and showed me how to solve the moral dilemma Rivka faces partway through the book. Oak Park Temple provided a haven to write in, three mornings a week while my younger son was downstairs at Glasser Preschool. I spent those hours in the blessed quiet of the upstairs library, surrounded by source material for my novel's Jewish characters, including Irving Cutler's *The Jews of Chicago*, and several Yiddish dictionaries (which I consulted whenever my father-in-law was unavailable). Any errors in my attempts to paint Old World Jewish culture in a rapidly changing, nineteenth-century American metropolis are mine alone.

No historical novelist setting a story in Chicago can do without the Chicago History Museum, whose extensive archives include photos, newspaper articles, drawings, city directories, and even the actual forms used by the Relief and Aid Society to determine who merited aid post-Fire and who did not. The ever-helpful staff members were happy to answer my questions and hunt for whatever I needed. The museum also hosts a website, "The Great Chicago Fire and the Web of Memory," that I cannot recommend highly enough as a starting place for deeper research.

Finally, I am indebted to several other authors whose works I consulted while researching *Shall We Not Revenge*. They include Karen Sawislak, Perry Duis, Donald R. Miller, and Richard Lindberg (who also let me pick his brain about what little formal police procedure existed in Chicago during this time period). For those interested in Chicago history, I heartily recommend their books, all of which are listed in the Historical Note. The Chicagology website and the Chicago Crime Scenes blog likewise proved invaluable, especially in tracking down tidbits such as which buildings survived the Fire and where the city's rougher neighborhoods were located. To the creators of those websites, thank you from a fellow history nerd.

Like all stories worth anything, *Shall We Not Revenge* was a struggle and a joy to write. I hope you'll find it a joy to read.

HISTORICAL NOTE

The Great Chicago Fire devastated much of the city between October 8th and 10th, 1871. The first few months after the Great Conflagration, as the newspapers called it, were a turbulent period. Widespread destitution occurred virtually overnight, coupled with an unshakable determination to recover and rebuild as swiftly as possible.

The Fire engulfed a significant portion of the city's southeast section, known as the South Division and bounded by the south and east branches of the Chicago River. It likewise destroyed a small part of the West Division and a vast amount of the North Division. None of this stopped Chicago's energetic citizenry from starting over as best they could. From late October, when the embers cooled, through most of December, parts of the city were rebuilt at dazzling speed. Spotty funding and the widespread failure of insurance companies kept the process unorganized and sporadic, with the greatest efforts focused on such vital engines of commerce as railway depots, lumberyards, warehouses, and the profitable commercial buildings and banks common throughout the downtown area between Lake, Wells, Madison, and State Streets. The city's geography at this time was haphazard compared to modern-day Chicago—blocks of office buildings might be found cheek-by-jowl with stretches of small shops and frame houses occupied by ordinary Chicagoans, as well as ramshackle emergency barracks and the dank foundation pits of burned buildings claimed by desperate squatters for the meager shelter they offered.

Politics and money, by contrast, haven't changed much. After the Fire, donations from around the world poured into the stricken city, but control of them was wrested within days from city government by the privately run Relief and Aid Society. Composed of prominent men from Chicago's elite native-born "Yankee" class, the RAS saw giving to all in need as harmful to the poor, encouraging a "spirit of dependence" that rewarded laziness and discouraged self-sufficiency. They believed in "scientific charity" to separate the "worthy poor" from the rabble and ensure that relief went only to the former. Those denied aid, and their families, were denied permanently. No recourse existed for appeal. Add to this the chancy nature of employment and skyrocketing rents in sections of Chicago untouched by the Fire, and you have a recipe for suffering. It is against this backdrop that the fictional Rabbi Kelmansky acts as he does, and unfortunately pays with his life. Ultimately, the Relief and Aid Society ended up with $600,000 in unspent fire-relief funds, which the organization kept for its own uses.

The Fire destroyed many landmarks and civic buildings, including the Court House and the public library. The consequent loss of documents and records greatly complicates historical research into exactly what was where in early 1872. In creating Frank Hanley's Chicago, I have relied on what sources I could, and fallen back on the "fudge factor" when necessary. Any resulting errors are my own. One deliberate change is the location of the police station where Hanley works. The actual address of the station was considerably west of the river, far from the areas where the bulk of *Shall We Not Revenge* takes place. I therefore invented a fictional version of the station and placed it just off Lake Street where the Chicago River branches meet, a locale that puts Hanley closer to the action of the novel.

Though most characters in this book are fictional, a few are known historical figures. Wirt Dexter and O.C. Gibbs were prominent members of the Relief and Aid Society, and Joseph Medill won election as mayor in November of 1871. C.P. Holden was a real alderman, with strong ties to the immigrant communities of the South Division neighborhood he served. Captain Michael Hickey commanded the First Precinct and was noted for corruption. The Comiskey Probe in 1868 cited him for running a bail-bond racket out of the original Armory station (though he never faced sanction for it) and, in 1870, he joined forces with up-and-coming gambling prince "King Mike" McDonald to crush McDonald's competition with selective raids on rival gambling houses. Sergeant Thomas Moore commanded the twelve-man detective squad, though little else is known about him. He became head of the only recently formed detective squad in 1865, and also served for a time as president of the Policemen's Benevolent Association (founded in 1861).

Readers wishing to explore Chicago's history further will find plenty to interest them in the following bibliography. However, it is by no means a complete list of every source consulted in the writing of this novel.

⅓∝

Andreas, Alfred T. *History of Chicago*, v. III (1871-1885). A. T. Andreas Company, 1884.
[available online: https://archive.org/details/historyofchicago03andruoft]

Asbury, Herbert. *Gem of the Prairie: An Informal History of the Chicago Underworld.* Northern Illinois University Press, 1986 (first printing 1940; reprinted in 2002 as *The Gangs of Chicago*).

Colbert, Elias, and Chamberlain, Everett. *Chicago and the Great Conflagration.* J.S. Goodman & Company, 1871.
[available online: https://archive.org/details/chicagogreatconf00colb]

Goodspeed, E. J. *History of the Great Fires in Chicago and the West.* Goodspeed & Co., 1871
[available online: https://archive.org/details/historyofgreatfi00good]

Lowe, David. *The Great Chicago Fire.* Dover, 1979.

Kogan, Herman. *The Great Fire: Chicago, 1871.* Putnam, 1971.

Cutler, Irving. *The Jews of Chicago*. University of Illinois Press, 1996.

Duis, Perry. *Challenging Chicago: Coping with Everyday Life, 1837-1920*. University of Illinois Press, 1998.

Flinn, John J. and Wilkie, John E. *History of the Chicago Police: From the Settlement of the Community to the Present Time*. Chicago Police Book Fund, 1887 (reprinted by Kessinger Press, 2007).
[available online: https://archive.org/details/historyofchicago00flin]

Lindberg, Richard. *The Gambler King of Clark Street*. Southern Illinois University Press, 2009.

———. *To Serve and Collect*. Southern Illinois University Press, 1998 (first printed by Praeger Press, 1991).

Miller, Donald L. *City of the Century: The Epic of Chicago and the Making of America*. Simon & Schuster, 1996.

Sawislak, Karen. *Smoldering City: Chicagoans and the Great Fire, 1871-1874*. University of Chicago Press, 1995.

Chicago Crime Scenes Project: http://chicagocrimescenes.blogspot.com/

Chicagology: http://chicagology.com/

Encyclopedia of Chicago: http://www.encyclopedia.chicagohistory.org

The Great Chicago Fire & The Web of Memory (a comprehensive web site on the Fire created by the Chicago History Museum): http://www.greatchicagofire.org/

GLOSSARY

Ano (Czech/Bohemian) Yes

Areyn/kum areyn (Yiddish) Inside/Come inside

Bar mitzvah (Hebrew) "Son of the commandment;" refers to the Jewish ceremony commonly held at the thirteenth birthday, when a boy assumes adult religious obligations. In Hanley and Rivka's time, the ceremony was held only for boys. Modern-day Jews celebrate *bat mitzvah* for girls as well.

Baruch Hashem (Hebrew) "Blessed is the Name" ("the Name" meaning God)

Bimah (Hebrew) Elevated platform at the front of a synagogue that holds the table, desk, or lectern from which the Torah is read

Bohemian Nineteenth-century term for the Czech nationality or language

Boxty (Irish Gaelic) A fried mashed-potato cake with onions

Boyo (Irish Gaelic) Boy; can be affectionate or derogatory depending on context

Bully boys Thugs, equivalent to contemporary "leg-breakers" or "muscle"

Bummer A shiftless vagrant, lazy person, or sponger; often applied to politicians

Bunco-man/bunco-steerer Con man, often a card-sharp; a bunco man frequently posed as a well-dressed gambler "down on his luck," or an "honest country farmer" new to the big city

Cantor One who sings and/or leads chanted prayers in a synagogue

Challah Traditional bread made for the Sabbath, often braided

Faro A popular card game common in nineteenth-century gambling houses

Footpads Street thieves, roughly equivalent to modern-day muggers

Fray/Fraylin (Yiddish) Mrs./Miss; similar to the German "Frau/Fraulein"

Gambling hell/gaming hell A gambling house

Golem Clay man from Jewish folklore, known for mindlessly carrying out any task it is given, often to the point of destructiveness. In some tales the golem protects a village against attack by Christians. In others, it rampages until stopped.

Goy/goyische (Hebrew/Yiddish) Literally "nation/of the nations;" outsider/non-Jew

Hashem (Hebrew) Literally "the Name," meaning the name of God (which observant Jews consider too sacred to utter or write)

Hashem in himmel (Hebrew/Yiddish) "God in Heaven"

Holchei rachil (Hebrew) A tale-bearer or slanderer

Ikh bet dikh (Yiddish) I beg you

Johnny Rebs Union slang for Confederate soldiers during the Civil War

Kaddish, mourner's A specific Hebrew prayer spoken to honor the dead

Kashruth Hebrew word for kosher; refers to Jewish dietary laws and food or drink that conforms to them

Lashon hara (Hebrew) Literally "evil tongue;" refers to gossip, usually derogatory, about other people

Maideleh (Yiddish) Little girl; used as an endearment toward a young, unmarried woman

Menorah A six- or nine-armed candelabra; the nine-armed version is lit for the eight nights of Chanukah

Minyan A gathering for prayer, daily or weekly, with at least ten Jewish adults who have undergone bar mitzvah; in Hanley and Rivka's time, this would have meant adult men

Mitzvah/mitzvot (Hebrew) Literally "commandment(s);" a good or righteous deed

Onen (Hebrew) Principal mourners, usually immediate family of the deceased

Onkl (Yiddish) Uncle

Panel shop Bordello with false interior walls, or "panels," that slide back to let thieves rob customers who are otherwise engaged

Pogrom Violent attacks on Jews by non-Jews; though more typical in the later 19ᵗʰ century, and most strongly associated with the Cossacks of Russia, pogroms occurred sporadically throughout Europe from the Middle Ages onward

Rav A term of the highest respect for a rabbi

Reb (Yiddish) Mister; a general honorific applied to men

Rebbetzin (Yiddish) Refers to the rabbi's wife, who had specific duties to keep the rabbi informed of needs, issues, and problems in the community

Shabbos The Sabbath, which in Judaism falls on Saturday rather than Sunday. The spelling used in this book reflects the Yiddish pronunciation Rivka's community would have used.

Shaytel (Yiddish) A wig worn over a married woman's hair whenever she is out in public, so that only her husband ever sees her natural hair

Shiva (Hebrew) The seven-day mourning period immediately after a death

Shomer (Hebrew) One who watches over the dead

Shtetl (Yiddish) A village or small town

Shul (Yiddish) Literally "school;" refers to a synagogue

Siddur (Hebrew) Prayer book

Tallis (Hebrew) Prayer shawl worn by adult Jews who have undergone bar mitzvah

Talmud Central text of rabbinic Judaism; a collection of commentaries on the Mishna, or Jewish Oral Law, interpreting the Torah

Tanta (Yiddish) Aunt

Torah In its narrowest sense, Torah is the first five books of the Bible; in its broadest sense, Torah is the entire body of Jewish teachings

Yeshiva (Hebrew) Institutions of learning where Torah and Talmud are studied

ALSO PUBLISHED BY
ALLIUM PRESS OF CHICAGO

Visit our website for more information:
www.alliumpress.com

Beautiful Dreamer
Joan Naper

Chicago in 1900 is bursting with opportunity, and Kitty Coakley is determined to make the most of it. The youngest of seven children born to Irish immigrants, she has little interest in becoming simply a housewife. Inspired by her entrepreneurial Aunt Mabel, who runs a millinery boutique at Marshall Field's, Kitty aspires to become an independent, modern woman. After her music teacher dashes her hopes of becoming a professional singer, she refuses to give up her dreams of a career. But when she is courted by not one, but two young men, her resolve is tested. Irish-Catholic Brian is familiar and has the approval of her traditional, working-class family. But wealthy, Protestant Henry, who is a young architect in Daniel Burnham's office, provides an entrée for Kitty into another, more exciting world. Will she sacrifice her ambitions and choose a life with one of these men?

◆

Company Orders
David J. Walker

Even a good man may feel driven to sign on with the devil. Paul Clark is a Catholic priest who's been on the fast track to becoming a bishop. But he suddenly faces a heart-wrenching problem, when choices he made as a young man come roaring back into his life. A mysterious woman, who claims to be with "an agency of the federal government," offers to solve his problem. But there's a price to pay—Father Clark must undertake some very un-priestly actions. An attack in a Chicago alley…a daring escape from a Mexican jail… and a fight to the death in a Guyanese jungle…all these, and more, must be survived in order to protect someone he loves. This priest is about to learn how much easier it is to preach love than to live it.

Set the Night on Fire
Libby Fischer Hellmann

Someone is trying to kill Lila Hilliard. During the Christmas holidays she returns from running errands to find her family home in flames, her father and brother trapped inside. Later, she is attacked by a mysterious man on a motorcycle. . . and the threats don't end there. As Lila desperately tries to piece together who is after her and why, she uncovers information about her father's past in Chicago during the volatile days of the late 1960s . . . information he never shared with her, but now threatens to destroy her. Part thriller, part historical novel, and part love story, *Set the Night on Fire* paints an unforgettable portrait of Chicago during a turbulent time: the riots at the Democratic Convention . . . the struggle for power between the Black Panthers and SDS . . . and a group of young idealists who tried to change the world.

◆

A Bitter Veil
Libby Fischer Hellmann

It all began with a line of Persian poetry . . . Anna and Nouri, both studying in Chicago, fall in love despite their very different backgrounds. Anna, who has never been close to her parents, is more than happy to return with Nouri to his native Iran, to be embraced by his wealthy family. Beginning their married life together in 1978, their world is abruptly turned upside down by the overthrow of the Shah and the rise of the Islamic Republic. Under the Ayatollah Khomeini and the Republican Guard, life becomes increasingly restricted and Anna must learn to exist in a transformed world, where none of the familiar Western rules apply. Random arrests and torture become the norm, women are required to wear hijab, and Anna discovers that she is no longer free to leave the country. As events reach a fevered pitch, Anna realizes that nothing is as she thought, and no one can be trusted. . .not even her husband.

Her Mother's Secret
Barbara Garland Polikoff

Fifteen-year-old Sarah, the daughter of Jewish immigrants, wants nothing more than to become an artist. But as she spreads her wings she must come to terms with the secrets that her family is only beginning to share with her. Replete with historical details that vividly evoke the Chicago of the 1890s, this moving coming-of-age story is set against the backdrop of a vibrant, turbulent city. Sarah moves between two very different worlds—the colorful immigrant neighborhood surrounding Hull House and the sophisticated, elegant World's Columbian Exposition. This novel eloquently captures the struggles of a young girl as she experiences the timeless emotions of friendship, family turmoil, loss...and first love.

A companion guide to *Her Mother's Secret*
is available at www.alliumpress.com. In the guide you will find photographs of places mentioned in the novel, along with discussion questions, a list of read-alikes, and resources for further exploration of Sarah's time and place.

THE EMILY CABOT MYSTERIES
Frances McNamara

Death at the Fair

The 1893 World's Columbian Exposition provides a vibrant backdrop for the first book in the series. Emily Cabot, one of the first women graduate students at the University of Chicago, is eager to prove herself in the emerging field of sociology. While she is busy exploring the Exposition with her family and friends, her colleague, Dr. Stephen Chapman, is accused of murder. Emily sets out to search for the truth behind the crime, but is thwarted by the gamblers, thieves, and corrupt politicians who are ever-present in Chicago. A lynching that occurred in the dead man's past leads Emily to seek the assistance of the black activist Ida B. Wells.

◆

Death at Hull House

After Emily Cabot is expelled from the University of Chicago, she finds work at Hull House, the famous settlement established by Jane Addams. There she quickly becomes involved in the political and social problems of the immigrant community. But when a man who works for a sweatshop owner is murdered in the Hull House parlor, Emily must determine whether one of her colleagues is responsible, or whether the real reason for the murder is revenge for a past tragedy in her own family. As a smallpox epidemic spreads through the impoverished west side of Chicago, the very existence of the settlement is threatened and Emily finds herself in jeopardy from both the deadly disease and a killer.

Death at Pullman

A model town at war with itself . . . George Pullman created an ideal community for his railroad car workers, complete with every amenity they could want or need. But when hard economic times hit in 1894, lay-offs follow and the workers can no longer pay their rent or buy food at the company store. Starving and desperate, they turn against their once benevolent employer. Emily Cabot and her friend Dr. Stephen Chapman bring much needed food and medical supplies to the town, hoping they can meet the immediate needs of the workers and keep them from resorting to violence. But when one young worker—suspected of being a spy—is murdered, and a bomb plot comes to light, Emily must race to discover the truth behind a tangled web of family and company alliances.

◆

Death at Woods Hole

Exhausted after the tumult of the Pullman Strike of 1894, Emily Cabot is looking forward to a restful summer visit to Cape Cod. She has plans to collect "beasties" for the Marine Biological Laboratory, alongside other visiting scientists from the University of Chicago. She also hopes to enjoy romantic clambakes with Dr. Stephen Chapman, although they must keep an important secret from their friends. But her summer takes a dramatic turn when she finds a dead man floating in a fish tank. In order to solve his murder she must first deal with dueling scientists, a testy local sheriff, the theft of a fortune, and uncooperative weather.

Bright and Yellow, Hard and Cold
Tim Chapman

The search for elusive goals consumes three men…

McKinney, a forensic scientist, struggles with his deep, personal need to find the truth behind the evidence he investigates, even while the system shuts him out. Can he get justice for a wrongfully accused man while juggling life with a new girlfriend and a precocious teenage daughter?

Delroy gives up the hard-scrabble life on his family's Kentucky farm and ventures to the rough-and-tumble world of 1930s Chicago. Unable to find work, he reluctantly throws his hat in with the bank-robbing gangsters Alvin Karpis and Freddie Barker. Can he provide for his fiery young wife without risking his own life?

Gilbert is obsessed with the search for a cache of gold, hidden for nearly eighty years. As his hunt escalates he finds himself willing to use ever more extreme measures to attain his goal…including kidnapping, torture, and murder. Can he find the one person still left who will lead him to the glittering treasure? And will the trail of corpses he leaves behind include McKinney?

Part contemporary thriller, part historical novel, and part love story, *Bright and Yellow, Hard and Cold* masterfully weaves a tale of conflicted scientific ethics, economic hardship, and criminal frenzy, tempered with the redemption of family love.

CPSIA information can be obtained at www.ICGtesting.com
Printed in the USA
BVOW07s1756150914

366833BV00003B/4/P

31901055678215